SOURCE AWAKENING

Source Rising Series, Book 1

Tracey Canole

D1527965

KORBEN SKIES PUBLISHING

Korben Skies Publishing

Years of dreaming and hard work are in these pages that you will never see—so much support people provided, conversations with friends, and advice they gave. For behind every writer, are the ones you don't see. The family that brings honesty, joy, and chaos to their lives. The friends that have no idea what the author's talking about, but supports them anyway. Or, the betas and editors that tell the writer when they've gone off their rocker, or are on to something magical.

I cannot write all of your names down, but this first book is for those who push me to be better than I am. For my children who keep me honest and bring light to every moment. To Quinn who loves me even when I am lost in the words. And to Autumn, Vanna, my accountability ladies, and so many others, you have helped more than you know.

Thank you for supporting me in this crazy endeavor. I see you all and am grateful.

Chapter One

The den of evil appeared before me. My shoulders slumped, and my mouth went dry as I forced myself to take a step. One after another, I approached the senior lockers, my emotions whirling in my chest. I had to get a hold of myself. This was high school, not a war zone, but I knew what was to come and I hated it. Maybe they wouldn't be there yet, but with my luck? I doubted it.

I had one job and, theoretically, it was simple. Give my ex-best friend his birthday present because my mother hated to have him wait. Plus, she likes to torture me. What she didn't grasp was the truth of how hard this was. Jaxson Beck, my best friend since we were born, was now the bane of my existence.

Tucking my hand into my pocket, I played with the box hidden there. The sharp corner sliced at my skin. I pressed the injury to my lips, the tang of iron pleasant on my tongue. Was this a premonition? *Maybe.*

"Hey, Reena!" Crissy, one of the girls from my group, called. Her perfect hair and makeup made her look like a doll.

"Hey, girl. I'll be right there. I just have to stop at my locker. You look totally adorbs, by the way." Inwardly, I grimaced. *Adorbs. Really?*

I smiled at the girl I barely tolerated. The girl who was supposed to be my friend, but in reality was just a pawn in my game to stay hidden in plain sight. It was all a show because there was no way I could be myself in this place. They'd destroy me. I'd learned that the hard way when the popular girls decided to make Jaxson and me their focus just over two years ago. In response, I'd ruined my longest friendship and changed myself completely, wiping away who I'd been before.

My gait quickened as I glimpsed my reflection in the glass of the gymnasium door. My tall, athletic, yet a little-too-thin body glided over the glass in a vaguely uncoordinated grace that made me self-conscious. I shuddered and increased my pace.

I reached the ramada that housed the rows of senior lockers. The tall structure shading the space from the hot sun stood between the parking lot and the gymnasium and, this early, only a few people lingered below it. I reached the far aisle where Jaxson's locker was. The red metal was chipped in places, the gray beneath peeking through.

Please let him be alone...

"Oh, look, Jaxson, the beauty queen is here," a snarky voice rang out.

Great. Just freaking great. I stood straighter and walked to the end of the aisle, Jaxson my only focus. *You just need to give him the box.*

"I need to talk to you for a second," I said.

Mike elbowed Sam in the side. "You know, I don't think dressing like that is acceptable under the dress code. I mean, what're you trying to do? Pick up a hot date off the corner?"

"Seriously, Jaxson? Can't you control your losers?" I said, feigning disinterest. I had to get out of here. If I stayed, I might just punch someone. That would be a definite no-no to my image.

"What, Reena? Can't handle hearing the truth? Or is it that the truth hurts?" Jaxson said.

As if we hadn't spoken at all, Sam said, "Naw, Mike, I don't think that would work for her. They'd probably just think she was a man in drag."

They laughed as if they were the funniest people in the world. Anger and hurt built within me. I fought to keep control. I fought to ignore the mean comments that brought out my deepest insecurities.

Jaxson smirked. "Shut it, Sam."

That was it? If this were two years ago, Jaxson would have hit Sam for a comment like that. Now? He was holding back a smile.

It's your fault, Reena. You did this to yourself.

Thanks, Conscious, you're super helpful...

"Oh, come on, Jaxson, she has to know. From what you've told us, she isn't a complete dimwit. Or maybe the years of hanging around with the popular crowd has made her stupider," Remus said.

"Stupider isn't a word." I glared at Jaxson.

"Errr, yes, it is," Remus said after a long pause.

"Well, it's not a very good one," I snapped.

Don't hit the idiot. Don't hit the idiot.

I looked up to meet Jaxson's eyes. Maybe if I focused on him, my urge to kill the dumbass next to him would recede. My breath caught, and I pressed my hand to my chest. Holy crap, I had to look up. When the hell did that happen? I realize that doesn't seem like an accomplishment but, being over six feet myself, I promise it was.

"What's a giant like you doing over here anyway? Feel like destroying a few villages?" Remus asked.

I lunged at Remus as blood rushed in my ears. Jaxson's arm caught me, wrapping around my waist before I could reach him. I yelled, "I'm tall. Not Godzilla, you idiot. And if you aren't careful..."

"Reena," Jaxson snapped. "Calm down."

What? How could he use that tone with me? Like I was in the wrong? My anger turned on Jaxson. My eyes met his, and I stopped cold. He was so close. His well-trimmed mop of blond hair fell onto his forehead, and the blue of his eyes shone. Those eyes felt like home. I ground my teeth.

"You know what? Nevermind," I said, swallowing the hurt. I spun and stalked back to my car. This day could go to hell.

My fingers ran hesitantly over the small box that lay on my belly. The rough, brown craft paper scratched my skin, contrasting with the smooth texture of the tape. I opened my eyes and stared up at my feet, propped against the pale green of my bedroom wall. The comforter underneath me was soft, the warm afternoon light filtering through my windows to caress my skin as if in an attempt to make me feel better. If only the images from the day would stop playing in my head. Each one made me want to shove a pillow over my face —either from embarrassment or rage, I wasn't sure. I had no idea how I'd failed so miserably. It had been such a tiny job, and I'd screwed it up.

I lifted the present so I could read the script on the front. The one word scrawled there made my chest swell with happiness one second before the wave of regret and loss wiped it out. *Jaxson,* it said. A name so familiar it was part of me. My best friend and confidant.

Not anymore.

My gaze traveled toward the ceiling to the collage of pictures covering the wall. The faces of my family and friends were filled with love, drawing my attention against my will. You could track my life by these pictures. Jaxson and I, five years old, swinging on the monkey bars. Me and my sisters sneaking up on Jaxson and his brother, Eric, with handfuls of water balloons. Their retaliation had ended with us soaked. Jaxson and me, eleven years old, on our first hunting trip with our compound bows. Then, our combined family adventure to the beach two years ago. In that one, I sat on Jaxson's shoulders, laughing, while Eric made a face in the background. Our smiles were so bright, and I couldn't help but think that was the last time I'd smiled with so much unfettered joy. It was, however, the last time I felt like myself.

Two years already? I huffed, closing my eyes. Two years since I lost my best friend. Two years since I'd ruined everything and made the biggest scene in our school's history. People still talk about that dance. And why wouldn't they? I mean, how often does someone manage to "trip" the sweetest girl in school—and Jaxson's crush—causing her to fall into the punch bowl and snacks, ruining her handmade dress. I'd hated to do it, but the mean girls had promised to spread some of Jaxson's secrets if I didn't. Secrets only I knew. Secrets that had slipped out after they'd cornered me in the bathroom just before to torture me first. They'd been so impressed by my display that they decided I was actually cool enough to bring me into their fold.

I'd hated myself for weeks after that, and I'd never apologized. I decided it was easier to join them than be a target. I was just happy to have the teasing taunts stop. That's when the change started. So, to say the incident from earlier proved we were no longer friends? It was true enough, and I couldn't blame him.

"Reena?" my mother's voice called from somewhere down the hall. It shook me from my thoughts, for which I was grateful.

I jumped, grabbing the box and shoving it under the pillow beside me.

"In here," I called. I snatched the book sitting on the bed next to me, opened it, and pretended to read.

Yup, everything is totally normal.

My mother's beautiful face appeared in the doorway. She wore a light cream shirt which looked amazing against the richness of her golden wheat skin. Her long, black hair was down, falling around her shoulders to frame her face. She had a beauty I only wish I had. Though I'd inherited a lot of my mother, I looked more like my dad. My skin tone was a lighter shade than hers and my frame significantly larger. My sisters, Lily and Kiera, resembled my mother more. Kiera, who was older, was a tiny, perfect replica of Mom. But Lily, who held the same face and eyes, looked like she'd be tall like my dad too. Never would I admit it to them, but I was jealous.

"Hey, you packed?"

I put the book down and sat up. "Yeah. I got everything in one bag and my backpack, but have you seen my bow?"

She leaned against the doorway and nodded. "Yes, your father finished packing yours and the boys' after Kim dropped Jax and Eric's off this morning."

Thanks for the reminder of what's to come. I grimaced.

"Well, my bags are ready."

"Good. Bring them out front and we'll get them loaded. Also, I wanted to let you know that plans have changed for dinner. Do one quick check that you have everything you need and then we'll head out."

"Head out where? We're leaving in like two hours anyway."

"That's true, but it's Jax's birthday. Kim managed to get off from work early so we're meeting them for a quick dinner. We'll head to the airport straight from there."

I shot to my feet. "What? No! You said we were celebrating when we got to the cabin."

The family cabin we shared with the Becks, Jaxson's family, was just outside of Portland, Oregon. We were headed there for the next two weeks where, I was sure, the constant awkwardness would make both our lives hell as we were forced to stay under the same roof.

Mom's expression went dark as she glared at me. She rested her hands on her hips.

I should've known better than to say anything. With the fit I'd thrown this morning over taking Jaxson his present, it would have been safer to stay quiet. But going out to dinner for his birthday? And here? What if someone saw me with him, or more importantly, what if my presence ruined his birthday?

"You've got to be kidding me," she said.

"Mom, someone might see me." *With him. The "loser."* "I don't want to go."

Her eyes narrowed, and I knew she could see those thoughts on my face. This was going to be bad. When she spoke her next words, I flinched.

"Did you give Jax his present this morning like I asked you?"

I could feel the heat of her gaze as I averted my eyes.

When I didn't answer, she threw her hands out, continuing, "Reena Novak! You didn't, did you? You didn't give your best friend his present on his birthday? Seriously? Did you even wish him a happy birthday?"

Straightening my shoulders, I took a deep breath. "You don't understand, Mom. We aren't friends anymore. We haven't been for a long time, and his cronies—"

She held up a hand. "No! I don't want to hear it. This has gone on long enough. We will be spending an entire vacation with the Becks, and I will not have you —and whatever this is—disrupting it." She stepped forward to place her hands on my shoulders.

I looked down at her, the distance my height provided doing nothing to protect against the anger radiating from her. Her back was tight, lips drawn in a line, and worry seeped from her touch. Chest expanding, she took a breath for patience and when she spoke, her voice was far kinder than I deserved.

"Jax is family. So, we're going to celebrate his birthday together, today. I don't know what's been going on, but you need to figure it out and soon. Reena, honey, you and I both know you haven't been the same since you two stopped hanging out. You were so much happier when he was around—"

It was my turn to interrupt. "Stop. I've told you before, things change. We grew up and we're different now. We grew apart." *Liar*, my entire being screamed. Each word was bitter in my mouth. They weren't wrong, but that didn't change the fact that I hated them. "Plus, my friends don't like him."

It's okay, Reena, they might not like him, but you're popular. You have friends, and admirers, and no one makes fun of you. They wouldn't dare. I turned my head away. *And who cares if you hate everything you've become, and you have no idea who you are. It's worth it. Right?*

Internally, I rolled my eyes. *You have some serious skill lying to yourself.*

"Well, maybe you need to choose better friends," she snapped. She released me and stepped back. "Get ready; it's time to go."

I swallowed hard, not missing the disappointment in her tone. I glanced down at my hands as I kneaded them together.

Before she left, she turned and said, "Do you really think any of those prissy friends of yours could ever hold a candle up to that?" She gestured to the collage of memories, hundreds of them, brightening the room. With one last tilt of her head, she disappeared.

I collapsed back onto the bed, my hair flying out behind me. I blinked away the burn of tears and the thickness in my throat. She was right; I knew that. I'd believed that the choices I'd made had been the right ones, but there was no denying I was miserable. I hated everything about who I was now. It was exhausting faking who I was every day or forgetting the things I loved to do. It was worse pretending the people I hung out with were my friends. Eventually, it would destroy me.

The only person who had made me feel whole was Jaxson, and ever since I'd pushed him away, I'd felt like something was missing. I shook my head, attempting to clear it.

Mom and Dad's voices echoed from the living room, a plan to leave in ten minutes reaching me. Pushing up, I went to the mirror over my dresser and checked my reflection.

I held back my wince, that invisible weight planting itself on my chest. I even hated my new appearance—the image I'd created. All so that I'd fall into the shadows, removing myself from the focus of those who'd tortured me in previous years. I ran my hand through my perfectly coiffed curls. My golden-almond skin was the same as ever, but my round eyes were encircled by far too much eyeliner. And my outfit? Ugh. I straightened the sequined shirt that fell off one shoulder. Even after all this time, I missed my ripped jeans and plain T-shirts.

Whatever. Suck it up and let's get this over with.

Before I took my bags out to the truck, I retrieved Jaxson's present from under the pillow. I shoved it into my purse and, before I let go, ran my finger over the paper. I hoped with everything I was that he loved it as much as I thought he would.

My dad was loading the SUV when I came out. Before he noticed me, I wrapped my arms around him from behind and squeezed. He grunted, then laughed.

"You okay, Bug?" he asked. His bright blue eyes met mine as he turned. "Ready for an adventure? For some hiking, hunting, and snow?"

Only a few inches taller than me, he was one of the only people I could look in the eye. I chuckled at the sight of his tanned ivory cheeks, pink from the exertion of packing so much into the truck. I doubted the sun beating down helped. For winter, it was an unseasonably warm year in Arizona. We had yet to pull out the heavy jackets here, which meant summer was going to be tough.

"Yup, to all of those questions. Especially hunting. It's been forever since we went deer hunting, and I've been itching to go," I said, stepping back so he could heft another into the back. "Do you need any help to get this train moving?"

"No, I got it, but I do have to ask, how can three women pack so much?" he asked.

I snorted. "Yeah, yeah. You and I both know you packed more than Lily and I did together. I don't want to hear it." I pushed his shoulder, and he grinned.

Before I walked around to get in, he stopped me. "Hey, you have Jax's present, right? I feel like I should check; otherwise, I might be down a daughter."

So, Mom had already told him about our argument. I rolled my eyes.

"Seriously though, Bug."

"Yes, I have it," I said, irritation in each word. I pulled the box out and showed it to him. He nodded, examining me and seeing more than I liked. I shifted uncomfortably before spinning and slipping into the car where Lily and Mom waited.

"Hey, Mom," I said. I placed a hand on her arm. "Listen, I'm sorry for not giving Jaxson his present this morning, okay? But think of it this way, now you can see his reaction when we give it to him. Isn't that better?"

Her shoulders relaxed, and the frustration in her expression melted away.

"I guess that's true. I'm still frustrated with you, but I can see your point. And either way, I can't wait to see his reaction!" Had she been any other woman, I would've expected a squeal to escape her lips, but it was Mom. Always in control. Jaxson was one of the only things in this world that could bring this side of her out and that was only because he was seen as one of her children. So giving him such a meaningful gift meant even more.

A wave of sadness hit me because I knew how the situation between Jaxson and I hurt her. He still came to visit, but it wasn't like it had been before—no longer almost daily and never with me in tow. I always hid in my room or went out. I swallowed the lump in my throat.

I'd never admit it to anyone, but I was just as excited to see his reaction. It was the perfect surprise. So, for once, I let my elation fill me. I ignored the hesitation and worry, choosing to revel in the fact that I was going to have a night with Jaxson before heading on vacation with all of my family, Becks included. Well, almost all. Keira was staying back, the jerk. I guess I just missed our joint trips; it had been so long since the last one.

Chapter Two

J axson and Kim were in front of the restaurant when we arrived. Kim was shifting from foot-to-foot with a grin on her face. Knowing her, she probably hadn't told Jaxson we were coming. This was confirmed when we approached, and she turned him to face us. His face lit up with a huge smile as Lily ran to him. Without hesitation, he picked her up and swung her in a circle. She squealed happily before he set her down, that big brother, little sister relationship shining in the daylight.

"Hey, Lily! It's been too long. What are you now, twenty?"

Lily harrumphed, placing her hands on her hips. "No. I'm thirteen, and you know it. That's stupid anyway. That would make me older than you and I know because it's your birthday!" She jumped up and down, then hugged him once more. "I was so excited when Mom said we were meeting you for dinner. I know we were going to celebrate when we got to the cabin, but it's just not fair to not celebrate *on* your birthday. You know?" Her speech was so fast I was only able to catch three out of five words, but because I was used to it, I could fill in the blanks.

Jaxson chuckled, released her, and then accepted embraces from Mom and Dad.

I stood back and watched the exchange, a sense of contentment at coming home filling me. This was my family. My entire family. Well, except for Eric and James, whom we'd see tomorrow. The Becks have been the second half of us since before I was born. Kim and James were a second set of parents and their boys, a mix of friends, siblings, and partners in crime. I rubbed my chest, wishing the action would remove the guilt and loss weighing me down. I'd caused the rift here. I wonder if anyone saw it like I did.

Releasing Dad, Jaxson reached for me, but stopped, realizing his mistake. A sharp pain lanced through my heart. I bit my lip, lowering my eyes to the ground. God, I missed him.

It's your fault, Reena. You did this to yourself.

Thanks, Conscious, you're sooo helpful...

Clearing his throat, his expression hesitant but happy, Jaxson said, "Thanks for coming. It means a lot."

I couldn't think of anything to say, so I just nodded. I could tell he was about to say more when a voice I despised rang out from behind me. Jax grinned, but it took everything I had not to scowl.

Great. Just freaking great. Dread spread up my spine like wildfire. I turned, and it was like a nightmare come to life. Jaxson's three best friends, Sam, Mike, and Remus approached. With a silent curse, I spun to follow my parents. Just the sound of Remus' voice brought back the mean words he'd spat at me this morning—the taunts and insinuations that I was a...

What, are you trying to pick up a hot date off the corner?

It doesn't matter. Stop thinking about it.

"Wait," Sam said. "Is Reena the Harpy here?"

Not wanting Lily to hear, I pushed her through the door. "Lily, go to the table. I'll be right there." She sent me a questioning look, glanced at the boys, then did as I asked. She'd have questions for me later.

"It is," Remus said, interest and a wicked glee in his voice. "Think she'll try to hit me again?"

My heart rate picked up, my breathing becoming deeper as fury swirled through me. I barely caught a growl. No doubt that would just add to their excitement. He had no idea how lucky he'd been that Jaxson stopped me from pummeling him this morning. No one calls me that and comes out unscathed.

He's not worth it, Reena. Don't ruin Jaxson's birthday. But I didn't have to do anything because Jaxson stepped in front of me. His giant form was so big he blocked my view of the guys. I fought a flush. Earlier my shock when I realized how tall and broad Jax had become had been a little embarrassing. I hadn't realized how thoroughly I'd been avoiding him until that moment. It was the first time I realized this wasn't the Jaxson I'd always known. This Jaxson was larger, stronger, and um, beautiful—definitely no longer a boy. I'd like to say there'd been no blushing or ogling, but even I wasn't that good of a liar.

I started to move around him, my hand pressing to his back. He glanced down to meet my eyes and I stopped, those blue irises holding me captive. In them, I read his intention, and I froze.

"Guys, stop it," Jaxson said to his cronies. "Whatever stupid crap you were going to say, just stop. Her parents and little sister are inside. If you can't be nice, then you need to leave."

He stopped his friends from picking on me? Seriously?

The three boys blinked, and, after a long moment, they vocalized agreement. Jaxson nodded and told them to go ahead.

I was still gaping like a fish when Jaxson turned to me. "I'm sorry about them. Are you okay?"

Yup, still stuck in that shell-shocked state. Clearing my throat, I shrugged. He reached out to touch my arm, but I stepped back, his expression falling instantly. I lowered my eyes and went inside, his steps echoing behind me.

Our table was long and set off to the side. The scent of freshly cooked pizza filled the restaurant, making my mouth water. The guys were saying a quick hello to Kim when we entered, so I found a seat next to Lily and across from Jaxson. I had to hide my flinch as Remus slipped into the chair beside me.

Thanks, Mom. I really appreciate you dragging me to dinner. This is exactly how I wanted to spend my night. I stayed tucked into myself as conversation picked up, and we all settled in. After we ordered drinks, I zoned out completely, thinking that if I didn't initiate, they'd forget I was there.

"Reena, honey?"

I started, straightening in my seat. "Mom?" I glanced up to find most of the table staring at me. Dad's was especially focused.

"You have his present, right?" she asked. "Honey, are you okay?"

"Oh! Um, yeah. And yes, I have his present." I pulled the small box from my purse and handed it over the table to Jaxson. "Mom saw this last week and couldn't resist. I was supposed to give it to you this morning, but..."

Jaxson's eyes darkened, and he bit his lip. I glanced down at my soda.

"Sorry, man," Sam said, and I was shocked that it sounded sincere. "I didn't know."

Shaking it off, I said, "Well, open it, or Mom's going to explode. You're lucky she hasn't internally combusted at this point."

With a grin, he turned toward Mom. "I can open it?"

"Of course!" she said.

Without hesitation, Jaxson removed the wrapping paper. It fell to the table, crinkling as he sat the box on top to untie the ribbon holding it closed. When he lifted the lid, his eyes went wide.

"Whoa," he said, and I couldn't hold back my smile. He reached in, gently caressing what was inside reverently.

"What is it?" Kim asked. She moved to lean over his shoulder.

"A compass." Jaxson ran his fingers over the intricate wind rose pattern covering the lid. Gently, he removed it from its cradle.

"Look at the other side," Mom said. She was bouncing in her chair.

Jaxson flipped it over and read the inscription.

"'Truth will always point you home, '" he said, voice deeper than a moment ago. The smile that broke across his face was breathtaking. It was a true smile; one I hadn't seen in ages. "It's perfect, Viti. Thank you."

"You like it? I'm so glad!" She got up and rushed to hug him from behind. "I was going to put something simple for the engraving, but Reena demanded I put this wording instead. She said that if I was going to put anything on it, it needed to mean something."

I felt everyone's gaze shift to me, but all I saw was Jaxson. Surprise looked back. I watched as it turned to amusement. He looked at the compass, then back to me.

"Third grade?" he asked.

I chuckled, then shrugged. "It seemed appropriate. That was the best short story either of us has ever written."

He started to shake, laughter reverberating from his chest. This was exactly what I'd hoped for.

"And now that you're officially an adult, I thought I'd remind you of that long-ago lesson."

He leaned his head back and chortled. He ran a free hand through his blond hair, his eyes sparkling. The rest of the table was silent, unable to figure out what was going on, but unable to look away. Then Kim got it.

"Wait, isn't that the story where the two of you had to fight off aliens with the help of the local squirrel population using only kitchen utensils?"

"Yes. Yes, it was," Jax said between breaths.

"That makes absolutely no sense," Sam said.

"Which is just about right for these two," Dad added from his spot down the way. His face was alight as he took in the exchange.

"That was *not* the best story you've ever written," Mom exclaimed, her voice exasperated. "Reena, how does this *mean* something?"

"It means more than you know, Viti." His eyes met mine, and the softness I saw there had me shifting in my seat.

"It may not be the best story ever," I said with a grin. "But Jax gets the inscription. Plus, it's obscure enough that he can add any meaning he wants to it."

Jaxson froze. He gripped the compass tighter in his hand. "You haven't called me 'Jax' in years."

Heat spread through me at the affection in his tone. I dropped my gaze, my cheeks burning. A long moment of silence passed before my father—God, I loved him— rescued me by asking to see the compass, stating that

Mom hadn't let him examine it before she'd wrapped it. I risked a glance at Jax as he handed it over and found he was still watching me. Additionally, I had to hold back a groan when I noticed the guys' eyes kept bouncing from Jax to me and back. What was I supposed to do now?

Thankfully, conversation picked up as the waiter arrived. I stayed tucked into my food, Lily the only one I spoke to. She'd been telling me about her day when Jax spoke.

"Wait. Lily, did I just hear you talking about some boy? Is there a boy you like?"

"No," she said, holding a finger up, but her quick response said everything.

Jax lifted his eyebrow in disbelief. "I did, didn't I? Do I need to meet this boy?"

Lily heaved a sigh. "No. No, you do not. You are not my dad, and I don't need another creepy protector embarrassing me in front of boys."

I coughed, barely holding back a smile.

"You may not need one, but you have one. I'm the closest thing you have to a brother and with Eric off at school, it falls to me. But... based on your reaction, I think the more interesting question is, what did Reena do?"

"Me?" I asked, placing a hand over my heart.

Lily let out a derisive snort. Apparently, no one bought my innocence.

"The last time I let a boy I liked meet her, she pulled out her compound bow and scared him off. He refuses to talk to me now." She crossed her arms over her chest. "It's been months."

"Not bad," Remus said, an impressed smirk lifting his lips.

"Well, no one looks at my sister that way and lives."

Remus froze, eyebrows dropping in thought.

Ha! One point for Reena. He can't tell if I was joking.

Jax shook his head. "Well, I think she'd do a better job protecting you anyway. She's scarier than I am."

"No kidding," Sam said under his breath.

Jax elbowed him in the side. He leaned over and said something to his friend.

"Sorry," Sam said.

I nearly choked on my drink. *Wait, Sam apologized? Well, crap, the world must be ending. Maybe vacation wasn't a bad idea.* I forced myself to release the breath I'd been holding.

I met Jax's eyes. In them, I saw more than I wanted to, more than I was ready to see, and definitely more than I was ready to reciprocate.

Was it possible to salvage some form of a relationship from this trip? Was it possible that even for a short time, I could feel like myself again? The hope that buzzed through me almost hurt as realization came crashing down.

No. What are you thinking? That would never work. I have to stay away from him. If you open that friendship again, you'll just hurt him more. When we come back from break, everything will just go bad again.

Because I couldn't be myself anymore. I'd spent too much time as this fake version of myself, and I didn't know how to stop. No matter how hard I wanted to be who I used to be, I couldn't. I was broken. I'd created this person I hated, held everyone I cared about at a distance—because they couldn't understand—and knew there was no way to change that.

That truth hurt more than anything, I think, but it was nice to have those few moments of normalcy. Those few moments where everything had been like it used to be. Maybe one day I'd find a way out of this prison I'd created.

Not long after, Keira, my older sister, showed up to see us off to the airport. She'd somehow managed to talk my parents into staying behind for break because she had to work. I didn't like leaving her—it felt dangerous to separate—but I understood her reasoning. She was in college with tuition and other bills to pay.

After some honest torment of Jax for his birthday, Keira left with a round of hugs. We loaded up to head for the airport. I didn't want to admit how much of a relief it was to see the guys drive away. I knew I was being a child, but the last few months had been hard. Because of some seriously bad choices I'd made, they'd decided I was Enemy Number One. I'd hurt Jax, and he was their friend. Part of me appreciated the way they protected him no matter how hard it was for me.

Mom rode with Kim, leaving Jax next to me in the backseat of the SUV. It was nice, though, the joy and contentment of the evening having settled our nerves. We sat in comfortable silence, me looking out the window and not watching him caress the engraving along the back of the compass, his face deep in thought. Every so often his eyes would shoot to me.

Chapter Three

The last quarter mile leading to the cabin was lined with trees that canopied the road. I sighed, enjoying the way the sun peeked through the branches above as they skated by. I felt the shift in my chest as the tension I'd carried all day changed to the joy of being back. It had been a long trip, and we were minutes away.

It was the day after we'd left Arizona for Oregon, and we were exhausted. We'd spent the night at a hotel, then gotten up early to go shopping for supplies. With everything we needed in hand, we left the city and headed toward the small town where our land waited for us.

Passing through the Columbia River Gorge, we made one stop—a quick hike Jax begged us to go on because it held his favorite waterfall. Tall and beautiful, the water had fallen more than a hundred feet into a small pool below. The droplets had bounced off the ice covering it, then shot across, making the entire thing look as if it were covered in diamonds. We'd had a lot of fun as, over the course of the hike, each of us had slipped, causing the others to break down into hysterics. When I'd fallen, then slid down a small hill, our laughter had filled the canyon. Mine had stopped only when Jax had rushed over to help me up. His worried "you okay?" had caused my throat to close. Instead of saying "yes" and "thank you" like a normal person, I'd snapped at him. Not my finest moment.

Which was why I'd been quiet the rest of the drive. But excitement rose in my chest the instant we'd made that last turn toward the house. There was a sense of coming home I only ever felt here. Then when my favorite place in the world appeared out of the trees, I released a breath. The large, two-story home was beautiful with its dark wood siding and huge front porch. The fading evening light was just enough to see by, the orange kiss of the sunset adding a magical feel to the land. Several of the lights were on, whispering of the warmth within.

I grinned as two men stepped onto the porch.

"Uncle James! Eric!" Lily called, jumping out of the car the moment it stopped. She ran up to Jaxson's dad and wrapped her arms around him.

He chuckled. "Lily Girl. How are you, honey? How was the trip?"

"Good! We miss you back home. When are you coming back?"

James had spent the last nine months on contract in Portland. He hated being away from the family but couldn't turn down the financial benefits, especially with Eric in college and Jax soon to be.

"Hopefully soon," he said, kissing the top of her head.

He looked healthy, having lost a few pounds since the last time I saw him. His skin was bright, and his eyes were filled with relief. I giggled when James spotted Kim and, as if none of us were there, he pulled her into a long kiss. It was sweet, if not a little gross to witness.

"Where's Kiera?" Eric asked, stepping up to Mom for a hug.

"She decided to stay home and work some extra shifts. She said to tell you she misses you," Mom said.

I wonder what Mom would say if I told her about the party Keira was planning. I wouldn't do that. Kiera deserved some time to herself after this semester and, in truth, I agreed the cabin was a little too small for all of us now.

"Isn't that right, Reena?"

Crap. Someone was talking to me. "Huh?"

"I was telling James that you've been looking forward to this trip all year."

"Oh! Yeah. It's been way too long since we've been here together. I've missed it." I sighed. "We were here at least twice a year for what? Ten years? And then nothing."

"We haven't had all of us together in almost two." Lily pouted. "Except for Christmas."

"Well, with my basketball schedule, Eric off at school, and Jaxson's swim team stuff, it just hasn't been possible." I wrapped my arm around her shoulders and squeezed. "But we're having one now. Well, except for Keira."

"She's a stick in the mud anyway," Lily said, causing me to choke.

Did she really just say that?

Lily perked up and continued, "And we're going snowboarding while we're here, right?"

"That's the plan," Dad said. "Why don't we get settled and then we decide what we're doing?"

"Sweet!" Lily said.

"But first." Eric stepped forward and, with one of his infectious grins, lovingly punched Jaxson in the arm, then hugged Lily so hard she squeaked. I shook my head. I had to admit that Eric was handsome even if all I saw was the jerk who treated me like a kid sister. To me, he was that older brother that liked to meddle. He set Lily down and faced me. "Reena..." *Turdnuggets. I knew that taunting tone.* I tried to run, but before I got two steps, he picked me up and spun me around as if I were six. I squealed as loudly as Lily had. It was a mirror of how Jaxson welcomed Lily to his birthday dinner.

Siblings...

"Eric! Stop it!" The high-pitched laughter that escaped my lips pulled the attention of everyone. I wiggled until he let me go, then smacked him in the arm. "I swear you're the only person in the world who doesn't realize how big I am now!"

"Munchkin, you're not big, and you'll always be little to me." He poked my side. I jumped out of reach.

"I see what you mean," I said, lightly tapping his tummy. "Looks like someone's getting a little comfortable at college. Is a girl doing this to you?"

Eric grunted to the sound of chuckles.

"You have to remember, you're not playing ball anymore. If you're not careful, you'll get fat," I said.

There was no way he was fat. He was tall, with wide, strong shoulders that served him well in his football days and although his belly did not resemble the six-pack he used to have, it wasn't exactly fat.

"I've only been back two minutes, and you start this?" In one quick move, Eric wrapped his arm around my head to place me in a headlock, then proceeded to give me a noogie. I punched him in the side. Hard.

"Oomph!"

"Ah! Stop it!" I yelled. *God, I missed him.* "I swear I will find a way to give your hulking butt a swirly. Jax will help!"

"You two are children." Jaxson chuckled. "And no, I won't."

Jax had begun unloading the trucks when Eric released me. I escaped to hide behind Jaxson, completely stopping his progress. I pressed my hands to his back. If Eric tried that again, we all knew I'd throw Jaxson into Eric's path. That was my M.O. and in return, Jaxson would find a creative way to get me back later. It was worth it. Jax rolled his eyes, meeting mine over his shoulder. Realizing I was touching him, I skittered back, a quick apology on my lips. His expression darkened.

Eric's eyes narrowed.

"Is this crap still going on? You two need to stop fighting." With that, he grabbed a bag and went inside.

Jaxson and I exchanged glances. His shoulders dropped, and his face became impassive. He reached down and picked up two bags, and I watched as he walked away, my stomach churning.

"Thanks, Eric," I grumbled, lugging my own set of bags toward the house.

It wasn't his fault. It was mine. Just like always.

Stepping into the cabin—okay, it was more like a big house—I dropped the bags by the front door. I'd take them upstairs later. I followed the sound of voices into the kitchen. Everyone stood around talking; a small TV on low sat on a table against the far wall. I stepped up to Lily, and something strange on the screen caught my attention.

"Emergency Presidential Report," the banner read. And there was President Dahill with a serious look on his face. I reached over and turned it up.

"Earlier today the Eastern Hemisphere reported a flash of light that caused havoc wherever it could be seen. 'The Flare,' as we call it, was reported at sixteen-thirty Eastern Standard Time and..."

"Hey, everyone!" I said, getting their attention. Using the remote, I increased the volume a bit more still. "Listen up."

They quieted, and the president's words came through.

"This is what we know. Ten months ago, a young scientist named Sean Williams at the University of Arizona noted an anomaly moving toward our solar system. Upon confirmation of the discovery, Dr. Williams contacted the appropriate authorities. Since then, international leaders and specialists across the globe have been brought in to collaborate with Dr. Williams and the United States."

"Turn it up," Eric said, leaning his elbows on the counter.

"...the anomaly's classification, size, speed, and trajectory were of the highest importance. After weeks of evaluation, it was identified that this anomaly"— President Dahill paused and took a deep breath—"was not a meteor as initially thought. The object was denoted a rogue planet and named Goliath. Approximately the size of Mars, it was headed on a direct path through our system." Panicked chatter exploded from the screen as the media attending the hearing went wild.

"Seriously?" Mom said. Her chest rose and fell quickly, the worry palpable. Dad wrapped an arm around her shoulders.

"Initially, it was thought that there was a chance for a collision with Earth."

Gasps came from everyone, both on-screen and in the room. Jax stepped up next to me, his arm brushing mine. I met his gaze, and I could tell we had the same thought.

End-of-the-world collision with Earth? There was fear in his eyes, the same fear I felt. His fingers linked with mine. He squeezed, and the world stabilized for both of us. It was just like when we were kids. Taking a measured breath, I brought my attention back to the announcement.

"An experimental rocket, named the Freedom, was launched earlier this year from Kennedy Space Station with the intention of traveling toward Goliath to deliver a series of nuclear warheads. These were to be deposited in calculated spots along its projected path in hopes of slowing Goliath enough to allow the Earth to pass safely out of range without risk of collision. The final missiles were to be placed within Goliath's atmosphere with the use of an unmanned aerial vehicle piloted by the Freedom."

Cool. It was hard not to find this fascinating, even if I was terrified.

President Dahill continued, "The Flare was the effect of the first detonation. It was the largest collection of warheads, closest to the surface of Goliath. Up to this point, and due to its unique makeup, Goliath has not been invisible to the naked eye. What the experts have said, and is the best description I can give, is that the surface of Goliath absorbs light. This means that the light from the Sun does not reflect off its surface as with all other objects—the Moon, for example. Because of this, the planet has been overall undetectable. What we did not expect was what happened when the first blast went off."

I leaned against the counter, needing the support. Jax did the same, our hands pressed between us. Lily slipped in next to me, and I wrapped an arm around her. Mom and Kim took seats at the breakfast table, our fathers standing next to them.

"Upon interaction with the warheads' electromagnetic pulse, the light of the blast field intensified and rebounded, causing the Flare. With it, this quality of absorbing light has disappeared, and cracks have appeared on its surface. The confusing part is the strange glow emanating from them." He paused to rub his hands together. "We are currently trying to determine the cause of this illumination but have yet to identify it. With that said, I would like to warn all of you that there are several additional detonations expected over the next twelve hours."

"What does this mean?" I whispered to Jax. He shook his head.

"At that point, we will perform a final calculation to verify our mission was a success." Dahill took a long, deep breath. His exhale was slow. "I know I've given you some very concerning information this evening, but I wanted to assure you that based on all calculations up to this point, the rogue planet Goliath is *not* going to collide with Earth. That risk was low, to begin with, but the leaders of our world decided a proactive approach was the best course of action." President Dahill shifted from foot to foot. He looked terrible. "With its documented size and the additional distance that has been created by the first blast, I want to assure all of you that Goliath will pass out of Earth's gravitational reach. This means that there should be no effect on Earth or the Moon due their proximity. There will be no interaction between the two objects. Should Goliath's speed stay at a constant rate, it should pass completely in two months' time. Please understand that come tomorrow, Goliath will be visible. Do not panic. It is large, but it is not a threat."

There was a long pause as everyone took in his words. "To verify all questions are answered properly, I will hand it over to Dr. Sean Williams and Dr. Thomas Walls. Thank you for your time and your hope." With that, he stepped off the stage and left the room. The press called after him, but he didn't return.

A young man with warm brown skin a shade lighter than mine and dark hair stepped up to the podium. The man, in his mid-to-late twenties, swallowed hard before asking for the first question.

I leaned forward, wanting to know everything, but before the entire question was out, the sound stopped and "mute" appeared on the screen. Eric held the remote. He stared toward his parents, worry in his eyes.

"What does this mean?" he asked, repeating the words I whispered earlier. The parents exchanged a look.

"For us?" James said. "Nothing right now. We'll act as we normally do. They state that this Goliath will pass, and that there's no threat. They're probably not telling us everything and we'll do some research to see what else we can learn, but I think that for now, we continue on as normal."

"I agree," my dad said. "Even if something happens, we'll deal with it together. Here at the cabin is the best place we could be in a situation like this."

He was right. We had supplies, and we were out of the big city. With this news, they'd probably have all sorts of problems. Hell, how many times had riots happened following sports events? The panic this would cause? I could only imagine what would happen. Fear did weird things to people. I thought of Keira. I'd have to call and check on her before bed—make sure she was okay.

"I'll call Keira and make sure she's okay and has a plan," Dad said as if reading my mind.

"But Mom?" Lily asked. "Don't you and James have to go back into Portland the day after tomorrow for a meeting or something? Do you have to go?"

Mom exchanged looks with the other adults, then said, "I'll call my boss in the morning, but probably. I wouldn't worry, though; it'll only be for a few hours and the meeting with my client shouldn't take long."

"Mine either. Don't worry, Munchkin, we'll be back before you know it."

"And you're planning to go snowboarding while we're gone, right?" Mom asked. We nodded. "Well, I don't think there's any reason for those plans to change. They said everything was going to be fine and if anything happens, it won't be soon. We'll make some preparations just in case, but you guys should go have fun. We'll see you when you get home."

"She's right," Dad said, but I knew he'd have each of us loaded with emergency packs, just to be safe. Okay, that wasn't all that different than usual anyway.

"Kids, why don't you guys set up the bedrooms, then head down to the basement? We'll bring down some food and we can talk more, okay?" Kim said. She was trying to get rid of us. "Bring down your day packs so we can get them stocked."

Called it. Super crazy day pack, here we come.

"Yeah," Eric said, bending to pick up a suitcase balanced against the wall. As he did, he glanced at us. His eyebrows rose when they locked onto our still-linked fingers.

Heat warmed my cheeks. As nonchalantly as I could, I dropped Jax's grip, then rushed to help with the bags.

Thankfully, Eric didn't say anything. Of course, the way I bolted out of there might've had something to do with it. At least I wasn't alone. Jax was right on my heels, Eric's chuckle following after.

The rooms were prepped, and stuff put away. I was about to head down to the basement but decided I needed a few minutes to myself. I shrugged on my jacket and stepped outside. If Goliath was now visible, would I be able to see it? I guess that would depend on if the clouds that usually haunted the Northwest region decided to clear. It had been overcast most of the day, but maybe I'd get lucky.

I stepped off the porch, and a gasp fell from my lips as I took in the sky.

"Hey, guys," I called to the house. "I can see Goliath. Get out here!"

Goliath was just breaking over the mountains, and it was massive. Most of it disappeared into the night, too black to really see with only a shadow at the edges that gave away its end. The cracks President Dahill mentioned were stark against the surface. Maroon lines shot out from two large focal points to snake farther and farther out. Some were wide and whispered of how deep the damage truly went. Others looked so small I worried it was a trick of the light. But what really caught my breath was how the deep color of the cracks contrasted with the vibrant blue-green light that radiated from sections of the exposed surface.

A wave of dizziness hit me, and I closed my eyes against a sharp pain between them. A flash of writhing, deep purple tentacles filled my vision, and I gasped.

What the heck was that? I lifted my gaze back to Goliath and I swore the light was moving. My stomach flipped. I had to be imagining it, but I knew this feeling. It was one I'd had before which warned me to be careful, to see what others couldn't.

We were in danger.

How much? I wouldn't know until the planet got closer and those sections became even more defined, but in my gut, I knew Goliath was about to change everything. I rubbed my arms and sighed at its beauty. It had a majestic quality to it and a pull that sang to something deep within me. That was never a good sign.

The soft snick of the door shutting brought my attention around. Jax came down the steps but stumbled when his gaze latched onto Goliath.

"Holy crap."

"Right?" I said with a giggle, hiding the panic which had overtaken me. "I can't believe we never noticed it before. I guess what they said was true. It was basically hiding. Where are the others?" I steadied my breaths, pushing back the image.

"On the way out." He stopped next to me. "Its appearance does make me question a few things. Like, are the 'properties' of the planet natural or something more controlled?"

I swallowed, and with a giggle, said, "I feel like I should add a 'dun-dun-duh!' after that comment."

He chuckled. "All right, fine. I'm being paranoid."

"Are you, though? I feel the same way. Like whatever that is"— I gestured toward Goliath—"is more than it seems. Who knows, maybe the government knows more than they're saying. Or maybe not. Either way, it doesn't change anything."

"What do you mean?"

"I don't know. I'm rambling." I rubbed my hands over my face. "I think I'm just scared."

Jax stared at the rogue planet endangering our world. Because that was what it was doing. Even if it was out of range, so many things could go wrong and most we couldn't do anything about.

"I heard one of the experts they were interviewing talking about its size and whether it would affect the Earth or the Moon. They say that Goliath isn't big enough to have much of an effect with how far away it is."

"Do you believe them?"

He sighed; my eyes were drawn to the movement of his shrug. His face was serious, his blond hair cut short on the sides but longer on the top. It flopped over his forehead, and I had an urge to push it back.

Clearing my throat, I shoved those traitorous thoughts away. This was Jax. My oldest friend and, more recently, my enemy. He wasn't some guy I got to stare at. I needed to keep my distance, avoid emotions that would further complicate the situation. Muddling my brain with hope—and other emotions—was not a good idea.

"Jax?" I asked, then paused. I found it interesting how, in the last twelve hours, "Jaxson" had once again become "Jax" in my head. The "Jax" from my childhood. The Jax that was once my best friend. I didn't fight it anymore and definitely not here in the place that had always been ours. "What do you think is going to happen?"

He tilted his head to the side, eyes taking me in. I shivered at his intense, knowing gaze. He was reading me, and there was no way to hide. He knew me too well, even now.

Crap. He'll see how scared I am.

And he did. Without a word, he pulled me to him. With only a moment of hesitation, I nuzzled into his chest, my arms encircling his waist. He was warm, his scent filling my nose a better relaxant than anything.

He smelled like my childhood. He felt like home. I sighed when his chin rested on the top of my head.

I knew I shouldn't let him comfort me, but I couldn't resist. He was the only one who could—who I'd let—comfort me. But this was dangerous.

"I don't know, Reena. I don't know. But we'll figure it out as a family just like we always have."

I nodded, then pulled away. The door opened and, a second later, everyone else poured out. It was almost funny how their eyes went wide one after another. Exclamations of surprise filled the air, and I found a spot on the porch steps to watch and listen as they discussed Goliath. There was a sense of fascination within each of them, but also fear mixed in too. That's how I felt. My guess was that this was how everyone around the world felt at that moment. Could we trust what we were told? Was Goliath really going to pass by? Would we survive if it didn't?

I guess we'll have to wait and see.

The next day flew by. After long hours of hiking and exploring, we had dinner and relaxed together watching crappy B movies. We bantered, played board games, and just enjoyed each other's company, all while trying to ignore the elephant in the room. Or more accurately, the approaching rogue planet. It was a great night. That was until, just before Mom and James left for Portland, Lily admitted she didn't feel well. Seeing as this was our first day in the cold, that wasn't all that surprising, but then she spiked a fever. Lily was upset because that meant she wouldn't be snowboarding tomorrow. Instead, she would be heading into town with Mom to see the doctor.

Lily was nervous to go into the city after what we'd learned yesterday. As expected, there had been riots, and she was scared. She didn't want to leave us, but Mom and Dad insisted she see the doctor. Eventually, Mom put her foot down, and they loaded up to leave.

Jax and I watched them drive away in silence. I couldn't explain why but letting them go didn't feel right. Something inside me said it was wrong, that it would be a long time until we'd be together again. I lifted my face to the sky, to where I knew Goliath lurked behind the gray blanket of clouds, and just breathed in the pine scent.

"They shouldn't be going anywhere," I whispered.

"It's only for the day," Jax said.

"It feels wrong." I rubbed my palm nervously. The swirling in my gut had me say, "Something isn't right."

"Another one of your feelings, huh?"

I stiffened. That tone of judgment set something off in me. I flashed to a few days before as Sam and Remus had taunted me.

"We're back to that?" I snapped. "Are you gonna call me a bitch, a slut, and all those other wonderful things Sam and Remus said the other day? Or are you considering adding to it this time?"

"Reena, no! I..."

I cut him off. "I don't want to hear it." Waving off anything he might say, I stomped away. The truce had only lasted forty-eight hours. Why was I not surprised?

Before I rounded the house, he called out, "I'm sorry. I should've stopped them."

I froze but didn't turn around.

"I should've followed you and made sure you were okay. Instead, I added to the mean things they said and didn't listen. And all you were trying to do was wish me happy birthday."

That wasn't one hundred percent true.

My shoulders dropped, anger disappearing, and guilt took its place. I let out a long breath. Without looking at him, I said, "I've said or allowed a lot more to be done to you. You aren't the one at fault here, Jaxson. Not completely anyway."

"Jaxson," he whispered, defeat in every syllable. If I thought I could sink any further, I would've been covered by soil. I rounded the house and disappeared from sight.

An hour of sitting outside alone did nothing to improve my mood, so I headed inside, grabbed my computer, and started to research. Maybe something I learned would help the family. I was there minutes before a large body flopped next to me. Jaxson shot me a sad smile, opened his laptop, then hit my knee with his. Hesitantly, I smiled back.

We spent the next few hours researching anything about Goliath. The tension drifted away slowly. The longer we stayed, the more we opened up, deciding to put the previous argument behind us. Sadly, we came up with very little that hadn't been reported earlier that morning on the news. Even so, we'd continued on. For hours, we talked about the Freedom, Goliath, and the conspiracy theories that had popped up in the last twenty-four hours. Unfortunately for us, little had been released, and what had been was over our heads scientifically. I'd like to say astronomy was a passion, but I'd be lying. Now, I wish it were. We stayed up even after everyone else had gone to bed. I hadn't realized I'd fallen asleep until I felt Jax brush a piece of hair from my face. He chuckled.

"Reena, it's time for bed."

I blinked away the sleep that had pulled me under. My head rested on his shoulder, and my body was pressed up against his. He was warm and smelled so good.

"Come on," he said quietly.

I pushed myself to a seated position and rubbed my eyes. Jax appeared in front of me and, forcing my eyes open, I took the hand he offered. He led me to the girl's room and was about to leave me there when I stumbled. His arm laced around my waist, then he helped me to my bed.

"I'm so tired," I whispered, leaning into him.

"I know. Let's get you to bed, and you'll feel better."

I flopped down to snuggle into the covers he placed over me. When I heard his soft steps retreating, I said in my sleepy haze, "I'm sorry, Jax. For everything. I miss you."

The last thing I remember was Jax's whispered words, "I know. I miss you too."

Chapter Four

"Reena, wake up."

A gentle hand brushed down my arm. I grumbled and rolled away from Jaxson. I'd been awake for a while listening to Eric, Kim, and Dad in the kitchen, but hadn't wanted to get up yet. I was so warm, snuggled in tight. I'd get up soon. I knew I had to get ready for the trip up the mountain, but up until that point, I hadn't cared. I was on vacation. So, I curled tighter into a ball and ignored him completely.

"You look terrible in the morning. You know that?" he said.

What? Really? Jerk. I hid my smile, rolling farther from him with a groan. I wanted to be mad, but I wasn't. I knew what was happening here.

"Come on, Reena, it's time to wake up. You're keeping me from kicking your butt on the slopes." He shook my shoulder this time.

Kick my butt? Yeah, right. He shifted closer. *Perfect, he's within reach.*

Getting a good grasp of the pillow, I spun, whapping him in the chest. A *whoompf* escaped him as he fell off the side of the bed and to the floor, landing on his back. In one full motion— and before he could react—I was on my knees, pouncing. I pushed him down and knelt above him, my hands pressed to his chest, holding him to the ground.

"I doubt that! I could beat you with my eyes closed," I taunted.

He grabbed my wrists and yanked me off balance. Next thing I knew, I was on my back with him straddling me. *Damn.* He pinned my wrists to the ground so I couldn't easily break free. I wiggled in an attempt to escape, lifting my hips to throw him off. No luck. I tried to roll, but nope. He was too damn big now, and I'd let him get me good and pinned.

"No fair," I complained. "I wasn't really trying to pin you."

"You started it." A wicked grin lit his face. "And besides, you're not really pinned."

I shook my head in exasperation. His hand shifted against my skin, thumb tracing my wrist. I don't think he was aware he was doing it, but it caught my breath anyway.

He leaned down, a gleam in his eye. "And considering you can't even walk with your eyes open, I doubt it would be smart to snowboard with your eyes closed."

When I struggled again, trying to get the upper hand, I felt his weight press down. He really hadn't been pinning me. And through it all, his thumb continued to caress my skin. *Why was he doing that?*

He leaned closer, only inches between us. "I don't know if you noticed, but you're not bigger than me anymore. I've got you by at least two inches and twenty pounds now. You'll have to up your game."

Challenge accepted. "That may be true, Jax, but I play dirty."

With that, I took a deep breath and blew it at him. Immediately, he let go of my wrists to cover his face, protecting his nose from my morning breath. He sat back on his ankles, still straddling me. Making a sound somewhere between a laugh and a cough, he said, "Ah! What's wrong with you? Girls should never smell so bad!"

I laughed. I'd won this round, and we both knew it.

Eyes sparkling, he leaned back over, placing his hand on the ground by my waist. He kept enough distance that my trick wouldn't work again.

"There's something so profoundly wrong with you." But amusement lit his face.

I was sucked into the shocking blue of his gaze as it traveled down me, taking in my body and the precarious position we were in. I lay in just a tank top and a pair of very short sleep shorts. The sheets were thrown everywhere from our play and my hair was splayed across the floor in a halo around my head. My shirt had risen just a few inches to show off the smallest amount of stomach.

Heat flushed my face. Jaxson—no, Jax—was looking at me in a way he never had before. It was heated, and I liked it.

As if it were a struggle, he pulled his gaze away from my body and up to my eyes. They fluttered to my lips, and his head tilted curiously. Our breaths, quick from laughter, sped even more. And yet, we were both frozen in place. The gleam in his eyes shifted—amusement changed to a fascination that was mixed with just a little confusion.

I, too, found myself staring at his lips, my own need to be near him muddling my thoughts. I bit my lip. His eyes tracked the movement, and I swear he began to lower himself.

"What's going on here?"

We jumped, Jax straightening in an instant. Apparently, we'd been so lost in each other that we didn't hear the steps approach. And there was Eric standing in the doorway with a quizzical grin on his face.

Jax jumped to his feet. He extended a hand, and I took it. I caught Jax's sweeping glance as I adjusted my shorts. He cleared his throat.

"Nothing. Reena was just showing me how awful her breath is in the morning. Let me tell you, it can peel paint." He pushed me playfully.

"It's not that bad. And that's what you get for waking me up." *I had to get out of here.* I could feel the blush on my cheeks. If I wasn't careful, stupid things would start coming out of my mouth as I began to babble. I needed an escape. I pushed past them and into the bathroom.

"Yes, it is!" he hollered as the door shut. Even through the door I heard his next whisper to Eric. "She plays dirty."

Eric chuckled and clapped Jax on the shoulder. "They always do, Jax. They always do."

I grinned. Their footsteps echoed down the hall, toward the kitchen. I pressed my back to the door, trying to calm my racing heart.

What had just happened? I rubbed my wrist. I felt branded from his touch. Smiling to myself, I went to shower.

Less than an hour later, we were on our way up the mountain. Our brightly colored outfits swished with every step as we headed from the parking lot to the lifts.

Ah, the sound of nylon in the morning. I couldn't wait until we'd warmed up a bit and could remove some of these layers. After my interesting and unexpected wake up, I'd showered and layered up. With our backpacks stocked, we'd eaten breakfast, spoken to James and Lily on the phone, and then headed out. Unfortunately, the call didn't go well. I guess, after her meeting, Mom fell, hitting her head and injuring her ankle badly enough to go to the hospital.

Dad had wanted to leave for Portland that instant in order to be with her in the emergency room, but Mom had nixed that idea. Due to the severity of the injury, they wanted her to stay overnight. Mom was irritated, Dad was worried, and that bad feeling in my chest had gotten worse. The good news was, Lily was feeling much better, and they decided to have James bring her home. Dad would pick Mom up tomorrow. With a soon-to-be broken person in the house, Kim decided to stay back from snowboarding and get everything ready.

While we talked to them, Eric had made a few calls of his own. Come to find out, there was a girl back in Denver. Her name was Arianna. I'd overheard parts of their conversation and afterward couldn't help but wonder about this girl who'd caught his attention. Was she good enough for him? As we drove up the mountain, I grilled Eric for details. He laughed at my demanding questions, but eventually relented. He was smitten.

"So, Eric. The question is, do you think we'll approve?" I joked.

"You better because Mom does, and she's the one who matters."

"Aw. That's both cute and offensive that you think she'd be more important than Jax and me," I said. Jax snorted, but Eric grinned.

"Don't forget," Dad said, interrupting our teasing. We pulled into the parking lot. "I'm meeting up with some old college friends around one o'clock. You guys can run off and cause trouble at that point. I'll meet you back at the lodge around four. Does that sound good?"

We vocalized our agreement, climbed out, and grabbed our stuff. After a few runs with us, Dad went off to find his friends on the east side course while we went to the main course on the west side. It had warmed up some, so my overcoat, ski mask, and gloves went into my backpack while Eric and I hopped on the lift. Initially, Jax and I had gone for one together, but when Eric started teasing us, I wimped out. Stupidly, I said something mean to Jax before I hopped on one with Eric instead. With a scowl, Jax did the only thing he could do—he climbed on alone. I sat watching him as the lift swayed back and forth with the movement of the wire and the wind.

"Think you can beat me to the bottom?" Eric asked.

"You know it. I've seen you snowboard, Eric, and considering how uncoordinated you are, I'm a little surprised you've survived this long."

He rolled his eyes. "Okay..." Then, he looked at me sideways, a devilish glint in his eyes. "So, uh, what was going on this morning?"

"Nothing." *Was my voice a little higher than normal?* "He woke me up, and I beat him with my pillow."

"That's not what it looked like to me." He winked, then raised his eyebrows suggestively.

"Shut up, Eric," I said, shaking my head. "You know as well as I do that nothing would ever happen between us. We aren't close anymore, and besides, he's like my brother."

I glanced toward the lift ahead to the lone figure sitting there. I was lying to myself, and I knew it. Jax had always been more than my best friend. He'd been everything.

"And that's not even considering all the crap I've done to push him away the last few years."

"People make mistakes. We grow."

Was that true? Could I fix this and get him back? Was there something more here now? No, there couldn't be. There had never been anything romantic between us exactly, but it had never been purely platonic either. As if to prove a point, Jax turned to us and smiled. I couldn't help but smile back.

"Uh-huh, sure. Reena? So you know, *that*"— he gestured to Jax— "is not the smile you give a sister. Neither is the way he was looking at you this morning. Or the way you look at him."

I choked a little but tried to hide it. "Whatever. You don't know what you're talking about."

"Hmmm. Well, whatever happens, at least you both seem to be friends again. You need to keep it that way."

"I'll do my best." And I meant it. I was tired of fighting our friendship. It had only been three days, and I already felt more like myself than I had in years. It was because of Jax—because of the way he allowed me to be me even when he was angry.

Wanting to change the subject, I said, "And, um, what about this Arianna?"

The sappiest look I'd ever seen appeared on his face. "I think she's a keeper. Smart, beautiful, kind. She's a handful—that's for sure—but it's worth every second. I wish she were here, but her family needs her. I think we'd both feel better if she were, especially with everything that's been going on."

"I'm sorry she isn't. That has to be hard."

He looked up at the sky, taking a long breath, then back to me. The overcast sky was bright. "Listen, Reena, I need you to remember something. You and Jax are better together. You always have been. Even if it's just as friends. You two need to keep working on whatever broke between you. I feel like something's coming and the only way we're going to survive is if we stick together. I need you to forget all the high school crap and remember who loves you, who your friends are."

I nodded, then rested my head on his shoulder. I agreed completely. I could feel the danger too. Was it because of Goliath or something else? Our world was about to change. I just hadn't figured out what it was yet. I could feel it in the ground, in the wind, and even in the sounds that came from the forest surrounding us. It felt like the world was balanced on the head of a pin and there was no way to tell which way it'd fall. My heart dropped, sadness leaking into my very being.

Jax turned and made a face at us. *How does he always know?* Warmth spread, wiping out that previous sense of helplessness. Him and me. It felt familiar. This felt right.

"Are you going to make it off this thing without face-planting?" Jax hollered at me. I glared.

"Focus on yourself, jerk."

He grinned. We reached the top and exited the lift where I barely managed to keep my feet. I'd been snowboarding since I was little, but for some reason the lift was always something that tested my coordination. We won't talk about the number of times I actually fell on my face.

"Nice job," Jax said as I joined him at the top of the hill. I shoved him playfully.

"Yeah, yeah. Put the sass away and let's go. I am ready for some fun."

"Then let's do this!" Eric said. With a wide grin on his face, he began his descent.

Jax and I followed a second later. We swerved, gliding over the snow, zigzagging to and fro. Bright white arcs of powder followed behind us. I loved being out there with wind, speed, and the guys' laughter echoing in my ears. It was heaven.

We'd just passed the halfway point when a wave of blue-green light shot across the sky. The clouds rolled with its movement, turning the sky into water. An instant later, a *boom* crashed through the landscape. I yelped as it hit my ears, nearly losing my balance. I managed to right myself until a much larger and closer *boom* slammed me to the ground. The earth beneath me began to shake. I screamed.

Jax appeared at my side and began to pull me to my feet. He was yelling, but I could barely hear him over the rumbling.

"Get up! Go, go, go, go! Over there!" He pointed down the side of the mountain. "It's an avalanche!"

There was no thought; I just moved. We needed to get out of its path *now*! We headed to the right. There was a large cliff with an overhang that broke up the mountain. Earlier, I'd seen some snowboarders jump off of it on their path down. It wasn't much protection, but it was something. Refusing to look behind me, I moved. The air vibrated, and the snow shifted beneath me.

Move. Move. Move! I chanted. *Don't look behind you. Don't do it. Just keep going.*

I veered to the right sharply.

One hundred yards. Come on.... Fifty....

I could no longer see Jax, who was somewhere off to my left. I screamed for him but couldn't hear anything over the noise. My muscles seized with a spike of terror like nothing I had ever felt. I fought it, focusing only on my destination.

Ten yards......Five.

The ground disappeared. For a second, I hung in mid-air, but then a wall slammed my back and I rolled. I hit hard, my breath pushed from me. Before the snow took me under, I heard my name. The world spun.

Jax. With that last thought, the world darkened.

I awoke with a start. My chest refused to expand with the impossible weight resting upon it. It was cold and my body hurt, but I managed to suck in a shallow breath.

Where am I? What happened? Seconds passed as I tried to remember.

Snow. Lots of snow.

Oh my god, the avalanche! Panic rose in my chest. *No, don't panic. You have to stay calm. Breathe.*

Focusing, I did just that. With each in and out, I calmed. Then, I took stock of myself. A sharp pain radiated from my thigh and up to my hip, but other than that, I seemed fine even as I lay face down, my legs twisted to the side in an extremely awkward and uncomfortable position.

See. Not so bad. Just think, Reena. First, calm your breathing a bit more. It's too fast. I had to slow it, or I would run out of air. The snow was pressed against my face, adding to my difficulty breathing. I had to clear it away from my mouth and soon. My right arm was wrapped in an arc above my head, hand close enough I knew I'd be able to. The other was pinned behind my back. Carefully, I shifted and cleared the snow away from my mouth. It helped. I could breathe better and, with it, was able to push the panic down.

Keep calm. Someone will come for you. Jax will come for you.

If he's alive. I choked on a sob. *Stop it. He* is *alive and he'll find you.*

As my clothes became damp, the cold settled deeper into my bones, causing the pain in my hip to worsen. I wished I could adjust and relieve the tension, but there was no way. I couldn't move. Time became abstract. It felt like hours passed, but it could've been minutes. I just had to stay calm. Either they would find me, or they wouldn't. I cleared more space around my mouth, the air becoming stale.

That's when I heard it. It was muffled and far quieter than I liked, but it was there. It was my name.

"Help!" I rasped. The pressure cocooning me refused to let my chest expand all the way, so the cry was weak. I tried again and was happy when it was louder this time.

Was that a response? I think it was. Please don't be a hallucination, I prayed. Long moments later, there was a weird scraping sound. *Someone digging?*

This went on for what seemed like forever. They didn't hear me correctly? Could they tell the right spot? I began to shake, and tears burned my eyes. I focused on the noises and prayed it was real. Then I felt it. The weight along my back lightened, and sounds of the world seeped back in. I hadn't realized how quiet it'd been. When the hand touched my side, tears froze on my cheeks.

"Here!" a voice exclaimed. The pressure lessened along my shoulders and head now. "Reena!" Their cry was pained. The sound of Jaxson's voice, so worried, tightened my throat. I squeezed my eyes shut. "Reena, are you okay? Please be okay."

Hands cleared snow from around my head and air rushed in, allowing the first of many deep breaths. In. Out. In. Out. I groaned as they cleared my legs. There was a click as my snowboard was removed, and I was finally able to adjust. They pulled me free and turned me over. Gentle fingers cleared snow from my eyes and face, and a true sob burst from my chest. Arms wrapped around me.

"I've got you," Jax said. Tears broke through at those words. Jax lifted me as though I weighed nothing, and I leaned into him as he carried me away. The world tilted again, and I opened my eyes. He'd set me down by the base of the cliff we'd been trying to get to before. His eyes were the first things I saw. They were scared and anxious. A quick smile, then he moved to examine me for injuries.

Eric appeared at my other side. His brow was furrowed, and a frown twisted his mouth. He lifted my chin, forcing me to make eye contact. "Reena, are you okay? I need you to answer me."

"Yes? Scared," I admitted. Eric kissed the top of my head.

"You're okay," Jax said, pushing Eric back.

"Yes, are you? What happened? Jax, I..." I felt out of control, spiraling waves of shock and fear. *I was out of my prison. I am out of that prison.*

Jax cupped my cheek. "We've got you, but we need to know how badly you're hurt."

"Um, not too bad. My thigh hurts like hell. My hip is sore. Probably from being in that position, but..." I shrugged. "How long was I in there?"

"Twenty minutes or so," Eric said. "I saw you guys fall. I got Jax out pretty easily, but I was worried you'd run out of air before we got to you. I'm sorry it took me so long."

"It felt longer than twenty minutes. I was able to make an air pocket, but it was getting thin." I took Eric's hand. "Thank you."

I scanned Jax to see if he had any injuries. Nothing I could see.

"Are you guys okay?" I panted. Jax was too distracted with checking me over to hear my question. I grabbed his arm. "Seriously, I'm fine. Are you? What happened?"

It was a fight not to pull back at the fear in his gaze. He looked to the sky.

"Oh my god," I whispered, only then seeing how truly screwed we were. A shiver ran up my spine. *How had I missed that?*

The sky was burning in waves of blue-green and yellow. The clouds had broken apart and swirled like water. Flashes of color exploded everywhere like popcorn, and I realized it was with each impact of small meteorites entering the atmosphere. The size of them determined the intensity of the shock waves that expanded out from their entry points. The sky was chaos.

Cold fear swept me at the sight of a very changed Goliath. Now in two pieces—one significantly larger than the other—they took up the entire horizon. The larger piece looked on the same path as before, but the other was coming toward Earth. It was huge, like end-of-all-life-on-our-planet huge. Or I thought so. It was hard to measure something like that.

"A piece of Goliath broke off," Eric explained. "I stopped here to wait for you to catch up and I saw it. It hit the Moon."

Dread. Absolute and utter terror. I shook, my mouth going dry. I glanced at the Moon. It was still where I would've expected to see it, but it looked so different. New craters scattered its surface, and a small chunk was missing off its side. Fragments floated in all directions with many being sucked into the atmosphere. This was bad, really bad. If it had been knocked out of orbit, we were in serious trouble.

"Everything looks so strange," I said in awe. "Look at all those colors."

Just like that, it clicked. There was a difference between the meteorites. Those from the Moon lit up with a white streak as they hit the atmosphere, but the Goliath pieces? They were bright green. A circular wave pulsed from each.

"What do you mean?" Eric asked, his eyes on the sky.

"It is so terrifyingly pretty," I whispered.

"This can't be happening," Jax said.

"It is, and Goliath is getting closer." My voice wobbled. The small piece of Goliath was caught in Earth's magnetic field and when it got here, everything would change.

Chapter Five

"Help me up. If the world is going to end, I want a good view." The miles wide chunk of Goliath, which had peeled off from the main section, was headed toward us. Between it and the main piece, it took up at least a third of the sky.

"Not funny," Jax said, but pulled me to my feet. I winced as I put weight on my left side.

The way they approached made me think of the times as a child I would hide in a box, and someone would slowly slide a lid over the opening. That feeling of claustrophobia, of panic and despair. And just like back then, my chest tightened; my breathing picked up. But this? This was the sky, and a lid was being slid over it.

"It's glowing," Eric said.

He was right. One entire side shone that same blue-green that had leaked from the cracks in Goliath's surface while the other shimmered with a brilliant mix of purple and yellow. Even from here you could tell how the two colors flowed like liquid.

"You guys are seeing this too, right? What used to be the inside of Goliath is a different color than the shell?" Green and white fire licked at its tips as it began its descent. It was coming, and there was nothing stopping it now.

"There's nowhere to go," Jax whispered. His hand slipped into mine, and on instinct, I stepped closer.

"No. We just have to hope nothing hits near us," Eric said.

"I'm scared," I admitted. Eric took my other hand, and I pulled him closer too. I needed them with me.

The forest went silent.

Goliath began to rotate. No, really. I thought I was seeing things, but I wasn't. It was turning to place what was left of the shell downward. It was like Goliath wanted to protect the inside substance. But why?

"That's not possible. Did you see that?" I asked. No one answered, because right then the outside layer hit the atmosphere. I slammed my eyes shut when the sky lit up to blind us. It faded quickly, but then we were staggering as the shockwave crashed onto us. Jax steadied me, his hand strong in mine.

"It's here," he said.

Yeah, no shit. The sky burst apart with color. Shades of green permeated everything around us. The light was so bright that Jax, Eric, and I skittered back to the cliff wall. We crouched down, ducked our heads, but covering our ears did nothing to lessen the roar. It growled and roared with so much fury I was afraid it would blow out my eardrums.

The chunk of Goliath screeched across the sky, heading southwest. We felt its passage with every fiber of our beings. The ground shook, the air was hot, and the smell of smoke surrounded us. I was pressed between Jax and Eric, their arms around me. I only knew the sound had lessened when Jax's heartbeat against my ear filtered through. Then the shaking rattle of the universe subsided.

I took a relieved breath. We released each other. When I was finally able to open my eyes, I saw the boys shift in unison to watch its descent.

Goliath flew impossibly fast, a line of dust and ash trailing behind it. Again, I swear I felt a shift in it. It changed its speed. Goliath couldn't be slowing down, but that's what my eyes—and more importantly—my instincts told me. Goliath *was* slowing down. It disappeared into the distance, the trail behind it all that was left. Absolute silence followed. That was until a detonation of sound rocked us again. I cried out, clapping my hands to my ears. I felt it in my bones as the entire world vibrated. There was another huge burst of light, and then nothing.

My heart beat. One, two, three...

It wasn't over yet. Debris from the collision reached the outer atmosphere. Pieces of all sizes sailed overhead, many falling in the surrounding mountains. Trees blew apart, earth shot into the air, and fires ignited. Explosions of all sizes could be seen in every direction. The entire region was being bombarded. A few miles away, a larger chunk hit and although the shock wave was nothing like Goliath, the ash cloud was more than visible.

I gasped. *This was bad. This was very, very bad.*

We stayed where we were, pressed up against the cliff face because really, where could we go? The only thing we could do was wait and hope that none fell too near or, God forbid, on us. It was hard to breathe. It was hard to think past the truth that we might still die as so many others were.

I had no idea how long the onslaught lasted. A while, that's for sure. I only looked up when something touched my face. It was soft and cold. An ash trailed Goliath. The ominous snow was ready to suffocate everything in its darkness as it shimmered, a mixture of a dark metallic purple and bright sun yellow.

I couldn't help it. I put my hand out and caught some. The moment that the dust touched my skin, a tingling sensation spread up my arm, then all over my body. The feeling wasn't unpleasant, just foreign. As I gazed at it, the dust changed. It shifted from the solid that fell from the sky to a swirling liquid. The smaller pieces collected, then rolled across my skin into oil-like droplets.

"It reminds me of mercury," I said, shifting my hand right to left, and then back again. "But it's cold."

"You know what mercury looks like?" Eric asked, watching my hand. I shot him an annoyed glare. He grinned. "Sorry. Seriously though, it's cold? You'd think it'd be warm."

"I've never seen ash this color. Let alone anything that turns liquid when it hits skin." Tilting my hand back and forth, the substance rolled. Wherever it went, it left a trail of shine behind.

Jax knocked the substance out of my hand. "It might be poisonous."

I turned to find him covered, ash resting at the ends of his long strands. I reached up and stroked through his hair. The flecks had the texture of ash, but when I touched them, the ash changed again. It rolled to collect on my fingertips.

"Nothing we can do about that now. We're covered in it," I said.

He startled. He'd been staring so transfixed at my hand that he hadn't noticed how the snow around us had changed from the bright brilliant white, to a dark purple that glinted with hints of yellow.

"It's everywhere," he whispered.

I flinched as another explosion racked the neighboring hills. Tears filled my eyes at the thought of my family in danger. Did Dad get caught in the avalanche? Did Lily and James make it home? Would Mom be safe in the hospital? What about Kiera?

We had to find Dad and get back home.

The ash was everywhere, but that didn't mean I wanted to be covered in it. That odd feeling I felt on my skin continued as I brushed it away. The exposed skin of my arms and face tingled. Even my hair felt strange. I'd released my ponytail in an attempt to shake off as much as I could and ever since, it felt like something was crawling over my scalp. I tried to ignore the sensation, but it was impossible.

Ugh...it feels like bugs walking in my hair. What is this stuff? Whatever it was, we'd been exposed to a lot of it. If it turned out to be poisonous, we were in big trouble. The boys weren't nearly as concerned as I thought they should be—with either the ash or Goliath's entrance. Come to find out, they weren't experiencing the same thing I was. When I mentioned the sensation on my skin, that feeling of tingling, they didn't know what I was talking about. Still, they worked to clean off as much of the ash as possible. Once we'd cleared most of it, we pulled our gloves and masks from our bags and covered up as best we could.

Afterward, we paced around our small spot of safety. We needed to figure out what the next step was. It had been more than an hour since Goliath passed and the sky turned dark. With the sun blocked by the ash, the temperature was beginning to drop. Soon it would be cold. Very cold.

I looked around, trying to take in as much information as I could, but over and over I found myself being mesmerized by the ash that still fell. It had slowed but was still working to cover everything in a coating of purple and gold. Each tree branch twinkled yellow in the muted light, which was amplified by the dark shadows covering everything. It was such a different scene than what had been here before. The bright white which shone in the sun now held a coating of dark purple. The sky now held a haze which blocked out the sun. The day had shifted to have an otherworldly quality that sent shivers down my spine.

"Guys, we need to make a plan. The temperature's going to drop fast with this stuff. Once the sun goes down, we're in trouble."

"Agreed." Eric said. "Plus, I think we should get out of the avalanche zone as soon as we can."

"Have you heard or seen any other people? Survivors?"

Eric shook his head. "There were a few other people that were near us when it hit. I saw one hit a tree. The other...I couldn't find him. We didn't see anyone else. It was a slow day on the mountain."

"Well, the phones don't work. My watch stopped too," Jax said.

I pulled my backpack off and opened it to check mine. *Yup, dead.*

"Is anyone else having a 'thank goodness for paranoid parents' moment?" I asked as I dug through the items in my pack—snack bars, trail mix, first-aid kit, extra socks, Ace bandage—until I reached the water. We all had a backpack filled with similar items. Our parents were more than willing to let us go off on our own, but ever since we were little, they'd required us to carry a backpack with some basic essentials. My dad had been even more paranoid about our packs today. He looked through each of them and added a few extra items including an LED flashlight and a small knife. Of course I'd also added a few items of my own.

"Yes, actually."

"We need to get organized. We need to decide if we are staying here for the night or trying to get down the mountain and find somewhere safer to camp," I said.

"We shouldn't stay here. It's too dangerous," Eric said.

I nodded my agreement. "Do you think anyone is coming to help?" I asked.

"No. Usually the response to an avalanche is pretty quick, but have you noticed anyone moving near the bottom of the mountain?"

"No. In fact, shouldn't we be able to see the main lodge from up here? Or the town in the distance?"

"Yes, we should. I've tried from a couple different spots, but it's not there. There's been no movement from the lifts or from any people at the bottom," Eric said, turning. His movements were tight, jerky even. "I think we're on our own. Look over there." He pointed through a row of trees down the mountain where the distant town should've been. His hand shook, and it was then I noticed what he did. All that was left was upended trees. That town was gone.

"I'm starting to think this wasn't a localized avalanche. I wonder if all of the mountains responded to Goliath's entrance like this one did."

"It looks like it," Jax said worriedly. "I hope Mom and the others are okay."

Exhaling slowly, I pushed down the well of motion threatening to clog my throat. I couldn't think about that right now.

"I agree with Eric. We shouldn't stay here. We should head toward the lodge, find somewhere to hide out for the night. Any survivors will head there."

"Definitely. We need shelter. It's going to be cold tonight," Jax said.

"Well, it's getting late. Let's get to the lodge. Maybe we'll get lucky and find more people," Eric said.

"Dad," I whispered. Both Eric and Jax stiffened. We'd been ignoring it, but I knew that they were as worried about Dad as I was.

"Your dad's a beast. No doubt he and his group made it through. Who was he meeting again?" Eric asked.

"Sydney and her son. Remember them? I think you guys only met her once."

"Not really. Sorry. But either way, the lodge is where your dad will head."

"Agreed," Jax seconded.

"Then let's get started." I rubbed a hand down my thigh and hip where I'd hurt myself. "I'm going to apologize now, though. I'm going to be slow."

"How bad is it?"

"I'll deal. But give me a minute, okay?" I walked back to where I'd left my backpack against the cliff wall. I pulled the waistband of my pants down to examine my hip.

A long bruise ran from my hip bone down and into my pant leg. A red inflamed scrape about three inches long stretched across the peak of my hip bone. I gritted my teeth. It hurt. Not only at the wound site, but deep in the joint. Thank goodness the memory of being thrown around like that was missing. I doubt it would've been good.

It's okay, Reena. You're only hiking in an avalanche zone with an injured hip. That is totally safe, I thought as I cleaned the wound with an alcohol pad. I hissed.

"How bad?" Jax asked again.

"It's fine—an impressive bruise and small scratch. Not too bad. I'll try not to slow us down."

"Let me see it," Jax said.

"I'm fine."

"Reena, just let me get a quick look. Just at your hip. We can get a better look at the whole thing when we make camp."

"Why? You're not going to be able to do anything for it." He glared back at me, his jaw set and unwilling to back down. I sighed. "Fine."

Carefully, I pulled my waistband down just enough to show him the bruise on my hip. Both Eric and Jax whistled in appreciation.

"That's nice," Eric said.

"See. Nothing you can do. Once we stop, I'll look at it closer, but right now, I just want to get going."

Eric slapped Jax's shoulder. "She'll tell us if it gets any worse. Let's go."

Jax was not happy. Ever since I'd broken my arm on a hiking trip when we were ten, Jax had developed a tendency to become a mother hen whenever I was injured. It was going to be a long day. Eric picked up the packs and handed me mine. He threw the other to Jax.

"Let's go. Reena, if you need a break, just let us know."

"It's not that far, Jax. I'll be fine." The annoyance in my voice made Eric smile.

We followed the trees to make our way down the mountain easier, but even then, it was slow moving. The snow was thick, and I hurt. I was grateful when Jax found a large tree limb that I could use as a walking stick. It was crooked and had a few small branches sticking out of it, but he quickly cut enough of them off to allow me to grasp it comfortably. The more we walked, the more my pants dug into the bruise and the more I knew there had to be another wound farther down. With each step, pain radiated from it, making me cringe. I wanted to sit down.

It took a little over an hour and a half to reach the spot where the lodge should have been. We walked around the spot, surveying the damage. There was nothing left. There had been a record amount of snow the last few weeks and every bit of it had come down to rest right here. The main lodge had taken a direct hit. Large beams stuck out from the snow at random, their sharp ends proof of the force which snapped. The lodge had been ripped apart. Another section had been buried.

We need to find something, somewhere that we can use for shelter.

I arced around to the left. A path had once been here. It led to a parking lot and along it, a small coffee shop had been hidden in the trees. If I remembered right, the structure had butted up against a hill twenty or so feet high. Maybe it had been enough to provide some protection from the onslaught. I rounded the small hill and saw a crater about thirty feet wide where the parking lot had been. A few lumps of metal were visible, but from where I stood, no cars remained. Either buried or swept away—I didn't know.

It was hard not to cheer when the mostly covered building appeared. Only a four-foot section of wood was visible where it stuck out from the rock.

"Eric!" I called, ushering him over to what I'd found.

"Nice eye."

"I bet there's a window along this wall. Snow isn't too deep and if we can get in, it'd be a great place to stay for the night," Jax added. He turned to me. "Not bad. Who knew you'd be so useful?"

I glared, lifted my walking stick, and hit him lightly on the shin. He grunted, holding back a laugh.

We began to clear the snow. After about an hour of digging, we found the outside frame. The glass appeared next. I was standing back, catching my breath as the guys cleared the window when, just as Jax looked up, a face appeared on the other side. He squealed and jumped backward, falling to the ground.

I couldn't help it. I knew it was mean, but I lost it. I was laughing so hard I thought I'd pass out.

"I think you broke her," Eric said to Jax.

I clutched at my stomach as giggles rolled out uncontrollably. In between gasps, I asked, "Jax, did she scare you?"

He grumbled under his breath as he got to his feet. Eric did nothing to hide his grin as he continued clearing the glass. The beautiful face looking out laughed. Her soft features were framed by curly blond hair. Her golden brown eyes shone.

Oh, I was gonna like her.

Within minutes, we were able to push it open.

"Thank you!" she cried. "We were starting to think no one was coming." She leaned out and began scanning the forest. She frowned. "Wait, where's the rescue party?"

Chapter Six

Four people survived in the coffee shop. Cassie, the girl at the window, was in her early twenties. She was the one working when everything happened. After introducing herself, she and the others came out to examine the damage to the lodge while the three of us headed inside to look around.

The shop was a single room with a door toward the back. The space was separated by a counter that wrapped through the center and around to the right. Two tables and chairs sat on either side of the door near the front window, and in the far corner was a small cast iron fireplace. If we could clear the snow from the shoot, we might be able to light it. A shiver of pleasure ran up my spine at the idea of being warm. It had been hours, and the cold that had seeped into my bones while buried in the snow still hadn't left me. Part of me wondered if I'd ever be warm again.

Cassie introduced us to the family that had been ordering when Goliath's boom rattled the landscape. Not knowing what exactly was happening, but following some emergency protocol, Cassie had pulled them around the counter where they hunkered down. The parents, Allan and Jia, were in their mid-thirties.

After meeting them, I'd expected they would take charge or at least jump in with ideas of what to do, but two hours in and they hadn't spoken more than a few words. Instead, they hovered protectively around their nine-year-old son, Thomas, as if any one of us were a threat to him.

Cassie told us that a few others had been in the shop too, but they'd rushed outside. She'd tried to call them back, but then, seconds later, they'd been swept away and the shop was covered. By her tone, I knew she felt responsible. The more she spoke, the more I found it interesting how, for her, the entire experience was a flash. Whereas for me, time had crawled. I'd felt every movement of the earth, every brush of wind, and every ounce of fear that poisoned my body.

"Were you guys just going to stay in here?"

"No." She laughed. "Initially, we tried to find a way out, but the windows and door were covered. There's a back door that leads into a storage room attached to the main lodge, but the noises that had come from there... Well, let's just say I didn't want to chance it."

"Good call," Eric said.

"Either way, if no one came in a few hours, I was going to start digging."

"What's in the storage room?"

"On the other side of the door, there's a small closet with food and supplies for the shop. I can reach that. The storage room down the hall? If it's still there, it has a few aisles of supplies for us, but mostly it holds the main lodge's random crap. I haven't really spent much time snooping in there. It was frowned upon."

"There might be stuff we can use," Eric said.

"If it's still there," Cassie said. "From what you're telling me, the lodge is gone. If that's true, then it might not be intact. That room was the bottom floor of the lodge. It's probably not safe to go in. The beams holding this place up aren't very happy."

"Then we avoid it if we can," I said. We sat in a circle on the floor, taking a few moments to rest.

"So, then, what's the plan?" she asked, scanning us. Cassie pulled her knees up to her chest. She fidgeted with a piece of paper, twisting it, then tearing it into pieces. She'd held things together so far, but she was scared. I could see it. She didn't want to be in charge and was hoping we would take some of the responsibility off her shoulders. She needed support, just like the others had.

"Let's get set up for the night. The sun's going down soon," Eric said.

I stood. "All right, Jax, let's make ourselves useful. There's enough light to scout the area a little. On our way, we'll collect firewood."

An amused smile appeared on Jax and Eric's faces, but Jax stood. Good to know he still accepted my orders so easily.

"We need to organize any useful supplies. Food, water, etcetera. This is going to be base camp until we figure out what we're going to do. Cassie, can you take care of that?" I asked.

Cassie nodded. "Jia, can you help?"

Jia smiled, nodded, and then both women disappeared behind the counter.

"Great. Reena, Jax, go on and be careful. Get enough wood to start a signal fire outside and also for that." Eric pointed to the wood-burning stove. "Allan, I need your help with something."

The look of indignation on Allan's face almost made me laugh. He didn't like being bossed around by a bunch of kids, but he hadn't exactly added to the conversation. Before I said something I shouldn't, I climbed outside, hiding my wince from the movement. I followed Jax up the slope to a higher spot perfect for surveying the area. The crunch of snow under Jax's feet and the sound of my breathing were all I could hear. As I followed a few steps behind, something caught my eye. A flash of light. What was that? I turned toward it, gazing toward Jax's boot. There it was again. It was almost too quick to believe. Just as Jax took another step, it happened again. I blinked.

What was that? Was it real or am I having a stroke? With each press of his foot, there was a minute flash. Nope, real.

Left behind was the contrasting boot print; a dark purple—almost black top—ringed by a fluffy white.

It looks like Oreos. I stopped and shook my head. *That was a ridiculous comparison.*

Yup, it's a stroke. I mean, come on, Reena, it's not even dark yet. How could you be seeing flashes of light? I rushed to catch up with Jax. The overlook he'd stopped at gave us a great view of the mountain and the range around us. There was no movement, no people we could see.

"This all seems so surreal. Look at that." I gestured into the distance. "The entire sky has changed in only a few hours."

And it had. This morning had been overcast with bouts of sunny patches. Then Goliath had destroyed the clouds and caused the light show. Since then, it changed to a thick haze of ash that darkened the sky and gave it a smoky quality. It was like looking through a snow globe, but with glittering black snow instead of white. Hours later, ash still fell in tiny pieces, allowing only scattered rays from the sun to pass.

"We've got maybe an hour before the sun drops too low."

"Yup, and we need enough firewood to last us the night. A good place to start might be over there." I pointed to an unharmed thicket of trees to the east.

"Sounds good."

"While we're at it, I think we should do something else too."

"Oh, Reena," Jax said quickly, the tone wicked. My eyes narrowed at him. "Even in the presence of all this destruction and chaos, all you can think about is making out with me. I mean, I knew you wanted me, but come on. Is this really the time?"

My jaw dropped. I blinked at him a few times, attempting to find *anything* to say. Nothing came. He'd said that with a straight face, but was he serious? A huge laugh erupted from his chest at my reaction.

"Ah ha! Finally, I've managed to turn the great Reena Novak speechless! Only took seventeen years, but I did it."

I chuckled, still at a loss for words. It had never been part of our relationship to joke like that, and the fact that he'd done it so smoothly startled me. I had to scramble for a response. "Well, seize the day, right?"

He responded by placing his arm around my shoulders in a friendly hug. I wrapped my arm around his waist, then rested my head on his shoulder.

"I cannot explain to you how worried I was when I saw you disappear under the snow." Jax's voice was barely a whisper. "I don't know what I would have done without my best friend."

I slipped my other arm around him, pulling him into a hug. With my face pressed to his shoulder, I said, "All I could think about was you. If you were okay. I..." I stopped, unable to find the words that could penetrate the block in my throat. "Thank you for saving me."

He pulled away just enough to look into my eyes. "Anytime. You know I'd do anything to protect you." He leaned down and kissed my forehead.

I was once again stunned. It had been so long since we'd shared that sentiment with each other. As kids, we'd always claimed we'd die for one another, but ever since I'd ruined things... well, I'd thought that had changed.

Was it still true? As I looked into his face and those amazing eyes, I realized that it was even truer than it had been all those years before. We may have been apart for far too long, but that had never changed my dedication—nor my affection—to him. There was a settling deep in my heart. I knew right then that anything that happened, we'd do it together. As we always had.

His gaze traveled over my face. I caught my breath. We were so close. My arms were still locked around him, with his around me. The hand that pressed against my back began to move in gentle circles.

There was something different here. I found those familiar, yet foreign eyes one more time, then stepped back.

With a sigh, Jax turned his back on me and ran his fingers through his hair.

With a steadying breath, I said, "Anyway, um... So, as we walk, I want to make some sort of sign or path to where we are. Make it easier for others to find us."

"I like that idea. We can point them to the cabin."

"Yeah. Well, then, let's do this."

We made a half circle around base camp. We filled our emptied packs of firewood, making several trips back when they, and our arms, were too full. By the time we headed back for the final run, we'd collected enough firewood for that night and the next day. We'd also created a number of rock formations to mark the direction of the cabin. The task reminded me of a time when we were eight, my father had taken Jax and me

out for some survival skill training. First, he'd tested us
to see if we could navigate in the forest. We'd failed
miserably. Then, he'd spent the rest of the day teaching
us techniques for marking your path. Things like the
marking of trees, breaking specific branches for
visibility, and stacking rocks to make cairns. They were
skills we'd honed over our many adventures, and we
hoped if Dad was still alive, he'd be able to find us
using them.

Jax set the final piece on the marking we'd been
working on. It was set in the middle of what I thought
was a ski pass based on the way the tips of trees stuck
out on either side. I set my hand on his shoulder and
leaned on him.

"All right. I think that's enough. Let's head back. It's
getting too dark, and I need to sit down," I admitted.

He nodded. "Let's head through those trees and wrap
back around. It's an easier walk."

"Don't worry, I'll be fine. It's just been a long day," I
said, unconsciously rubbing my leg.

"Sure you are. When we get back, we're taking a real
look at that injury. Maybe there is something we can
do, wrap it or something."

As if talking about it could make it worse, the pain
intensified. I guess I'd been blocking more than I
realized. The pain radiated from my hip bone down
more than halfway to my knee. There was no doubt in
my mind that a secondary cut existed farther down.
The way my pants pushed into the spot with each step
was approaching unbearable. I needed to rest.

A few steps down the path he'd indicated, and I sank
into the snow on my weak side. A gasp of pain escaped
me as the leg nearly gave out. Jax's strong hands
grabbed me, holding me up. He must have been
hovering near my elbow, ready to steady me if I needed

it. His arm wrapped around my waist. He lifted me out, then steadied me until I had my balance.

"I've got you," he said.

"Thanks," I grumbled, exhaling in frustration. "This is ridiculous."

All day, I'd managed to keep the fear and uncertainty at bay. I just couldn't do it anymore. I was so tired; my emotions were running wild. My body hurt, and I was scared. Scared for us, scared for my family, and scared for everyone else out there in the world. I couldn't imagine how many people had died today.

"What's ridiculous?"

"I shouldn't be hurt. I can't be hurt." My voice cracked a little. Being the friend he was, he didn't acknowledge it. "I need to be strong. Otherwise, how can I continue to believe everyone is okay? How am I going to help Dad? Or Lily? Or...our moms? You've been so calm and collected through all of this, but I know you. You're just as worried as I am. Jax, I'm trying..."

Jax's arms tightened around me. "You're right. I'm not okay, but all day you want to know what kept running through my head?"

"What?"

"Your dad's voice telling me that, 'all you can do is work with what you have right now.' You and Eric were safe, and that means we're okay. We'll figure out how to get through tonight. The shop has more than enough supplies to last a few days. It's shelter and warmth. We have help. Tomorrow, if he hasn't found us yet, then Eric and I will go look for your dad. We'll find him. Then—and only then—will we tackle the next step." As if he knew I was about to protest, he continued, "You will stay and rest. As soon as we find him, we'll head home and make sure Mom is okay. She has plenty of supplies and things to do, but I'm sure she is freaking out."

"Does your mom ever freak out?"

He grinned.

He's so warm. The thought hit me and without meaning to, I leaned closer.

"She does when it involves us." He took more of my weight. "Listen, I know you keep saying that you're okay, but I don't believe you. I need to look at your leg."

Something sarcastic nearly slipped from my lips, but then the intensity in his expression registered, and I asked something else. "Jax, what's changed? I mean, less than a week ago, we couldn't be in the same room without fighting. We couldn't even talk. The day we left..."

"Hasn't it always been that way? We fight, we never really make up, but we're always—*always*—there for one another. It's what we do."

Dropping my gaze, I whispered, "Unless other people are around."

A small grunt. "Well, a lot has changed in the last twenty-four hours. Maybe this could be one of them. I don't know about you, but I hate not having you in my life."

"Me too." Blinking quickly, I stepped back, squeezed his arm, and started walking.

It took another five minutes before we reached the cabin. Outside, a fire burned like a beacon for anyone coming down the mountain. The roof of the shop was exposed, and a small metal flue spit smoke in a steady rhythm.

When Eric noticed our approach and my use of Jax as a crutch, he pointed to me. "Inside now. Rest. Allan and I are taking first watch."

"First watch?" I asked. "What? Are we in a war zone now?"

He chuckled. "Not exactly, but it is a good idea to keep an eye out for anyone or anything that comes close."

"All right, all right, General Eric. Let me get her settled and I'll be back out."

"No. Take care of her, then get some sleep. You'll be second watch. That way, we'll get some rest before we head out to find Dan."

Cassie opened the window at our approach. Jax climbed in first, then half-lifted me into the room. The warmth hit me, and I nearly moaned. A wave of exhaustion hit me.

So beautifully warm.

All I wanted was to lie down and sleep right here, but I knew I needed to stay awake. I could hear Jax asking for a first-aid kit.

Soon, dear sleep. I will let you take me. I snorted internally. When had I become a poet?

Cassie pulled what looked like a large fishing box from behind the counter. "We may only be a coffee shop, but we are the closest contact to the eastern slopes. It was not uncommon for us to get a lot of injuries. Is she all right?"

"We think so. When she was buried in the avalanche —" Jax started but was interrupted.

"She was buried in the avalanche?" Thomas asked excitedly. He'd stood in the far corner, a look of awe on his face.

"Yup. She hurt her leg, and I want to see if there is anything I can do. She has a pretty nasty cut on her hip."

"So noble of you," I said sarcastically.

Jax stuck his tongue out at me. "Come on, wimpy girl. Let's get you checked out." He rummaged through the kit a bit more. "Aha! Ace bandage." He waved it at me.

I passed Cassie on my way to him. "Are there really that many injuries here?"

"Snow, ice, horribly uncoordinated people trying to fly down a mountain on flat pieces of wood... hmmm... yep!"

"Fair enough."

Jax had pulled out several large bandages, alcohol swabs, an Ace bandage, and a few other items we may or may not need.

"Can we go into the hallway? Yes, it's probably more dangerous, but I'd rather not do this in front of strangers."

"Sure. Are you okay with me looking at it or do you want Cassie?"

Do I want to take off my pants in front of Jax? No. No, I did not, but I trusted only Jax and Eric here, and having Eric do it would be creepy. Plus, Jax had dealt with enough injuries with rock climbing and during Eric's football days that I knew he had some experience. He'd even shown a real aptitude for it.

"For all the people here, I trust you most, but I swear —" I stuck my finger in his face. "You make any fat jokes, and you'll lose a tooth."

He rumbled with laughter. We gathered everything up.

"But inappropriate jokes are okay? Well, then, I am good to go."

"Uh..." was my only response.

Carefully, we opened the door to the hallway. The beam of my flashlight showed there was no snow or damage visible. From our door to the one at the far end approximately thirty feet ahead, it was clear. Creaking sounds echoed, but nothing that was too alarming. We walked in and placed the flashlights to shine toward the ceiling. I removed my jacket and reached to untie my pants.

Just as the bow released, Jax sang, "Hot..."

I reached out and smacked him hard in warning.

"What?! Okay, okay, I'll be good. And really, it's not like I've never seen you in a bikini."

He was right, of course. Even then, I was wearing long johns under the waterproof pants. I slipped the pants off and set them to the side. A few patches of blood stained the leggings I still wore. I definitely had another wound.

He knelt, lifted the edge of my shirt, then gently lowered the edge of my waistband near the wound I'd cleaned earlier.

"This is much worse than I thought. How far does it go?"

I shrugged. "Pretty far, based on the blood on my leggings."

"I need to look at it. Clean the wound and check the bruise. We need to keep an eye on it to make sure it doesn't get worse." His eyes met mine.

"Fine, but if you say anything, I'll kill you. Turn around for a sec."

He did. I hissed as I pushed them to my knees and then off. I took a moment before telling him to turn around.

Stop being weird. It's just Jax. There is nothing happening here.

Okay, I knew that, but didn't *know* that. Standing in a hallway in just your panties was one thing. Being there in the dark with Jax—my very grown up, oldest, and best friend—while he examined my leg and hip was something very different. We'd spent our entire lives together; summers at the pool, sleepovers on the weekends, but this was new. He was no longer the "jump-into-everything-without-thinking" kid. There was so much more to him now.

"How have you been walking all day with this?" Jax said after a few moments.

There was a four-inch cut farther down on my thigh. Not terrible until you considered the bruise that encircled it. The sensation as Jax traced the bruise with his fingers was both painful and absolutely distracting. It started at my hip, trailing down my thigh, until a few inches above my knee. Then, it wrapped toward my inner thigh. Keeping my breathing even was nearly impossible.

"We need to get these cleaned."

His gentle hands were steady as he treated each cut, then placed a bandage over them. The cooling sensation of the antibacterial ointment was such a relief that I nearly sighed.

"Thanks," I said. My long johns were still warm as I slipped into them. "So, who knows if this will help, but can you wrap my hip with one of those Ace bandages? It really hurts, and I think the pressure might help."

"It's not going to be pretty."

"You know how, right?"

"Yeah, a guy on Eric's team had to have it done. It was one of the days I was helping out."

"Please?"

Jax nodded and retrieved the larger Ace bandage from the kit. He placed it on my thigh and began to weave it around my hip. My hands rested on his shoulders for balance as he started, then re-started the wrap. It took him a few tries, but with his guidance and some adjustments to my stance, it was soon tight and secure.

"How does it feel?" he asked, getting to his feet.

"Actually, a lot better. The pressure feels nice. Not too tight, though."

"Good."

We gathered up the supplies we used and went to find a place to sleep. Jia and Cassie were talking quietly when we entered. Thomas and Allan were nowhere to be seen.

Jia smiled. "Thomas and Allan are out for first watch. Which leaves you two a little more room to relax and lie down."

"That sounds great. Thank you," I said.

With them along the far wall, Jax and I had a clear spot to lie down. We slid down the wall and to the floor. It was the closest spot to the window, but it had more than enough space for both of us. At this point in the day, this hard sticky floor was heaven.

"Is there anything to eat?" I asked no one in particular. I could get one of the remaining granola bars I had in my pack, but I wanted *real* food if possible.

"Oh! Yes." Cassie pulled out two disposable cups and proceeded to pour hot water from a can sitting on the top of the stove into them. "It's not much, but it's something."

"Oatmeal?"

"Yeah. It's on the menu. Many find it a good match to their coffee in the morning, though I don't know why." Cassie looked like she'd taken a bite of a lemon.

Noted, not an oatmeal fan, I thought, stirring the lumpy liquid. *Can't say I disagree.*

I grinned. I liked Cassie. She inclined her head to us and returned to her seat.

"There should be enough food for breakfast, but we'll need to figure something out after that. We only have a few muffins and small sandwiches left, so unless we get into storage..." She shrugged. I was about to say something when she looked at me and said, "Eat, and then get some rest. We'll deal with everything else tomorrow."

We ate in silence, then lay on the floor. I stretched in a vain attempt to get comfortable.

Jax stretched out next to me, his face inches from mine. Just before sleep took me, he said, "You better not snore."

I rolled my eyes and drifted away.

Chapter Seven

T he blast of cold air that slid up the back of my neck woke me. I flinched away, only to slam into something soft. I forced my eyes open and found Jax's shirt pressed to my face.

Right. Cabin. Sleep.

I shifted so that I could see him fully. He still slept softly, his face relaxed. His hair fell gently across his forehead. Behind him at the window, Allan was passing a very asleep Thomas to Eric. Dark circles ringed Eric's eyes and when he saw me staring, he smiled.

"Think you can take watch?" Eric asked.

"Sure." My voice was gravelly. "How long have we been asleep?"

"It's close to three in the morning. So, maybe six hours? With how tired you were, I figured I'd let you sleep."

"What? Eric, you must be exhausted. Why didn't you wake us earlier?"

I shook Jax gently. He didn't respond, so I placed my palm against his cheek. His eyes opened slowly and met mine.

"Our watch," I said, removing my hand. "Oh, and you snore."

"Liar," he responded through a yawn. We stood and headed for the exit.

"Take these," Eric said. He handed each of us a mug of coffee. "Not the best coffee you've ever had, but drinkable. Cassie's the pro, not me."

I leaned down and took a whiff. "Smells great to me."

Damn, it's cold out here, I thought. *Thank you, Eric, for keeping the fire going.* I rubbed my hands together, warmed them on the fire, then shoved them into my gloves.

The ash had turned the forest dark. With the sun down, the effect was even more complete. It was like we were in a bubble. Nothing existed beyond the light of our fire. The sky, the trees, everything beyond it pitch black and ceasing to exist. There was no sound, no rustling breeze or flutter of wings. No distant howls of wolves who owned these woods.

The coffee slowly kicked in, and as it did, Jax and I began to talk. We talked like we used to. Not about anything in particular really, but the conversation flowed with an ease I missed. We had two years of catching up to do, and it seemed like that night was where we would start. Our conversation shifted from movies, music, and plays to embarrassing or interesting stories from school; amusing situations we'd either experienced or witnessed. It felt like it used to be.

Eventually we talked about the important things. We didn't talk about friends or family back home and what they were going through specifically, though you could tell it was on both our minds. Instead, we theorized what the world was like after Goliath. Based on its path, the largest piece probably fell in the Pacific Ocean. Considering the size, the flooding had to be bad. Who knew how far the tsunamis traveled inland?

If it was as bad as we guessed, much of California was gone now. Also, seeing as we weren't dead, it obviously didn't cause a wave of fire to spread across the globe. Nor did all the volcanoes in the world erupt, but who knew if that was in our future? Terrifying thought, I know, but with how large Goliath had been?

We discussed the smaller meteorites. No doubt they ranged in size and magnitude of damage. Hell, even one the size of a baseball could leave a crater fifteen feet wide. The ones the size of cars? Well, let's just say millions were probably dead or dying by now.

"What do you think the waves of light were?"

"Waves of light?"

"When Goliath entered. You didn't notice how huge waves of green and blue pushed out from it almost rhythmically?"

He shook his head.

"Could you tell the difference between the moon pieces and Goliath pieces? They had a different color to them. The fire or trail or whatever."

"Reena, there was no difference. At least, not that I noticed."

"I'm not crazy."

He held up a hand. "I'm not saying you are. I just didn't notice. When Eric wakes up, let's ask him if he saw what you're talking about."

"Okay..." I couldn't stop the wave of embarrassment at his admission. "And what do you think about the ash?"

"I'm not sure. It has the same texture as ash, and it collects on everything like ash. Even the snow." He gestured around himself as if to say "see." "And the way it changes when it touches the skin? I'm not sure what to think."

"Did you feel anything when it touched your skin?"

"What do you mean?"

"I felt a tingling sensation. It tickled everywhere it made contact. Even in my hair."

Jax's expression shifted to surprise.

I searched for the right words. "You know when you get a sunburn and you put on aloe? There's that feeling on your skin. Not a burning, but like you can feel your skin absorbing it, drinking it in and sighing in relief. Well, it felt kinda like that."

Jax was quiet for a moment, watching me, then said, "No. I didn't notice anything, but is that really a surprise? You've always been more aware than most, that strange sixth sense."

It was true. Even as a child I'd been able to sense the world around me in ways no one could explain. Whether it was being able to tell the chiropractor exactly which vertebra was out or having a sense that something was wrong with the river we were planning to swim in. That time, after walking away disappointed, we'd learned that the river had a serious chemical leak just upstream from where we'd been. Sometimes I just knew. I'd always assumed it was a mixture of instincts, paranoia, and sheer dumb luck.

More dumb luck than anything. Whatever it was, that weird sense had saved us or others on a number of occasions.

"Do you still feel that sensation?"

"I've been focused on other things the last few hours."

"Your hip," he said knowingly. "It hurts more than you said."

I nodded. It had been agonizing in the end but complaining wouldn't have done anything. Okay, yes, over the last few years I'd become a spoiled, prissy, whiny girl, but this experience had smacked me right out of that. This wasn't high school. I couldn't act like that anymore. I needed to be smart. I needed to be useful.

"What if it's poisonous?" I asked.

He opened his mouth as if to say something, but I started first.

"Remember when we were...I don't know, six years old? We were in the kitchen, and we broke Dad's thermometer. This substance spilled out, and we began to play with it. He freaked out and told us it was mercury."

"Yeah, he made us wash our hands over and over because mercury is poisonous."

"Exactly."

"Reena, we haven't seen any reaction yet."

"I'm not so sure," I said thoughtfully.

I reached down to scoop up a chunk of undisturbed snow, making sure to leave the top intact. Yellow sparkled from the depths of the purple substance. With the tip of my gloved finger, I lightly tapped a particularly large piece of ash. There was the faintest flash of light. Using my teeth to remove the glove, I proceeded to touch another section of ash. No light.

I lifted my finger and watched as the ash mutated. Over a few seconds, it changed, leaving the liquid-ash stuck to the tip.

So, skin makes it change, but movement makes it flash? Or is it the pressure?

Slowly, it began to roll down my finger. I tilted my hand, guiding it to my palm. The world disappeared as I focused. There it was. It was milder than before, but there was a tingling on my skin wherever the oil passed. It was a relief to know I hadn't imagined it.

"Reena?"

I jumped, startled. Somehow, I'd forgotten Jax was there.

"Huh?"

"Are you okay? You've been staring at your hand for a really long time."

"Oh...Yeah. I'm fine, but I want to try something. I am going to touch this piece of ash right here. When I do, tell me if you see anything. But don't look right at it. I seem to see better if my eyes aren't directly focused on it."

"You see what?"

"Just tell me if you see something."

"Okay..."

Retrieving my glove, I pressed it to the new ash. Just like before, there was a quick flash. I glanced up.

"Did you see it?"

"No, what did you see?"

"A burst of light. It lasts for only an instant. The first time I saw it, your steps were causing it."

Frustrated, I dropped the handful of snow. Again, there was a flash.

"Maybe you just need a little more sleep. Why don't you sit back down?" He tried to make his tone playful, but I could hear the hint of worry underneath.

"I'm not crazy, Jax! I don't know what is going on, but out of everyone I need you to believe me. There is something weird about this stuff."

"Can you feel what you mentioned before?" he asked.

"A little? It's not quite the same as before. Can you?" I took his hand and dropped the oil into it.

His expression tightened in concentration. After a few moments of moving the oil across his palm, he said, "Not what you described. I believe you, Reena. I may have no idea what any of this means, but I believe you. I would recommend that you not tell the others just yet. They might assume a head injury."

The smile spread across my face against my will. He was right, of course. Everyone would think I'd hit my head. Maybe I had and didn't remember? No, this was linked to this ash. I could feel it in my gut.

As if to solidify that thought—or make me lose my mind—a burst of light in my periphery drew my attention. I jumped to my feet and took a step toward it before I realized I'd moved.

Jax was immediately alert. "What is it?"

I shook my head.

If there was one, maybe there would be more. Then I wouldn't be crazy.

"Did you see that?" I stepped toward the trees. "There!" I whispered.

"No. Where? What did you see?"

At least someone is in his right mind, I thought when I noticed Jax had drawn his knife. I drew mine as well.

"Way back in the trees. There are flashes of light like I told you."

A snap of a branch off in the dark made me jump. I grabbed Jax's arm.

"They look like steps."

This was followed by a larger burst of light about waist high.

"It sounds like a person moving in the woods," Jax said.

It took a few more minutes for the person—I was sure it was a person by that point—to come into view. I was mesmerized by the steady gait illuminated by the ash. The figure broke the last line of the trees and entered our bubble of light.

"Reena?"

"Dad!" I exclaimed and ran into his arms.

No. Let me rephrase. Stepping past Jax, I wobbled uncoordinatedly to him. My arms encircled him at the exact moment his did me.

Oh, thank you. Thank you. Thank you.

"Hey, baby." He held me for a long moment. "Nice markings. They pointed me right to you."

He sounded so tired. I smiled into his shoulder.

"Give Jax the credit. He did most of the work."

"Maybe, but it was your idea," Jax said.

My father released me, then pulled Jax into a hug. Jax may not be one of his children by blood, but he loved him as one.

"You took care of my girl for me. Thank you."

"Always will, you know that. Plus, there's not much to do. She takes pretty good care of herself."

My grin grew. "Ha! Jax, I'd still be in the snow if not for you and Eric."

Dad's eyes widened in worry. "Is that why you're limping?"

"Yeah, but don't worry. It's been taken care of." I waved away his concern. He looked back and forth between us until I continued. "Come to the fire and we'll tell you everything."

"You said Eric is all right?"

"Yes. He's in the cabin sleeping."

"Cabin?"

I pointed toward the exposed window. The glow from the wood-burning stove was barely noticeable. A look of shock and pride lined his face. Taking his hand, I led him to the fire.

Jax retrieved our makeshift coffee pot and began working to heat up some clean snow. He added the coffee, then set it next to the fire to steep.

"I'll be right back," I said.

Jax stopped me and said, "Let me get it. Go sit down."

He disappeared into the cabin.

Dad was warming his hands on the fire. He looked unhurt, but there was a hunch to him that had never been there before.

Give him a minute to warm up. You can hound him after that.

I was adding wood to the fire when Jax rejoined us. He handed my dad a hot cup of oatmeal. When I looked back up, he was eating ravenously.

"Good?" I asked, teasing.

He grunted in response.

"Do you want to talk about what happened or wait until Eric is awake?" Jax asked.

"Let's wait. Give him a bit longer to rest," Dad said.

"We can make room for you in the cabin."

"No. Now that I've eaten, I'm good to go. I was resting up on the hill when I noticed the glow from your fire. Tell me what happened to you. Then we will wake Eric up and make a plan to help those I left behind."

Jax and I exchanged glances.

"Those you left behind?" Jax asked.

"Yes. They are safe enough for now. Once it is light out, it will be easier to help them anyway. Start talking, kids. I want to know everything."

So we talked. Our story continued until the sky lightened and throughout, we answered his questions. He nodded along, clearly relieved by the end.

"I am so happy you are all okay and that you were able to help those here. With that said, I think it's time to wake everyone up."

Chapter Eight

Jia and Allan were beginning to stir when we entered the cabin. I nodded to them before kneeling and shaking Cassie, then Eric.

"Time to wake up. Eric, we've got good news."

"What's up? Is Jax all right?" Eric asked groggily.

"Fantastic. He's sitting by the fire with Dad. Looks like we've got a long day ahead of us."

"What?!" Eric shot up.

I had everyone's attention now.

"He came into camp an hour or so ago. He saw the fire from up the hill where he and some other survivors made camp. He followed the light right to us."

"Other survivors?" they all said, surprised.

I grinned. "I don't know much yet. We got him some coffee and food. He wanted to wait until you were awake to talk. So hurry up. I want to hear what is going on."

Within minutes, the adults were around the fire. On her way out, Cassie grabbed some breakfast sandwiches and a larger pot for coffee.

"I was worried, Old Man," Eric said, embracing Dad. "I figured I'd have to scour the whole mountain just to find you."

Dad chuckled. "Sure you did. Don't worry, Son, you'll be tired of me and this mountain by the time I'm done with you."

I introduced everyone, and we settled down to hear his story. Cassie handed out the food, and we ate as Dad spoke.

"Thankfully yesterday was not a busy day at the lodge. At least, not like usual. Still, there were a fair amount of people here. I headed to the east side to meet up with some friends. There were six of us total. We made a few runs before Goliath hit. Sydney, her son Camden, and I were still at the top when everything went to shit. Tom, Jake, and Bill had already started down and were caught in it." He looked up to the mountain, which was just visible in the morning light.

"Based on what I see here, the avalanche on our slope was nothing like this one—tiny in comparison. But, between the avalanche and some serious falling rocks, anyone not at the top disappeared in the snow. I tried to see where people fell, but there were few survivors. When we thought it was safe enough, we headed down. We spent hours searching. We managed to find Tom. He's hurt, but alive. The rest of our group was lost."

"I'm so sorry, Dad."

"We found three others, though. I'm worried. The older man we found has a head injury. He's not really coherent, and his balance is shot. A man who's maybe twenty-five isn't speaking. From shock, maybe? But otherwise I can't find anything else wrong with him other than some bruises. It's the last one I'm most concerned about. She's in her teens and was pinned to a tree. She was in so much pain we couldn't move her. So we set up camp around her and did our best to make her comfortable."

"That doesn't sound good." *I hope we can get to her in time.*

He shook his head. "By the time the sun went down, we had a fire and everyone was resting."

Cassie handed him a mug of coffee.

"Thank you," he said. "Not long after that, I saw your fire. I was anxious to find you and some help."

"You shouldn't have made that hike in the dark," Eric said. "We were planning to head your way come morning anyway."

"I couldn't wait. I needed to know if you three were okay. I knew you'd head to the lodge first and try to signal me."

"We weren't trying to signal *you* exactly." I winked, then sobered. "But anyone coming down the mountain."

He grinned. "The good news is I know where to head. We need to get there as soon as we can. The fire and Sydney are the only things keeping them alive. But before we go, we need to rig something up for Tom. I splinted his leg, but he can't put weight on it. The rest will have to walk."

"Are you worried about that?" Allan asked.

I was surprised. Allan was quiet and rarely added to the conversation. He seemed like a good guy, but I'd only heard him speak a few times. I wondered if he'd opened up last night to Eric. I'd have to ask.

"Some. The older gentleman was having trouble balancing. That's not an easy thing while walking downhill. If I pair him up with someone, he should be fine."

I shifted uncomfortably, then gave up and stood. To take the pressure off my hip, I started to pace. Sitting, doing nothing, was driving me crazy. With each step, I tried to settle my nerves and release the ache.

Jax followed my movement. He knew me too well and knew I was freaking out.

"So, what should we do?" Jia asked. "Other than getting to them, what do we do?"

I was shocked when it was my voice that rang out. "There's a lot to do. One, we need to find some sort of stretcher or sleigh to bring Mike back down the mountain. Two, we need to get up that mountain and get everyone down safely. And three, we need to find a way to feed and shelter everyone once they're here. The coffee shop just isn't big enough to fit that many. Based on that, we'll probably have to be here at least one more night. So, we need to collect more firewood, or we'll freeze to death." I could feel all their gazes track me as I moved. I made no eye contact as I spoke, just kept walking. Finally, I faced them with my hands on my hips. "If we can manage all of that, then we can go on to the next step, getting home."

I sighed, making eye contact with them each one at a time. "I think we need to get into that storage room. See if there's anything in there we can use."

Silence. For way longer than I expected. Jax was the first to speak.

"See, Dan? She does a fine job taking care of herself." Humor was thick in his tone.

The grin Jax sent Dad made me uncomfortable, but not as much as the look on my father's face. There was a little bit of shock, a fair amount of amusement, and hell of a lot of pride mixed in for good measure. Completely uncomfortable in that moment, I turned to Cassie.

"Cassie, do you remember what was in that storage room?"

"If it's still there? Some. But the noise that came from there was intense."

"Yes, but if you tell me it was empty, we won't even try. But if you remember anything good, then we'll go for it. There might be items we can use. We need every advantage we can get."

"Okay. There was coffee, supplies for the shop, more oatmeal, and granola bars. Further in, there was all sorts of different stuff, but I never really paid attention. We would get in trouble if we snooped around, and I'm still pretty new."

"It's worth looking into," Jax said. "There may be something we can use for a stretcher. And either way, we need the food."

"Thomas and I will work on collecting wood," Allan said.

"No," I said. "Jia can work with Thomas to collect the wood. They shouldn't be anywhere near the cabin while we're in there. A few of us will try to open the door first. See if we can even get in. If we can, then I think we'll need everyone else to collect anything useful as quickly as possible."

I sat next to Dad, who was listening carefully, his lips pressed together in what looked like amusement. I was a little surprised he hadn't stepped in yet, but I guess I hadn't given him the chance.

I continued, "I want to be one of the ones going up the mountain, but I'm not sure that would be a good idea. I think Jia, Thomas, Cassie, and I can get this place set up. If we don't find anything in there to use as shelter, then we might have to fabricate something. The rest of you"— I gestured around the circle—"need to go help get the others down."

Eric grunted his agreement. "Then why don't we get started? Jia, can you wake up Thomas? Once everyone is outside, Dan and I will make our way in to see if it's safe. If there are no issues, then we will work together to get out as much as we can."

"We need food, water, or bottles of any kind, rope, bags, and anything else that might be useful," Dad said.

"If it hasn't collapsed yet, then why do we need to move it all out?" Allan asked.

"Because it could collapse at any moment. The creaking noises the ceiling was making in that hallway tell us the beams are not happy. There's a lot of weight sitting on those beams," Jax explained.

"Exactly. They may not hold forever. We need to make our move now and get what we can," I agreed. Eric, Jax, and Dad stood. It was time to get started.

Jia was helping Thomas climb out the window just as we approached.

"Morning, Dude," I said as he passed me. I lifted my hand for a high-five. He obliged. The four of us climbed in. Jax and I waited inside the shop. Eric stopped halfway down the hall. My flashlight shone at their feet, allowing the light to extend all the way down.

"Ready?" Dad asked.

The doorknob turned, and Dad gently pushed it open a few inches. When nothing happened, he swung it the rest of the way. Dad froze, waiting. A groan that sounded like a cat mewling echoed through the entry, but then nothing else happened. There was no crash, no feet of snow pouring through the ceiling or rushing through the door. Dad's figure relaxed, and a collective sigh escaped us. It was time to get to work.

Chapter Nine

C assie had been right about the storage room. It was huge. The first twenty feet were organized into rows of shelves that housed all sorts of supplies. Past that, it opened into a space used for equipment for the lodge.

Dad had taken a quick look around before letting any of us in. The damage was extensive and the room unstable. The far wall opposite our entry point was gone. The snow had ripped it apart and collapsed part of the roof. Snow had poured into the space, knocking some of the farther shelves over and spilling their contents to the floor. Some of the main support beams near the center had held, but most of the equipment or supplies past them were inaccessible or damaged. With every step into the room we took, noises of strain on those beams radiated. It was terrifying.

"We need to be quick," Eric said.

Over the next half an hour, we did a review of available supplies and began removing them. Anything thought to come in handy was pulled from the space. We moved with speed, none of us wanting to be in there a second longer than necessary. The flashlights didn't diminish the cold darkness of the space which was made more ominous by the eerie sounds that vibrated through the air.

This place is dangerous, it whispered.

First anything edible was removed: a few boxes of oatmeal, various bars, and the last of the wrapped muffins. Some coffee, tea, and other drinks were removed as well. From there, we spread out and searched for anything useful.

The sense of claustrophobia grew the longer I stayed in this room. *Maybe this wasn't the best position to be in right now. Dangerous, Reena. So dangerous.*

Of course the shelf I lay underneath didn't help that feeling. I was on my stomach, and it arched menacingly over me. My flashlight pointed inward, searching the darkness for its hidden treasures. Supplies were strewn across the floor. I'd crawled in here because of the battered tent and two backpacks I'd first spotted. They were my first finds, but there was more up ahead that looked promising.

I shimmied deeper under the shelves and grabbed a box near the back. It took some finagling, but with just the right amount of force, I pulled it free. It scraped against the ground, then ripped at the seam.

Jackpot, I thought.

"Allan, are you back yet?" I called. He and I had teamed up throughout this adventure. We laughed and joked the entire time, easing the tension we both felt, while still managing to collect a lot.

"Yes, what do you need?" he asked.

"I'm pushing some items out. Can you make a pile?"

"Sure," he said. I felt his hand touch my leg, letting me know where he stood.

I wiggled farther in, then pulled one rope after another out of the box and slipped them to him.

I squirmed even deeper into the darkness.

"Be careful," Allan said.

I opened another box and nearly cheered at what I found. Maybe a dozen carabiners and a half dozen six-inch-long stakes that looked like something out of a vampire movie.

These could come in handy. I pushed the box to the side and saw it. A second tent. We needed that tent, badly.

"I've got one more thing to grab, and then I'm coming out. Okay? You might have to pull me out, though."

"No worries. Jax just took everything else to the cabin. Once you're out, we are calling this adventure over."

"Sounds great to me."

I grabbed a hold of my final prize. It was stuck beneath the first shelf—not pinned fully—but it would still take some effort to get it out. I tugged a few times, but it didn't budge.

One big pull and it's mine.

The small tent bag broke loose. I'd yanked so hard that I slammed my head against the shelf above me. Pain erupted in my skull, but I didn't linger on it. Just then, a bone-shattering *boom* made me jump.

Shit, shit, shit! One of the support beams just broke...

The sound changed. It became that of shifting metal and snow. The shelf began to shake, then slide. Right. Toward. Me.

"Pull me out!" I cried to Allan.

Hands were on my ankles. One strong pull and I was out. A sharp pain lanced through my hip and down my leg. I yelped but pushed it down.

The instant my head cleared the shelf, it collapsed. Our momentum caused Allan to fall backward into another row. The sound of his impact ricocheted and then was quickly followed by that shelf collapsing. Each row fell like giant dominoes.

There were cries from the others and the sound of pounding feet as they ran toward us.

They can't come in here!

"Stay back!" I screamed just as Jax rounded the corner. With no hesitation, he raced for us.

Stupid boy doesn't listen for crap. Whatever, we need to get out.

"Allan, come on!"

Allan stared up at the remaining wooden beams that were beginning to splinter. His face was frozen in absolute terror, his breathing heavy. There was another snap. Crap, we only had seconds.

I shot to my feet, grabbed his arm, and started to move. With all of my strength, I yanked Allan to his feet.

Before we made it five steps, the beams snapped. Snow and debris tried to cover us. The largest of the beams fell, hitting Allan across the shoulder. He was slammed to the floor.

I skittered to a stop, turned around, and reached for him. I dodged out of the way of some falling debris, ducked, and barely missed a beam that had snapped in half and swung at my head. It came to a stop with a resounding *thwump* on top of the shelf next to me.

Snow fell onto Allan, covering him. I grasped his fingers but couldn't get purchase. Something hit me on the back, and I felt my breath shoved out of me.

I was going to die. We were going to die.

Out of nowhere Jax was there. The weight on my back disappeared, and I was yanked to my feet. My back pressed to his chest. His arm wrapped around my waist, and then my feet left the ground. He swung me in the direction of the door and set me down.

"Run!"

The roof gave another groan as the structural beam to our left cracked like a gunshot.

A warm tingling sensation spread up my spine. Then, I was flying through the air as if I'd been thrown. I heard Jax's scream of pain and surprise just as I hit the far wall. I fell in a lump to the floor. My chest burned as I sucked in a painful breath. I forced myself to my feet, attempting to turn and find Jax, but before I managed it, something slammed into me, and I was back on my knees. I cried out. With sheer determination alone, I got to my feet. I leaned into whatever was hammering me as another hit me, but I kept my feet this time.

This wave wasn't as strong. They're getting weaker. Finally, I turned, needing to find my friend. I froze, shocked.

Jax crawled on his hands and knees. His shoulders were tight, his jaw clenched so hard lines appeared along his jaw. He was in agony. A moment later, he flinched as a wave erupted from his body. Then another. Every few seconds, a surge of pale green light exploded outward from his heart, traveling in all directions. With each explosion of power, the debris trying to encapsulate him was pushed back.

And again, I knew they were getting weaker.

Jax crawled toward me, only a few feet from me now.

When I tried to step closer, he yelled for me to stay where I was. I wanted to ignore him as he had me, but I couldn't move. My screams were barely audible over the roar of the destruction around us. The wetness on my face felt thick as the tears poured from my eyes.

"Get out, Reena!"

"I'm not leaving you. Hurry the hell up!"

Time slowed. Helpless, I watched until he was close enough for me to grab. Clasping the back of his arms, I kicked off the ground with my legs and flung us backward into the hallway. He landed on top of me. We pushed ourselves up enough that I was able to pull us incrementally down the hallway.

Cries from those in the cabin urged us to keep moving.

Jax tried to help, but he was barely able to lift himself. The waves that had escaped him were now so weak they felt like a gentle brush on my skin.

I had to use all of my strength to drag him out. Finally, hands grabbed us and hauled us into the cabin where someone slammed the door.

The rumbling continued, and the cabin walls shook. My heart pounded as we waited for it to give way. We huddled together, unable to move, until the world calmed.

I wiped my face with the sleeve of my shirt, clearing the grime, sweat, and tears from my face. My other arm was still wrapped around Jax. I shifted both of us until we knelt, facing each other. Eric and Dad stood over us. I could hear them speaking but was unable to follow any of it because in that moment, only Jax mattered. I needed to know that we'd made it out unharmed. I hugged him to me and immediately knew something was wrong.

Jax didn't hug me back. Instead, he folded into me. His face pressed to the hollow of my neck. The heat of his breath stung my skin. He was panting hard, and his heartbeat was far too fast.

"Jax," I whispered in his ear. "What was that? Are you okay?"

"I don't feel right," he whispered. His entire body shook, and a second later, he collapsed.

I fell backward by the unexpected weight of his body on top of mine. I grunted, trying to slow our fall. I barely kept us from slamming into the counter.

Eric helped lower him to the ground. "Jax?"

"Jax? Jax!" I shrieked.

I touched his cheek. No response. I checked his breathing. My tone approaching hysteria, I said, "You're breathing. He's breathing."

"Let's get him by the fire. Does he have any injuries?"

"I don't think so."

"What happened in there, Reena?"

"I don't know."

They shot me a concerned look, then hurried to move him. I cradled his head as the two men carried him around the counter. Now that the roaring in my heart had stopped, I could hear those outside calling to us from the open window. I ignored them.

We laid Jax on his back, placing his head in my lap. Unconsciously I stroked his hair as my father did a check for injuries, but he didn't have any.

Whatever that was, it saved me. But if I don't fix this, it might kill him.

"What happened?" Eric asked. I could feel the force of his gaze on me.

"I was under a shelf. I found another tent. When I pulled on it, the shelf shifted, and that caused the beams overhead to buckle. Allan—" I paused, my voice cracking. "Allan was helping me. He grabbed my ankles and yanked me out. He saved me, but in the process fell into the other aisle, causing it to collapse too. Then everything came down."

My throat was thick, and it was hard to breathe. Tears filled my eyes, but I held them back.

"Allan was covered. I tried to get to him, but..." They stared at me in horror. "A beam hit my back, and I fell. I thought I was dead, then Jax appeared and..."

My voice trailed off as a sharp, emotional wail broke my heart. Jia's cry for Allan was one that I will remember for my entire life. I hunched, the weight of that sound—of Allan's death—too much to bear. But I had to. I listened to her pain, but it was the questioning voice of Thomas and the quiet "no," that forced the tears from my eyes.

I leaned down to Jax and set my forehead to rest against his. I felt Eric's hand on my shoulder.

"It's not your fault," he said. I shook my head, closed my eyes, and absorbed the pure radiating pain of those outside.

It was my fault.

"I'll be back in two minutes," Dad said. "Stay with Jax and make sure he's okay. Get that fire going again, too."

I focused on the sound of Jax's breathing as tears for Allan fell and I prayed that Jax would be all right.

With the soft skin of his cheek under my fingertips, his words from yesterday were bright in my mind. "I don't know what I would do without my best friend."

Chapter Ten

T he world faded away as I focused on Jax. I curled
into him and as I did, I felt something strange
where our foreheads touched. I recognized it. It was the
same sensation as in the storage room; the tingling
power that had spread up my back just before I'd been
thrown across the room. But it was weaker.

The waves came from him, I realized.

I searched his face but couldn't see anything
radiating from him like I had before. So, I closed my
eyes and placed my forehead to his again. There was a
pulse of energy. When I touched him, I could feel where
it vibrated a few inches from his skin, like a field
protecting him. It beat in a pattern that matched his
heartbeat.

I tried to think. From what I could tell, there was
nothing physically wrong with him. The only change
had been the shield he'd created to protect him—no,
us.

*A shield...*Jax had said he didn't feel right just before
he collapsed, and it got me thinking. *What if he'd just
worn himself out? To keep the snow off him, he had to have
used a lot of power. What if he was still doing it? Just not as
intensely?*

Knowing I couldn't see whatever this was, I followed my gut and tried to use my other senses to feel for it. I pushed away everything, praying to find the source of the problem. After only a few seconds, I felt it again—a hum. It was familiar to me just as Jax was. I took my hands and placed them on either side of his face, my fingers tingling when they hit his energy.

"Reena, what are you doing?" Eric asked.

I barely heard him. Deep in my mind, I felt something click. I understood what this was, and somehow, I knew how to help. Well...sort of, but how?

As if in answer, and for only an instant, the scene before me changed. The cabin disappeared, and I was standing on a hill, a gray forest to my left and a field of alien-looking flowers to my right. I jumped as something wrapped around my ankle. Before the image disappeared, I saw a rope of purple and gold absorb into my skin.

I blinked, and the image was gone, the memory faded like a dream. Only my quickened heartbeat and rolling stomach proof it had happened.

I shook my head, focusing back onto my task. I'd have to think about that later. Right now, Jax was more important because this was pure energy escaping him. His energy. It felt like life and emotion. It was him. It's hard to explain what I did in that moment; my reaction was part desperation and part instinct. I let go, using those instincts to guide me.

I extended myself outward, and the room around me lit up. The field he'd created buzzed against my skin, so I pressed it. It responded, falling back inside him, giving me an idea.

Let's see if I can do this.

Wherever the energy leaked, I wrapped my mind around it, then wound my own energy with his. I held his energy, calmed it, then took control of it. I pushed it back into his center, to a place I could only visualize. With gentle coaxing, I soothed it, so it no longer spread out from him, but was instead worked within. I focused on his heart and steadied its beat.

Beat with me, I said to it. *Flow through him and repair the damage done.*

I put my whole heart into it, pulling everything from within and around me. My head began to ache, but I didn't stop. His heart took up a rhythm that matched mine. He needed more. I don't know how I knew this, but I did. I manipulated the field within him, pouring more of my energy into him, speeding it faster and faster. It was delicate work, but I could feel the energy building within him. Somehow, I was replacing what he'd lost.

Eventually, his heart reclaimed a steady beat. It overcame my own, and his breathing shifted to even, full breaths. Cold spread up my legs as I continued to mold the field within him. I didn't know how to stop, when to stop. I groaned, my heavy breaths so loud in the quiet room. The world became foggy.

Suddenly, a hand touched my hair, and I jumped. I lifted my head to find Jax's striking blue eyes staring into mine, the few inches separating us amplifying their effect.

He's awake. Relief spread through me. His hand caressed my hair again.

I let go of the focus I held and had to hold back a flood of dizziness as I did. It didn't matter. The sight of his eyes open and gazing at me was all that mattered.

"What did you do?" he asked so quietly I almost couldn't hear. "I could feel you, but what..." he trailed off, unable to finish his question.

"I don't know. What did you do?"

"I don't know." We chuckled at our ignorance. I leaned to press my cheek to his for just a moment.

"I'm so glad you are okay." My hands slid to rest on his shoulders. I sat upright so that I could look down at him. I ran my hand through his hair. The world began to come back to me.

In the distance, I could hear crying. Jia's soft voice speaking to Thomas, full of emotion. Cassie was talking to Dad right outside the window, but I couldn't tell about what. I remembered the sound of Eric, Dad, and Cassie's voices while I worked, but had no idea what was said. All I'd been aware of was their worry. It had fueled me.

The sound of a metal door closing brought my attention to the far corner. Eric had just put another log on the fire. He looked worried.

"He's awake," I said.

Startled, Eric moved the few feet to sit next to us. He leaned down and smiled at his brother. "You okay, Little Brother?"

When Eric placed his hand on Jax's arm, Jax turned to him. "Yeah, just tired."

"What happened? How did you get out?"

Jax and I exchanged glances. In that simple exchange, I knew we were both on the same page. Neither of us knew, let alone could explain. And if we tried, no one would understand. Hell, we didn't. So I spoke.

"Jax ran into the room even though I told him not to. He flung me out of the way and tried to reach Allan, but it was too late. I'm not sure how, but he managed to get to me against the far wall before everything fell on us. I pulled him the rest of the way through the hall and that's where you guys came in."

Eric looked skeptical. He knew us well enough to know when we weren't telling him the whole truth, but he had no idea what we were keeping from him. He gave a resigned sigh.

"Fine, don't tell me," Eric said. "Just get some rest. If you two are okay, I'm going to help Dan get ready. We still need to head up the mountain today."

As Jax started to sit up, Eric and I pushed him down.

"Jax, you're not going. You need to rest. Cassie agreed to come instead. It'll be up to you and Reena to get camp set up, but only *after* you get some rest. I doubt Jia and Thomas will be of much help. They aren't doing well. Reena, it's your job to make sure Jax doesn't overdo it."

"I can do that. I'll keep an eye on Jia and Thomas too. I feel so bad."

"It wasn't your fault," Eric said.

"Yes, it was. I shouldn't..."

"Stop," Jax whispered. "We all knew the risks, and he still tried to save you. Allan was a good man. It's a tragedy, but all we can do is take care of his family for him. Be there for them."

His gaze held me captive as he spoke. I knew he was right, but there was no way I would ever not think his death was on my hands.

To change the subject, I asked, "Did we get anything good out?"

Eric nodded, then gestured to the far wall. I could see several stacks of provisions that had been haphazardly arranged.

"On top of food and drinks, we found some good stuff. The two old backpacks and two tents are the big items. Another first-aid kit. We also found an old-style collapsible litter." At my look of confusion, he explained, "It's what the military calls a stretcher. This one is old. We'll need to make some adjustments to make it stronger and easier to use in snow. Go through everything and get it organized."

"Is everyone else all right?" Jax asked, his voice gravelly.

"As good as we can be. It was just the two of them in the room when it collapsed. We heard Reena scream for us to stay back and tried to stop you from running in."

"But of course he didn't listen," I said. My voice was tired and sad.

"If I hadn't, you wouldn't be here." His eyes looked up at me with so much emotion. I ran my fingers along his jaw.

"I know. Thank you."

For the next hour, we worked to get Dad, Eric, and Cassie ready to head up the mountain. Their packs were filled with food, water, and first-aid supplies.

The litter was upgraded by adding tree branches to the sides, then weaving smaller ones through and underneath the fabric. The base we built supported the person while keeping him or her out of the snow. After a few additional changes, we even managed to add some ski-like pieces so it glided over the snow.

Was it going to be easy with someone inside it? No, but at least it was better than nothing.

Jax rested while we moved about. Every few minutes, we found a reason to go check on him. I was still so worried his breathing would change and I would find him non-responsive. I think Eric was too. Every time we went in, we found him fast asleep, his color slowly returning.

It was still early morning when they left. Jax was sleeping off his near-death experience, so I went off to find some firewood.

As I wondered, the silence of the forest began to overwhelm me. I heard Allan's laughter and his screams for help. I heard the roar of the roof as it fell toward us. Then the quiet plea from Jax saying he "didn't feel right."

I shook as I tried to hold back the tears. It took so much effort to hide that pain and fear. I just couldn't do it anymore.

The guilt of Allan's death was tearing me apart. It made me question every decision I'd made; every action I'd taken. I had been the one to tell him he was going in there. I had sentenced him to death instead of letting him collect firewood as he had offered.

That's why you'd teamed up with him. You wanted to protect him, I thought. *You did a shitty job.*

I looked up to the sky and took a deep breath. The clouds were heavy and dark, but the air was finally clear.

Stop it, Reena. You can't change what happened. You tried to save him and almost died, too. You have people depending on you, and a pity party won't do anything.

That was better. Anger and determination to help who was left would have to be enough. Enough for now, at least. I needed to be strong no matter what. I just had to keep moving.

Not too far from camp, I found a pile of cut logs in a fenced-off area. It was down the main trail from the lodge, and one wall of the fence had been knocked down.

Thank you for small favors. There was plenty of wood to keep us warm here. A few days at least.

My luck held. At the base of the pile, I found a small circle of plastic jutting from the snow. It was half buried, but once I dug it out, I realized it was a children's sled made of bright pink plastic. A rope was tied to one handhold.

Finally, a break. This will make collecting wood so much easier.

With my hip hurt and the new pain along my back from where the beam had struck me, I couldn't overdo it or the next day would be hell. Another severely injured person was not what we needed right now.

I filled the sled with as much as I could fit and headed to camp. After three trips, I called it. I was so tired. My hip hurt, my back ached, and the headache from helping Jax was pounding. The various other bruises I'd acquired from the storage room all sang in beat with my heart.

The first thing I noticed when getting back was that the fire was nearly out. No one was outside, and camp was quiet. I put some more wood on the fire, then headed to the cabin.

Jax was asleep on the floor. He was curled on his side, his back to me, but he was alone.

Where were Jia and Thomas?

Confused, I closed the window and scanned the area.

"Jia? Thomas?" I called. Maybe they went for a walk.

There was no answer. I walked up the hill for a better vantage point. I scanned the surrounding area and nearly gasped. Two sets of prints, one smaller than the other, were visible heading away from camp and down the hill. The path they'd taken was in the opposite direction of where I had been. Jia and Thomas were gone.

I ran a hand through my hair. In the hour I was gone, they'd left. After losing the most important person to them, they had snuck away and were gone. They were too far away to catch them by now. I felt terrible.

Something hit me. I ran back down the slope, only to dive into the cabin. I tried not to wake Jax up, but in my haste, I stepped on him. He screeched in surprise.

"What's going on?" he asked, alarmed.

"Sorry."

Please, have only taken what you needed. Please, have only taken what you needed. Please, don't take your anger out for me out on the others.

Terrified, I dropped to my knees at the pile of supplies. I did a quick inventory. Relief swept through me, followed by a new guilt.

I'd assumed that she, out of spite, would damage or take all the supplies we needed. My first instinct was to doubt a woman who had been nothing but kind and helpful, but she hadn't. Jia had taken one of the backpacks. The other sat lonely against the wall. A note laid on it.

We are leaving. We could not stay here another moment. I did not take much, just enough to last us until we get back into town. Good luck to you all.

My heart sank. I crumpled the letter in my fist. Jax extracted the note from my hand and read it quickly.

"This isn't your fault. It was always their plan to leave today. At least they have a few supplies."

"That's true, but they're leaving without him."

Jax wrapped his arm around me, and I pressed my face to his shoulder. We stayed like that a long time.

"I assumed that she would damage everything—all our supplies—in revenge. Jax, what is wrong with me?"

"You're scared." He looked down at me. "You know that you also almost died today, right? You have the right to be a little on edge."

"Still..."

"How are you feeling? Physically, I mean," he asked eventually.

"Sore. My hip and back hurt. I've also had a wicked headache ever since..."

"Since you... did whatever you did to me?"

"Yeah."

Neither of us spoke. I wasn't ready to talk about it, and truthfully, I didn't really know what happened. Jax seemed to understand my predicament. He squeezed my shoulder and stood.

"Why don't we get organized? Since I'm feeling better, let's get the tents up."

I nodded. "Yeah, they'll probably be back soon."

We set up the tents, securing them to the ground with the stakes I'd procured. They weren't large, but they were meant for cold weather. A few small holes were easily patched with duct tape from the shop. Someone had found a few thermal blankets. We threw those and the curtains from the windows into the tent. They wouldn't be much, but it would be better than nothing.

We organized the remaining food on the counter, then separated a portion, marking it for the trip down the mountain. The first-aid supplies and food were split into the backpacks as my father had indicated. We prepped for leaving in any way we could, knowing that our focus in the morning would be on getting the others up and moving. With how far we had to go, we wanted to make sure we had plenty of time.

By the time we were done, it was early afternoon. Jax and I had a small lunch, then waited.

Chapter Eleven

"Look there," I said to Jax. I pointed up the hill to where three figures had come into view.

"Start some tea. That way, they have something warm when they get here. I'm going to go meet them."

"I'm right behind you." Once I had the water on, I headed to catch up.

Jax pulled the litter, a very tired Eric walking beside him. The unconscious Tom, the man who had broken his leg, lay within.

I went to help my dad, who was trying to steady a man in his sixties. He seemed to be having trouble balancing. Dad held his elbow firmly, but when he passed a branch in the snow, he tripped, falling to his knees.

Sydney, my parents' friend, bent and helped pull him to his feet.

"Hey, Reena. Good to see you again," Sydney said.

"You, too. Can I help?"

"No," Dad said. "But you can go help Cassie."

"Sure."

Sydney smiled as I passed. I hadn't seen her in years but remembered the stories my mom had told of her. Her kindness and soft temper had not only helped my mother through some tough times but had helped unite my parents. I was glad she was okay.

"Hey, Cassie," I called.

Cassie walked farther back from the group with a man in his late twenties. He looked healthy enough. Or... that's what I thought until I got closer. When he turned his head, I had to hold back a gasp. Bruises spread along the side of his face. They started at his cheekbone and disappeared into his hair. Their dark color weaved around his eye, then just over his nose.

"Hey, Reena, glad to be back." The aggravation in her voice told me how hard the trip had been.

Cassie grasped the man's arm and steered him toward me. Almost instantly, he began to weave to the left. She corrected him again, then sighed.

I took my place on the other side and, with me there, he didn't weave as much.

"Where is the girl you told us about?" Jax asked from the front.

"She didn't make it," Sydney said, her gaze falling. "I think she had internal bleeding. She passed away last night."

That poor girl.

Silence fell, each of us not knowing what to say. Only when we entered the camp did conversation pick up again.

"Jax and Eric, can you help me get Mike inside? We need to get him warmed up."

"Definitely," they said in unison.

The rest of us settled by the fire. I handed Sydney and her son, Camden, some warm tea. That's when I noticed Eric and Dad arguing by the cabin.

"Give me a minute and I'll get you all something to eat."

"Thank you," she said. I nodded, then joined the two men.

"So, what do you want to do?" my dad said, frustrated.

"I want to head out. If we leave soon, we can get to the house before dark."

"No, Eric, we can't. I want to get there too, but we can't leave yet. These people can't make it any farther today."

"So, let's leave them," Eric stated coolly.

"What?" I said, shocked. "Seriously, Eric? You just traveled all day to help these people and now you just want to leave them up here with nothing?"

Eric winced. "They'll be safe in the cabin. Plus, we can move faster without them, then send help."

"We can't leave! These people can't take care of themselves. And without knowing if we'll find anyone to help..." I pressed my fists to my hips. "No, we aren't leaving them."

"I know." Eric sighed. "It's just, twelve is a big group to move and keep on a good pace."

"Ten," Jax said, sneaking up on me. "Jia and Thomas left after you guys headed out."

"Wait, what? And you didn't stop them?" my father said.

"They left while I was out gathering firewood and Jax was sleeping. They took a backpack and some muffins, but not much else. They left a note that said they couldn't stand being here anymore. If you go up there, you can see their footprints heading downhill," I explained.

Dad dropped his face into his hands and rubbed.

"All right, ten," Eric cut in. "It'll take forever, but fine. We get home, then find out what's happening out there." I knew Eric didn't really want to leave these people, but the need to know about our family was killing him.

"I agree with Reena. We can't abandon them. If we do, they die," Jax said.

"We can't get there tonight anyway," Dad added. "On foot it's almost a six-hour walk and that's without snow, downed trees, and injured people. The roads are probably a mess. We'll get some rest, then leave first thing in the morning."

"Then what? What do we do after we get to Kim?" I asked seriously. "We can stay there for a while, but not forever. Plus, Mom's in Portland, and my guess is she won't be able to get to us. Lily and James were probably on the road. What about Kiera and everyone back home?"

Dad touched my arm. "Remember, we can only take one day at a time. Right now, we need to get these people help. Then we'll head to the house and check on Kim. As for everyone else, we'll just have to wait and see what we can find out."

Eric was nearly shaking with frustration. I placed my hand on his arm.

"Come on," I said. "You need a break."

After a long moment, he nodded. It was rare for Eric to lose it like that, but of anyone, I had the highest probability to calm him down. Just like Jax, their tempers could keep them from seeing clearly. Over the years I'd become a pro at calming both of them down.

Jax shot me a grateful smile.

I followed Eric up the embankment. His slumped shoulders and distraught expression made my heart hurt. The day had taken its toll both mentally and physically. But it was more than that. Something in his eyes told me his anger was also directed at me. He'd

had the whole day to think about what had happened
with Jax, and he was pissed that we'd lied to him.

"So, what's up?" I asked.

We'd reached the top of the hill that overlooked
camp. A large rock stuck out of the snow, and we sat on
it.

"Just frustrated." He took a long breath. "Today was
hard. When we got there, the fire was out. Camden had
been trying to find wood, but it was all too wet. Sydney
was attempting to get everyone ready, but the issues
they each have... Our two catatonic friends are barely
there, Reena." He shook his head. "Mike was in so
much pain. Getting him in the sled was hell, and it only
got worse as we started moving. He kept passing out.
In his sleep he kept talking about death and the end of
the world."

I placed my hand on his.

"Not really the time to hear stuff like that," I
whispered.

"No, it really freaked me out. His leg's bad. If we
don't get him help soon, he isn't gonna make it."

"Is that why you were pushing Dad so hard?"

"No, not completely. I just can't stop worrying about
Mom and Dad. Plus, I need to know how bad the world
out there is, where Arianna is. I can't lose her."

Eric had mentioned that the weather in Colorado
was unpredictable at the best of times. If that was the
case, what would a giant, menacing, life-altering piece
of space rock do to it?

"I'm actually glad she's up at her family's cabin. With
everything that's happened, who knows how people in
bigger cities will react?"

I rested my head on his shoulder, not really sure what
to say. He laid his head on top of mine and sighed.

"It'll be all right. She'll be all right. From what you've told me, she's strong. She'll survive. But I agree with Dad. We can't freak out when we really don't know what's happening out there. We need to get more information before we start making plans on what we're gonna do after we get home."

"I know. I know."

The cold breeze that ruffled the nearby trees burned my cheeks. My constant motion usually kept me warm, but the longer we sat here, the more I felt the cold. I shivered.

"We should probably get..." I started to get up. He stopped me.

"Are you ever going to tell me what really happened in the storage room?"

I sat back down.

"What about what happened in the cabin? I know something happened. I saw your faces, and I know you're lying."

"I..."

"What happened, Reena?"

I froze. There was no way I could explain it. I didn't know myself.

"What are you talking about?"

He snorted. "There it is again. You just lied, and you're a terrible liar, Reena. Would it help if I told you I felt something weird right before you two appeared in the hallway?"

I sat up straighter, then scooted sideways to face him.

"What do you mean?"

"Something has changed in you. Dan noticed it last night too. He asked me what was going on, but what was I gonna tell him? I know that whatever happened in that room is more than just the luck of running to the door before the roof caved in. I heard your screams, Reena, and I felt something." He paused to look into my face.

I couldn't speak.

"But it's not just then. There have been other changes in you and Jax. Though most of them have been you. You're acting different."

"How?"

"It's hard to explain. It seems almost subconscious, like you're not aware of it. For instance, whenever you sit down, you pick up and touch the ash. There are times you just stare at it. Then there are times you collect it in your hand and roll it around on your palm. We've had to stop you a few times when your fingers turn blue from the cold."

"I do what?"

"Jax pointed it out. I know it hasn't been long yet, but the more you play with it, the more focused you seem to get. More aware of your surroundings somehow."

My eyebrows had to have knitted together in irritation and confusion because he let out a quick laugh before continuing.

"You started taking charge with so much confidence. It's a little shocking."

"That's not weird. I've always been bossy," I said.

"Not really, and it's not just that. It's hard to explain. It's like you see the detail no one else can. You watch everything differently than you did before."

Was he right? Was I acting that differently?

"I wish I could explain better." A curious expression spread across his face.

I followed his gaze and gasped. At some point, I'd taken off my gloves. I didn't remember doing it, but I'd scraped off a layer of the ash from the snow next to me.

As a result, I held a rather large glob of the purple-gold liquid ash. I moved my hand in careful circles back and forth, rolling the substance around and around. The tingling sensation whispered the path the substance had taken.

My heartbeat picked up. Fear and panic rose.

What am I doing? Suddenly, I needed it off my skin. I shook my hands violently, flinging the substance in all directions. I stood, my arms stiff at my sides, my fingers extended and every muscle tight with shock.

This isn't happening. I haven't been playing with the ash. No, no, I would have noticed.

My mind spun with denials. I mean, how could I have been doing this, regularly by Eric's account, but never been aware of it?

"I told you. Something's going on, and I need you to tell me everything. I won't think you're crazy." He gestured for me to sit.

It took me a long moment to collect myself, but when I did, I sat back down.

"When you were in the storage room, I felt something. It was like energy flooded the hallway. When it hit me, I felt jittery, keyed up. You started screaming for Jax, and it happened again. A few seconds later, you pulled Jax into the hallway. Your eyes were so wide, but that wasn't the disturbing part."

"What was?" I asked.

"They were unfocused. It was like you were trying to see something out of the corner of your eye. Or... like you were trying to see something that wasn't there."

Interesting, I thought. *Everything had been so vivid and clear. So bright.*

In those moments, I saw everything almost in slow motion. I saw the beams snap and the shelves crumple.

Even the movement of a single snowflake hadn't missed my notice.

"When I touched Jax after you pulled him through," Eric explained, "he felt weird. It was like a jolt of energy passed into me, but it wasn't until he passed out that I realized something was going on. We laid him down with his head in your lap. You placed your head on his, and there was a tangible shift in the room."

"Okay..."

"You jerked up, then your eyes got weird again. You put your hands on his face, and suddenly the room got cold. Like really cold. It was like all the heat in the room was being sucked into you. I could see my breath, and the fire went out. But you and Jax? There was warmth radiating from you two."

I was stunned to hear the events from someone else's perspective. It was fascinating and actually answered some of my questions. Eric had felt the wave of power from Jax but couldn't see it. He felt the connection I made with Jax. He knew I was trying to help Jax, but not how.

This made sense. What happened in the storage room had opened a flood of power from Jax. His instincts had kicked in to save himself, but then he couldn't stop it. All I knew was that if I didn't stop it, Jax would die. I had no doubt that if Jax had kept losing energy, he would have lost himself. In my head, I'd kept thinking that I needed to keep him warm and alive.

"This is serious, Eric. I need to know you won't tell anyone," I said.

"I won't unless you say I can."

That was the best I could expect.

"Okay. So first, Jax saved us. Well, it's more complicated than that." I stumbled over my words. "I guess I should start from the beginning. You need to know that I have been seeing things since the first ash fell. Maybe even before that. At least since The Flare."

"Seeing things?"

I gathered my courage and explained. "When Jax and I spoke about Goliath's entry, I mentioned to him I saw a green wave spread across the sky. Do you remember anything like that?"

"No."

"Jax didn't, either. Then I started seeing something weird. Anytime the ash is moved or touched, there is a tiny burst of light."

"Okay..."

The doubt in his tone caused me to cringe in embarrassment.

"You promised you would listen with an open mind."

"I am. Sorry."

"When Dad found us? I saw him approach long before he stepped into the light of camp. I could see his steps in the snow because of the flashes of light they created." I glanced down at my hands. "Today in the storage room, everything slowed down for me. Allan fell, and I tried to get to him, but he was pinned. Something hit my back, and I thought I was going to die. Then Jax was there. He lifted me and swung me toward the door. All of a sudden, a warmth ran up my spine, and I was thrown fifteen feet into the far wall."

"What?"

I nodded.

"It's true. When I was able to turn around..." I clenched my fists. How was I supposed to explain this? "He... well, he hadn't thrown me exactly. A wave of pure green power originating from his chest had flung me to safety." Eric's jaw dropped, but I continued, "The waves kept coming. I think they were in line with his heartbeat. Each one got weaker. These waves? They kept the snow and debris off him. They held back everything, giving us time to escape. By the time we were back in the cabin, his energy was almost gone. I could barely see them anymore. That's when he passed out."

"Wow. Um...okay. So, what happened after we moved him?" Eric asked.

"She saved me," the voice came from behind me.

Shit. Jax. I cringed.

"Well, aren't you getting good at eavesdropping today?" Eric said.

"I know we agreed not to tell..." I exclaimed. He held up his hand to stop me.

"I know. It's all right, but I want to hear this part." Jax sat on my other side, our small circle comfortable in its familiarity.

"Okay. Let me see if I can explain. When I put my forehead on yours, I could feel the energy you were emitting. It was slowly leaking out of you. I'm not sure how I know that, but I do. When Eric saw me lift my head, I was trying to see it."

"That would make sense since that's when your eyes got weird," Eric said.

I faced Jax and said, "When I focused, I could sense that the energy was coming from every part of you. It was pushing out in all directions. So, I wrapped myself around it. My mind or my own energy. Hell, I don't know." I couldn't look at him anymore. "My only thought was that I had to stop it. I held it so it couldn't escape anymore. I focused on your breathing and heartbeat. Then I pushed my energy into you and kept doing it until your body was able to take over again. At least that's what I think I did."

His hand touched mine, and we made eye contact.

"That's when I felt you," Jax said softly.

Eric's eyebrows rose in surprise. He was glancing back and forth between us.

"What do you mean?"

"After I collapsed, I wasn't really aware of anything. I don't remember being moved. I do remember a shock when your head touched mine. Then everything calmed. No, that's not quite right. It was calmer, but then this sensation of warmth spread over me... It started at my skin and moved into me. When it got to my heart, it started beating so fast. By the time I was aware enough to stop whatever you were doing, I felt like my body was vibrating. Like I'd just taken the best nap ever and drank thirty cups of coffee while asleep."

"Wait. So, she healed you?" Eric said, dubious.

"No," I said. "I think I did something else. I think I used my own energy to stabilize him, allowing his own body to balance itself. That's why he was still so exhausted afterward."

"Why do you think you gave him your energy?" Eric asked.

"When I was doing it, cold spread up my legs. You said the room's temperature dropped? I know this is a longshot guess, but what if I somehow pulled the heat from the air?"

"Is that possible?" Jax asked.

"I've read enough crappy sci-fi books to make the connection." I laughed because it really did sound like something out of a story. "And anyway, when I was done, I had a crazy bad headache. If Jax hadn't touched my head, I don't think I would have stopped. I wasn't fully in control of what I was doing. I think, like Jax's rescue of me, it was emotion driven."

I rubbed my temples. If I wasn't careful, the headache would spike again. For the last few hours, it

had just ached at the edge of my consciousness, but
retelling the story was making it pound again.

"I'm probably way off." I shrugged.

"Wow. I have no idea what to say to any of that," Eric
said. "But I think you both should try not to do
whatever you did again. At least until we know more.
This could be dangerous."

We grunted in agreement, then sat quietly, absorbing
everything we'd discussed. The sky changed as the sun
began its descent below the horizon. Some of the ash
cloud had cleared in the last few hours, which allowed
us to watch the eerily beautiful sunset.

"Emotion driven, huh?" Jax teased. "Are you trying
to tell me something?"

"You just wish," I said. I leaned over and pushed him.
"And don't tease. What you did was weirder than what
I did."

Jax just grinned, our comfortable rhythm settling
back in place.

"Pretty sure this situation confirmed it. You're both
freaks, but that's not a shocking development," Eric
said.

"Sorry to break it to you, Eric, but you might be one,
too. We just haven't figured out how yet," I said.

Eric shrugged in neither acknowledgment nor denial.

The three of us sat there until the sun dipped,
splashing every color into the sky, then fading into that
beautiful deep blue of night. As I watched the detail of
the world around me fade into darkness, my mind
rolled over everything we'd talked about. It all felt true
and yet lacking. There was something missing here.

Eventually, I stood and headed back to camp. They
wanted to stay back a little longer, so I left them where
they were. Their soft voices trailed after me.

Chapter Twelve

Upon returning, I found Sydney and Cassie in the cabin. Tom's leg had been re-splinted, and they were moving him to the far corner. With him there, there was far less chance of anyone accidentally hitting his bad leg.

"He doesn't look good," I said to Sydney.

"No, he doesn't. He's in shock. I've given him some pain meds, but we don't have anything strong enough to really help. All we can do is keep him warm," she said.

"And get him to a doctor as soon as we can," Cassie added.

"Yes, we do." Sydney smiled gently at us. "Thank you both for your help."

"No problem. Cassie, I think we should get everyone some dinner. Will you help me?"

She nodded and followed me out. We cooked enough for everyone, then passed equal amounts of what we made using the disposable cups from the shop.

"Good news! We're having oatmeal again," I said with a fake smile.

Jax, who was around the fire again, laughed. "Your favorite."

Approaching the two men who had yet to speak, I handed the older one his food first. He stared blankly into the fire, swaying back and forth with a gentle motion that reminded me of a ship on the water. The younger man ignored my offering, so I placed it next to him on the ground.

"Do we know their names?" I asked.

"His name is Walter," Dad said, pointing at the older gentleman. "But we haven't been able to get him to speak yet."

I stared at the younger man intently. There was something off about him. Something that just wasn't right. I tilted my head ever so slightly as if this would allow me to see what was wrong. A familiar tingling started at the base of my neck, then spread up and out across my skull. When it hit my eyes, my senses expanded and unfocused. My mind took over, and the world changed.

A hum of life appeared around each and every person, plant, and animal in range. Somewhere in my mind, I noted the small field mouse in the distance, then a bird in a nearby tree, but the image of those around the fire was what I focused on. They were beautiful, varying shades of light which vibrated in the air. That was for all except for the younger man. He was different.

Neat.

"No, Reena," Eric said forcefully. He placed a hand on my arm and squeezed.

"What?" I asked, my voice far off. Eric shone with energy when I glanced at him.

"Don't. You're doing it again. You need to stop."

"Huh?" My mind felt foggy. He was trying to tell me something, but what?

"What's happening?" Dad asked.

No one could figure out why Eric was scolding me, but by the way he and Jax sat, it was clear something was wrong. What, though? It was the weight of Jax's glare that made me realize my mistake, pulling me out of this haze.

Oh. "Sorry," I said. I shook my head to clear it and stood.

Maybe movement was all I needed. I began to circle the fire. Each step made the ache in my hip ping worse, but this helped clear my head. After a few loops around, I, without realizing, sat next to the younger man. The impulse was too strong to refuse as I placed my hand on his arm. One touch and I felt his energy. I assessed it as I had Jax earlier, reaching for it by instinct.

"No, Reena!" The harshness of Jax's voice broke me completely out of whatever had taken hold. I blinked, yanking my hand away.

"What's going on?" Cassie and Dad chorused.

"Nothing," I said. The boys both glared at me. What was wrong with me? Almost immediately, I'd broken our agreement. I avoided their judgment and turned to speak to the young man.

"Your name's Sean, right?"

He blinked rapidly, the clouded and scared quality clearing as he met my eyes. It was like the light inside them changed as I watched. He stayed silent, but for the first time since he'd been here, there was someone inside.

Everyone around the fire watched with rapt attention.

"Okay, Sean. I know you don't feel well. I know you're tired and scared, but I need you to eat something." My tone was one a mother would use on a small, terrified child.

I lifted the cup from the ground at his feet and pulled the spoon from it. Sean's gaze never left mine as the spoonful of thin, tasteless oatmeal I lifted reached his lips. Very slowly, he parted his lips and took a bite.

"Good job, Sean. Can you take another?" I asked, bringing the spoon up again. He opened more readily this time. I smiled gently.

"Great. Now, I need you to finish this. Then I'll take you into bed, all right? We need you to be strong for tomorrow."

The entire group gasped as he nodded, then took the cup from my hand, and started eating. When I turned back to the fire, all eyes were on me.

"How did you do that?" Sydney asked.

"I didn't do anything."

"Then how did you know his name? We've been trying to guess it all day. The whole walk I kept throwing names at him, but he never responded," Cassie exclaimed.

"I didn't do anything," I said again, dropping my head. I wished everyone would stop asking me questions because my head still felt fuzzy, my thoughts jumbled. But it was the look of awe mixed with rage on Jax's face that made me want to run and hide. He was pissed.

Nothing I can do about that now.

When the older man tilted violently, almost falling off the log, that strange vision reappeared, and I could see the issue so clearly. His balance was so off he could barely control his body. From one second to the next, that same sensation spread up my spine and my hand reached out.

"Reena!" The angry scream from Jax filled the air, but he wasn't fast enough.

I touched Walter's leg, and a shock shot into my hand and up my arm. The air was shoved out of me as if I'd been kicked in the stomach. The power of the contact made me dizzy. I pulled my hand back and shook it. Before I knew what happened, Jax grabbed my arm and dragged me from the fire. Eric's angry gait followed behind.

"Boys! What's happening?" Dad called, worry lining his voice.

Eric stopped and, to my dad, said, "Give us a minute and I'll explain." Then, reaching the trees, turned furious eyes on me. "What were you thinking? After everything that happened today, you do that?" It was nearly a yell.

"What did I do?"

You know what you did, Reena. And I did. With distance from the others, I could see what happened.

"What's wrong with you? We don't know what this is, Reena! It could hurt you." His voice shook with emotion.

"I'm sorry. I didn't... I just—"

"We warned you when it started! Then you still went over and touched him," Eric snapped.

"Guys, I didn't do anything! Not really."

"Then how did you know his name?" Jax asked.

"When I touched him, I felt his energy, and it told me his name." I shrugged.

"It told you...? Whatever." Eric rubbed his face in frustration. "But then you started speaking to him in that creepy melodic voice and he responded!"

My words must've derailed Jax a bit, because he asked, "What did you feel when it was happening?"

"Nothing. I touched him, knew his name, and tried to draw him out. He was lost."

"Can you hear yourself?" Eric asked.

Jax ignored Eric's question. "What happened with Walter?"

"Now that, I'm not sure. When we touched, there was a shock. He was out of balance, uncontrolled. All I did was touch him."

"Come on, Reena. We know you better than that," Jax scolded.

Anger bloomed in my chest.

"What the hell do you want me to say?" I exploded at them. "Less than forty-eight hours ago, a rogue planet enters the atmosphere, probably destroying our entire world as we know it..."

Why can't they understand I have no clue what is happening! I stomped back and forth in front of them, continuing, "...dropping a weird ash that probably flicked some switch on in my brain. Then while helping me, some young father dies, and my best friend tries to save me and almost dies along with him." My voice was loud and angry now. "Then we add more people to our sad group—one of which is dying, and two others that are almost catatonic—and I want to help them but feel completely useless. Then apparently that sets my brain on fire, and I pull one guy out of his head and balance the other!"

My throat closed in frustration, my fury vibrating within. Okay, I'd hit my limit.

"Balance?" Eric asked.

My shoulders sagged, and I started to cry. I tried to turn away, but Jax reached out and gripped my shoulders, refusing to let me hide my tears.

I hate crying. This is so embarrassing. I'm weak.

"Eric, give us a minute," Jax said, and Eric retreated. Jax's soft whisper made me flinch when he continued, "I'm sorry. I shouldn't have yelled at you. I'm scared, and I don't want anything to happen to you."

I didn't respond.

Jax's hands slid down my arms, then dropped to his sides. I barely heard him when he said, "Tell me what to do."

From the corner of my eye, I saw him step back. No, this couldn't happen. I reached up and grabbed his shirt, stopping his retreat.

"I can't," I whispered.

The distant crackling of the fire and soft whistling of the wind helped to settle my thoughts. I pulled him closer and wrapped my arms around his waist. He responded immediately. My cheek rested on his shoulder as I let the frustration seep from my eyes. This was my best friend. We'd been away from each other for a long time, but I still had him. His warmth, his worry, and his heart were still mine.

"I think we have a new team motto," I said once I'd settled.

"Oh, yeah, and what's that?"

"'I don't know shit.'"

His laugh rumbled under my ear.

"Seems appropriate." Jax leaned away just enough to use his finger to raise my chin so I would look at him. "Are you okay?"

"Yeah, and I'm sorry."

"Me too," he said gently. He brushed a hair from my cheek. Warmth lingered wherever his skin touched mine.

He's so amazing. I thought, then I caught myself. *Stop this. It's Jax. He's your friend and nothing else.*

Embarrassed that he might be able to read my thoughts, I released him.

"I'm exhausted and need to go to bed. Do you think they'll let me sleep?" I asked.

"I'll make sure of it."

When we got back to the fire, I was afraid to look up. I'd always felt like crying was a weakness and I knew everyone would be able to see the tear tracks on my face, but only Sydney and Sean remained. I breathed a sigh of relief.

"I got Camden and Walter to go lie down in the cabin, but Sean won't move. He just kept staring in your direction."

"I've got it," I said. I knelt next to Sean. "Hey, Sean. How are you doing? It's time for bed. Let's go to the cabin, okay?"

Sean stood, and we walked together. Eric was inside speaking with Walter. I was able to find a spot for Sean to lie down. It was by the window, but with the fireplace burning, the room was more than comfortable.

"Get some sleep. We'll talk more in the morning," I said and brushed some ash from his cheek.

Sean smiled, and I felt it in my chest. It may be tiny, but it was something, and I had done that.

Eric waited for me just outside the window. He half-lifted me through, then pulled me into a hug.

"Love you, Little Sis."

I squeezed him back, then walked toward the tents.

"Are these claimed? I'm exhausted," I asked.

"Cassie and I are taking that one," Sydney said. "But you can have the other."

"Do you care if I join you? The boys and I are taking shifts," Dad said.

That is when I realized how terrible he looked. He was easily going on forty-eight hours without sleep and with our little show, he was worried about me now too.

"That's a stupid question. Of course you can," I said. I shot him an exasperated look, then followed it up with a hug.

"Eric?" I said.

"Yeah?"

"Tell him what's going on, all right? I need to lie down."

"Will do, but only after you both go get some sleep." He motioned for my dad to head to the tent. "You've been awake longer than all of us. Go on, Dan. I'll wake you up in a few hours."

Even though my body was drained, my mind kept spinning. I lay there, convinced I would never fall asleep. When I finally did pass out, my sleep was restless. At some point in the night, someone came in, woke my dad, and lay next to me. When I glanced over my shoulder, I saw Jax trying to get under the blanket.

That won't help, I thought.

"I'm so cold," I whispered.

Jax rolled to his side and pulled me against him. His jacket was still warm from the fire. My back pressed to his front, and I sighed. His hand rubbed my arms, then wrapped around my waist. He pressed his face into my hair. With the help of his body heat, my eyelids became heavy, and I finally fell into a deep sleep.

Chapter Thirteen

Warmth. Comfort. Contentment. That was not what I expected to feel when I awoke. I'd fallen asleep so cold and lost, but as I came to, there was no shivering or painful aching in my muscles. My mind was clear and my heart happy. Afraid this was a dream, and it would disappear, I didn't move.

Is this real? I took stock of myself. *Nope, not a dream.*

The ground beneath me was hard and uneven. The tent's fabric rustled in the wind, and soft light of morning filtered through the canvas. The air that touched my face was frigidly cold, but the rest of me was blissfully warm.

I was curled into someone—Jax—I realized, our thin blankets wrapped around us both. My head rested on his arm with my face pressed to his collarbone. Our arms were wrapped around each other, our legs tangled beneath the blanket.

Okay. Wow. Um...

At some point, his jacket had been unzipped, and I had snaked my arm underneath it and around him. I was pressed solidly against his chest with the jacket half-covering me.

Based on the way his arms draped over me, it was clear he was still fast asleep. His breath was slow and deep where his face was buried in my hair.

My mind whorled at the sensation of being in his arms. Never had anyone held me like this and never had I thought he, of all people, would.

It's just because it's cold. You're just friends, I thought. *Then why does it feel so good?*

I didn't want to wake him. I didn't want to move. This was the most comfortable I had ever been. In my groggy haze, I pressed my hand to his back and pulled him closer, secretly wishing this moment would never end. His shirt had risen during sleep so two of my fingers brushed against the long lean muscles there. Tingles shot into my fingertips. My body responded automatically. I pressed my face closer into him, unconsciously nuzzling his neck.

How does he smell so good?

In response, Jax tightened his arms, pulling me in, too. The sound of his groan sent shivers through me.

What is wrong with me? This is Jax! What are you doing? I scolded myself.

Jax began to move as he came awake. He shifted closer as if not wanting to break our pocket of heat, either. He burrowed into my hair, took a deep breath, and then sighed.

It was impossible to resist the urge to touch him. My hand moved upward to brush the bare skin of his back just under his shirt. The tips of my fingers grazed the indentation of his spine, and I felt him shiver.

Seriously, Reena, what are you doing? A small noise escaped, letting him know I was awake.

He stretched his legs for a moment, then returned them to wrap with mine.

"Warm enough?" he asked. His voice was scratchy from sleep.

"Mmmmhmm, I don't want to move," I admitted.

His small chuckle rumbled under my cheek. "Don't have to yet. You sleep okay?"

"Better once you joined me," I said honestly. I pulled away only enough to look at him. In doing so, I found our faces inches from one another. The blue of his eyes captivated me, but the mere millimeters between our lips was far more intriguing.

Never had I felt like that. Never had I expected for Jax to be the one to bring it out. A weight settled in my chest, one that pulled me closer and pushed me away.

His eyes were sleepy but changed as he gazed at me. It was as if he could read my thoughts. I wanted to look away but couldn't. He scanned my face curiously and with a heat I felt deep in my chest. This was not the boy I'd grown up with. This was a man. A man who saw the world for what it was. Who never gave up and was dedicated to those he loved. He'd grown into something more. And right now, every ounce of this newfound intensity was focused on me.

My face flushed.

Sensing I was uncomfortable, he blinked and shifted back just a touch. "Are you feeling any better today?"

"Better? Oh, you mean after my breakdown yesterday?"

"That wasn't a breakdown," he said. He smiled softly. Without seeming to know he'd done it, Jax lifted his hand to gently brush away the hair from my face.

The gesture stopped any reply. I was too focused on his expression and the path of his hand as it trailed down my arm to stop on my waist. I bit my lip.

You need to move away. Get some space.

The light in his eyes shifted. The corner of his mouth rose as he teased, "I have to say, you don't look bad for someone sleeping in a tent. Especially considering how you usually wake up."

I choked back my laugh. *Jerk.* Okay, this I understood.

"Funny, I can't say the same thing about you," I replied.

To that, his smile grew wider. The humor in his gaze sparkled. Then it shifted again to something far more serious. It was like some battle warred in his head. From one second to the next, he made up his mind and acted. He moved the final inch to brush his lips against mine in the softest kiss I'd ever experienced.

Instantly, I was lost. I knew I should pull away, but instead, I tightened my arm and slid my hand farther up his back under his shirt. Stunned by both the fact he'd kissed me and the intense heat that lit my body in response, I kissed him back. And it felt so right.

The hesitation he'd had only seconds before disintegrated. His hand tangled in my hair, deepening the kiss. He shifted, rolling to hover over me. The feel of his muscles flexing under my touch ignited something within me. I lost myself in his embrace, in his lips.

As if cold water was being thrown over me, my mind came back to me. This was wrong.

Jax was kissing me. He was kissing me in a tent, in the middle of nowhere, after the world was probably destroyed. After we'd been stuck in an avalanche zone. Only one day after a man died trying to save my life, while we had no idea if the rest of our family was alive or dead.

I pulled away, forcing myself to separate from him, removing us from the intimate position we'd been in. A

blast of cold air snapped me farther back into reality as
I left his arms. I sat up in the small space.

"Jax," I said, breathless. "What are we doing?"

Jax was breathing heavily. His eyes held joy and
surprise, but there was also hesitation. He closed his
jacket, then sat up to face me. Unconsciously, he licked
his lips before he spoke. When he did, it was tinged
with worry.

"I'm sorry. I had—I just—" He was stuttering. It was
cute.

"You just what?" I couldn't tell if I was mad or not.
Was I mad he kissed me? No, not exactly. In fact, that
was the best kiss I'd ever had. I just knew that right
now, in the midst of all this craziness, was not the time.
How could I trust anything I was feeling?

"I... I'm sorry. I had to. You're amazing and beautiful
and... I know you think of me like a brother. I'm sorry,
but..."

"I've never thought of you as a brother," I said
without thinking. He froze and watched me carefully. I
tried to find the right thing to say. "To be honest, Jax,
I'm not sure how I feel. I know you're my best friend
and I love you, but I can't help but wonder if we really
want this or if it's just the stress."

He was offended. His posture closed off, then his
expression smoothed into something calm and cool. I
hated it. He was trying to hide from me, and it was my
fault. My reaction had hurt him. I messed up everything
again.

"I'm sorry," he said. The regret I saw hurt more than
the words. "I didn't mean to make you uncomfortable."

My heart ached at those words. Jax was my friend
and always had been. One of the people I loved most in
this world, and I'd just hurt him. I scanned his every
feature, wishing I could understand, but it was like

there was a block in my head. My body demanded more of that warmth I'd felt in his arms, but my mind was stuck. Stuck in the past. Stuck in the stupid choices I'd made over the years. I just wasn't good enough. *This is so unfair.* I reached out and touched his cheek. Jax tried to pull away from my touch, but before he had the chance, I shocked myself. I just couldn't let him go. I couldn't miss the chance to taste him again. My fingers flitted to tangle in the soft hairs at the back of his neck. In the next instant, I pressed my lips to his. *Please...*

His shocked groan caught me off guard. I sank deeper into the kiss, parting my lips. He didn't hesitate. This kiss was different. It was so incredibly sweet and yet dangerous. Jax pulled my body against his. His hands roamed up my back and into my hair.

I shifted onto his lap and gasped as his heartbeat thundered against my chest. The heat between us built in a way I never expected. He broke away to breathe and used the opportunity to kiss down the line of my neck. I arched my back, allowing him more access.

As he found my lips again, the thought, *my Jax*, filled me. I nearly moaned at the thought.

"Reena, Jax?" Our tent shook. The canvas flapped as someone grabbed the edge and proceeded to shake it. Jax and I froze instantly. "It's time to get up. We've got a long day ahead," my dad hollered cheerily, completely unaware of what was happening mere feet from him.

My eyes went wide when I realized there was only the thin fabric of the tent between us. I tried to calm my racing heart, but that wasn't easy. Especially since I refused to look away from Jax.

"All right, Dad. We'll be out in a minute," I yelled. I managed to keep my voice calm.

"Sounds good." The sound of his footsteps faded as he headed for the cabin.

Jax examined me as if I were someone he didn't know. I still sat on his lap with my hand resting along his jaw. Slowly, I moved my fingers to gently brush against his lips. His eyelids fluttered closed.

Jax... I wish I knew what to do.

In a low whisper, I said, "With everything that's going on, I honestly don't know how I feel, but I can tell you one thing. You are *very* important to me."

He sat stunned as I got up and slipped through the door. When I looked back, he stared after me, a small smile playing at the edge of his mouth. He was so tempting, but I forced myself to walk away.

Chapter Fourteen

I went for a walk to clear my head. The entire scene ran through my mind over and over. I was dizzy with everything that had happened. When I was out of sight, I found a tree to lean against. My fingers rose to brush my lips.

What just happened? My thoughts were jumbled. My feelings swirled so fast I felt nauseous. *Get it together. You have to keep going. You can figure this all out later.*

I shook my head. I had no idea how I was going to handle this too.

"Hey, baby," my dad said as he walked through the trees. I jumped. "You okay?"

I nodded. "Just a little overwhelmed. It's going to be a long day."

"It will, but we'll get through it. What are you doing out here?"

"Nothing. I was just heading back to help pack up." I pushed off the tree.

"Sounds good. I think Cassie could use some help in the cabin."

I nodded. Jax and Sydney were breaking down the tents, and Camden was putting out the fire. Jax glanced up as I passed, and I could see everything I felt mirrored in him. I bit my lip and continued on.

"Hey, Cass, can I help?"

"Absolutely!"

We worked in silence. We stocked all the backpacks to the breaking point, then gathered the remaining food, drinks, and other supplies. Using the curtains, we created makeshift bags to carry the rest. It was our hope that we would make it back to town before sunset, but with the injured, we weren't sure. So anything we might need for a night outside was coming with us.

I was piling the final items onto the purple sled when Cassie finally spoke.

"So, are you and Jax a thing?"

I nearly choked at her question.

"What? No, why would you ask?" My "no" sounded more like a question to my ears.

"Just curious. You two are always together. You sleep in the same tent, but you don't really act like it."

"Um... well, we've been friends since we were born. We grew up together." I shrugged. "The last few years have been tough on us, but we are still close."

"So, he's more like your brother?"

"I mean, I guess." I dropped my gaze and fiddled with one of the ropes.

I mean... yeah, if by brother you mean an amazing guy who you would die for. One you just made out with in a tiny tent in the middle of nowhere. Then yeah. Brother. Totally...

"Does he have a girlfriend? I know Eric has Arianna, but I haven't heard Jax mention one."

I gaped at her. Cassie wanted to make a move on Jax. We'd known her for what, two days? Anger flared inside me.

He isn't yours, and can you blame her?

"Nope. No girlfriend. So, you don't have a boyfriend?" I asked.

Just then, Jax walked past the window. Cassie and I both stared, transfixed. He was tall and lean. His long body moved with strength and grace. He'd removed his jacket, and even through his long-sleeved shirt you could see the muscles of his arms bunch and stretch.

"He is pretty," Cassie said, distracted. "And to answer your question, no. No boyfriend. I'm only here for break, and there's no one back home."

"Are you a student?"

"Yup, UCSD. You?"

"Seniors in high school back in Arizona."

"High school, huh?" she paused, still admiring the view out the window. "He said he was eighteen. Do you think he would ever be interested in an older woman?"

Now I did start choking. I shook my head and shrugged my shoulders awkwardly. "Um... You'd have to ask him."

Cassie laughed, obviously happy she'd caught me off guard. We finished packing in silence. We lifted the sled out the window, but she stopped me before I climbed out.

"I know this will sound weird, but I want to come with you guys wherever you all head next. I'm alone here. And the only family I had was in California. Even if it's still there, I can't make it alone."

"I'm sorry to hear that. Of course you can stay with us."

"Thanks."

Cassie was cool. Even though she'd asked my permission to hit on Jax, there was no way I could leave her on her own. We just didn't do that.

Within the hour we were on our way. We started in a large group, but quickly paired up and spread out. Dad walked with Walter, who was no longer unsteady on his feet. He even conversed openly with those around him. Eric, Jax, and Camden—who I now knew was thirteen —switched off to pull the litter which contained the unconscious Mike.

Sean walked with me. He no longer stared blankly, which was nice. He glanced around, taking in anything and everything he could. He tried to talk, but each time it was like the words clogged his throat. No matter how hard he tried, the words just wouldn't come. So, I spoke to him. I told him about anything I could think of: home, family, the plants around us, anything. He just listened and smiled at me.

A few times, I caught Jax looking in my direction, but he glanced away each time when I caught him. The two times I tried to approach him, I lost my nerve and retreated to the back of the group.

The trek got a little better once we got to the road. The snow wasn't as thick, but ice was a problem. Finding a grip in certain spots was difficult. Then, downed trees littered the road and rockslides blocked a few sections. Several times we had to carry the litter over something. It was exhausting. I hated not being able to help much. My hip ached and pain shot down into my knee. But I stayed quiet, sticking with Sean or helping the others when they'd let me.

After a few hours, we came across our first vehicles. They were a mile or so apart. One had been abandoned, but the other held two bodies. My dad checked to see if they were okay, but unfortunately, the occupants had not survived. When he tried to get the car working, the engine wouldn't turn over.

On our second stop of the day, we huddled next to a thick line of trees. The wind had picked up, and the temperature had dropped. My fingers ached with the cold. We pulled out some food and water and passed it around.

After making sure everyone was set, I headed toward Jax. This time, I would talk to him. That idea flitted away when I saw Jax and Cassie talking animatedly. They both laughed at some story she was telling, and she leaned close to him. Her posture screamed flirting, but Jax seemed unaware. He continued his conversation as I passed. He met my eyes, and this time I looked away.

"Hey, Eric, can I join you?" I asked. He sat on a huge log twenty feet or so away from the rest.

"Absolutely."

I sat next to him, pulled out my muffin, and started to eat.

"What's happening over there?" Eric asked, gesturing toward Cassie and Jax.

My fist clenched. "Cassie thinks he's hot. She basically asked for my permission." Bitterness snuck into my voice even as I tried to push it back.

Eric's head snapped to me. He chuckled. "Seriously? And what did you say?"

"In simpler terms, I told her that he wasn't mine to claim."

His eyes narrowed. "Isn't he?"

"No. Why would he be?"

"I dunno. Just a feeling."

"What did he tell you?" I asked sharply. I was so mad I could barely speak. If Jax told Eric what happened, I was gonna kill him.

"Nothing, but you just did." Eric laughed. "So, who kissed who first?"

My face heated, and I knew I was blushing. I dropped my head into my hands and groaned. My hair fell to hide my face from the others, a dark barrier that did nothing to hide my embarrassment from Eric.

Through my hands, I said, "The first or the second time?"

"Ha! Finally!" Eric shouted.

I slapped my hand over his mouth and glared. Eric realized his mistake as everyone turned to look at us.

"I... uh... I finally got her to admit I am a better shot than she is. You know, with her bow. I've been trying to get her to admit it for years."

So, blaming our battle for superiority normally would have worked, seeing as we'd been doing it for years, but as most of the group didn't know us well, I guessed that we'd failed miserably. The strange looks we received would've made me laugh, but Jax's curious gaze held me immobile. With how red my face was, I knew he knew the truth. Only when Cassie started talking and he looked away could I move.

"Eric, I swear."

"Come on, I knew it already. You just confirmed it. All morning you two have been refusing to look at each other and not speaking. You do know that is the universal sign for, 'don't notice something big just happened between us,' right?"

I rubbed my temple. "I don't know, Eric. I don't know what to think. We've never had that kind of relationship, especially not the last two years. How can I trust my feelings with everything going on? And now there's Cassie." I forced myself to stop rambling. I pulled at my hair, the pain calming me.

"What does your gut say?" Eric asked.

I glanced away. *Who knows?*

"You guys will figure it out. You always do. You just have to be honest with yourselves."

"If I'm honest..." Disappointment littered my voice as I spoke. "If I am honest, he's too good for me. I don't deserve him."

Eric leaned over to wrap me in a one-armed hug. "Not even close to the truth," he said with finality.

I ducked my head to rest on his shoulder and tried to sort out my own heart.

The wind blew in large gusts as we entered town. The sky had darkened ominously, and ash-colored snow covered us from head to toe. My hair was frozen, and my entire body ached. The last ten hours had been a test of will.

An unsettled feeling rose in me as we approached town, and it didn't wane as we entered it. Only two days had passed since Goliath, but it looked like weeks had passed. No one was in sight, and it was far too quiet.

"That's what it is," I said to myself.

"What?" Cassie asked.

"The power's out. That's why it's so creepy. That humming sound of electricity is gone."

"Hmmm. You're right."

A line of shops flanked the main road. Their dark windows gave a sense of quiet judgment and despair. In the distance, several damaged buildings had crumpled into the street. Charred sections hinted at the kiss of fire.

I wonder what started it.

Thankfully, the clinic was still intact. It was the only two-story building in town, and I thought I could see light coming from the windows.

"Looks like someone's home," Eric said.

We pushed the doors and entered a dark room. Chairs lined one side of the waiting room in shades of maroon and tan. Curtains with geometric patterns hung from the windows. A candle sat on a side table, letting us know someone was here.

"Hello?" Sydney called.

Quiet voices came from behind the swinging doors, which separated us from the hallway. The voices came closer, then a man in scrubs appeared through the doors followed by a woman with chestnut hair. They took in our battered appearance.

"Where the hell did you guys come from?" the man in scrubs and heavy boots asked.

"Up the mountain," Dad said.

"What? You guys were on Mount Hood? I'm surprised anyone survived with all those avalanches. Hell, you could see them from here."

"No one else has come back?"

"Not from there at least."

"Then we might be the only ones. Listen, we need some help. A few of us are injured."

"We'll do the best we can," the man said, glancing at the woman next to him. "Right now, we're trying to re-establish our backup generators. They failed a few hours ago. By the way, I'm Doctor Travis McCormick, and this is Cindy Gonzales. How can we help?"

Dad led them over to where Mike lay. They examined him quickly, then Cindy disappeared into the back. She reappeared with two large men. Without a word, they carried Mike and the litter away.

"Where is everyone else?" Sydney asked Travis. "It's so quiet."

"Goliath caused all sorts of problems. The power went out. Actually, everything electronic stopped working. The town isn't big, so we were able to check on most of the townsfolk." He sighed. "Some of the houses collapsed, and a few died in car accidents or from falling debris. Others, we can't find. Luckily this place had backup generators that weren't on when Goliath entered. With the influx of injured, we took those with minor injuries to town hall where we set up a relief shelter for the locals. This is a close-knit community, so they were willing to help watch after them. Those who needed more extensive help are upstairs. You're the first new people we've seen in a while."

"Has anyone named Kim come in?" I asked.

"No, why?"

"One of our group stayed back. I wanted to see if you'd seen her."

Jax and Eric exchanged glances.

Travis nodded. "Well, not that I've seen. Does anyone else need to be checked out?"

"Walter and Sean. Reena should probably have someone look at her leg too," Dad said.

"No, Dad. Jax and I have it covered," I said.

"Reena..." he scolded.

"She's walking, talking, and isn't bleeding. More importantly, she doesn't have anything sticking out of her. We'll check out the other two now. If you get worse, come back."

"I'll be fine, doctor."

Eric stepped up and asked, "Is having people come in with things sticking out of them a common problem here?"

I held back my grin at Eric's dry tone but noticed my dad turn away.

"Sadly, yes," Travis said seriously. All the smiles in the room disappeared. He nodded, then turned and gestured to Walter and Sean to follow.

Sean began to panic. He started to stutter, "No. No. No. Ree, Ree, no." Sean shook violently. His gaze shot back and forth from me to the doors and back. Sean calmed when I took his hand. I pulled him toward the door.

In the calm voice that I'd used on him before, I spoke. "It's okay, Sean. These people are here to help. I could come with. Would you like that?"

"Ree, Jax, Ree, Jax," he said.

"You want me and Jax to come with you?" The surprise I felt was mirrored on Jax's face, but without hesitation, Jax joined us.

"We got you, Sean," Jax said. He patted Sean on the shoulder. He visibly relaxed, turned, and followed Travis.

The hallway was lined with five triage rooms, most empty. Mike was in the first room. Walter and Sean were taken to the next two.

"Sean, can you sit down?" I asked when he stopped in the middle of the exam room. He did so, and the doctor gave me a strange look.

"I'll be right back. I'm going to go check on your friend first. Are you okay here?"

"Yes," Jax said. He hovered near the door

"Sean, are you okay?" I felt an attachment to him, a connection that linked us. As strange as it sounds, I could feel how he needed Jax here just as much as I did.

"Go. With. Reena." The words were forced out of his mouth. There were long breaks between each word as if he had to work to pronounce them. He glanced around erratically, only meeting my eyes when the next word escaped.

Jax's eyes widened in surprise. This was the first real sentence Sean had said, so when Jax came to stand next to me, I was grateful.

"Sean, you need help. You hit your head. We need to make sure you're okay," I said gently.

"No. No, no, no. You help. Brought back."

"What?"

"She brought you back? Is that what you're saying?" Jax's scowl was one of confusion, not anger.

Sean nodded so violently I was afraid he'd hurt himself. "Yes. Reena. E. M. Jax. Protect."

E.M.? What in the world did that mean? Sean knew something and was trying to explain, but between his fidgeting and broken speech, it was hard to understand.

That tingling along my spine told me I could help.

"Jax, I need you to trust me. I have to try something. I *need* to."

Jax's eyes were hard when he said, "No. What if it hurts you? What if it hurts him?"

"I probably won't be able to do anything anyway, but I have to try. He knows something about both of us. Why else would he want you here? Think about it. He wasn't there when the collapse happened, so how does he know you 'protect'?" There was a pleading quality in my voice as I attempted to make him see.

Jax ran his hand through his hair.

"But..." Jax paused, staring into my eyes. "Fine. But if I see you freak out like you did before, I will stop this."

"Yes! Protect. Protect!" Sean's voice rose even with his stutter.

That confirmed it. "Do it," Jax said.

I placed my hand on Sean's chest, unfocusing my eyes, and the world lit up. I extended out my senses in an attempt to feel for Sean, and it hit me with an unexpected strength.

"Woah."

He was out of control. His energy spun so fast I could barely get a handle on it. It swirled, pushing against me and making me nauseous.

"Okay, I'm gonna try something," I whispered to no one in particular. This was so different from what I did with Jax.

Catch it, some inner voice whispered. *Catch it and calm it. Catch it and calm it.*

I reached out, wrapped myself around the unstable power and, the moment I did, I felt my knees go weak. Somehow, I kept my feet.

I'm doing something wrong. Eric had said that the temperature had dropped in the cabin. We guessed that was because I'd pulled energy from around me. That was why my feet had gone cold, and the fire had died. *I needed more energy. But how did I do it before...? You pulled...*

I took a deep breath and squeezed my eyes closed. Jax's hand touched my back.

"No, Jax." His hand disappeared.

A few seconds passed before I felt the change. Something flooded into my feet, then traveled up my body and into the link with Sean. He gasped as I began to focus on him. I slowed his field—the opposite of what I'd done with Jax—and felt as more of Sean returned.

Jax took a step away. Without breaking my concentration, I opened my eyes and looked at Sean.

Sean was focused directly on me. His gaze didn't stray; he didn't fidget.

"Explain," I panted. I could feel my hold slipping. "Fast."

"You helped. Speed Jax. Slow my field. E.M." Sean's voice was more normal, but still clipped. Plus, he wasn't making any sense.

"I'm confused."

"E. M. Power."

With his last word, I lost the connection. My mind went blank, and the world flashed with darkness. I heard Jax's cry of alarm, then felt him catch me before lowering me to the floor. The world spun again as he picked me up and moved me to a chair by the window.

My stomach rolled as the image of falling rocks filled my head. Bright flashes of light followed by the rumble of thunder. I flinched at the rattle deep in my bones. I shook my head, then slowly opened my eyes. Slowly, the world materialized around me again.

What a weird dream. Deep breaths. In and out. My head rested against the wall. I opened my eyes slowly. His mouth was moving, but I couldn't make out his words yet.

"I'm fine," I said. My voice was so soft I could barely hear it.

I looked past Jax to Sean. He sat on the table, fidgeting worse than before. On the floor, a ring of ice shimmered, two boot prints etched perfectly inside.

"Ree!" Sean said.

"I'm fine, Sean," I said louder. With those words, he calmed ever so slightly.

"No, you're not. Your nose is bleeding."

Chapter Fifteen

"We're good to go," I said as I walked from the back.

My dad and Cassie sat in the waiting area. The others were nowhere in sight.

"Where did everyone go?"

"Town hall. They said we could drop off Sean on the way out."

"No!" Jax and I said in unison.

"He's coming with us," I said, calmer. It was nice to know Jax and I were on the same page.

He'd been quiet since he'd scraped the ice off the floor, before the doctor had come back. Then, he'd stood by the door as the doctor examined Sean. Travis explained that his head injury was severe, considering his symptoms. There was a possibility Sean would recover, but there was no guarantee. He wanted to do a scan, but the equipment had been damaged along with all the other electronics.

"I don't know, Reena. These people are more qualified to help him," Dad said.

"Dan, he's coming home with us. Reena and I will watch out for him." Jax patted Sean's shoulder. "Won't we?" he said to Sean.

Dad rubbed his hands together thoughtfully. We stayed on either side of our friend, refusing to back down and, eventually, he shrugged.

"Fine. I'm too tired to argue." Dad rubbed his face. "Did you get checked out, Reena? You feeling okay?"

"We talked about what happened. Travis gave me some bandages and stuff. I just want to go home."

"Then let's go."

I'd thought I was tired before, but as we headed the final two miles to the house, my energy crashed. I felt weak. My whole body hurt. My head ached with renewed vengeance. After a quarter mile, I fell back. My limp was more pronounced, and I dragged my feet.

Sean stayed next to me, and when I nearly fell, he latched on to my arm for support. His jerky movements made walking interesting, but we laughed at our attempts until Jax appeared on my left.

"You two are ridiculous," he said with a grin.

We turned down the tree-lined street that led to the house. The driveway was covered with untouched dark snow. When the house appeared through the trees, Eric ran for the door.

I could feel Jax's need to rush forward. "Go, Jax. Sean's got me. Go find Kim."

He was torn, but after a gentle squeeze of his arm, he jogged to the house.

I sighed. "Sean, what am I going to do with him?"

"Pro-protect," Sean replied, his face serious.

Always, I thought. *Always.*

The boys called out. There was an excited reply from within. Pure joy filled me as three people burst from inside. Kim and James were followed by a petite form.

"Lily!" I screamed. I let go of Sean and ran up the steps.

Lily jumped into my arms.

A second before I'd been about to collapse, but the sight of her changed everything. She was all right, and that was all that mattered. Hugs were exchanged all around, followed by extensive questioning of why I looked about to fall over.

Cassie and Sean watched with amused smiles. They were introduced, and soon we were all shuffled through the kitchen and down to the basement. The warmth of the wood-burning stove and the smell of jasmine told me we were finally home. Candles sat between us, making the room flicker with a calming light.

We made it.

We all squeezed into the space. Eric, Jax, James, and I shared one couch while the others fought over the other. Sean and Cassie decided to take the floor, not willing to get involved with all the excited banter.

"I've been so worried," Kim said. "I knew deep down that you'd be okay, but not knowing..."

"We've taught the boys well, Kim. Plus, with Reena and Dan with them, there was no doubt they'd be okay." James' grin was bright and happy.

Chatter broke out as we all started to speak at the same time.

"So, what happened to you guys?" Eric asked. "I'm glad you were here, Mom, but what happened? And to you, Dad?"

Lily spoke first, her excitement of a good story energizing her.

"Uncle James and I'd been driving back when everything happened. We crashed when a bunch of trees and snow fell onto the road. The car wouldn't move. I was so glad that Uncle James was there because I didn't know what to do. I was so scared."

"You never showed it," James said.

She dropped her head. Lily leaned against Dad's side and curled under his arm.

"You weren't hurt?" Dad asked.

"Not at all. We grabbed everything we had in the car and started walking. We made it to that little Shoppe N' Café. The one with the really good pie," James explained.

"And oh, how we ate pie." Lily's statement made me laugh.

James continued, "The power was out, but they were more than willing to let us stay overnight. We ate like kings, didn't we, Lily?"

"Yes. I just wish we'd brought some home."

"It took most of the next day to get here. We've just been hanging out waiting for you guys to get back," he said.

"That, and learning that Lily had become a Monopoly shark," Kim grumbled.

Lily laughed. "I warned you. Um... Hey, Kim, can we get them something to eat? Reena looks like she could use it."

I missed my Lily. And I could use it. I rested my head on Jax's shoulder.

"Can I help?" Cassie asked.

"Sure." Kim stood, picking up a small oil lantern. She headed out of the room, Cassie on her heels. Kim gently brushed my hair back as she passed.

The conversation continued as Dad and Eric grilled them for more detail. The story eventually switched to the retelling of our adventure. I listened silently until the food arrived.

"These should hold you over until dinner," Kim said.

An echoing of "thank you" resonated as we all dug in. After I'd scarfed two peanut butter and jelly sandwiches, I leaned back. The words of the conversation weaved in and out of my consciousness as exhaustion overtook me.

There's no way to tell how long I was out. When I woke, I found myself in a very interesting position. I lay, my legs sprawled across Eric's lap, and my body pressed against Jax's side. I was on my right, my arm resting around Jax's waist. Both men were still talking with the group as if they weren't pinned down by me. With a groan, I lifted my head.

Jax stroked my hair. "It's all right, Reena. Sleep. I'll wake you when it's time for dinner."

My eyes couldn't stay open. I cuddled back into his chest and sighed. Cassie's annoyed face was the last thing I saw.

The sound of our parents laughing with Lily as they stomped up the stairs was what woke me. Eric had somehow escaped my imprisonment, but Jax was where he'd been. Cassie sat on the floor next to us, flirting outrageously with him, her sweet voice teasing.

I didn't want to listen, but I definitely didn't want them to know I was awake.

"I love how close your families are. It's got to be like having sisters." Her expression fell. "I had a brother once. He died when he was young and my mother... well, she couldn't take it. She never had any more children."

Jax was about to say something when she spoke again.

She waved away his sympathy and said, "It happened a long time ago, but it's still nice to see a family like yours."

"I'm sorry to hear that. That must've been hard," Jax said. "As for sisters? Lily has always felt like one. A little sister to protect. But, Reena, no. She's always been something else. My best friend."

"Are you guys together? She said no, but..."

Jax stiffened beneath me, then said, "N-no, we're not together." I heard the tiniest hint of a lie.

"Good." Cassie bit her lip flirtatiously. "Well, I'm going to see if your mom needs help. Need anything?"

"Um... No, thank you."

Trying not to move, I glanced up to see the shocked smile on his face. I must have failed.

"How long have you been awake?" When I continued to pretend I was asleep, he said, "I know you are."

"Not long."

The hand on my back rubbed up and down. I closed my eyes.

He cleared his throat. "Not together, huh?"

There was no malice in his eyes when I met them, just curiosity.

"She kinda caught me off guard. She kept asking me if you had a girlfriend. It was right after... I had no idea what to say. She seems to like you, though."

Stupid, hot girl flirting with Jax.

Stop it! This is Jax.

His eyes narrowed as they took me in. I moved to sit up, but the arm resting over me tightened. He moved closer until our lips almost touched. My breath caught.

He sniffed and wrinkled his nose. "You stink. You need a bath."

My laugh was loud. I pushed off his chest to sit up, grabbed a pillow from the floor, and swung. Before I made contact, one hit me in the side. My butt hit the floor, but I was up before his next swing.

"You should talk! You smell like stinky man!"

Moments passed as pillows flew through the air. Our laughs and grunts were muffled by them. When the barrage finally stopped, we sat on opposite sides of the couch. His hair was a mess, his eyes full of laughter.

"Seems like you're feeling better," he said.

"The food helped and the sleep. I think getting cleaned up will help even more. And what are they cooking up there? It smells amazing."

Jax nodded. We picked up the mess we'd made. Blankets and pillows had been flung to all sections of the room.

"I feel so much better knowing they're safe."

"Me, too. Did I miss anything?"

"Not really. We told them what happened to us. Not in complete detail," he said quickly as I flashed him a worried look. "Then we just talked. You fell asleep early on. It was kind of funny actually. Both Eric and I became your personal pillows."

"Well, that's all you two are really good for anyway. Proved that when we were ten." I regarded him over my shoulder. He stuck his tongue out at me.

Once the room was in order, we headed for the stairs. Cassie and Kim were in the kitchen. Kim was explaining that dinner would be cooked in the firepit out back. They looked up as we entered.

"Kim, is there any way I can get cleaned up? Jax says I smell. I told him the smell of stinky man was worse, but he doesn't believe me. He says I need to take care of my issues before we worry about his stink."

Kim grinned, a wicked glint in her eye. "Jax, my love, you know you're wrong. Why would you argue with her? I mean—really, honey—I can smell you from here."

I sent Jax a triumphant smile.

Cassie's grin widened, too. "She's right, Jax. You do stink. That's why I kept you downwind all day."

Jax pressed his hand to his chest in mock offense. He glared playfully at us while we chortled. He held up a finger as if to say something, shook his head, and then pressed his hand to his forehead.

"More women, more trouble." With that, he backed slowly out of the room like a frightened animal. He must have met Eric in the hallway because we heard him say, "You don't want to go in there. Three women with knives and sassy tempers."

Another wave of laughter spread over us.

"I think I have an idea of how we can get you all clean. I have water heating over the fire now. Give me five minutes," Kim said.

Kim met me in the upstairs bathroom. It was freezing up here, but after we added several pots of water to the tub, steam filled the room. Getting the dirt and grime off me was amazing. Washing my hair was heaven. My wounds had finally scabbed over, but I made sure to clean them thoroughly. The rest of the night went like that. A few jokes here and there, but clearly everyone felt better after they'd bathed.

Cassie joined Lily and me in our room while Sean followed the boys. Cassie took the top bunk of Lily's bunk bed. Like me, she sighed dramatically when she collapsed on the mattress.

"So much better than the ground," she whispered.

I grunted my agreement, pulled my comforter up to my neck, and reveled in the warmth and comfort around me.

Chapter Sixteen

The next few days were full of research on the outside world. Every day a few of us would head into town and speak to the locals. We traded stories, helped around town, and spent more time with Sydney and Camden. As they were staying with these people, they had heard news of passersby. Not many, granted, but a few had passed through, providing interesting insights into the area around us.

First and foremost, we'd learned that all electronics were dead. Like, everywhere. They'd verified that two of the nearest towns had been destroyed. One by a meteorite, the other by an avalanche. Sadly, there had been no updates on Portland to come in yet.

Dad was losing his mind. He paced and tinkered, then started to pack. Several times, we'd had to stop him from leaving for Portland alone.

"Dan, once we have some strong information, we'll go get her. But going in blind is a suicide mission," James said. He squeezed Dad's shoulder. "Your girls need you."

Dad had flinched, set the bag down, and disappeared upstairs.

"Low blow, James," I said.

"It worked, didn't it?"

Rubbed my temple. "Yeah, it did."

I took the bag back to the garage. It felt wrong to use us against him, but James was right. I knew he wanted to find Mom, but it was just too dangerous. After the confrontation with Dad, a few of us left for town. I walked into town square and immediately knew today was going to be different. A man stood on the far side, speaking to Sydney. She waved me over.

"Reena, this is Mayor Gonzales. You said you wanted to speak to him."

He looked terrible. Dark bags lined his eyes. His hair was a mess. His shoulders straightened as I held my hand out.

"Mayor, it's nice to finally meet you."

"You as well. I heard your harrowing story. I'm glad you all made it back safely."

"Thank you. So, I wondered if you've had any contact with the outside world."

"No. With the phones down and roads closed, we're completely cut off."

"I had a question about that, actually. Doesn't anyone in this town have a ham radio? I would think the police or someone would have at least one for situations just like this. For when the lines went down or something." My companions perked up. *Was I really the first to think of this?*

The mayor's face went blank, then he smacked himself in the forehead. "I can't... How did I never think of that?" He pushed through us. "Follow me."

Mayor Gonzales ran toward the tall two-bay firehouse a few blocks down, the exhaustion vanishing from him.

Cassie ran next to me. When she whispered, she mirrored my thoughts exactly. "Seriously, no one thought of this?"

"Look at him. I doubt he's had time to sleep. Let alone think."

As if his thoughts aligned with ours, Gonzales said, "I can't believe I'm such an idiot! The entire fire crew was out on a call outside town when everything happened. We haven't seen them since. And the two deputies were injured in a landslide." He pushed the door open and stepped inside.

The air inside was stale, confirming no one had been here in a while. The silence of the space was made stronger by the clean, almost clinical, set up. We headed toward the chief's office off to the right. Cabinets lined the far wall, a huge desk sat in the center, and another table stood beneath the only window.

For such a small town, these are really nice digs.

"It should be in here," The mayor said.

Cabinets opened and closed as Eric and Jax began their search.

"Cassie and I are gonna look around." The guys didn't acknowledge us. Leaving the boys to their search, we headed upstairs. The kitchen took up one whole side of the building. Next to it, a storage room held pallets of food, water, and other drinks.

"We need to show this to the mayor. He'll need this food in town," I said.

"Yes, but would it be bad of me to say we should hide some of it and take it back to the house? There's a lot of us," Cassie said.

"No, I wouldn't. We'll leave most for town, but I agree. What we have right now won't last forever. Even one of these pallets would last us two weeks."

We organized two pallets of food, then hid them underneath a sheet in the barracks. A case of water and sports drinks went with it. Everything else—which was a lot—would go to town.

Entering the office again, I spotted Jax holding something. "Jax, what's that?"

"Portable emergency radio. Eric found the station's setup, though. It should have a lot better range."

A black box with knobs and dials sat along the back table. Dust fluttered in the light coming through the window above it. A microphone that looked like something air traffic control would use sat next to a small, ancient square speaker.

"Does it work?" Cassie asked.

"I think so. These work differently than the newer models. They're usually kept off until needed and since this one isn't wired in, we might be okay," Eric explained. He pulled a black box from under the table.

"Sweet," he said. He pulled out several batteries and slid them in. A sharp screeching erupted from the speaker, and we all winced. Eric turned the dial, and static replaced it.

I found a spot near the wall next to Jax. I held my breath as Eric began to turn the knob. *Please, let there be someone on the other side.*

Click. Static. Click. Static.

Click. Static.

Click.

"Coastal cities are destroyed."

We straightened, leaning in. The volume rose as Eric spun another dial.

"All reports say Japan is underwater. The tsunami that hit Asia took out all of the Polynesian islands," a calm, collected man's voice said.

"Echo-Sierra-Echo-Two-Two, how far inland did it go? Any reports?" another voice asked.

Everyone was silent, trying to understand the strongly accented voices. Out of the corner of my eye, I saw Jax shift nervously.

"Negative, no report available. Thanks for the update." Eric reached for the knob to join the conversation, but before he could, the person said, "Echo-Sierra-Echo-Two-Two, out."

Eric let out an aggravated sigh. We'd only gotten the last of the conversation, but at least what we'd heard told us a lot. Without prompting, Eric moved the dial again.

My foot jumped in nervous anticipation.

The speaker squealed loudly, and a new voice came through.

"This is Charlie-Hotel-Romeo-India-Sierra-Four-Two. Come back?" a male voice said. The voice paused, then repeated.

"Hello? We hear you. This is Eric Beck. We're just now getting up, no known call sign, can anyone hear me?"

There was a pause, then a click. "We can hear you, Eric Beck. Where are you located?"

"An hour outside Mount Hood, Oregon. What's your location?"

"Durango, Colorado. We've been acting as an information collection source on this frequency. What's your situation?"

"Our town is intact. Some injured, some killed. Very few survived in the area around us due to rockslides and avalanches."

"Understood, Mr. Beck. How much do you know?"

"Very little. Can you provide an update? Is anyone coming to help?"

"I'm sorry to tell you this, but no one is coming. There's been worldwide destruction. Flooding, meteorites, earthquakes. I've even heard of a few volcanic eruptions. Luckily, the U.S. seems to have missed out on that one. Even so, we've only been able to reach a few people over the air."

"Can you explain?"

"Some. We've confirmed sightings of tsunamis as far inland as Las Vegas. Which seems impossible, but from what we've heard, it was more than one. One after another only hours apart. The east was hit by them too, but we're unsure how far inland those came. There's been severe flooding upstream in rivers. The worst is the Mississippi. It's no longer just a river. It's part of the ocean."

I tasted blood where I chewed on my lip.

"How's that possible?" Eric asked.

"I don't know, but reports are that the water isn't receding. From what we can tell, California is underwater, and Vegas is now oceanfront property." There was a click as the man went silent.

Not wanting to miss the opportunity, Eric said, "Have you heard anything about the Portland, Oregon, area?"

"Yes. Some serious flooding. Reports that the Columbia River's level rose fivefold, and a large meteor fell on the Vancouver side. The extent of the damage hasn't been confirmed. Our contact hasn't come back online to report."

I pressed my hands to the wall behind me. Maybe they could hold me upright. When that didn't work, I paced, the movement settling my nerves.

Portland may be gone. My mom may be gone.

"Meteorites blanketed the U.S., a worldwide EMP took out all electronics, airplanes fell from the sky, trains derailed, and untold numbers of fires were started. Mr. Beck, the world as we know it no longer exists."

"Any advice for those stuck out here?"

"Not really. The government has been silent, and we don't know how much is left. Keep checking in for updates and good luck out there. If you learn anything new, let us know."

"Will do. Thanks." Eric cut the transmission.

The only sound was the sharp click of Cassie's nails on the desk. We were all stunned. Everything was gone, and we were on our own.

In a daze, Eric turned off the radio.

Mayor Gonzales' expression was even more distraught than before. "I need to get back to city hall."

"Mayor? We found some food and water in a storage room near the back. I think it could come in handy. Can I show you where it is?" Cassie asked.

He shot her a sad smile. "Show me where it is, and I'll send someone for it." He bowed his head to us all, then left the room.

"We need to check this thing regularly. Keep up to date," Eric said, raising to shaky legs.

"Can we take it back with us?" I asked.

"No. Let's leave it. The mayor needs a way to contact the outside world, but we'll take the portable one Jax found."

"So, Cassie and I hid some of the food we found so we could take it back to the house. I think we should also grab any jackets and blankets we can. They could come in handy."

"Agreed," Jax said.

With a lingering sense of helplessness, we gathered up what we could and started home. The entire trip I locked down the terror that ran in my blood. I knew that if I let even an ounce out, I would break down. And soon I'd have to tell Dad about Portland. This would not be pretty.

It sucked telling Dad and Lily what we'd found out. We all sat around the kitchen table and took turns explaining the day. Their expressions fell ever so slowly as the story unfolded. Dad was hunched over, his head in his hands.

"I know there's not much hope, and we don't know if she survived, but..." Dad lifted his head, meeting James' eyes. "I have to go. I have to try to find her."

"I know. I know," James said. "You're not going alone."

"I can go," I said.

"No!" Dad exclaimed.

"Dad."

"No!"

I shrunk down in my seat. I hated that tone. After everything, he was going to pull the "dad voice" out.

"I know you want to come, but I need you safe. You will stay here with Kim and take care of your sister."

Kim bristled. Her tone was sharp when she said, "You can't make that decision for me, Dan. She's my best friend, and I am just as capable as you are."

Dad placed a hand on her arm. "I know. That's why I need you here to take care of my girls."

How he didn't shrink away from the force of Kim's glare, I had no idea.

"I agree with Dan. We trust you to keep these kids in line. If you're not here, they'll cause all sorts of trouble," James said.

Kim huffed, knowing he was trying to make her laugh. "So just you and Dan, then?"

"No, I'm coming too," Eric said. Before any protests started, he continued, "I'm old enough to decide for myself and more than capable to handle a trip like this. I'll just follow."

Jax and I moved to stand, but Dad held his hand up, stopping us before we could speak. I ground my teeth. This was stupid! I could handle a trip like this!

Dad looked at me. "It's just too dangerous. This is going to be a quick trip. In and out. If it's too dangerous or we can't find her, we'll head back."

"Fine. I don't agree, but it doesn't look like my opinion matters much here," I snapped, grabbing my jacket. I shoved open the door and stomped onto the porch. No doubt the conversations had shifted to how they would stop me from following.

But I wouldn't. If Mom and Dad weren't here, I'd have to stay. I was all Lily had left.

A few minutes passed before the door into the kitchen opened. The scent of sandalwood hit my nose.

"Dad, I don't like this," I whispered.

His arm slipped around my shoulders, and he pulled me to him. "I know, but you have to trust me. I have to try to find your mother, and I can't do that if you are in danger, too."

"And what happens if you can't?" Pain slammed into my heart at those words. I weaved on my feet as my breathing became tight. This was something we might have to deal with.

"Then we meet back here and figure out what the next step is."

He took my hand and pulled me to the chairs, which lined the porch. The wood was cold on my fingers as they ran them along the arms. The cushions had a light layer of ice that cracked when I sat. When I faced him, the world dropped out from under me and my stomach lurched as the scared expression on his face registered.

"I need you to promise me something. You need to take care of your sister. You are a strong, amazing woman, and I couldn't be prouder to call you my daughter. You and Kim are the only ones who I trust to leave her with, but she needs you more. She will need you more."

"You're talking like you're not coming back."

"That's not it at all. I just haven't been able to talk to you since everything happened. Since Eric told me what was going on."

I held my hand up to stop him before he said anything we didn't want others hearing. "Let's go for a walk."

"I'll grab our bows. If we're out, we can hunt, too."

Always practical.

The weight of the bow was both familiar and comforting. I'd been hunting with my dad since I was a little girl, so as we walked, a sense of contentment settled over me. The smell of pine. The crunch of snow. The normality of it made me feel connected to him like nothing else ever did.

"Eric didn't tell you everything. He doesn't know everything," I told him. We'd reached the top of a hill about a half mile from the house. It overlooked a small valley that was technically part of our land.

"Okay. Then tell me."

I hesitated for only a second. We'd always been close. So, I felt like this was something I needed to speak to him openly about. I told him my story, start to finish, leaving nothing out: the ash, my work on Jax, and the incident at the clinic with Sean.

A weight lifted as the entire truth, fears and all, streamed from my mouth. I explained how it felt to initiate the power and how drained I felt afterward. I didn't realize how much I'd held back when speaking with Jax. And so many pieces of the puzzle had fallen into place over the last few days. Things became clearer the more I'd thought about them.

"I think it's the ash. I feel like it activated something crazy in us. Jax and his protectiveness? Then, me." I stopped to gather my thoughts.

Dad sat quietly, waiting for me to continue. His knees were raised, his arms hung loosely over them.

I reached down and plucked a lone piece of grass. Weaving it through my fingers, I continued, "Do you remember when we were in Yellowstone? The day I stopped that girl Brittany and Eric from stepping into that hidden underground hot spring? I tried to stop all of them."

"Of course I do. That's hard to forget. Samantha didn't listen to you because she thought you were just some stupid kid."

"I was."

"But you knew something was wrong. If she'd listened, she wouldn't have stepped into a hot spring and been burned across most of her legs."

I could still see her being loaded into the chopper as it landed in the parking lot. I'd dreamt of her screams for weeks.

"Do you remember what I said after, how it felt?" I asked. He nodded. "I guess it feels kinda like that. Ever since The Flare, something changed. I'm seeing and feeling things that don't make sense." My gaze found his. "Dad, I feel the ash. Actually feel it."

I took a breath, then rubbed my face, pushing my hands into my hair and pulling at the strands.

"I'm going crazy. I have to be," I rambled.

"I don't think you are. Your instincts have always been strong. You've always been able to see things others can't. We just haven't had time to figure this all out yet." He reached out and drew circles on my back. I leaned my head on his shoulder. "What do I always say, huh? We are only ever as smart as what we know today."

I rolled my eyes, and he laughed.

"Honey, there is obviously something else to this. So, I have a question for you. Other than the big things that have happened, what else do you 'feel'?"

"What do you mean?" I asked.

"Well, you said you're 'feeling things stronger.' What are you sensing? Have you tried seeing or feeling anything when you aren't in an emotional situation?"

"No," I said honestly. I hadn't had time.

"Try it. It might help you explain what this is. Or, at the very least, give you more information."

"Okay, um... on what?"

He stood and pulled me to my feet. Then he said, "Doesn't matter. Open up your senses—as you said—and see what happens."

His calm, cool tone settled my nerves. Not once he freaked out over anything I'd said. My dad was the best.

Exhaling, I leaned gently against the tree behind me. My senses expanded, but nothing happened.

Focus on your breathing. Sense what's around you. Again, I pushed them outward. This time, something changed. First was the tangible feel of my father watching me. Then there was the slightest tingle along my back. It was so faint. I opened my eyes, and the world changed.

Snow fell like a dream. A glow radiated from everything around me. The trees and bushes all took on a different hue.

It looks like one of my snow globes.

A flutter up the next hill caught my attention. It was so quick I barely followed it. I bent, grabbed my bow, and headed for it. I had no idea what it was, but I was gonna find out. As I hiked, I pressed my hand to the trees I passed. With each brush, their glow flashed brighter. My fingers tingled. My pace increased when another flutter of light flashed near the top. There was something up there; I just didn't know what.

It's so pretty, I thought. *Like feathers in the air.*

I reached a line of tall bushes. They blocked the view of what lay beyond, but I didn't go farther. My dad stepped behind me, watching.

This is where I am supposed to be.

Another burst, the light only another fifty yards in front of me. Then it moved, dimming. It went behind a bush.

As quietly as I could, I pulled the bow up, removed an arrow from its quiver, and nocked it. With one final breath of concentration, I let it fly. The bright red arc of light and the *thwump* told me I hit home.

I stepped around the bushes to find a large mountain quail lying with an arrow sticking from its heart.

"Interesting," Dad said, wonder in his voice. "How did you do that? I never heard it or saw it."

With a quick burst of effort, I unfocused my mind again. He gasped, but I was too distracted by the glow radiating from his skin. With every move, it flickered as if the energy pulsed with his movement.

"I—for lack of better explanation—saw its energy."

"Woah. That's not possible."

"None of this is possible," I agreed.

"You need to see what you did to the trees." He bent to grab the arrow out of the bird I'd killed. It hung limply, an instant kill shot. I was glad for that.

We retraced our steps. I followed, only stopping when he pointed to one of the trees in my previous path. I took in the sight of my fingers burned into the bark.

No, not burned. Where my fingers had touched, a gray discoloration covered the bark. I went to the next tree. This one, I'd placed my entire palm. My heart pounded, and suddenly I felt so cold.

"It's like the tree died where you touched it." His fingers traced the memory of my fingers. As if realizing what had happened, he asked, "You used the tree, didn't you?"

"There wasn't much to use; they're all asleep." I felt his attention as he rolled over what I'd said in his mind.

We walked back. With each new tree we passed, a gray handprint was burned into its bark. This didn't make sense. I'd only touched them for a second.

"How are you feeling after all this?" Dad asked. "You look pale."

"Better than last time. Last time, my nose bled."

He grasped my arm to stop me. I turned to face him.

"You need to figure out what this is, but you need to do it smarter. Maybe it's a practice thing. Maybe not. You have to be careful."

"I'll try. But Dad, something's coming. I can feel it. I'm scared that whatever this is, it is dangerous and with you leaving... What am I supposed to do?"

He pulled me into his arms. "Hope. Learn what we can and stay true to who we are. That's all anyone can do."

Chapter Seventeen

"We'll be back soon." Dad squeezed me tight, then kissed my forehead. "Be safe, take care of your sister, and keep working on what we talked about."

"I will. Good luck," I whispered before he let me go. I got a hug from James and Eric, and then they were gone, too.

I stood out in the cold long after their figures disappeared into the distance. The wind was ice against my cheeks, the cold seeping into my bones. And yet I stayed. My gut rolled as a feeling I knew too well swept over me.

Warning, it said.

"He's not coming back," I whispered. The wind grabbed my words and took them away. In that moment, I just hoped that the power in them did not seal their fate. My head dropped.

Sean, who had stood with me from the moment we'd walked outside, placed a hand on my shoulder.

"Trust *them*," he said.

"It's not about trust," I said, rubbing my hands together. "Can I tell you a secret?"

Sean's expression told me all I needed to know. The "duh" in it nearly made me laugh.

"I've been having dreams. Bad ones. Falling rocks, bright flashes of light, and thunder. Actually, the first time I saw them was in the clinic right before you saw the doctor."

He scowled, and he began to twitch more violently for a few seconds.

I placed my hands on his shoulders. "Don't worry. It's not because of you. It's just weird, you know? They feel different than normal dreams."

Silence fell as we leaned against the fence that ran along one side of the house. It took me a long time to wrangle my emotions into something I could control.

"You know, Sean, I'm glad you're here," I said with a weak smile. "You're a good listener. Plus, you're sorta my comic relief at the moment."

His eyebrow rose in question.

"The one-word responses? I bet if you started shouting profanities, no one would think anything of it. Actually, that might be fun!"

Sean scoffed and playfully pushed me away. His grin faded, then he said, "Not. Funny. Don't *like*. Feels bad."

Shame. What was wrong with me? I'd watched him the last few days. I'd known he was miserable, frustrated, and lost. His speech took so much effort that it balanced on the edge of being painful.

"I'm sorry. I didn't mean to be cruel." I placed a hand on his arm. "You're getting better every day. Maybe soon it won't be like this."

"Will," was all he said.

Part of me wanted to argue, but I knew better. I was angry for him. He didn't deserve this. And my frustration only grew when I'd heard Cassie talking about him being "slow." She didn't know him. She barely spoke to him. Most of the time she just pretended he wasn't there, but Sean and I had spent a lot of time together. He wasn't slow. He sure as hell wasn't stupid. The more we talked, the more I felt like his mind was on overdrive. He absorbed everything, processing it at a speed we couldn't understand. And that's why he couldn't interact. The speed of his mind was too fast for his body to keep up with.

Speculation, I know.

It had been four days since Dad and the others had left. Just like we had the last three mornings, Sean and I sat staring down the driveway as if by some miracle they'd be back already. Somehow, he'd known that this was what I'd needed. I was grateful for his presence and his friendship.

"Reena, Sean?" Jax called from the porch. "It's cold. Why don't you come in for a bit before we head out?"

After shoving to our feet, we headed toward him.

"I'm not heading into town today. We've been there every day listening to that damn machine, and I need a break. I don't want to hear about how bad the world is today. Not when Dad is out there." My boots *thunked* on the stairs.

"I agree but, Reena, they'll be fine."

"I know." *You don't know that.*

"So why don't we get your mind off everything? Our haul from the firehouse was great, but I think we should get some meat. Cassie thinks she's ready to try hunting now that you've taught her everything you know."

Chuckling, I asked, "So her arm is all healed up?"

As the days had passed, we found ways to entertain ourselves. We began training Cassie on the extra bow. She wasn't bad and seemed to enjoy it. At least until she accidentally hit her forearm with the bow string. The wicked bruise, the entire length of her arm, was her reward. She'd danced around in pain while Jax and I laughed. We'd both done this to ourselves many times and knew how bad it hurt. When Jax had played the "we told you to wear an arm guard" routine, she'd thrown snowballs at him. That had started a war. Snowballs flew for a good hour. Lily, Kim, and even Sean joined in —against their wills, of course.

"Not fully, but she says she can move her fingers again. I think we all want to get out, and we're getting low on meat. Lily heard Cassie bragging and is now demanding a lesson herself," he explained.

"Of course she is." I laughed. "So, are we going together or splitting up?"

"Lily wants me—she says you're a mean teacher—" His eyebrow rose in accusation, and a snort escaped my lips. "And Cassie says you're the pro since you always come back having caught something. So, she wants to learn how to hunt from you."

"Okay. Sounds like a plan." I turned to Sean. "Do you want to join us?"

Sean shook his head. "*Stay*! Help Kim."

"Then we have a plan."

We stepped into the house to find Cassie and Lily prepping our packs. Snacks, drinks, bows, and arrows.

"Hey, ladies, you ready?" I asked.

"Just about," Cassie said. "You okay with being paired up with me?"

To be honest, I really liked Cassie. Were there times she annoyed me? Maybe, but she was funny and passionate. She was a good listener and had proven to be a hard worker. I respected that. The hard parts for me were when she either hit on Jax or knocked Sean.

"Of course! It'll be fun to have some girl time." I glared at Jax, and he lifted his hands in placation.

"Hey, I'm the one outnumbered here. Sean and I— sorry, Bud—are outnumbered. And stuck in this house with all you women. It's terrifying."

Cassie and I both rolled our eyes.

"I heard that, Jax! You ain't no saint either, mister!" Kim called from down the hallway.

We burst into laughter.

"Seriously, though, Cassie. It'll be fun. I was thinking we could go a few miles out. There doesn't seem to be much near the house. Are you up for it?"

"Yup. I'm ready to go."

We called goodbye to Kim and headed out. Cassie and I headed east. A few miles in, we came to a spot I'd hunted at before. When nothing showed, we followed the creek for another hour. We stopped for a break. I sat a few feet from the stream, eating a snack and staring at the ice crystals along the bank.

This is dumb. How have we not found anything? Not even a bird? I thought.

"A bird!" I said to myself, the excitement spreading within me.

What if I could see them with my gifts? The way I did with Dad! I shot to my feet. I hadn't attempted this with others around since the last time I'd been with Dad.

"Are you okay?" Cassie asked.

"Yeah. Uh...hold on."

My senses unfocused so much easier this time. The practice was helping. The first thing I noticed was Cassie. She glowed. It was similar to what my dad looked like, but where he had been white, Cassie shone red. Every shift or move of her body released a small burst of light from her skin.

Red. Red as in evil red, or... not evil. We spent a lot of time with her last week. Cassie was daring, willing to learn, and passionate like no one I'd ever met. We'd debated about everything and anything, but never had she attacked my thoughts and beliefs. She listened.

Cassie's eyes narrowed, and she stood. Her worried expression caught me off guard. "Are you okay? Reena, your eyes."

I spun, hiding whatever she saw there. I scanned our surroundings, feeling something out there. A flicker of light caught my eye. Far up the incline on the other side of the creek, there was movement. It was just like what I'd seen with Dad.

I stepped up to the bank, waiting for it to happen again. It did. I scanned the water. It flowed freely in the middle but was flanked by a foot or so of ice and rock. Several paths across appeared in my mind's eye, and without thinking, I hopped lightly from rock to rock to rock.

"Reena! Be careful!" Cassie exclaimed, my sudden movement a shock.

I reached the other side and couldn't help but smile at the look on Cassie's face.

"What the hell, Reena?"

"I got this. Stay here for a minute. I'll be right back." My tone seemed strange to me. Flat.

I jogged up the hill in the direction of the animal. When I was about thirty feet away, I stopped and crouched behind a downed tree. As silently as possible, I lifted my bow, nocked the arrow, and released it. A grin spread across my face as the quick flash of red light told me I hit home. A second flutter, and without moving from my spot, I let go another arrow. Flash.

Holy crap. I just got two quails! And they were big!

I released my concentration, then recovered my prey. Returning to the creek, I lifted the birds for Cassie to see. A huge grin spread across her face.

"All hail the Great Reena!" she sang.

"Why, thank you. Thank you," I said, bowing exaggeratedly. "I know I am amazing, but really, this is too much."

She laughed. "Seriously, though, how did you see those?"

"It's complicated." I shrugged and walked back to the edge of the water. "Can I throw these to you?"

It wasn't that far. The creek, fifteen feet or so wide, had rocks sporadically placed throughout the water. If I was careful, I could step out and throw them to her. But as I looked at my previous path, I froze. How the hell had I gotten over this without falling in? Every rock was covered in a thick layer of ice and some of the transitions were not easy.

"Sure. But why are you looking so terrified by the stream when you so nimbly crossed it before? Which was kinda freaky, by the way."

I shrugged. "Well, these birds are big, and those rocks are slippery. Falling in that water would be bad. So, I'll get on that first rock, then toss them to you, okay?"

"Sure," she said, moving into position on the bank.

I managed to pass the first few jumps with little difficulty. Reaching a somewhat larger stone, I got my balance and tossed the first bird to Cassie. She almost missed it, so when I went to throw the second one, I stepped onto the next rock with my right foot. I leaned forward, hoping this time she would have no trouble.

My calculations were off. Way off.

The bird's weight threw me off balance. Just as I let go of it, my boot slipped, and I was falling.

Cassie called out and tried to catch me, but she was too far.

I screeched as the cold hit me. The creek wasn't deep —maybe a foot and a half there—but that meant nothing when you landed on your butt. Water rushed up my back and into my jeans. I was soaked from the waist down. My chest constricted, and pain lanced through my muscles as they spasmed in response. I slid backward, the current much faster than it looked. So, I rolled to my knees, water splashing my face. My hand slipped, and the water streamed across my chest and into my coat. I fought for purchase, slowly making my way to the edge.

Cassie was screaming encouragements at me, but I couldn't focus on them. All I knew was my breaths, fighting to get out, my legs failing as I forced them to push against the current, and shivers so violent my teeth ached.

Finally, Cassie was close enough. She grabbed the back of my jacket and yanked me toward her. Only a few more feet and I'd be out. She took a step back and pulled again. I helped as much as I could, and it was enough.

I fell to the ground, no longer in the water, but drenched all the same. It had only been seconds, and my body was falling apart.

"Oh my god," I said, pressing my head to the ground. My whole body hurt.

"Come on!" Cassie said as she pulled me farther up the bank. "Come on."

"Wasn't so nimble this time, huh?" I said, but my words were so garbled Cassie couldn't understand them, the chattering of my teeth too loud.

"Do you trust me, Reena?"

"What?"

"Do you trust me?" she screamed.

"Y-Y-Y-Y-Yes," I stuttered.

Cassie nodded, turned, and ran in a circle, grabbing pieces of fallen wood as she did.

She pulled me to a sitting position, then said, "Take off your coat. Quick!"

I had no real control at the moment. My body had fully checked out. I knew that if I didn't get warm soon, I would die here. We were just too far out to get help.

Cassie removed my jacket as gently as she could, but I still moaned.

"Sorry," she said, leading me to the small pile of sticks she'd collected.

"Don't freak out," she said.

Huh? Already freaking out, Cass.

Cassie glanced nervously at me, then held her hands over the sticks. She stood perfectly still for a long breath. When nothing happened, she shook her hands out as if to release tension, then rubbed them together briskly. Her brow tightened in concentration. Then, after a few seconds, something flashed near her palm.

What the... And the pile of sticks burst into flame. My eyes went wide. *Cassie's been keeping secrets.*

Cassie came over and helped me move closer to the fire, worry lining her features.

"Think we need to talk after this," I said.

"Yeah, probably. I need you to trust me, okay?"

Like I had an option.

Cassie removed her own jacket. Then pulled me to her. I didn't fight. I couldn't fight. Cassie yanked down my jeans. She helped me out of them, which left me there in drenched long johns and an undershirt.

She hung them near the fire and said, "I'll dry these in a minute."

What did that mean?

"Don't freak out," she said again. Cassie wrapped her arms around me. Being so much shorter, her face pressed into my chest, the top of her head just under my chin. She leaned in, her entire body pressed to mine.

Between my chattering teeth, I asked, "Are you taking advantage of me? What will the boys think?"

She chuckled. "Shut up and let me concentrate."

Warmth. Beautiful warmth. It started at my abdomen, then it spread to everywhere she touched me. It leaked into me. Second by second, my body warmed, calmed by the heat emitting from Cassie. I sighed as the shivering slowed. I leaned into her, needing to be closer, warmer. My head rested on top of Cassie's, and my arms wrapped around her.

She didn't pull away. She held me as my body came back to life.

"Do you think that's enough?" she asked, strain in her voice.

How long had we been like this?

"Oh! Yes. Thank you. I think the fire will be enough now." I released her.

She stepped away, then sank onto the boulder near the fire. Bags had appeared under her eyes, and her shoulders slumped.

I sat next to her. I rubbed my hands down my thighs, only then realizing they were dry. Wherever Cassie had touched—my skin, my clothes—was dry.

"Hand me your jeans."

I did as she asked.

She took them in her hands and said, "Let's see if this works. I haven't done this before."

Cassie threaded her arms into the legs of my jeans, bunching them close to her body. Her expression changed, and a second later, steam began to emerge from the ankles.

She's drying them. I gaped.

"Here," she said, handing them back.

They felt like a pair that had just been pulled from the dryer. I slipped them up my legs and nearly moaned, the warm blissful fabric everything in that moment.

How was this possible? In minutes, Cassie had saved my life, dried my clothes, and made a fire. Okay, I'll say it. Cassie is amazing.

"I see we've both been keeping secrets." I bumped my shoulder against hers.

After this, I knew I could trust her. She'd just saved my life. I owed her honesty if nothing else.

"Maybe a little." She gave me a wry grin. "It's okay. I didn't trust you, either. But time's up, and I'm tired of hiding. I couldn't now, anyway."

"I'll tell you mine if you tell me yours," I said playfully.

A choke of laughter from Cassie. "Deal."

We spent the next hour talking. I filled her in on what had happened to me—without exposing Jax's secret—and she told me her story. Come to find out, her discovery had been an accident just like ours had. On the hike down the mountain to come home, Cassie had stepped in some water. Even freezing from the knees down, she hadn't told anyone.

I got angry that she hadn't told us, but she just said, "What could you have done?" She was right, of course. Didn't mean I wasn't still angry.

She explained that as she focused on it, her leg had begun to heat up. Then later on, when everyone else had been complaining about the cold, she was perfectly comfortable. Being able to control one's body temperature was not that strange of a skill, but then one day she'd inadvertently created a spark using the friction of her movement. Since then, she'd been playing with it. Trying to see what else she could do.

"I'm always so drained afterward though," Cassie told me. "Headaches, dizziness, even soreness in my fingers. Does this happen to you?"

"Yeah. Once when I was helping Sean, I got a nosebleed. It seems like the more power I use, the worse my response is."

"Well, at least I'm not the only one."

"How is it that you have developed abilities?" I asked. "You were in the cabin when the ash fell. If the ash is what's causing this, it doesn't make sense."

"Actually, the ash was still falling when you guys got us out. Not hard, but it was. Then, while you and Jax were out getting wood, I explored a little. I couldn't help but play with the ash. It was so interesting."

"True, but I worry what this all means."

She shrugged. "Who knows. We can't change it now. We just have to figure out how to control them."

"Yeah." I looked up at the sky. "Well, are you ready to head back? It's getting late."

"Yes, but can we keep this between us?"

I nodded. "Please. No need to scare the family with a thrilling tale of my stupidity."

Cassie chuckled, getting to her feet. We put out the fire, collected our kills, and headed back.

The day had taken an unexpected turn, but somehow it turned into something good. Cassie saved my life and opened up to me. It felt like she was another ally, a friend.

Plus, we'd come back with two large quail. Dinner tonight was going to be good.

On day six, my world changed again. The last two days had been great. Cassie and I had become closer as we worked to develop our abilities. She was brilliant, and over those hours we'd really bonded. During the day, we hunted or trained, and in the evenings, we'd spend time listening to the radio. Every day we discovered more about the world left behind. A large meteorite had fallen forty miles outside of Denver. The casualties were extensive and downtown Denver had erupted into violent riots and looting. From the sound of it, people were beginning to band together into smaller communities. Sadly, but not unexpectedly, many of these groups were then being attacked. The larger ones would do what they could to take them in, but it was dangerous out there.

Similar things were happening in Las Vegas. An organized group was working to balance the city, but they too had been hit hard. From what we heard, this one had been mostly successful because of the military base located just outside town limits. It gave me hope.

"Waters have yet to recede." The radio clicked, paused, and then the speaker said, "Las Vegas reports that the ocean, which now butts up to it, has waves and a tide. This is making getting their infrastructure up and running difficult."

Then there were the reports of people acting erratically. That channel had been choppy. What we could understand was confusing. People were attacking each other for no reason and then kidnapping them. There was something said about a link between the reactions and the ash, but the channel had dropped before any real information had been gleaned. What we did understand was extremely concerning.

When we could no longer handle bad news, we played board games. For hours and under candlelight, we battled each other with all sorts of games and filled the house with laughter. That night, I'd offered to stay and clean up. We'd made a mess after I'd beaten Cassie at a game of Gizmos.

"Are you sure?" Cassie asked.

"Yeah. I still need a few moments to bask in my victory."

"Of course you do," Jax said.

"Twice!" I gloated.

Jax rolled his eyes, Kim snickered, and they disappeared upstairs.

I closed up the board games, put them back on the shelf, then picked up the pillows that were all over the floor. I took my time. A quiet basement had become such a rare occurrence that I couldn't help but enjoy the few moments alone. On my way up, the stairs from the basement creaked. Reaching the kitchen, I grabbed a bottle of water and began my ascent to the second story. I yawned, so ready for bed.

I nearly tripped when I turned into the hallway. My knees locked, my feet stuck in place at what was up ahead.

In the dim light, I saw Cassie pressed to Jax's front as she pinned him to the wall. She was kissing him. And I mean kissing him. There was no space between them. Her arms were wrapped around his neck, and his rested on her hips. She moaned.

It could've been the sound of my sharp inhale or the resounding *thump* as I dropped my water bottle that caused them to pull apart. I didn't know. Nor did I care.

An apology burst from my lips, and I bolted back the way I'd come. My thundering footsteps were a blur in my mind. As was the cold night air as I escaped outside. It felt like a knife was buried in my chest. With each pant, the tears that burned my eyes threatened to make an appearance.

Why was I reacting like this? I've seen Jax kiss other girls. It never bothered me before.

I rubbed my arms absently. The gently falling snow tickled my skin, helping to calm the torrent within.

But it does now. He kissed Cassie. He kissed Cassie. With that realization, I felt the freezing trails of my tears and tried to wipe them away. If I did, they wouldn't be real, right?

I paced back and forth, my flashlight scanning the ground with every turn. When that wasn't enough, I headed out in the direction of the storage shed.

If I am out here, I might as well walk. Who cared if I got hypothermia? I didn't. My breathing slowed, but that didn't last long. I cringed when I heard the click of the door shutting behind me. I quickened my pace.

"Reena." Jax's voice was a whisper.

No doubt he didn't want his "older woman" to hear him. That's the term Cassie used before, right?

Really, Reena? Who cares? Faster, I walked deeper into the trees. Wetness licked at the hems of my jeans, and the house disappeared. I didn't turn. I didn't want to see Jax or hear what he had to say. It hurt too much.

Jax grabbed my shoulder to stop me. Not acknowledging him, I pulled free and continued to walk. This time he stepped in my path.

"Reena," he pleaded.

"What, Jaxson?" I snapped.

He flinched, head dropping. I stepped away when he lifted his hand as if to touch me.

"I'm sorry. I..." Snow speckled his hair. It attached to his eyelashes, the contrast against his skin beautiful. Even in the darkness, I could see the sorrow and confusion in his eyes.

"For what, Jaxson? You're allowed to kiss girls. I've seen you do it before." It killed me to keep my tone flat. I wanted to scream. I wanted to rage. I wanted to claim him.

But I couldn't.

"But I..." Jax said.

I cut him off. "I have no claim on you. Never did. I told her that." I tried to wiggle out of his hold, but he refused to let me go.

"She kissed me. I stopped her."

I grunted my disbelief. "No, Jax, I stopped her. You were all into it." I paused as I heard the anger seeping out. I forced my voice to sound supportive instead of hurt. "And you should be. She's beautiful and funny and —"

This time I was cut off.

"And not you," he stated, gaze boring into me. His voice left no misconception. No argument.

That caught me off guard.

In my moment of weakness, Jax acted. He slid his hand around my waist, pulled me into him, and kissed me as though his life depended on it.

It was the single most important moment of my life. I wanted to melt into his touch, savor his kiss. I needed everything he was. But that was a dream now lost.

Cassie and Jax pressed together in the dark. This wasn't right. My anger ebbed. I growled, pushed against his chest to break away, then slapped him across the face as hard as I could.

"I will not be sloppy seconds!" I screamed.

The shock at my actions hurt more than anything I'd ever experienced. His face fell, pain and regret written in every cell of his being.

I turned and ran back to the house. Tears poured from my eyes as the inner monologue I knew so well started up all over again. For years this pain, doubt, and hatred for myself had been my only friend. Why had I thought it was gone?

Always confused. Always unsure. Always running from the best things in your life. Stupid, stupid girl. Never will you deserve him.

I stumbled onto the porch. Just before I stepped inside, I glanced back. Jax hadn't moved. He stood, arms down at his sides, head bent. The snow falling around him made his silhouette ghostly. I swiped at the heat of the tears that burned my soul.

What have I done?

Hiding was my only option. There was no way I could explain what had just happened, and I was afraid to find Cassie or someone else awake upstairs, so I ran down to the basement. I grabbed one of the blankets and made a bed behind the couch. No one would see me here. I was safe for now.

Never had I thought I would feel this way. Never had I thought things would go like this. Cassie pressed against him, Jax chasing after me, my slap, his kiss, his words...

*And she's not you...*I was being torn apart, and I wasn't sure I'd ever be okay again.

Chapter Eighteen

When I woke the next morning, my eyes burned, my back ached, and my very being felt broken. I jumped when I noticed my sister, Lily, sitting on the floor nearby, a knowing expression saddening her beautiful face. Without saying anything, she scooted over and wrapped her arms around me. She ran a gentle hand down my back, soothing me. Telling me she was there.

My eyes closed. No tears fell as they were all dried up. We didn't speak, just leaned against each other, hidden behind a couch in the basement.

"Breakfast?" she asked eventually.

She helped me to my feet, then out of nowhere pulled a damp rag out. She handed it to me, and I cleaned my face. My hair was next. I swept it into a messy bun.

"Thank you," I said.

She shook her head. "Time to face the day."

With a gentle hand, I stopped her from leaving. "How did you know?"

"I'm not as blind or young as some of you think I am," she said with a sad smile.

I took a breath, then headed for the stairs to join everyone at breakfast. Cassie was happier than usual,

Sean was ever watchful, and Jax looked miserable. He tried to get my attention, but I didn't acknowledge him. I feared what I would see: hatred, longing, anger, frustration? Any of these and I'd break. So, I ignored them all.

The worried glances and whispers were getting to me, so, in an attempt to distract myself, I flipped on the ham radio. After a few minutes, everyone but Sean left the room, and I was finally able to take a deep breath. He patted my hand before I started fiddling with the dial. With each blip of sound, I prayed someone would distract me. There was a screeching, and then an urgent voice came through.

"Hello? Hello, is anyone there? Can you hear me? We need help. Hello?" The voice was male and panicked.

In the background, there was a sound of creaking metal followed by a loud crunching sound. Immediately, a flash of the roof collapsing in the storage room rushed through my mind.

"Is anyone there? Please, we need help," the voice begged.

I looked up and saw Sean staring at the radio. He met my eyes, and I knew we were on the same page. He motioned for me to pick up the radio.

"This is Reena Novak near Mount Hood, Oregon. I can hear you. What's your location?"

"Mount Hood! Seriously?" the voice exclaimed with a sigh. "Finally, someone who's close! We're just north of Punch Bowl Falls along the Dee Highway. We need help. We're stuck in an old workshop and can't get out."

Sean ran out of the room to get Kim and the others.

"Okay. What's your situation?"

The others entered the room. Kim glanced down at the notes I'd jotted down on the pad of paper we kept on the table.

"There are four of us. Two injured. One has a bad leg injury, but I think they both have hypothermia. Snow has blocked all the doors, and the roof sounds like it's ready to give way." A groan of metal in the background confirmed his words. "We're low on supplies, and I can't build a fire. Please, we need help."

Kim met my eyes. Punch Bowl Falls wasn't that far, maybe four hours on foot. We could make it.

"Please. It's so cold, and there's no one else," he said. "I've been trying for hours."

Kim took the radio from me. With a frustrated glance to us, she said, "It's been snowing pretty hard here the last few hours, so expect that it'll take us around five hours to reach you. Stay calm and warm. We'll do our best to get to you. Where exactly are you located?"

The man provided us with the details of their location. We listened as Kim took charge, asking additional questions and making a plan. When she finally signed off, she looked to each of us in turn.

"We're going on a hike," she said, then left the room. "Pack for cold."

We scattered. Supplies appeared on the kitchen table, collected from every part of the house. Backpacks were stuffed with all sorts of supplies; an extensive first-aid kit, food, water, sleeping bags, and blankets. Two small tents were tied to their exteriors. Jax added rope and a foldable shovel to the pile. He even pulled out my walking stick.

At the last minute, I decided to re-wrap my hip. It was feeling better overall, but with the storm outside and the heavy backpack, I felt it necessary. A little extra support wasn't a bad thing. I was in my room, attempting to wrap it myself, when Jax burst in.

"Reena, it's time to go," he said. He froze when he saw what I was doing. Without a word, he walked over and took the wrap from my hand. "I told you I would help you with this."

He didn't meet my eyes; he just took the Ace bandage and began to wind it around me. I braced myself on his shoulders. His entire body was tense.

"I'm so sorry," I whispered.

He didn't acknowledge my words or slow his movements.

"Jax, I... I'm sorry. I never should have hit you."

"Forget about it," he snapped. Finished, he turned and headed for the door.

I stepped forward and grabbed his hand. He wrenched it away, making me gasp in surprise.

He hesitated at the door and said, "You know, I thought you finally got it. That you understood. I'm such an idiot." He disappeared into the hallway.

Stunned, I rubbed my chest. I slumped onto the edge of the bed.

Great job, Reena. Great freaking job.

When I entered the kitchen again, I went to Kim and said, "We should stop by town on our way out. We can drop off Sean and Lily to Sydney, then pick up the litter."

"Good idea," Kim said. "We'll need it."

When I saw Lily was about to argue, I said, "I need you to take care of Sean while we're gone. He likes to cause trouble."

Lily and Sean had bonded. They communicated better than even I did with him. Hell, he'd become as protective over her as he was of me; just another big brother to torture us. She snickered.

"Fine. He's better company than you anyway," Lily said, deadpan.

"Hey!"

"Kids," Kim said, getting our attention. "There's a pretty strong storm out there. The hike will be long and cold, so grab anything you'll need. I want to be there, or on our way back, before dark."

She was right. The wind was insane when we stepped outside. On the way to town, Kim instructed us on how we would travel should it become a full whiteout. Once we found Sydney, dropped off Lily and Sean, and picked up the litter, we made our way to the highway.

Holy crap monkeys, the storm was terrible. Hours in, and it still pushed against us, the wind so strong we lost ground with each step. Hiking in a line, we used the draft from each other's bodies as a shield, conserving any energy we could. At one point, we thought the forest would make things easier, but when we tried to hike near the tree line, we realized the snowdrifts were so deep that walking was nearly impossible. Snow clutched at our shoes and tried to pull us down. We sank in, then tripped on hidden branches or rocks.

"The road was easier," I screamed through the roaring wind.

Kim nodded. "It's getting harder to see. Let's tie up."

And that's what we did. We pulled our ropes out and looped them through the carabiners linked to harnesses we each wore. All connected, we could confirm no one would get lost or left behind. It also made it easier to communicate. A tug or two on the line and we knew what was coming. Kim took the lead, followed by me, Cassie, and then Jax.

I nearly cheered when I spotted the first sign pointing to Punch Bowl Falls. It was hard to see, and I'd worried we missed the turnoff.

About a half-mile from the exit, Kim disappeared from my view up ahead. A second later, and the rope that connected us tightened. I was yanked from my feet. I hit the ground hard and dug my heels in as best I could. I slid along the snow, pulled in her direction, and knew that if I didn't stop this, I would go over with her.

There was a hole. Kim had fallen into a crater of some sort, but I had no idea how deep.

My foot caught on something, and I grunted. Inches. I had only inches. I clasped the rope, slammed down my other foot harder, and pushed back using my body weight to stop our progress and keep her from falling farther.

Small arms encircled my waist as Cassie planted her feet, adding her weight to stabilize us.

Through the rope, I could feel Kim fighting to get a grip on the wall. Based on the way it jerked, she wasn't having any luck. I gritted my teeth.

Hold her, Reena. Hold her!

Jax popped into my view. Yelling over the wind, he said, "I'll get her!"

Jax unhooked himself, then dropped to his belly. He reached over the edge, and the rope stilled. A second later, Kim's hand appeared, followed by her arm, and eventually, her entire body was pulled over the side. The rope went slack, and my arms let out a sigh of relief. I collapsed back into Cassie, panting from the exertion and the adrenaline running through my system.

I scurried over to Kim and asked, "Are you okay?"

"Fine," she said between gasps.

After confirming she had no injuries, we spun to examine what she'd fallen into. As if knowing we needed it, the storm dissipated. With each breath, more was revealed until five feet, then ten, then thirty were visible.

"Woah," I whispered.

A crater nearly as wide as the three-lane highway appeared before us. It was at least thirty feet deep, the jagged edges telling of the extreme heat which made it. I slid to the edge of the meteorite landing site. Melted asphalt ringed the sides, the path of destruction more than a quarter mile long. Trees on either side were burned or broken and to the left, broken beams jutted out of the snow. Their edges were splintered and blackened by fire.

The remains of a building. A sign balanced precariously over the edge of the hole read, "Lou's General."

I took the hand Jax extended to me. He helped me up, then spoke in my ear.

"You okay?"

"Yeah." I held out my hands, curling them a few times. They burned a bit, but the gloves protected them well enough.

Jax pulled off my glove and examined my pink palms. His fingers caressed my sore skin.

"Red, but not too bad. You okay otherwise?"

I nodded. They'd be sore, but not for long. Jax's thumbs trailed to my wrist, and a wistful grin lit his face. I bit my lip.

"That was a close call," Cassie said.

With those words, Jax came back to himself. He released me and stepped away. "Glad you're okay. Nice save by the way."

"Thanks." I brushed the snow off and moved toward the burnt building. "This must've been a general store."

"Based on the remains," Kim said, walking through the ruins, "it went up quickly. I wonder if anyone got out."

There was a shriek from Cassie. We rushed to her. There on the ground, a man and woman lay burned and broken. Their faces frozen in a silent scream. It was the most awful thing I'd ever seen.

"I wish we could bury them or something," Cassie said.

"Me too," I admitted. "But we don't have time."

I felt terrible walking away, but with the numbers of people dead and dying, there was nothing I could do. This would not be the last time I came across a scene like this and no matter how much they deserved it, I couldn't bury everyone.

Not long after we'd passed into Punch Bowl Falls, a strange feeling spread over me. Kim had stopped to review the map when my chest tightened. There was a pull near my heart as if someone had reached in and grabbed a hold. It was a longing—a need—so intense I forgot everything else. Unsure if I was imagining it, I stepped back the way we came. It lessened. I took a few steps forward. It strengthened. Three steps to the left, the pull vibrated. Five steps to the right, and it calmed.

Weird.

"Reena, are you okay?" Cassie asked. "What are you doing?"

"Shhhh!" I said, waving my arm around crazily to get everyone's attention. They fell quiet. I tilted my head back and forth as if listening. Whatever this was, it felt familiar. It was like the sense I got when I was hunting or when using my abilities.

"Reena?" Jax asked.

"Do you guys feel that?" I tapped my chest. "Right here?"

They shook their heads, concern filling their eyes.

"I'm okay, but I need to go check something out. I *have* to go check something out."

"What is it?"

I met Cassie's gaze. She must have seen something in my eyes because hers went wide. I stared into the distance.

"None of you can feel that?" I asked again, extending out my senses. My vision stayed normal this time; I was using the part of my power that felt the energy. Apparently, my practice sessions were successful because it worked.

"What do you feel?" Jax's stare was heavy as he tracked my movements.

"Hard to explain. It's a need. Like something's pulling me. There are two points though. One is closer than the other, but the pull to the farther one is stronger." I faced the others. "I need to see what they are."

"That's not safe."

"There's not much that is anymore," I said and began to walk toward the first.

Jax ran his hand over his face in frustration and said, "Okay, then. I guess we're right behind you."

I led them off the main road and into the woods. We hit a stream, and I cursed. Moving up it, I tried to find a bridge or low spot to cross over. This stream wasn't as big as the one from the other day, but I wasn't willing to chance another dip in the water. A half-mile down, we found a bridge and crossed over.

The tug in my chest increased, the vibration telling me I was moving in the right direction. Both in the same direction, but the sensation to the farther one became even more electric the closer I got. It hummed in my blood, a comforting song telling me everything was all right. Which made absolutely no sense.

The farther one's moving, I thought. *It's shifting back and forth. Back and forth.*

"In here," I said. I hopped over a fence and entered an automobile graveyard. "Almost there. It's right over there. After we check this out, we'll go find who we came for."

My mind was foggy with power and the need to keep going. To learn everything I could.

"Would you believe me if I told you I know where they are?" I asked, my tone distracted.

"With the way you're acting, no," Cassie admitted. "Jax and I got you, Reena. Kim looks confused as hell, but she's with you, too."

"Wait, you know?" Jax asked Cassie, surprised.

It was my voice that responded. "Yeah. There was an incident. I fell into a freezing river after catching another bird without seeing it. She saved me, and we bonded. She knows about me; I know about her." My voice sounded drugged, lazy. When I was done speaking, I cursed. I'd said too much. "Sorry, Cassie. Didn't mean to tell."

"Don't worry, babe. Keep doing your thing. You seem focused elsewhere right now. Just don't overdo it."

I made a noise of acknowledgement.

"There." I pointed. I unfocused my senses, eyes shifting to see the energy which called to me. There on its side, bottom facing up and a blanket of snow disguising it, was my target. And I knew exactly what it was.

Waves of blue light pulsed from the large flat end. It wrapped back around in an arc to connect to the side pressed against the ground. The giant magnet looked exactly like the pictures from science class. Secretly, I'd loved learning about the science behind them. The unique quality of two objects being pulled toward each other, almost like magic. I just hadn't realized that they really did look like the picture. Energy pulled one end to the other as if reaching for it and pulling away from it all at the same time. I started to laugh.

"What?" Kim asked.

"Jax, do you remember learning about magnets in Mrs. Waldon's class freshman year?" I asked.

"I try not to," he said.

I snorted. "Well, I think we need to start remembering her lessons. Looks like it's going to have real-life applications after all."

I reached down and brushed the snow off the giant magnet. The large, flat side sat at a forty-five-degree angle and was three feet in diameter. It was the largest magnet I'd ever seen. The energy it gave off—though smaller than it might've been when turned on—tingled along my skin. There must've been some residual current leaking from the line to keep it active. Either way, this had once been used to lift cars. Cool.

"I have an idea. Jax, what do you think would happen if I did to this what I did to you?" I asked, and his eyes widened. And it hit me. This would work. Probably not in the way I expected, but I knew there was a correlation between living things and this magnet.

"Do you think that would be smart?"

"I don't know, but I think it would be interesting to find out." I grinned wickedly.

The field was so steady and strong. There was no shifting or changing, or bursts of energy release. It was perfect. Nothing like what the body gave off. I held out my hands and wove myself into the field. The energy was cold and constant, not flowing with life. I grabbed onto it, and then pushed, focusing on one point of contact.

The response I got was not what I expected. It began to spin. Slowly, then faster and faster. I continued to press into the field.

"What in the world," Kim whispered.

Faster still. The snow resting on its surface flew off in all directions. A terrible whining filled the air, increasing in volume the faster it spun. I covered my ears and backed away.

"Everyone behind me," Jax demanded. He pulled me behind him.

With my senses heightened, I saw Jax release a pulse of green from his chest, a shield shining and ready to protect us. I giggled.

The magnet began to wobble. Grooves cut into the ground as the magnet shifted, and dirt sprayed into the air.

The cringe-worthy sounds resonated through the air, and I gasped as the powers within me ignited again. Light burst from everything, then a haze of purple fog rose from the soil. Was I imagining this? I closed my eyes to block it out, but that didn't help. There was a sharp pain in my head, and I was taken back to a dream. A landscape I recognized, but now changed. Barren soil, once a forest, disrupted by winds and lined by those strange alien flowers. I looked to my feet, and just like before, the tentacle of gold and purple slid around my ankle. The scream caught in my throat, but before I could release it, the vision shattered, disappearing in the instant the magnet stopped. Suddenly and completely.

The Source is here. The voice echoed in my head.

Okay, I was losing it.

For a heartbeat, everything went still. Then a painfully loud crunching rumbled across the field as the piece of metal collapsed in on itself. It folded and bent down into a crooked and uneven clump on the ground. Then there was silence. Now the field I saw was uneven, uncontrolled. Because of my interference, one side had pulled the other inward with frightening strength. The shape left behind, beautiful in a malevolent way. That was unexpected.

"Okay, I think I've seen enough. We can go now," I said, barely controlling the terror and awe thrumming through my veins. Was I scared or excited? The jury was still out.

Jax's exasperated glare had Cassie releasing a hysterical giggle.

"Seriously! Seriously? That's it? You think you've seen enough? What the hell was that?" Jax snapped.

I gathered myself, knowing there was no way I could tell them the truth. They'd think I was crazy. So, I played it off as if my initial curiosity was still what drove me.

"What? Dad told me to collect more information. That's what I'm doing."

"What could you have possibly learned from that?" Jax looked down at me, fire and frustration in his eyes.

"I'm not sure yet. I need to think about it, and then we can talk."

"Fine." He pointed at me. "But you won't get out of this."

I rolled my eyes. "Understood."

He spun, kicked the hunk of metal, then stomped back toward the road.

I touched his arm as he passed. "Your shield is beautiful. You've been practicing, haven't you?"

He shot me a wry grin and said, "I don't know what you're talking about."

I returned his smile with an amused one of my own. "Sure, you don't."

"Are we done here?" Cassie asked. "I'm getting cold."

"Yes. Let's find these people and get home. Good news, I know where they are," I said, bouncing on my feet. I was pumped. My experiment had been awesome. I could affect a magnet. If that wasn't cool, I didn't know what was. But I needed to know more, and the only way was to find the other energy source and see what it was. Maybe then I would finally understand my powers.

"I am so confused. What do you mean you know where they are? And what the hell just happened?" Kim asked.

"I can feel them. Or I can feel one of them. He's pulling me to him," I said, gazing in the direction we walked.

"He?" Jax asked.

At the same moment, Cassie asked, "That sounds creepy. What exactly do you feel?"

"Okay. So, the best way I can explain it is I can feel them. Just like I can with the rest of you. I can sense Cassie when I pay attention, but the rest of you all the time." I tilted my head in thought. "Though I think I've always been able to do that."

"You know you sound crazy, right?" Jax asked.

"After what you just saw, you think we aren't all a little crazy?" With that, I spun on my heels and started away, Cassie's laughter following behind me.

Chapter Nineteen

I f the sound of the stream nearby, and the exact description the voice had given didn't tell us we were here, the sharp pull from the mysterious person inside would have. It had taken twenty minutes to reach the land with the metal workshop. The farmhouse nearby was completely destroyed, burnt and broken like others we'd seen. The barn had also caught on fire at some point and lay in rubble.

"They're in there," I said, pointing to the metal structure half-covered in snow.

Only a foot or so of the two garage doors peaked out. Ice hung from the roof and filled the joints between doors and walls. The overhang that had once arched over the door and window had been ripped from its place and was bent downward, pinning it to the wall. I circled the building, hoping to find another door, but with the way the snow had collected at its sides, there were none.

"They're in there, but I don't see an easy way to get them out," I said.

Jax went to the litter and retrieved the folding shovel and crowbar. After some discussion, we made a plan to clear the snow away, then use the tools to break away the ice. Once the first section of the garage was uncovered, Jax and I began to chip away at it. Unfortunately, it was thick and far harder than we expected.

"I've got an idea. Jax, can you step back?"

"What? Why?"

Cassie met my eyes, sighed, and said, "Because I am going to melt the ice."

Cassie had hoped to keep her powers to herself for fear that Jax would freak out. As I wasn't going to tell her about his abilities, I'd stayed quiet. This was her decision to make.

"Are you sure?" I asked.

"Melt the ice? How?"

"Like this." Cassie held her hand out, and a flame appeared on her palm. It was bright orange and flickered in the wind.

Jax and Kim's mouths fell open.

Ignoring them, she went to the door and held the flame against the ice. Within seconds, steam erupted from her hand, and water poured down the metal. I joined her, breaking off the bigger pieces whenever possible. Cassie worked in silence, moving methodically down the door. Once she'd finished the edges of the first segment, she sat back, gasping.

"You've gotten so much better!" I said, helping her to her feet. "You held it twice as long as last time."

"Wait. You can create fire?" Jax asked Cassie, stunned. Then his gaze swung to me. "And you knew about it?"

We nodded.

"So, when you said there was an incident and she saved you, you meant what?"

"I mean that I fell into a stream, drenching myself. Cassie pulled me out, warmed me up, and started a fire.

Without her, I'm not sure I would have made it back. Don't worry, nothing inappropriate happened," I assured him.

"Well, that's not entirely true," Cassie cut in. "Technically, I did take your clothes off and had my hands all over you."

"Oh. Right. I forgot about that," I said, inclining my head to her.

"Your chest makes a great pillow, by the way."

Jax's eyes glazed over, and he swayed just a bit. His expression shifted to that of someone thinking far too hard. No doubt images were flashing through his mind. *Men.*

"Great, now he'll be useless to us," I said playfully. Cassie giggled.

Kim approached Cassie slowly. From her body language, I couldn't tell what her reaction would be.

"That was *awesome!*" Kim said, separating each word out for emphasis. "You two are throwing a lot at me today, but holy crap!"

Kim kept talking, telling us how cool she thought it all was. She spoke so quickly that Cassie and I could only laugh as her questions got more and more outlandish.

Jax stayed motionless. He just watched us, blinking slowly as if he were trying to grasp everything we'd said. Girls. Clothes off. Warm up. *Poor guy.*

"You okay over there, Jax?" I asked.

"All right. While Jax pulls himself together, why don't we start on that door? Reena, you take the crowbar," Kim said. She leaned toward Jax and whispered, "Breathe, Jax. Breathe."

"Shut up, Mom," he said softly.

I snickered, grabbed the crowbar, and went to work. I fit it in between the sections and used brute force to pry them open. With the ice gone, it worked great. Once the hole was large enough for a person to squeeze through, I crouched down.

"Hello, anyone there?" I called into the darkness below. Jax bent the piece more, then joined me. I shivered at the sensation of someone watching me.

"Reena Novak?" The voice was melodic as it bounced around the metal structure. "I didn't believe you'd come."

"I said I would."

A quiet laugh came from the other side of the workshop. The sound made chills spread up my spine, and the hair on the back of my neck stand up.

"Can you come where we can see you?" I asked.

"Oh. Yes, sorry."

There were footsteps, and then a face stepped into the angle of light cast by the opening. To get a better look, I shone my flashlight down on the figure.

Green eyes were the first thing I noticed. They almost glowed in that handsome, grime-covered face. His well-trimmed brown, almost black, hair was longer on top. From this angle, I got the impression he was tall.

And gorgeous. But there was something more to him —something that both excited and scared me. *He's the one I'm drawn to.*

There was something, a rope of energy, which extended from me to him. I found myself unable to take my eyes off him. Even worse, I wanted to go to him. To be near him. To touch him.

"Hi, there, I'm Rembrandt, but please call me Remy. I'm the one you talked to over the radio."

"Hey, Remy. Based on what you said before, you're not alone down there. So, where are the others?" I asked.

"Two are in the van back there. Best place to keep them warm if we can't have a fire. We improvised." He paused. "Why don't I get something to help you down?"

Remy disappeared into the darkness. A painfully loud scraping came from the direction he'd gone. As the noise got louder, he appeared, pushing a large metal table.

That would work. Then it's only a few-foot drop.

"Be careful," Jax whispered in my ear.

Just as quietly, I asked, "You're coming too, right? This is a little creepy."

"A little?"

Getting on my stomach, I shimmied through the opening feet first. With Jax's help, I lowered the few feet to the table. The instant my feet touched down, strong hands grabbed my waist to steady me. A shock of electricity where he made contact made me jump. I sucked in a breath.

Woah. I spun to look at him, his hands still resting on my waist. Time slowed as we watched each other. Jax cleared his throat, and Remy released my waist. He extended his hand to help me down the rest of the way. I took it and jumped from the table. Everywhere his fingers brushed, my skin tingled with electricity.

"Thanks," I said, grinning at him. He was tall, close to my height, and he was mesmerizing.

Remy inclined his head with a wisp of a smile, then he looked toward the table.

Jax was already standing menacingly above us. He handed me one of the flashlights, and I took it. Then we helped Kim and Cassie through the opening.

To Cassie, I asked, "The litter?"

"Tied to the tree outside. Also secured a rope to help us back out." She pointed to the opening where a thick brown rope hung loosely.

Awesome.

"Hi, I'm Kim. This is Jax, Cassie, and Reena," she said, pointing to each of us in turn.

"I'm Remy. I really appreciate you coming. I was starting to worry that we'd never get out of here. We've been trying for days, but the snow just kept getting higher and higher."

"Where are the others?"

"Over there." He pointed to the shadow of a large passenger van nestled between a workbench and old rusted motorcycle.

I scanned the room. Almost instantly, I noticed an outline of another person. "And him?"

"So, this is the rescue party?" a nasally male voice said. The words were slimy and crawled like spiders over my skin.

Slow controlled footsteps came from the darkness. A short man with balding hair slinked into view. His back was hunched as if he'd spent too many years in front of a computer. His blond hair swept up and over his head in the worst comb over I'd ever seen. His breathing sounded like someone who'd been dependent on an inhaler for most of his life, and if I had to guess, he was in his late thirties. Just the way he moved made me wary. He let out an unamused chuckle. The sound reminded me of a stalker in a movie cornering his prey.

"Pretty sad rescue party. A couple kids and an old woman," he scoffed. His eyes roamed over us, stopping a little too long on both Cassie and I.

"We can leave right now. See if anyone else comes to help," Kim said. Just like mine, Kim's creeper senses were tingling.

Remy stepped forward. "Ignore him. He's been bitter since we got stuck in here. He blames me for it."

"And who is he?" Jax asked.

"My name is Lenard." He enunciated each word slowly as if we were stupid.

"Hmm, Remy and Lenny, huh?" I smiled, hoping my lame joke would lighten the mood. Oh, how wrong I was.

Lenard's head snapped in my direction. His face hardened, and his eyes focused on me with a violence that scared me.

In the calmest and cruelest voice I'd ever heard, he responded, "No. It's Lenard."

Jax stepped next to me protectively. At Jax's advance, Lenard dropped his eyes and smoothed out his expression. He cleared his throat.

In a much different tone, he said, "Well, then. I guess it's time for you to meet the rest of us and figure out what to do next. Thank you for your help."

Sociopath, maybe? It was like he was a completely different person. Instead of cold and cruel, his voice was friendly.

Jax and I made eye contact. The look of, *Be careful. There's something wrong with this man,* spoke volumes.

"I'm sorry about him. He's..." Remy searched for the right word. "Unique."

The van Remy led us to was old and rusted, the back seats long removed. The back doors creaked as they opened, revealing two men. Each lay wrapped in, for lack of a better term, garbage. Old, dirty towels, stained cushions, newspaper, and paper towels had been scrunched up around them, providing a barrier from the cold. A too-small sleeping bag lay draped over them both.

"I know it looks bad, but that's all I could find. I was afraid to start a fire with nowhere for the smoke to go," Remy admitted.

"Not bad," I said. "So, what's wrong with them exactly?"

"When we were crossing the stream out back, they fell into the water. Chris—the one on the left—slipped on a rock a few days ago and impaled himself on a large piece of wood. Louis was the one trying to help him across. We ran out of first-aid supplies two days ago, so I haven't really been able to clean the wound since."

"You've done fine," Lenard said, deadpan. It was like he was trying to console Remy, but his tone said he really didn't care.

It was strange.

"So, we get them warm," Cassie said. "Then what? We can't make it back before dark, especially if the snow picks up again."

"We go with plan number two. We set up camp outside, have a good meal, and leave tomorrow. We have plenty of blankets to keep them warm until we get back. The doctor in town can look at them then," I said, and the others nodded along. "Chris will be in the litter, but Louis will have to walk."

"And who made you boss?" Lenard said.

My hackles rose at his tone. I'd been near this man for less than five minutes, and I was holding back the urge to punch him. Instead of doing it, I said, "I did. You have a problem with that, feel free to start walking. We're here to help *you* and *your* friends. You don't like how we operate? Too damn bad."

Remy covered his laugh with a cough—unsuccessfully, I might add. But a disturbed smile stretched Lenard's face. It was one of warning and one of excitement. This man did not like being told what to do. He held my stare, hatred glimmering from within.

Kim spoke. "Cassie, why don't you help Reena with these two?" She glanced at me. "You have the first-aid kit, right?"

"Yes." I broke away from Lenard's stare-down but could still feel his eyes on me. I swung my backpack from my shoulders.

"Good. Patch them up and when you're done, let us know and we can move them out. If you need help, let us know. Remy, Lenard, and Jax, start gathering firewood and find a good spot to set up. I'll be up in a moment to help," Kim said, motioning for them to leave.

The men moved toward the opening, Lenard muttering under his breath the whole way.

I released the breath I didn't know I'd been holding.

Kim spoke so that her voice didn't carry. "Ladies, we need to be careful around this guy. You especially, Reena. After only a few minutes, you seem to have gotten under his skin. So, here's the rule: we stay together and never set down your weapon. You both brought a knife, right?" We nodded yes. "Never alone. This guy's dangerous."

We watched Kim leave in silence.

"That was creepy, right?" I asked.

"Very," Cassie said.

"Well, we might as well see what we've got here." I climbed into the van.

Both men shivered even while heat radiated off their skin. The last two days of constant cold was catching up with them.

"First, we need to get them warm," I said. Almost instantly, the temperature in the van rose, and my face started to thaw. "Seriously, Cassie, that's so freaking cool."

A smile quirked her mouth. She knelt over Louis and put her hand on his chest. Her eyebrows knitted together in concentration. Her energy tingled along my skin.

While Cassie worked on Louis, I examined Chris's leg injury. It was okay, considering their supplies, but it wasn't nearly enough. Crimson had soaked through the bandage, and blood had dripped down to puddle on the carpet beneath him. There wasn't much, but it was concerning, nonetheless.

First-aid supplies ready, I removed the soaked and dirty bandage, exposing a wound that was red and swollen. It oozed a creamy white, tinged pink, but it was the smell that got to me. *Diseased.*

"It's infected," I said to no one in particular. Chris shifted in sleep as I cleaned the wound, but when I poured alcohol over it, he shot up to a sitting position. He cried out.

Antibacterial ointment, followed by a gauze dressing and tape, and I was done.

"It's okay, she's almost done," Cassie said. She pushed him down, holding his shoulders.

While I worked, I was absently aware of Cassie warming him. His violent shivering slowed until he was able to relax back into sleep.

As she did, I examined him more closely. My instincts said there was more I could do here. So, I tried. I opened my senses and instantly felt the energies I was becoming familiar with. This time, though, I found two different rhythms within him. They were almost indistinguishable from one another. His natural one was strong and filled his entire body. The other was quieter. There was a main focus near the wound, but I could also sense it flowing through his body.

Am I feeling the infection? No. That can't be. After more examination, I realized I was right. *That's the infection.*

The world faded away as Chris's energy field became my project. As I had for Jax, I increased Chris's ability to fight the infection by pressing his immune response into overdrive. Due to the cold, his body hadn't responded normally, so the infection had gotten out of control. With the help of Cassie's heat and a push from me, his healing could finally begin. That statement felt true deep in my heart. I wasn't healing him; I was just activating his natural processes so that *he* could. I winced as my head pounded.

Just a bit more. His breathing calmed, and, sensing the change, I released the power. I shook my head to discharge some of the pressure. He opened his eyes.

"Hi, Chris. I'm Reena, and this is Cassie. We're here to help," I said. "We're gonna get you out of here and to a doctor. Do you think you can take some medicine?"

He nodded. We got him upright and gave him some pain medicine. He sighed as water touched his lips.

"Thank you," Chris said, lying back down.

"Just rest," I said, placing my hand on his forehead. "We're gonna move you outside soon, okay?"

"Okay."

Cassie and I moved to the back of the van to sit on the edge, our legs dangling.

"Well, that was interesting," Cassie said.

"Understatement." I rubbed my face as if I could swipe away the residual side effect of using my power. It didn't.

"So, um, Reena? I wanted to talk to you about last night. I didn't mean for you to see Jax and me. I'm sure it made you uncomfortable to see your brother like that."

My back stiffened, my discomfort at the use of the word "brother" running far deeper than I could let her know. But in truth, this situation had me reeling. Jax was not my brother—that was certain—he was something more. I just couldn't admit yet what that was. And I hated myself for it.

"It's not the first time. Of course, it's never been in candlelight with him pressed against the wall."

It took so much effort to keep my voice level. "I told you, we aren't together. I don't even know if that would be possible for us."

Big fat liar, liar-pants.

She frowned at me.

If you keep lying to yourself like this, you'll break us forever. Was this the point of no return? Maybe. *You slapped him.*

"Well, I'm sorry." Her eyes became very far away, and she smiled again. "And I'm not sorry. I really like him."

"You better or you'll have to deal with several angry siblings." Abruptly, I stood, then stomped toward the opening leading outside. "I'm gonna see if camp's ready."

There was no way that wasn't suspicious. I pushed down my rolling emotions and climbed onto the table. Looking out, I called for Jax.

Remy appeared instead. "Well, hello down there," he said cheerfully.

"We're ready to move them out. What about you guys?"

"Tents are up, fire is ready, and firewood collection is ongoing, but yeah, it's a good time. The better news is the snow has almost stopped."

This guy was not like his companion. His smile was too genuine and kind.

"Help me up?"

Remy bent, grabbed hold of the back of my arms, and pulled. I was up and out in the next second. My weight combined with the force he used caused me to fly forward to land on top of him as he fell to his back.

"Oomph."

"Sorry!" I scrambled off him and jumped to my knees. I held my hand out to help him up. The moment our fingers touched, a blast of electricity shot through my hand and up my arm. I froze, my nerves on fire. We stared, transfixed, our fingers still touching. Bolts of sensation crawled up my arm in waves.

"Can you feel that?" he asked curiously.

"If that's some kind of pick-up line, it's terrible."

A grin quirked his lip. He didn't let go. In fact, he took a small step toward me. "I never expected that such a beautiful woman would be my rescuer, but more importantly, I never expected her to be like me."

"That was better," I said and dropped my hand. I brushed the snow off my clothes. "Except for the creepy 'like me' part. What does that even mean?"

"You know, someone who can sense and manipulate magnetic fields."

My hand froze on my thigh. My gaze shot to him.

"Come on. I've been able to sense you for a while now and from the look on your face, you sensed me, too."

Wait, what? I couldn't speak, my mind racing to comprehend the words he'd just uttered. *Sense and manipulate magnetic fields? The magnet, the people, and animals I have been sensing. Everything had some sort of magnetic field. Right? But from what I remembered from science class, they weren't strong enough for humans to see or feel them. Electromagnetic fields?*

"But what you did in there, Reena"—he pointed to the workshop—"that was impressive. Delicate. I could never do something like that."

My mouth went dry. I stepped back. "I don't know what you mean."

"You manipulated Chris's magnetic field. I'm not really sure how, but it was cool to watch. Beautiful even. I could feel it. See it. What were you doing exactly?" he asked, head tilted in interest.

"Um..." I took another step back.

"Hey, the best I've been able to do is create a magnet and make it float. It's pathetic."

"Jax!" I yelled, not looking away from Remy. Anxiety was layered in my tone. "Come here, please."

Remy flinched.

I was freaking out. I had the right to. This person I'd known for like five seconds knew more about my abilities than I did, and he'd seen me use them!

Remy moved closer, hand extended as if to console me. "I'm sorry. I didn't mean to scare you."

I tried to dodge his touch, but it was too late. A sharp spark of energy popped between us, electricity exploding through us both and from us. The wave burst from the point of contact, propelling us away from each other.

We landed several feet away and rolled to a stop. Finding my side, I struggled for air. I pressed my forehead to the ground as my mind was sucked somewhere else. Images flashed in a volley that made me nauseous.

A ball of flowing, swirling purple and yellow liquid.

The great rock where it sat.

Vast blue water. So much water.

A shimmering field and a powerful storm. And a forest which grew and died.

Power radiated from the sphere, calling to me. The pure energy it released reverberated through me, making me crave more. I began to vibrate with its power. The urge to start walking rose like a song in every cell of my body. Then two words filled my mind, and with the knowledge of its name, the demand increased.

The Source.

Silence for two whole breaths, then I blinked, shaking it off. I pushed to a seated position and felt the air as it crackled between us. With effort, I curled my hands into fists and worked to settle myself. If I didn't, it might happen again. Power rolled through me, making me tingle as if I held a live wire.

I was about to yell at Remy when his expression stopped me. Not only did he look as shocked and scared as I was, but he was glowing.

Yes, glowing.

Lines of colored light arched from him. They reached out to connect with me, making purple glimmer from my fingertips. Then from one blink to the next, they were gone.

"What just happened?" Remy asked, clearly out of breath.

"I was going to ask you the same question. Are you okay?"

"Little freaked out, but physically fine. You?" His eyebrows were lowered in a scowl. "Because you're kind of glowing."

"Would it make you feel better if I told you, you were, too?"

"Not really." He stood and I followed.

"I feel like my skin's vibrating," he said, shaking out his arms.

"That's a great way to describe it."

"Can we not do that again?"

"I think that would be smart," I said, rubbing my temples.

"Reena! Remy! Are you all right?" Jax was running in our direction. "What happened?"

"We don't know, but we're okay." I glanced at Remy.

"I freaked her out. It was my fault. I guess I should've told her I could do what she can in a little less shocking way," Remy said.

To Jax's obvious confusion, I said, "We can talk about it later. I just need a minute."

"You sure you're okay?" Jax stepped between Remy and me. He placed a gentle hand on my back, his face lined with worry.

"Don't worry, it isn't the farthest I've been unexpectedly thrown recently. I'll be fine," I said, patting his arm. He rolled his eyes. "Is camp ready? Chris and Louis are ready."

"Yeah. Go rest. I'll help them up and get them settled," he said. He smiled softly, then turned to the workshop with a torn expression on his face.

As Jax lowered himself down into the darkness, I glanced back at Remy.

"Boyfriend?" he asked.

"No, best friend." I could no longer see the glow of his skin. It had faded, but I still felt the pull to him.

"Interesting," he said with a flirtatious smile.

I glanced away. Was he flirting with me after what just happened? No, it couldn't be. And yet, it felt like he was. It should've freaked me out and made me want to stay far away from him, but I didn't. Whatever this connection was, it made me want me to be near him, to touch him. To feel the electricity in his skin and the tingling of mine in response. The need unnerved me. I was drawn to this stranger, and it was connected to something called *The Source*.

Chapter Twenty

C amp was set up under a thick grouping of trees that provided some protection from the wind and snow. The tents were erected in a circle as close to the fire as was safe, popping and crackling happily as we cooked dinner. In a pot Kim had brought, the remains of the quail I'd caught simmered into a nice broth. Potatoes and carrots were added—I know, fancy—and cooked until soft. The scent of the stew made my stomach growl, but it was the loaf of bread Kim pulled out that had me kiss her cheek. It was exactly what we all needed.

"So where are you from?" Kim asked.

"Washington. We were on vacation when everything happened," Louis said.

Remy nodded, then took over. "Right before Goliath's entry, we crossed the Columbia River. A few hours later, a wave came upriver. It flooded the town we were in. No one had expected something like that so far inland. I still can't wrap my head around that one." Remy shook his head. "Everyone had stayed in their homes in the lower lying valley, but when the water kept coming, they freaked out. The whole area was destroyed."

"I never would've thought it was possible," Louis added. "A bunch of people died that first day, then more over the next week from the cold and contaminated water. Then people started to organize."

"Yeah, and those people got attacked. That's why we left. We'd met up with four other guys and had been working together. They were getting desperate and decided to attack a small group of families. I wasn't okay with that," Remy said.

"So you left?" Kim asked.

"Yes. Like a bunch of cowards," Lenard mumbled.

Remy rolled his eyes. "You didn't have to come."

"I'm your uncle. My sister would've killed me if I left you."

Remy closed his eyes, exhaling slowly in frustration. Louis just shook his head.

"We left with hardly any supplies," Louis said. "A few days max. We'd hoped to find tents, sleeping bags—hell, anything—along the way."

"It was my idea to go into the workshop when Chris and Louis fell in. I didn't want to leave them behind, and I figured it would be out of the storm."

"And it was a stupid idea," Lenard interjected.

"Love you too, Lenard," Louis' sarcastic tone nearly made me smile.

Lenard glared fiercely at his nephew. "I don't want to hear the rest of this. Which tent can I take?"

"The yellow one," Kim said. "Remy's sharing with you."

With a grunt of irritation, Lenard left us.

I turned to Chris and Louis and said, "I think it's time to get you two set up in the tent, too. You need to rest. Tomorrow's going to be a long day."

Louis stood on his own while Jax and I helped Chris into the tent.

"I feel like a child being tucked in by my parents," Chris said.

In a teasing tone, I said, "Don't worry. I'll be nearby in case you have any nightmares. Get some sleep and don't let the bedbugs bite."

He snorted, then wiggled into the sleeping bag. "Thanks, Mom."

Coming back to the fire and unable to help myself, I sat down next to Remy. I'd meant to sit next to Cassie. It freaked me out that the pull was getting stronger. It made me want to reach out and see if he was real.

"Sorry about Lenard. He's a pain, but he's family." Remy stared into the fire as he said, "My aunt made me bring him on this trip so he could 'get some fresh air.' I still don't get what she sees in him."

Ah. This I could understand. Family by marriage.

Remy continued, "He was pissed when I saved Chris and Louis. He thought we should have left them and kept walking."

"What? He wanted to leave them?"

"Lenard is a special individual. He's spent the last few years stuck in my aunt's basement playing video games and forgetting what it's like to be around people. He's always been a little strange, but it's getting worse. Plus, he's always had a different set of morals that don't sit right with most people. And I agree with those people."

"But he listened to you anyway and went into the garage?" Cassie asked.

"Barely. I think the only reason was because he promised my aunt and mom before we left to"—his voice shifted to a higher octave—"look after Remy and his friends or there will be hell to pay." He chuckled, then his voice was back to normal. "Lenard knew I wouldn't leave them behind."

"Why didn't you head home?"

Remy's face fell. "We learned that our town and the ones near it had been destroyed by falling debris. There was no reason to go back."

"Oh, I'm so sorry," Kim said.

An uncomfortable silence overtook the clearing. No one knew what to say. Everyone Remy loved was dead, and he was stuck with Lenard. That had to be hard to accept.

I leaned back, holding onto the log, my fingers extended. I shifted again, accidentally brushing Remy's thigh. He tensed, and I pulled away.

"So, what did you mean earlier? That you are like me? You know, before I blasted you."

"Technically, I think we 'blasted' each other, but I still can't figure out why." Remy's eyes narrowed, then unfocused. I sat up straighter.

"Is that what I look like?" I asked Jax. He nodded. "How about you start from the beginning? You said magnetic fields?"

"Actually, that was Lenard. He's read and studied more random topics than I could ever dream. When I told him what was happening, he made a guess, and it was a good one. And I think he's right."

"When what started happening?" Jax asked.

"If I was to guess, the same thing that's been happening to Reena." Remy turned to me. "You saw the waves of light when Goliath entered the atmosphere?"

I nodded.

"The strange colors of the meteorites as the ash fell? The weird flashes of light when the ash was disturbed? What about feeling people and objects?"

Again, I nodded.

"There are a lot of other little things, but for me, it wasn't until right before we'd left town that Lenard figured it out. We'd gone to the hospital with a friend after he'd been attacked. They were still trying to help people there. We figured it was the safest place to take him. While we waited, I felt a pull toward a different wing of the hospital."

"A pull?" Kim asked.

"That's the best way I can describe it. It was like a longing pulling me in a direction. Kinda like what I feel from Reena."

I swallowed hard and pushed down the flush I felt stirring when Jax shifted uncomfortably in his seat.

"Lenard followed me. We came upon a room that was meant for imaging. You know MRIs, CTs, whatever? When I went in, the room was alight. Lines of power radiated from the machine. From the magnet inside it."

"That doesn't make sense," Jax said.

"Actually, it makes perfect sense," I said before Remy could continue. "I saw the magnet in the field. You guys say my eyes go all weird, right? Well, when that happens, I can see things. Sometimes it's just a burst of light, like with the birds. Sometimes it's fainter, but steadier like with you guys. Dad is a white light, Jax a pale green, and Cassie is reddish color. With the magnet, it had arches of blue that swooped from one end to the other. Or it did until... well, you know."

"Until what?" Remy said.

I glanced from Cassie to Jax. I didn't know if I should tell him. Jax shrugged, giving me a "might as well" look.

"Until I pushed on the magnet's field and made it collapse into itself," I explained.

Remy's eyes went wide.

I tried again. "You can feel the fields, right? Well, I sort of wrap myself around them and push. With a person, like what you saw with Chris, it—I don't know —speeds up their normal processes or their natural response, allowing them to heal more efficiently. But when I pushed the magnet's field, it threw it out of balance."

"And it collapsed in on itself?"

"That's what it looked like."

"Can you show it to me tomorrow on the way?"

I gave a noncommittal shrug and tried to lead the topic back. "So, what happened then? In the hospital?"

"Oh, well, I could see it. There was no power in the place, but it was clear as day. I told Lenard what was going on, and he pulled me back into a small break room he'd seen in passing. He walked over to the fridge and pulled a refrigerator magnet off. He held it out to me, and I could see the same thing, but on a much smaller scale." Remy pulled two pieces from his pocket, then held out two magnets the size of quarters. "Lenard tried to explain to me what was going on, but my knowledge of physics is... minimal at best. I've never been the scholastic type, but what he said was that magnets have two poles. Opposites attract and like sides repel. So, I kept them and started playing with them."

The magnets lifted into the air and began to dance. They rose together, then proceeded to rise and fall in rhythm.

"The field is so small."

"I know, right?" Remy said, eyes squinted in concentration. From his hand, small bursts of energy pushed upward toward them.

"I get it! You're creating an opposite magnetic pole with your hand! You're not controlling it; you're just grabbing hold of it and forcing it upward with an opposite charged field." I leaned closer, trying to see.

The magnets dropped to his hand. I looked up to find him scrutinizing me.

"I didn't know that's what I was doing exactly," he admitted.

"Makes sense though, right?"

"It does. But for some reason, though, it only works when they're on my hand in this direction. If I turn them over, nothing."

"Hmm. Can I try?"

Remy placed them on my palm in the same orientation he'd held them. I focused, but nothing happened. They stayed glued to my palm no matter how hard I tried to make them move. After a while, I exhaled in frustration and handed them back.

"Don't worry. It took me a few times, too. Plus, from what I saw earlier, you have another focus far more interesting than mine." He placed his hand on mine.

Tingling. Always tingling. My gaze locked with him. Well, until Jax cleared his throat. I pulled my hand away. I stood, then stepped away.

Remy didn't mind. He spoke to Cassie. "What do you do? Since I was outside, I couldn't really see it, but she's right. You're red. The color of passion." He winked playfully.

"Wouldn't you like to know?" she said. Cassie examined him thoughtfully, then responded, "All right, fine. I play with fire."

She rubbed her ungloved hands together. She placed them a few inches apart and focused. There was a burst of red, and then a small flame appeared on her palm. She leaned down, adding it to the fire.

"Interesting. Anyone else special in this group?"

I spoke up. "Nope. Just Cassie and I are freaks."

I caught Jax's gaze and knew he understood. Yes, we were sharing tonight, but this stranger did not need to know everything about us.

"I need to go for a walk. Cassie, want to come with me?" I asked.

"Sure," she said, pushing to her feet.

Jax watched us go. Kim and Remy kept talking, and eventually I heard Jax join in.

We walked toward the burned barn. The light of camp was blocked out by tall trees and the silhouette of the workshop. Reaching the ruins, I looked down to realize my hands were shaking.

"Cassie, I'm freaking out. What just happened? I mean, we find someone out in the middle of nowhere with a creepy uncle, who can do what I can do, and for some reason whenever he touches me, my skin tingles. And..."

Cassie giggled.

"What?" I asked, annoyed. How could she be laughing right now?

"Someone has a crush, and I think it goes both ways."

"I repeat, what?" I asked, annoyed now.

"Come on, Reena. I see it. Jax sees it. And I don't blame you; he's a hottie. Plus, he seems to get this magnetic field thing."

"I have no idea what you're talking about. I've known him for two seconds. And you don't get it, my skin physically tingles. Not like 'oh my gosh, a boy is touching me' tingles." I paused and thought for a second. "Okay, maybe there is a little bit of that too—but no—that's not what I mean."

She laughed out loud at that. My anger flared. I was about to yell at her when Jax walked up.

"You two okay?" Jax asked.

"Yeah. Reena's just freaking out."

"Uh!" I threw my hands up and stomped toward the trees.

"Can you give me a second with her?"

"Sure," Cassie said, chuckling as she walked back to Kim.

Jax caught up with me. He grabbed my shoulder and turned me to face him.

Frustration so high, I immediately sank into his arms and pressed my face to his shoulder.

"This whole thing..." I groaned into his skin. My hand rested on his stomach. His arms slipped around my waist. "There's something weird about Remy. I'm so confused."

"I know what you mean. It seems a little strange that we just happened upon someone who can do what you can or at least close enough."

"It's more than that. Remember how I told you I could feel something before we got here? It was him. It was like I was being pulled to him."

Jax pulled back. "I don't like it. There's something else going on here."

I broke away and started to pace.

"I know. But there's more. When we were flung apart earlier, something happened. I saw something."

"What did you see?"

"The Source. I think it's what's left of Goliath."

"The Source?"

"That's what it's called. I know that doesn't make sense, but I saw it. And now I have the urge to find it. I can feel which direction it's in." I ran my hands through my hair. "Like I'm a compass and it's my north."

"You're a compass?" he choked, trying not to laugh.

"It's not funny!"

He grabbed my hand and stopped my pacing. "I'm not making fun of you. Much. Listen, it'll be fine. We'll figure it out, and when we get back home and meet up with the others, we'll tell them everything and figure out what to do next."

"Okay," I whispered hesitantly. "The problem is my gut tells me Remy *has* to come too. Has to. It scares me, especially since that means Lenard will be there, too."

The thought of Lenard being with us for longer than absolutely necessary made my skin crawl. Him being near Lily made me want to rage.

I exhaled, stepping closer again. "Remy knows about Cassie, but I think we need to keep him in the dark about you."

"Why?" Curiosity filled his voice.

"You're too important, too special. I don't want either of them knowing." As I said this, I looked into his beautiful face, then ran my fingers along his jaw.

He leaned into my touch, his scruff scraping against my palm.

I kept it there for a few more breaths, then reluctantly removed it. It felt like everything in my body, everything about me, was conflicted. My very essence was fighting for purchase. If I wanted to, this moment could change everything. Instead, I stepped back, breaking the intimate moment.

"I need to take a quick walk. Will you wait for me?" I asked, motioning to the woods.

He looked confused, then understanding lit his face.

"I came out here for a reason, you know, other than freaking out. Girls have to pee sometimes, too."

Jax spoke as I started away. "Watch out for poison ivy."

"It's winter! Seriously?"

"Rabid bunnies, then."

I groaned, and his chuckle floated after me. I grinned.

Jax waited where I left him. When I came back, he was lost in thought. He held a piece of metal that shone in the dim light. He examined it carefully, looking down, then back up, then down again. His eyebrows knitted together in confusion. Before he noticed me, I saw him look up and turn in a circle as if verifying his direction. A branch snapped under my boot which broke his concentration.

"What's wrong?" I asked.

"Nothing. Just looking at my compass. I must be turned around."

"The truth will always point you home," I said, reaching him.

He blinked as if shocked, glanced down one last time, then snapped the compass closed. He placed it in his pocket.

"Definitely," he agreed.

There was something in his voice that confused me. I was missing something big but had no idea what. As I passed him, I elbowed him in the side.

He laughed, then wrapped his arm around my shoulders. "So, no rabid bunnies then?"

"Not tonight."

He was quiet for a moment, then said, "I knew you were the one that came up with the engraving."

I laced my arm around his waist and hugged him to my side. We walked back to the fire that way. As we entered the circle of light, he released me and went to sit next to Cassie. She leaned into him, bumping his shoulder and making him laugh. I scowled at the rush of jealousy but managed to push it down before anyone saw.

Chapter Twenty-One

"Hey, honey," Kim said. Her hand gently brushed my shoulder as she approached the fire.

"Hey." I leaned toward the warmth, elbows on my knees, scanning the landscape and occasionally utilizing my ability to sense anything approaching. I'd watched two squirrels wrestle in the dark for a while, laughing when one did a backflip over the other, then shot up a tree.

"You okay? You look a little lost."

"Just a lot on my mind. Is everyone asleep?"

"Yup, and it's our watch." She examined me for a minute, then said, "Talk to me. You've been quiet the last few days, but I know you. Are you worried about your parents?"

Shrugging, I said, "Definitely worried about Mom and Dad. Actually, Cassie asked me if I was close to my parents. She thought I should've been more worried."

"Well, she doesn't know you like we do. We know you're freaking the hell out."

"I am. I'm so worried about Mom. How is she going to travel with her ankle broken like that? Then I keep having these dreams about Dad..." I trailed off. "Then there's Lily I worry about and everything with Jax. I'm just..."

A knowing smile lined her lips. "And what do you have to worry about with Jax? You guys seem to have healed your friendship."

"What do you know?" I asked, scanning her face. She grinned.

"Nothing, but I'm not blind. I see how you guys are together and how Cassie flirts. She's interested in him," she said. Her ponytail fell to the side as she tilted her head. "I also see how you don't like it."

My shoulders dropped. "I don't know what to do. I like Cassie. She's funny and sweet. And I'm... What if she's who's best for him?"

"Best for him? Reena, what are you talking about?"

"I've done so much damage, Kim. Made so many mistakes. What if our relationship can't recover from all that?" I rubbed my hands over my thighs nervously. "Can I tell you something? Something I'm not proud of?"

"Anything."

"I slapped him," I said, unable to look at her.

She laughed out loud, and my head snapped up. It took her a full minute to control herself.

"I told him it wouldn't be easy. And knowing you— and my son—he probably deserved it." She placed a gentle hand on my arm. "Honey, I think you're overthinking this. Stop asking if you're good enough for him and instead ask yourself if you two are better together?"

I had no response to that. Yes? No? There were just so many factors to consider. And now a new one had been thrown into the mix—Remy.

"Just be friends and see where it goes." Kim stood and patted my shoulder. "Stop telling yourself that it has to be one way. No relationship is just one thing."

There was nothing, and I mean nothing, I could say to that. But her words repeated in my head as I finished watch, made breakfast, and even as we packed and headed back home.

We were about two hours from town when the clouds started rolling in.

"Looks like we have some severe weather headed our way," I said to Kim.

Nodding, she agreed. "We should pick up the pace. We don't want to be outside when that hits."

As if hearing us, a blast of lightning flashed horizontally across the length of the storm. It was beautiful but unnerving. Snow with lightning was rare and never a good thing. So, I set a quick pace, taking turns pulling Chris in the litter. He apologized profusely, but we kept telling him it was our pleasure. Everyone needed help sometimes.

I was scouting a safe path for the litter when Remy appeared at my side.

"How old are you?" he asked.

"Seventeen. Why?"

"Just curious. You don't act like you're seventeen."

"I think if you knew me better you would say differently."

"I doubt that. Your group treats you older than you are and seeing as they're family, that's rare." He didn't speak as we climbed a small hill. Once at the top, he said, "So, where are you from? Are you from around here?"

"Why are you asking me so many questions?" I led everyone around an outcropping of rocks which lined a small ravine.

"Just making conversation."

"We're from Arizona. We were here on vacation at our cabin."

"Arizona, huh? You guys handle the cold weather well for being desert rats."

"We've spent a lot of time in Oregon, especially in the winter."

Conversation waned as we scaled the next hill, the incline much steeper and snow deeper. I was breathing heavily by the time we reached the top. I turned to check on those pulling the litter.

Jax and Cassie laughed hysterically as with each step Jax sunk into the snow up to his knees. Cassie, with her small frame, continued to walk over it with ease, barely indenting the powder. It looked grueling, but funny as hell for the rest of us. When he reached a spot on the top where he could take a rest, he fell to his knees, trying both to control the laughter and catch his breath.

"So, what about you? How old are you?" I asked Remy.

"Nineteen. You already know I'm from Washington. I dropped out of college last year and have been working for my dad in his law firm. I was going to go back in the spring, but I don't see that happening now. Oh, and no girlfriend."

With that last sentence, he leaned over to me and batted his eyes. He was so ridiculous it was cute. I rolled my eyes, holding back my giggle.

"Obvious much?"

"The world almost ended a little over a week ago, and who knows what's going to happen tomorrow? Might as well flirt with a pretty girl when I can. Plus, I feel a pull to you." The grin he shot me made me suck in a breath. He was handsome, charming, and funny, and it wasn't hard to want to get to know him.

Needing an escape, I stood and approached Jax. "Why don't Remy and I take over for a bit? Give you a break after that hill. Looked like the hill almost won."

"Almost," Cassie said, still chuckling.

"I..." Jax started, stopped, and then turned to Remy, ignoring us. "You taking over for a bit would be great. Thanks." He tried to act like our teasing bothered him, but I knew it was all for show when he pushed my shoulder playfully.

"It was beating you, wasn't it, Jax?" I taunted. Cassie and I shared a look.

Jax made a face at me but didn't say anything else as he joined Kim. So, like the adult I was, I picked up a snowball and threw it at him. Bulls-eye. Out of nowhere, another slammed into his shoulder. Cassie.

He turned to find both of us, innocent looks on our faces as we pointed at Remy, our designated scapegoat. Remy held his hands up in denial. So we shot Jax an "I don't know where they came from" look.

"Sure, you don't," he said sarcastically. "I'll get you two back later, you know that, right? Snow in your beds tonight. Don't forget, I know where you sleep."

We burst into laughter as he continued toward his mother. Kim was biting her lip, trying not to laugh.

"Next time, we'll gang up on him when he least expects it," Cassie said to me.

"Ooh, an ambush. I like it," I said, rubbing my palms together. We laughed again as a snowball, thrown by Jax, missed us both.

"You know I can hear you, right?" Jax said. This did make Kim laugh.

A harsh, irritated voice broke up the banter. As Lenard walked past us to continue down the hill, he said, "Stop acting like children."

The glare I received from Lenard gave me goosebumps. The sneer pulled at his lip, exposing his yellowed teeth.

There's something seriously wrong with that man. But it was too late; Lenard had sucked away all the fun.

Later on, when Louis asked for another break, I couldn't turn him down. His gait had slowed, and his fever spiked again. So I helped him find a comfortable spot to rest, then went to find my own.

I, however, chose a rock removed from the group which looked out into the woods. I sat there and I drifted, my mind finally blank. That was until something moved. Down the hill and to the left was an animal. In case I was seeing things, I reached out with my ability. When the lights of life lit around me, I was instantly drawn to the white-tailed deer. This was a chance we could not miss.

"Everyone, shoosh!" I snapped. "Jax?"

Jax and Kim ran to my side. I pointed in the direction of the deer that I'd seen. It wasn't close, but not so far that you wouldn't be able to see it.

"Dinner?" Jax asked.

"That depends. You wanna go hunting?" I said, smiling.

"Absolutely!"

"Keep everyone here. We'll be back in a bit," I said to Kim.

I hopped off the rock. I jogged down the hill as quickly and quietly as possible, Jax by my side. The deer, which was moving away from us, was upwind and moseyed along contentedly. Not wanting to accidentally make our presence known, I activated my sight to verify its location.

My sight. What am I, a freakin' superhero?

The deer passed through a thicket of trees in front of us. With only hand movements, we made a plan. Splitting up, we took up spots on opposite sides of the animal. I took the first shot and missed. I heard a snort from Jax as the deer ran in the opposite direction. This opened a perfect shot for him, and he took it. The animal fell. We rushed to it, and Jax bent down to the now-still creature. He lay his hand on its neck for only a second, whispered a small "thanks," then readied it for travel. It felt good to see that small gesture for the life lost. It was one we'd learned from our fathers, and we'd never forgotten.

"Do you remember our first hunting trip?" I asked, pulling out my knife.

Jax squeezed my hand and said, "Every time I hunt. Now, let's get this done. I want to get home."

"Especially now with the meal we have coming."

He agreed, and we readied our kill for transport.

"The hospital is right over there. Ask for Dr. Travis," Kim said.

Remy nodded and led his group to the clinic while I disappeared to find Lily and Sean. They were in the town hall conference room playing a card game with Camden that seemed to be cutthroat.

When I walked in, Lily glanced up, and instantly the game was over and she was running to me. Camden smiled as she embraced me.

"You're back! Everything go okay?" she asked.

"Yup, rescue accomplished. We're heading home; it's time to go." Lily's face fell at my words, but lifted when I asked, "Do you guys want to come back with us and stay? I feel bad that you've been staying here."

Sydney chuckled. "No. We chose to stay here. We don't want to be a burden. Plus, here, we can be of more help. So many need help with their homes. Plus, I try to help Travis whenever I can."

"Will you let us know if that changes or if you need a few extra hands?"

"Of course. Also, can you let me know when your dad and the others get back okay?"

"Will do." I started away, but she stopped me.

"Hey, do me a favor. If and when you all choose to leave and head back to Arizona, can you let us know? Camden and I will want to head back with you. My mother lives there. Plus, California is gone, and so is our life there."

I hugged her. We headed back to the clinic, hoping the housing situation had been figured out. Lily, Sean, and I arrived only to walk in on the mayor and Kim's conversation.

Mayor Gonzales spoke. "Do you have enough room to house them for a night or two? I can work to get them settled here, but it will take some time. I'm trying to... well, figure stuff out."

Kim, Jax, and I exchanged looks. *Did we have the space? Yes. Were we okay with sharing? No. But Lenard.*

But Lenard.

"Two nights. Then we'll re-evaluate," Kim said.

"Perfect. Thanks. I should have things figured out by then," the mayor said.

As we readied for the final trek home, I noticed Lenard. He stood in the corner, his back pressed to the wall, and his eyes tracking Lily. I stepped between them, forcing him to look at me instead. I glared a warning.

"You go near her, and I'll kill you," I whispered only loud enough for him to hear.

His reaction was not what I expected. Surprise.

"She looks like you, but is not nearly as interesting," he said, just as quietly. He stepped forward, invading my space. I backed up, but not before I noticed him take a deep breath.

Is he sniffing me? I hid my shiver. *And what does that mean? Interesting how?*

"Are you two ready to go?" Jax asked, placing a hand on my back. I nodded, and he led me away. "Good because I'm ready for a nap."

Come to find out, Chris had been taken upstairs to be looked at more closely. There was concern the infection was now in his bloodstream. Louis was okay overall, but Travis wanted to watch him for a night or two. So, we said our goodbyes, then headed home. We'd barely made it through the door when the storm hit. Wind rattled the windows, trees swayed, then cracked with its force, and lightning lit up the sky. The thunder was so loud you could feel it in your bones. Because of that, a nap was off the table. We spread out and locked down the house. We checked the shutters, secured the shed door slamming in the wind, and even covered the windows in the main living areas with blankets, hoping to hold the cold out. Then we organized sleeping arrangements for the newbies.

Remy was helping me upstairs when I realized something. He was a spoiled brat. He'd offered to help with some chores, only to find out that he didn't know how to do any of them. He tried but was really of no help. Somehow it was endearing instead of annoying. We laughed at his attempts while talking about life. He was as charming and funny as I'd suspected. We worked companionably until Kim came in and told us it was our turn to clean up.

"Reena, upstairs bathroom. Remy, basement bathroom," she explained.

With one last jab at his independence, we separated. An hour later, I was leaving the restroom when I'd rushed around the corner and ran right into Remy. I slammed into him, bouncing off and hitting the wall. His hands grasped my waist as he steadied me. I reached out to rub up and down my side where we'd hit. My hand stopped on his, and I glanced up.

"Sorry. I wasn't paying attention. Kim wanted me to bring this stuff up," Remy said, motioning to the blankets he'd dropped. "I forgot you were up here." His voice slowed as his gaze captured mine.

My cold, wet hair, which I'd haphazardly cleaned in a pot of warm water, pressed down my back. The smell of my soap filled the air around us, the light scent of the one he'd used mixing in the small space.

"I... I was just cleaning up," I fumbled. "Remember?"

He shifted closer as if unable to help himself. He reached up and brushed some hair from my face. The hand on my hip shifted to my lower back. The sensation made me take a deep breath. He was so close, so warm in the cold air.

"You're beautiful," he whispered.

The wall was hard against my back. He smelled good.

"No, I'm not."

"Yes. Yes, you are," he breathed. He moved slowly as if afraid I'd run.

I exhaled as his lips brushed mine just once. Wherever our bodies touched, my skin prickled with electricity. He was about to lean in again when Jax's voice came from down the hallway.

"Hey, Reena?"

I jumped away, removing myself from Remy's arms. I turned toward the stairs just in time to see Jax come into view.

When Jax appeared, his brow furrowed. He hadn't seen what happened, but it was obvious enough that he'd interrupted something.

"Yeah? What's up?" *Thank the heavens my voice was steady.*

"Everything okay up here?"

"Yeah, why wouldn't it be?" I glanced back at Remy, and he smiled coolly.

"Okay. Well, Mom needs your help with something. Can you come downstairs?"

"Sure, I'll be right down."

Jax's eyebrows knitted together as he looked from Remy to me and back. Eventually he gave up, turning to go back down the stairs.

I watched him go, only then realizing this was the exact spot I'd discovered him and Cassie. That was some crazy irony. Clearing my throat, I bent to pick up the blankets on the floor and handed them to Remy.

"I should probably go," I said.

"Okay," he said, disappointed. The green of his eyes shimmered in the dim light, and I knew that if I didn't look away, I would be pulled into them once again. Resisting the urge, I spun on my heels and went to find Kim.

Chapter Twenty-Two

The storm raged for nearly two days. It had been over a week since my father had left, and with every second they remained gone, the pit in my stomach deepened. They'd estimated the trip at a little over a week, but something inside me screamed that something had gone wrong. It was near the end of our second day back when I heard a strange noise. The storm was howling, but not with the intensity of the day before. Then the same sound hit my ears, and my head snapped up.

Was that a voice? I opened the shutter to the kitchen window.

"Kim, Jax! I see someone. Get up here!" I hollered. There was stomping as people from all parts of the house ran toward me.

I opened the door against the wind and ran out, unable to feel the cold through my excitement. I met the tall man at the base of the stairs and wrapped my arms around Eric, uncaring of the snow which covered him from head to toe. Eric released me, and I led him into the house. The outline of another figure followed. We could continue with hugs where it was warm.

Eric and then James walked into the small space. Ice covered the floor as they began to remove their hoods. When James shut the door behind him, a shiver ran through me.

The door *thunked* closed. It was like an elephant sat on my chest. Where was Dad? Both men, hesitant in their movements, were quiet as they worked to remove their gear. James removed his ski mask and then, hesitantly, met my eyes.

"No," I said, my voice cracking. Pain like nothing I'd ever felt spread with that one look, confirming what I'd felt a day ago. Something had gone seriously wrong. I swayed, dizzy.

The others entered the room but skittered to a stop at the expression on my face.

"No." I said again, unable to look away. "No!"

My vision clouded as tears filled my eyes. Eric took a step forward, but I stepped back.

"What's wrong?" Lily asked from behind me. "Where's Dad?"

All eyes shifted to me, the weight of their gazes too much. My breathing became heavy, chest fighting for air, as I started to hyperventilate. The room swam. I reached out a hand and placed it on the counter. I tried to hold back emotion, but I couldn't. I was losing that battle. The first sob burst free right as Eric grabbed me and pulled me into a hug.

"I'm so sorry, Reena. We tried. I swear, we tried," he said, tone filled with regret. "The storm, it-it..."

Lily collapsed, the sound of her knees hitting the tile so loud in the stunned silence. Kim bent to console her as Lily began to weep.

I pushed away from Eric and turned, searching. The room was full, everyone in the house squeezed into the small space, but the faces there were foreign, all melding together.

Where was he? I searched for the only one I knew would make the world stop spinning.

He was already there. Jax strode forward and pulled me against him.

His arms wrapped tight, and my body sagged against him. Only he kept me upright. I felt his tension and sadness join mine. My face pressed into his shoulder; my arms pinned between us. I was ugly crying now—harsh sobs that wracked my body.

"Let's go upstairs," he whispered. I nodded into his neck, still unable to pull away.

Everyone retreated when James went to Lily and scooped her up. He carried her upstairs, Kim following behind.

I let myself be led to the girls' bedroom, where Jax sat me on the edge of the bed. Jax knelt in front of me, then reached up and cupped my face. He wiped away the tears, only to have new ones slide over his fingers.

"I don't know what to say. I'm so sorry. I..." He choked up. This was a hit for him, too.

I leaned forward to press my forehead against his. I rested my hands on his shoulders. My fingers dug into his skin.

"I'm so sorry," he repeated.

His presence kept the world from spinning out of control. As we sat there, inches from each other, I used his breathing to steady mine. I closed my eyes as his thumb brushed along my cheekbone.

Eventually, my sobs slowed. The tears still fell, but I was finally able to think again. All I could feel was loss. Loss of my dad and, by her absence, my mom. The loss for my older sister, who was still an enigma. We'd yet to hear anything from back home, and it was killing us.

They were gone. All of them and what was left was broken. Hell, I even missed our simple life back home. The one we would never live again.

Jax moved to sit next to me. He wrapped his arm protectively around my shoulders, his fingers running through my hair in a comforting rhythm.

"I'm alone now," I whispered.

He stiffened. "No, never alone. You have family. You have me and Eric and Lily. Kim and James may not be your parents, but they love you. We all love you."

I sniffed but didn't move. "I wanna know what happened."

"You will." He kissed my hair and rested his cheek against my head.

"I love you, Jax."

The words were the truest thing I'd ever said. I may not have understood them fully yet, but it was still true. And if there was ever a time to say it, it was right then. He had proven that every time I needed him, he would protect me and support me, even when our relationship was broken and confusing.

"I love you too, Reena."

I sighed, the absolute surety in his voice warming me. He told the truth. It was the love we'd always held for each other. That absolute devotion that comes with a lifetime of friendship. But this time, I heard something more, and a secret part of me loved it. I squeezed his side.

"I need to check on Lily. She's my responsibility now." I looked up into Jax's face. "How can I be what she needs, Jax? I'm not them. I can't..."

I'm seventeen. Hell, I wasn't even able to take care of my best friend.

I thought back to the times I'd failed Jax—when I'd allowed my school friends to corner him or when I publicly ignored his request for a truce, instead pouring a soda on his head. But worst of all, when I wasn't there for him after his grandmother died. They'd been so close. I'd known he was struggling, but I stayed away. And still he was here with me.

He ran his hand down my back and shifted to face me.

"Reena. Lily, she..."

I couldn't fix the past with Jax, but I could be there for her. I would be strong for her.

He tried again. "You can't be them, but you don't have to be. Just be her sister, be there for her."

"Will you come with me?" I didn't want to move, but I knew I needed to go to her.

"Of course."

He helped me up, and we walked down the hall to the master bedroom where Lily had been taken. I took a few breaths before I knocked on the door and heard Kim's soft voice.

"Come in."

Kim was on the bed, Lily's head resting on a pillow on her lap. I walked over to sit next to them. Jax shadowed me. I put a hand on Lily's back.

Lily moved to sit up, and when her eyes met mine, I saw the pain I felt mirrored in hers. Her face was red, eyes swollen. Her hands were clenched into fists. A tear fell from my eye and slid down my cheek. She dove for me. I wrapped my arms around her, and she clung to me. Her tears soaked my shirt and burned my skin.

That's when I started talking. I told her that it would be all right. I told her that we weren't alone, that we'd always be together. I said everything that I could think of, whispering over and over that I loved her.

Jax and Kim didn't leave. They just sat there, their presence alone confirming my words. Kim rubbed circles on Lily's back, and Jax sat as close as he could to us. Eventually, Lily's crying slowed, and she released me. She moved clumsily to Jax, who embraced her.

"Don't worry, little Lily," he whispered. "You have an amazing sister, and she'll take good care of you. So will I."

"Promise?" she croaked.

"Promise," he said.

She clung to him as he rocked her gently. I held Lily's outstretched hand. Even as Jax pressed his cheek against Lily's hair, his eyes stayed locked on mine.

I couldn't help it. I reached out and brushed my fingers through his hair. The longer I watched him, the more his words sunk in. He would always be there for us. No matter what.

After a long while, Lily fell asleep. Jax picked her up, and we tucked her into bed. Before I left, I whispered in her ear what I'd said before, then gave her one last kiss on the head. She was such a strong kid, but also so young and naive. And now, it was up to me to keep her safe. My dad's words from before he left echoed in my head.

Take care of her, Reena. She needs you.

Could I be what she needed? It didn't matter; I had to be. It was my job to protect her now.

I stood, took a deep breath, and went to find out what happened to my parents. If I didn't do this now, I wasn't sure I'd be able to later.

Chapter Twenty-Three

Have you ever stood at the edge of a cliff when your world just changed, and you knew—knew it in your bones—that the next big decision would set you on the path you were always meant to take?

That's how I felt. I stood there, gazing back at Lily, finally able to see that I had been waiting for this. No, not my father's death, but some event that would shock me into action and prove there was something more expected of me in this life. Either by my protection of Lily or by my movements forward in the future.

Standing there, I could see that nothing I was before mattered. Instead, it was who I wanted to be that was important, because I always knew something would push me in the right direction. For me, it was my father's death, and it hurt more than I could ever imagine.

"I need to know what happened," I said to Kim and Jax, who'd waited in the hallway.

"Honey, you don't need to do this now," Kim said.

"Yes, I do. I need to know."

Her soft features were so warm and loving, but behind them was strength and some significant irritation. She could see what I was doing. She could see the wall I was constructing to block away my sorrow. It was a skill I'd mastered. One that in instances like these I cherished. It's how I faked strength. It had taken me years to learn, but now, only those closest to me knew my true emotions. Kim and Jax were some of the few.

"We aren't waiting for anyone anymore, and we can't stay here forever. I feel like what they say will outline everything."

"What do you mean?" she asked.

"I don't know."

Kim scanned me, attempting to figure out what was going on in my mind. She put a hand on my arm and gestured for the stairs.

The floorboards creaked as I entered the basement. Conversation stopped, and all eyes went to me. I gathered my strength before glancing up and meeting Eric and James' eyes. They were resting on one of the couches, heads down, expressions broken. Their lips were chapped, and I could see a few scratches on their faces. Dark circles lined their eyes. Blankets were thrown over them, and yet still they shivered.

Cassie, Sean, and Remy sat on the other couch, but they moved off to the side to allow me to take their spot. My lip curled as I spotted Lenard in the corner, an amused scowl on his face.

I sat next to Cassie. She grabbed my hand and squeezed gently. I sent her a soft smile of thanks. She understood the pain I was in. She, too, had lost people she loved. I faced James.

"Tell me what happened. Now. Start with Portland. I take it you didn't find Mom."

James took a calming breath, then spoke. "The reports of Portland were right on. The western part of the city was destroyed. The rest has serious flooding."

He rubbed his palms together. "A few of the people confirmed a tsunami made it up the river. It was bad. People were rioting and looting. They started attacking each other."

"Fear rules there now," Eric said, his eyes on the floor.

"We went to my townhouse to see if your mom was there. There was no sign of her. So, we headed to the hospital."

"Or tried to." Eric took over. "No matter how many different ways we went, we couldn't get there."

Kim sat forward. "Why?"

"Flooding mostly. The water was..." James fought to find the right word. "Polluted. There were bodies and sewage. That was on top of being dangerously cold. It just wasn't safe. We kept trying, but we'd go one way, and a fire or riot would push us in a different direction."

Eric spoke up. "Then we got stopped in a section of the city where all the buildings had collapsed. The people had turned them into a defendable fort." He was shaking his head. "After a short scuffle, we got away."

Kim and I exchanged a look.

"On the last day, we found a group of kids following us. They wanted our supplies. They were armed, and there were a lot of them." James rested his elbows on his knees. His dirty hands caught my attention. "We were only a few blocks from the hospital when the fight got bad. From what we could see, the bottom floor was flooded. The rest seemed intact, but it looked abandoned. We tried, but we weren't able to get there."

"We ran, Reena. We had to," Eric added.

Nodding slowly, I asked, "What happened then?"

"They jumped us. We fought but were so outnumbered we had to run. Some of them were acting so strange."

"Dan didn't want to give up. I didn't either, but it was too dangerous." James met my eye. "We don't know about your mom. We had to run."

"Okay..."

"We made camp a few miles outside the city, but—stupidly—still along the highway. That night, two people snuck into camp. Dan was on watch. When we woke, he was fighting them. They were deranged, unstable. We got them off him, but your dad got hurt when he stepped in to help Eric."

Eric pushed his sleeve up his arm. A jagged wound the shape of teeth was imprinted on his forearm. "One of them bit me."

I traced the mark with a finger.

"Dan got stabbed. We got away, but just barely," Eric finished.

James looked around the room. "There was something wrong with these people. Their eyes were crazed. They kept screaming that Eric tasted like The Source. They were Deranged."

"'The Source, The Source,' they screamed, 'it will kill us all.'" Eric shook his head.

I froze. The Source? The thing which I'd been seeing in visions and dreams for weeks now? Flashes of an island with frozen waves surrounding it. Purple and gold swirling together, reaching for my skin.

This was it.

"The what?" Remy asked, suddenly interested. My gaze snapped to him.

"The Source," Eric repeated.

In that split second, I knew Remy had seen something, too. He'd heard its name.

"Did they say anything else about it?" Remy asked.

"Not yet," I snapped at Remy. From the corner of my eye, I saw the others' shocked faces at my tone.

Remy's eyes hardened, coming to the same understanding of me that I'd just made of him.

I turned back to James and Eric. "What happened then?"

"We ran. Dan had been stabbed in the side and was bleeding. Once we were far enough away, we stopped to get him patched up. Then a storm hit." James continued, "We found an area a ways from the road. It was an overhang in the side of the mountain just large enough to provide a break from the wind and some cover from above. It was easily defendable. We stayed there for a few hours, but it was too cold. We cleaned up Dan's wound and tried to get warm, but the tent was left behind."

James got up and paced the room. His pants swooshed with each movement, and his boots left small imprints in the carpet.

"After a few hours, something changed. I can't explain it exactly. The air felt different. The storm was getting stronger. Dan was still bleeding, and no matter what we did, we couldn't get it to stop. So, we decided to wrap it and start walking. We were doing pretty well until the wind shifted direction and the lightning started up again. But this time it was right over us."

He stopped pacing. He sat on the coffee table inches from me and licked his lips.

This is it.

"You know where the road travels right through that narrow canyon?"

I nodded, my eyes glued to his face.

"We were there when lightning struck the cliff above us. Rocks fell, and we ran. Eric and I grabbed Dan to keep him moving. At one point, I ran ahead, leading them to the easiest path. Lightning hit again. More rocks fell, and your dad..." He looked down, then back up again. His voice shook as he said, "...the rocks were falling toward Eric."

A sound of pain escaped my throat. Tears filled my eyes, and the world dimmed just a bit.

Voice almost a whisper, but shockingly stable, I said, "And he pushed Eric out of the way."

"Your dad saved my life," Eric choked out. "He shouldn't have."

Kim joined Eric on the other couch.

"He did what he always did. He protected his family," I said simply. Throat aching, I forced myself to pace.

"We tried to help him, but we couldn't get him out. He died right in front of—"

My hand shot up, stopping Eric.

"Dad died for those he loved. He died to save you," I said. I knelt in front of Eric.

Eric's head dropped, and tears carved harsh paths down his face. His head dropped to my shoulder.

I brushed back his hair. If I wasn't careful, Eric would blame himself for the rest of his life. But it wasn't his fault. It was a choice. Dad's choice. One I would make without hesitation, and one I could never regret.

"There's one last thing," James said.

I released Eric and returned to my spot on the couch.

"The last thing he said. It was for you. He said to tell you to 'stand strong. See what you can see and set it right because truth will always point you home.'"

My gaze shot to Jax. He reached into his pocket and pulled out his compass.

But, set what right? I asked myself. *What am I missing here?*

"Thank you for telling me." I rubbed my forehead. There was a throbbing behind my right eye. I ran a tired hand through my hair. "Okay, I have a question. It might not make sense why I am asking right now, but... was that night—and from the attackers—the first time you'd heard the phrase 'The Source'?"

Yup. Caught everyone off guard with that one.

They each shifted; sat straighter, shuffled their feet, clenched their fists. Every single person reacted. Remy's eyes lit with excitement. Lenard's jaw clenched, but a gleam of desire peaked out. He licked his lips, and the glimpse I had of what was within him was terrifying.

"Why?" Eric asked.

"It's not, is it? You've all heard the phrase. From where?"

"We heard it a few times in Portland, but no one knows what it is," James explained.

"Anyone else? Cassie? Lenard?" I put a lot of emphasis on Lenard's name. At my tone, he squinted, then a small, amused smile quirked his lips.

He's hiding something.

Cassie leaned forward and said, "It was a dream. I woke one morning, and it was like the only words I knew were 'The Source.' I've seen it every night since we got back. What is it?"

"Remy?" I approached him. "What did you see?"

"What do you mean?" His tone betrayed him. He knew what I was talking about.

Damn, Remy had a mask on. To everyone else, he probably seemed normal, but to me? I could see the truth.

Lenard slithered next to Remy, and I knew this was Lenard's doing. He whispered in his nephew's ear. Just before he shifted away, Lenard took in a deep breath as if he were smelling Remy. His eyes closed slowly, only to open and lock onto me.

Creepy. Okay, time to see how far this goes.

"Let me guess. Uncle Lenny told you to keep it a secret? Why?" This was a bad idea. Sadly, all good ideas had been killed by the stress of the day. I needed to know. So, I continued, "Is Lenny scared?"

Lenard surged forward, slamming me against the nearest wall. The wood slats bounced with my impact, and one arm pinned me across the chest. His other hand gripped my throat.

I forced a dark grin. *I guess it was true. He really didn't like the name Lenny.*

Calls of alarm and everyone was moving. Eric and James were moving with anger lighting their eyes. In another moment, they'd have Lenard on the floor, bleeding. No, I needed to test this. I needed to know how far The Source reached and what they knew.

"Stop!" I hollered. I raised one hand to stop them. "Trust me."

"What?" James asked. I shook my head. They froze, though they were not happy about it. Jax was the only one who didn't immediately listen. He approached menacingly, definitely ready to throw Lenard through a window.

"I knew it." My tone was calm. Even a little cruel. "You want it, don't you? I knew you heard our conversation that first night. Remy's and mine, but you also followed Cassie and me. Kind of stalker-ish, isn't it?"

His eyes narrowed, and his breathing quickened.

"You were there when Jax and I spoke, too." I leaned as far forward as I could. "You see, you're not as sneaky as you think you are, Lenny." I dragged out his name. I knew I shouldn't bait him, but I had to know the truth. What and who was Lenard?

A guttural growl reverberated through him. He wouldn't hurt me then and there, but he wanted to.

"Let go of her, Lenard," Jax said, slow and deadly.

"It's okay, Jax. I think he's figured something out. He may not have the abilities Remy, Cassie, and I have, but he can feel them. Just like he can feel The Source. Its pull?"

"Shut your mouth," he snarled. "You're just a stupid girl who doesn't know what she's talking about."

"Maybe. Or maybe I just understand you better than you think. Maybe I see your jealousy. Your envy over the fact that not just your nephew has powers, but some stupid girl. And let me guess, you think it has to do with The Source." His arm pressed harder, but I continued anyway. "You think that if you can get to it, you'll finally have the powers you've always wanted. Don't you, Lenny?"

He slammed me against the wall again. My head hit with a *thump*.

I grunted softly and blinked off the pain. That was the end of it.

Before I knew it, Jax broke Lenard's hold on my neck. In the same instant, Remy pushed between us. Remy disconnected Lenard's other grip, allowing Jax to pull him away and drag him out of the room.

Lenard broke loose for a second, trying to get back to me, but Jax punched him in the face, causing him to fall to the ground. That didn't stop Lenard's threats or attempts to get at me. James went to help. They pulled him up the stairs with Eric and Kim right behind.

I was too busy watching the scene to notice Remy trying to speak to me. It was only when Remy physically turned my face to him that my attention was brought back.

"Reena, are you all right?"

"Yup."

He scowled at my nonchalant response. "What the hell's wrong with you? I know you can see something's wrong with him!"

"Yeah, he's a jerk. He kept smiling at me as if he loved watching us fall to pieces. Then, there is the fact he is clearly manipulating you. It's not okay, Remy! And I'm not afraid of him." I was almost screaming.

"Maybe you should be! I won't let him hurt you, and no one else here will either, but you need to be careful. Look at him." He pointed to the stairs. "That's not a normal man."

His fingers trailed from my face and down my neck to touch where Lenard had held me. It was tender, the spot throbbing with my heartbeat.

"I don't want to see you hurt. Even this is too much." His eyes saddened as he traced the mark wrapping my neck.

You need to stop starting fights. Just calm down.

The feel of his fingers along my collarbone made me shiver. It traveled down my arm to stop at my hand. I held my breath. Focused on his touch. It was hard to notice anything else in that moment.

"What did you see?" I asked.

He was gazing at our clasped hands but snapped up when I spoke. He shook his head, exasperated. "Fine. I'll tell you, but not right now."

Sighing, I scanned the room. Cassie and Sean were still there. Cassie, however, was focused on the stairs, the sound of fighting drifting down. Her eyes flitted to us every so often, making sure I was okay with Remy. Cassie didn't trust him, either.

Sean watched us intently, his fidgeting harsher than normal. He walked to us, searching first for Remy and then me. He was trying to see something, to figure something out. Sean tugged on the sleeve of my shirt, his thoughts visibly whirling in his eyes.

"Sean, can you check on Lily for me? Take Cassie with you?"

Sean stopped his examination. For a few long seconds, he tried to speak, but nothing came out, so he nodded. Passing Cassie, he spat out a quick "come" for Cassie to go with him. With one last look, she followed Sean up the stairs.

I slumped against the wall, lifting both hands to my face. "I'm fine. But I need you to tell the truth about what you saw and explain why Lenard's having you keep it from us."

"Ugh, fine." Remy was about to say more when boots hammered down the stairs.

"Reena, are you all right?" Jax asked, bursting into the room.

"Jax, I'm fine. Don't worry."

Jax's eyes locked on Remy. For a second, I thought he was about to go after Remy, but instead, his face smoothed out.

"Thanks for stepping in. I don't know what's wrong with that man, but I swear," he snapped.

"No problem. I'm just glad Reena wasn't seriously hurt. I'll talk to him," Remy said.

"Not tonight. He's sleeping in the shed. We can't chance a crazy person in this house, especially around Reena or Lily, or Cassie for that matter. It's just not safe."

"I agree, and again, I'm sorry."

"I know," Jax said. He patted Remy on the shoulder, then asked, "Can you excuse us? I need to talk with Reena."

"Sure," he said. Halfway up the stairs, Remy turned to look back.

Jax took me by the shoulders and scanned me. His gaze stopped on my neck and they narrowed, furry lighting within them. The muscles in his jaw clenched, and I sighed.

"I told you, Jax, I'm fine. Lenard's not as strong as he thinks he is."

That only irritated him further. "It's not funny, Reena! He could've hurt you, and you just kept antagonizing him. What were you thinking?"

He reached up and brushed the hollow of my neck. His fingers were warm and gentle, full of a totally different emotion than the one there moments before. The feeling was familiar and so wonderful that my heart jumped.

Not thinking, I rested my hands on his chest. I flattened my fingers against his shirt, cursing at the new confusion filling me. *Get a grip, Reena.*

"I wasn't planning that. I just wanted answers from Remy. There's something about him."

Jax's expression grew darker. It scared me.

"What?" I asked.

"Something about him? Something about him?" His volume rose. "You've known this guy for three days! And it's not just that. Do you know he watches you? Every move? Every word?"

Jax stepped away, my arms dropping to my sides. But he was back a second later.

"Come on. You know better. Hell, look at what just happened with his uncle. What if he's just like Lenard?"

"He's not."

"How do you know?"

"Why are you so upset? I appreciate your help, but..." I reached for his hand; he pulled away. My confusion grew. "I'm sorry. I didn't mean to..."

"You don't get it, do you, Reena? You never have. And now this creepy guy and his psychotic uncle show up, and you're just mesmerized or something. You can't see it, and I don't know why."

"Jax. What do you want from me? Everything has turned to crap and I... What did I do?" I choked out. My face was reddening, and tears began to well in my eyes.

Guilt filled Jax's eyes. He'd realized I was about to lose it. He took my hands and squeezed gently.

"No, I'm sorry. I shouldn't be bothering you with this right now. But I need you to listen to me and really hear what I'm saying. Lenard is dangerous and I don't trust, let alone like, Remy. The way he looks at you isn't normal. The way he watches you isn't normal. Cassie told me that you feel like you're connected to him. I don't like it."

"She said what?" I was pissed.

"She thinks it's innocent, but I can tell it's more. There's something wrong here. Reena, you're too important to me—"

"Stop!" I shouted. "I know you're confused about what's been going on between us, but... You know what? I'm just going to say it. I'm not good for you. You deserve someone worthy. Someone who can be as amazing as you are. Like Cassie." My voice cracked on her name. "I'm weak. I hurt you for so many years. I changed myself into someone I hate and all so that I could fit in. Then this happens, and you have to save my ass, twice! And why? Because I was stupid. I wasn't fast enough, smart enough."

I shoved my hands in my hair and pulled. The words might be true, but they burned my throat and tainted my blood. I inhaled deeply.

When I spoke again, I sounded helpless. "And now I have to be a parent to Lily, and I can't do it alone."

Jax touched my arm, about to say something, but I kept talking. There was no stopping the flow of emotion after it had started.

"And through all of this, I will always depend on you to keep me from falling, but you shouldn't have to do that. No one should have to do that. Especially when all you get in return is a slap to the face. You shouldn't waste your time on me, Jax. And even though I know that's the truth, I'm afraid of what would happen if you weren't there." My throat closed, causing my voice to crack. "I'm broken."

The despair in his eyes was more than I could take. I could see the words he would say. They were written all over his face—words that would try to convince me that I was more. Words to try to win my heart. I could never allow myself to believe them. Before he could say anything, I jerked my hands free and ran upstairs.

I pushed past Cassie, who stood at the top. I passed Kim and James. Then Eric and Remy. Their shocked and worried expressions pushed me faster. I ignored their attempts to stop me.

Eric followed, catching up to me in the hallway as I attempted to shut the door to our bedroom in his face. Behind me, Lily slept on, her angelic face the only light in the room.

"Reena," he said for the hundredth time.

"No, Eric. Today has been enough." I forced the words out. "My dad died, I got into a fight with a psychopath, and I've ruined one of the best things that has ever, even potentially, happened to me. It's my fault, and I'll never get it back."

"What are you talking about?"

"Jax. A lot has happened since you left. I'm not sure he'll ever forgive me, let alone be my friend again, and every day I get more confused. More unsure. It's like I told him, I'm broken, and I can't handle any more. Especially not today. I just want to sleep."

With that, I closed the door in his face. Only when his steps retreated did I slip under my comforter. The ache in my chest made it hard to breathe. I closed my eyes and thought about it all.

Where would we go now? Who would I be? One last thought before my mind finally drifted off. *And what the hell was The Source?*

Chapter Twenty-Four

T he sound of voices woke me the next morning. The late morning light came through the window, blanketing me in a golden glow.

Looks like the storm finally passed. Lily must have opened our shutters. My head was fuzzy, my eyes sore, but the room was silent. I sighed, taking that in. *I'm alone for once. It's been weeks since I've had this level of quiet.*

Out the window, Lily was playing a game with Eric and Cassie. Jax and Remy worked nearby, calling out to competitors. Lily grinned and laughed, but I could see the sorrow underneath even from here. I was grateful they'd all banded together to support her. She deserved all she could get. But after last night, it hurt to watch them.

I shoved the comforter off me. A flash of pink caught my eye, and I glanced down. My nails were chewed to the quick, and the last vestiges of my manicure were what had drawn me.

"You screwed up big time, Novak," I said to myself. "What are you going to do?"

Chores, I thought, pulling my last clean outfit free. *Scavenge, wash clothes, then decide next steps.*

"You need to follow Dad's advice. Keep moving and set things right. But first, you need time to think and that can't happen here."

Once dressed, I snuck down the stairs, grabbed my bow, and slipped out the kitchen door. The crunch of the snow under my boots made me cringe. It sounded like an alarm going off, one that pointed directly to me. I headed for the trees as quickly as I could, making sure I was out of their line of sight. Once in their shelter, I ran. Time far away was what I needed. After a few minutes, I slowed to a walk, taking solace in the green and white of the forest.

I went south toward town and not into open wilderness. We'd talked about checking the abandoned homes for supplies, and that was something I could do on my own. It would also provide me with productive alone time.

Luckily, I knew this entire area like the back of my hand. Jax and I had spent most of our time here defining different paths both to and from town. Without thinking, I chose Jax's favorite. It looked different covered in snow, but I had fun finding the markings we made as children. Small notches in the trees that grew higher and higher each year.

I was almost to the first house when I heard the snap of a branch behind me. Followed by a *thump* as someone fell into the snow. I pulled out an arrow and nocked it.

"Who's there?" I called.

A familiar face stepped out of the trees. Immediately, I dropped my bow and released the string, returning the arrow to its quiver.

"Sean, what're you doing here?" I asked.

Another crunch of snow and Lily stepped out. My shoulders fell in a sigh.

"You two. I swear," I said. "What're you doing here?
And how did you even know where I was?"

"I know you better than you think. I heard what
happened last night. I knew you'd try to escape. So, I
had Sean sitting by the back door waiting." Lily
shrugged. "Not that you noticed. He signaled me, and
we snuck away."

"Did anyone follow you?" I asked, pulse picking up.

"Doubt it. They're all busy. I said I had to go to the
bathroom, and they let me go."

Simple and effective.

"What if Lenard followed you?"

"He didn't. James took him to town this morning to
see Dr. Travis. The fight with Jax last night got pretty
bad after Eric joined in. James thought he should be
looked at. He also wanted Lenard away from you." She
stepped forward. "You caused one heck of a scene."

"Of course you know everything." I looked at Sean.
"Is this your doing?" He shook his head.

"We need to talk, Reena, and with Lily here, we can.
It's too hard otherwise," Sean said.

My mouth dropped open. His speech was perfectly
clear. It was a little fast, but precise.

"I have a lot to tell you and even with Lily here, I
can't do this for long. Where can we go?" he asked.

"Uh, we're almost to the Robins' house. No one
should be here; they rarely come in winter."

They followed me through a thicket of trees and onto
a pristine, white covered lawn. A small pink house with
white trim sat in the center. It looked like something
out of a fairy tale. This was my favorite house in the
area. I became friends with the owners years ago just so
I could see inside the home.

I knocked. As I'd suspected, no one was home. I went
to the side of the porch and started digging. I finally

found one of those special rocks that people leave a key in for when they lock themselves out. I turned it over and found what I needed. They'd shown me this one summer when I watched their cat for the weekend. I unlocked the door and headed inside.

It was just as cute as the outside. Comfortable furniture made up the living space. The small kitchen was decorated in gentle blues and greens with pops of color here and there. It was a calming home. Every time I visited, I'd come check on the Robins, but this time felt wrong. They'd probably never come here again.

I took a seat on the coral armchair while Sean and Lily took the beige couch.

"All right, what's going on?" I asked.

"Sean told me about what you can do. He also told me about what he thinks Jax can do," Lily said.

What he thinks Jax can do...

"Okay, now I have so many questions. Let's start with how can he tell you about it? He's moving too fast to speak. The last time I tried, I nearly passed out."

"I know, but I need you to trust me for a second," she said. "Look at him now. You know, in that weird way you do."

"Why?"

"Just do it, okay?"

Pride for her swelled. That and sheer curiosity made me agree. There she was, so young and sweet, and yet her jaw was tight, her eyes determined. She was so strong. I took a deep breath, closed my eyes, and unfocused my senses.

I lay a hand on Sean's, grounding me to him. The energy within him spun so fast that it made me dizzy. It was similar but tasted different than before. There had to be a variation, some change, since last time. I sifted through it all.

There. Right there. A new focus in his brain that was steady and calm. It was still spinning, but much more normal. I released his hand.

"Lily, are you doing that?" I asked, awed.

"Not on purpose. Everyone kept saying that there was something wrong with him, but to me, he was normal. Other than that, he doesn't talk much, but I can't blame him for that. I never noticed anything weird, though. Remy was the one that told me I was doing something to him. He pointed out the difference from when he is with me versus not."

"Remy?"

"Yeah. He said there was something special about me. He said Sean was clearer when I was around. It took me a while to realize what he meant."

I turned my power on her this time. I had to lean close, but I could see it, too. Lily was definitely special. Her aura was stabilizing, bright and beautiful. It reached out to Sean and draped over him like a shawl. Wherever it touched, he calmed.

"She slows down my mind," Sean said. "It's like you thought. I can't communicate because my mind is moving too fast, not because it's too slow."

Yeah, no kidding. Sean was brilliant. You just had to watch him to know that.

"I don't have much time. Lily shouldn't do this for long." His voice was deep and melodic. I liked it. "First, you and Remy. You can do similar things, but not the same, right?"

"Yes."

"That's because you two are polar opposites of each other. I've suspected it since you told me how you found them, but last night confirmed it. You feel a pull to the other, kind of like a magnet, because opposites attract. Last night, it was like you two couldn't back away from each other no matter how hard you tried. At least until you calmed down some. This is dangerous, Reena. Since you're living and not metal, you have to be careful. Something tells me that eventually something will happen to unbalance your fields. When they do, who knows what will happen."

"I know what happens," I said. His eyebrows rose in interest. "We're shoved away. The day we met, I got upset. He kept telling me I was like him. It creeped me out, and I panicked. When we touched, we were thrown almost ten feet."

Sean's slow nod said that I made perfect sense.

"Maybe your emotions or thoughts were too aligned. Remember, Reena, if opposites attract, then like magnets repel."

"That means he must have been as freaked out as I was. But I don't understand. How did you know about all that?"

"Most everyone acts like I'm not there. I've heard everything. And I think you are right. Being upset probably threw you off balance." His speech sped up a bit. "On to the next thing. She's getting tired. Pay attention to the toll it takes. You seem to have figured out how to supplement power, but the others haven't yet."

Supplement power? Yeah...kinda.

"Lastly, The Source. It *is* part of Goliath. You already figured that out though, but there's more. The pull, I can feel it, too. It's calling to us. Everyone here has heard it, but not those in town. Why?" We shrugged, unsure. "The Source. It wants all of us here, but especially you and Remy. I just don't know why yet. It needs us to do something. We just need to figure out what." He was almost too fast to understand now. Whatever hold Lily had was fading quickly.

"That would indicate that The Source is intelligent," I said. My heartbeat sped faster and faster in time with his speech. I wiped my sweaty palms on my jeans.

"Not necessarily, there..." The hold snapped. Sean's shoulders fell, his eyes slammed shut, and he rubbed his temple. A second later, Sean began to fidget uncontrollably.

Lily slumped in her seat, her face pale.

"Go." Sean tried to say more but was unable. It was like the first day I met him with his words a jumbled mess of sounds. Giving up, he leaned back against the couch.

When Lily collapsed, I'd slipped from my seat to kneel next to her. Brushing her hair back, I asked, "Lily, are you okay?"

Her breaths were steady. She leaned against the soft cushions, the beautiful brown tint to her skin next to my similar shade. It made my heart ache. She looked like Mom.

I had to do better than this. It was my job to protect her, not let her get hurt.

"I thought you didn't do this consciously. That it didn't hurt you!" I snapped.

"Usually, it doesn't. I can just be near him, and he focuses fine, but this was more advanced. It was a long conversation, so I had to think about it."

"You shouldn't have done this. You could've hurt yourself."

"I had to. You need to know. We want to help, but he can't without me. *This* is all I can do, Reena. You want to protect me, well damn it, I'm going to protect you, too."

"Don't curse," I said, but was grinning. "Mom and Dad would tan your hide for that."

Lily laughed. "You won't, though."

"Not this time, but in the future..." I placed my palm to her cheek.

She was clammy and looked about to fall asleep. I tucked her hair behind her ear and saw something that took my breath away. A drip of blood from her ear.

Sean's hand touched mine. He'd seen it, too. The "look see" expression had his words running through my head all over again. *Pay attention to the toll it takes.*

"Thank you. Let me find you a snack, and here's my water. Stay awake, okay?"

We propped her up and Sean helped her—as best he could—with the water. I think more ended up on her than in her mouth, but she didn't seem to mind. The kitchen was small, but well stocked with snacks and canned goods. I relaxed only after she ate a bar, and her color came back.

"Sean, do me a favor. Keep watching. Be my spy. I have a feeling what you find out will help us figure out everything. I know it's a lot to ask." I hated making him do this for me.

"Not! Lot," Sean said in his forceful fashion.

As they watched, I began to empty the cabinets, piling up the rice, beans, and canned veggies.

"What are you doing?" Lily asked.

"Shopping. We need more supplies, especially if we are going to make the trip." Three containers of almond milk, ten pouches of tuna, and a bag of quinoa.

Healthy eaters, I thought, adding it to the pile.

"Trip?" Lily asked. She stood and joined me.

"We leave in two days. We're heading south toward The Source. Sean agrees that we need to go."

Their eyes went wide at my understanding of his rant.

I continued, "I've known it for a while, too. I just couldn't leave Dad, Eric, and James. I'll tell them tonight. Whoever wants to join can come. Whoever doesn't can stay."

Lily released a slow breath. Her eyes dropped to the pile I'd built. I'd added batteries, candles, and two boxes of matches.

"Sean and I are with you. No matter what, but they won't be happy."

I smiled. "You're right. But here is my question. Why are you so willing to accept this?"

"One, because I know you. You would never risk us. And two, because you're not the only one who feels the pull. This decision feels right."

I stared, dumbfounded. *When had my baby sister grown up?*

"Now, how can we help?"

Over the next few hours, we scrounged the house. As Lily and Sean organized what we'd found for transport, I went to the next house. And the next house.

Armfuls of canned goods, bottled water, powdered drinks, Cream of Wheat, noodles, rice, bandages, flashlights, a collapsible shovel, knives, a two-person tent, and even a large backpacking rig were piled in the small living space.

"This is a lot," Lily said when I told her I was done for the day.

Part of me felt bad for stealing, but the probability of anyone coming back here was abysmally low. Plus, I planned to take anything we didn't need into town. Because really, there was only so much we could carry.

We stuffed the backpacking rig full, then used a combination of trash bags and pillow cases to carry the rest. On the way back, Lily carried the tent and the sleeping bags. As the backpack fit me better, I carried it. The rest of the supplies were split between Sean and me. It was a lot, and we both hurt by the time we made it back.

The closer we got, the slower my footsteps became. My boots dragged, and the base of my neck itched. What can I say? I was nervous to tell half my family I was leaving in two days' time, with or without them.

Chapter Twenty-Five

"You know, you're not sneaky when you leave footprints."

I stumbled at the sound of Eric's voice, dropping one of the bags I carried. I righted myself and looked up to find Eric leaning against a tree a few yards ahead.

"Was I trying to be sneaky?" I asked.

Eric pushed off the trunk and approached me. He bent down, picked up the bag I'd dropped, then grunted at its weight.

"What did you do? Go shopping at the surplus store?"

"Just a little breaking and entering," I said.

He laughed once, then glanced at Lily. "And you brought your kid sister along?"

"Family bonding," I said. He took another of the bags I carried, then led the way. I continued, "The way to pick a lock is an extremely useful skill. As is the knowledge of how to open a window silently."

"Glad she's on the right life path. Burglar is a very lucrative job."

"That's what I told her."

Lily giggled. "I would prefer the title of 'Expert in the Re-appropriation of Vital Goods.'"

We froze mid-step and spun to look at her. I blinked slowly, having to hold back my laugh. Eric seemed just as lost for words. He opened and closed his mouth a few times, but nothing came out.

"That *awesome!*" Sean said, patting Lily on the back.

"What? Dad loves crime shows. Sometimes I watch them with him." Lily passed us on the path. Her steps slowed, then her head fell minutely. As if to herself, she said, "Loved. He loved crime shows."

My vision swam as I watched her shake her head, speed back up, and disappear into the house. Eric and I shared a pained look, then followed.

"Where is everyone?" I asked, clearing my throat.

"Dad and Lenard are in town. Cassie and Jax thought you went hunting, so they tried to catch up. Mom and Remy are around here somewhere."

"Hunting sounds fun. Maybe Remy will want to go, too. I need to speak with him anyway."

"You shouldn't go alone," Eric said. Sean, who walked on the other side of Eric, nodded his agreement.

"You're always welcome to join," I said, entering the house. We placed our haul next to Lily's. "I'm sure Sean can hold down the fort while Lily takes a nap."

"What am I, five?" Her voice dropped an octave. "'Okay, Lily, it's quiet time, time for your nap,'" she said in a mocking tone. Her head tilted as if considering. "You know what? A nap does sound nice. You can take care of all this." Smiling, she left the room.

"Let's leave these here. I want to look through everything later anyway. Figure out what else we need."

"For what?"

I grimaced, my back stiffening. Should have known better. I hadn't planned to tell him yet. I figured it'd be easier to tell everyone at once.

"You know I'm going with you, right?" Eric asked.

Hesitantly, I glanced into his kind face. His dirty blond hair stuck out from his cap, but it was the determination in his eyes that caught me off guard. They were so filled with warmth. I squeezed his arm.

"And you know it's creepy that you know me so well, right?"

He pulled me into a one-armed hug. "Yup. So, where are we headed?"

"South. We need to head out of the mountains. The flooding comes up too far to go through California. So maybe head toward Las Vegas? I don't really care as long as it's south. We'll figure out the rest later."

"And what's south?"

"The Source."

His eyes went wide, his posture straightening. "What do you know that we don't?"

"I'm not sure yet. But pay attention today, and maybe we can put some of the pieces together. I'm going to talk to Remy. Meet me out back in fifteen."

"Okay," Eric said thoughtfully. He began to rummage through the bags and the grunts of approval as he dug through them made me smile.

I stepped onto the porch. I knew he was there by the pull I felt inside. I always knew. It reminded me of that feeling you got when someone was watching you, but instead of a creepy vibe, it felt comforting.

"You're beautiful when you smile," Remy's voice said from the chair next to the door. His green eyes scanned me from head to toe. "Where have you been all day?"

"Out. I didn't want to be around people, and we needed someone to go shopping."

I cleared the snow off the chair next to him and sat. Remy's hand slipped into mine, startling me. Heat rolled like waves from his touch. He played with my fingers as if they were fascinating. My breathing became heavy, my heart picking up.

"So... um," I said lamely. "We need to talk."

"Yeah, we do."

"Remy, I want to trust you, but I need you to tell me what you know. Lenard's manipulating you. If you continue to follow his advice, this will never work. You'll need to leave."

His gaze captured mine. There was so much pain and confusion behind that look. Lenard was all the family he had left. He may not be perfect, but he was still family. I understood that even if I didn't like it.

Remy lifted my hand and kissed my knuckles. The moment his lips made contact, his expression changed. Resignation? Affection?

"The Source. I saw purple and yellow swirling just like the ash as it floated mid-air surrounded by the ocean," he said. "I saw the power it held in the heat and waves that surrounded it. I could feel its strength, its field. It was a pure power that craved control."

"What do you mean?"

"The energy felt unstable. Thirsty." He shook his head as if the motion would release the words and make them come easier.

"Can you explain? Did you see where it is?"

"No. I feel the pull toward it, but I can't tell its direction. Especially when you're nearby. Then, all I can focus on is you."

I wrinkled my nose, embarrassed.

Was he hitting on me? Because if so, that was cheesy. But his stare was so open and honest. My face flushed.

I tried to think through everything we knew. Our powers were the same, but different. We'd seen similar things, but not exactly the same. I'd felt The Source's power, but to me that had seemed unimportant. To

Remy, it had drawn him in. He didn't know its direction, but I did. I could sense it every moment of the day. It was like a beacon pointing me toward the right path.

I feel like a compass. That's what I told Jax. The statement still feels true. It just doesn't point north.

"Do you feel the urge to go to it like I do?" I asked.

He was nodding when Eric stepped from the house. Eric scanned us, and his eyebrows rose.

Crap. My hand was still in Remy's. I shifted in my seat, using it as an excuse to pull my fingers free. I rubbed them against my cold jeans.

"Ready to go?" Eric asked.

"Not quite yet. Eric, can you sit down? I want you to see something. Remy, do you have your magnets?"

"Yeah, why?"

"I want you to show Eric. I don't think he's gotten the full story yet. Plus, I want to test something."

Shooting me a questioning glance, Remy removed the magnets from his pocket.

"Eric knows everything about my abilities. We've talked in detail about it," I explained. "Please just show him. I'll tell him everything anyway."

Remy's hair fell into his eyes as he focused on the magnets. His face evened out, and a second later, they lifted from his palm. They danced in the air, moving up and down, first in synchronization, then separately. The movements were fast and jerky.

"Since you left, we've learned a bit more. First, Remy can do what I can. We can see and manipulate electromagnetic fields. His power is a little different than mine, but I think I finally figured out why."

I reached out and grabbed the small disks. I placed them in the same orientation that he'd used. Feeling the power tingle in my palm, I focused, then flipped my hand over. They stuck. I shook my hand upside down, but the magnets stayed glued where they were.

Remy was inches from me, eyes excited. Eric had also stepped forward too and leaned into our space.

"Now watch," I said. I flipped the two magnets over, so their poles faced the opposite direction.

"It won't work that way," Remy said.

"Just watch."

The tingling of the magnetic field felt stronger on this side. It was easier to see and easier to manipulate. I pushed on it, and the magnets rose away from my skin. This time, the objects shifted smoothly around each other in a gentle circle. They separated and swirled, moving in opposite directions.

Cool. But ten seconds later, I was tired. I released my hold, and they settled on my palm once more. I glanced up and found both men's dumbfounded expressions.

"Explain, please," Remy said.

"Actually, Lenard kinda already did. You said that opposite poles of a magnet attract, right?" I laced my fingers together and rested my chin on my clasped hands. "Here's my theory. You and me? We're like this magnet, but you're one side, and I'm the other. Remy, you and I are polar opposites. That's why you can only affect the magnets in this direction."

I put the magnet down on the arm of the chair.

"And I can only affect them like this."

I put the second magnet down in the opposite direction.

"It's also why this keeps happening to us."

I lifted the magnet that represented me and held it close to the other one. Finally catching the attractive force, the one on the chair jumped to attach to the one in my hand. Out of the corner of my eye, I saw Remy's crooked smile make an appearance.

"It's physics." He winked and my face heated. "But then, what happened at the workshop?"

I ignored the grunt from Eric and said, "We're not magnets. We're human, so that means we get out of balance. Sean gave me the idea after I told him about the magnet in the field."

"What do you mean Sean gave you the idea? He's not exactly all there," Remy said.

My jaw tightened with his derision.

I ignored the comment, instead saying, "You know how we stopped to look at the one in the field on the way back? Well, Lenard said that the magnet at the car lot had its field pushed off balance, causing it to collapse. I did that. I destroyed it by changing its field to favor one direction. I think that's what happened to us. I was upset, out of balance. Sean thinks, at that moment, we were too similar, so we repelled each other. The field we created couldn't handle it, so it pushed us away from each other."

"The other night we seemed in sync, and it didn't happen then," Remy said with a wink.

I rolled my eyes. "That's not the same."

"What happened the other night?" Eric asked.

"Nothing," I snapped before Remy spoke. "But it makes sense. Think about it."

"You're right. It does," Remy agreed.

"What happened the other night?" Eric asked again.

I stood, retreating down the steps and toward the woods. I refused to look at him. "Let's go hunting."

Remy just waved off Eric's questions, then followed.

Eric caught up with me and handed me my bow. "Might need this," he said. He bumped my shoulder. "You're embarrassed."

"No," I growled. "I'm beyond confused."

I pinched the bridge of my nose and Eric chuckled, then shook my head as we walked up the hill. It was time to find Jax.

We had a great time hunting. After following Jax's trail, we split off from it to follow a hunch of mine. The path produced four jackrabbits for dinner, two by my bow and two by Eric's. Remy, though impressed, was clearly sickened by the whole process.

We were nearly home when we spotted Jax and Cassie up ahead. He towered over her, their packs at their feet. They stood inches apart, their positioning intimate. She was gazing up at him gently, her beautiful face amused. She spoke, then reached up as if to pull him down for a kiss.

A pained grunt escaped my lips. I turned my head away, but not before Eric's head snapped to me. He'd heard it. Damn.

"Ew! Cassie, don't touch that!" Eric called out. He may have said it teasingly, but Jax and I both heard the underlying note of anger.

Cassie laughed, letting go as she said, "What are you guys doing?"

"Trying to find you and get dinner."

"I see you were successful on at least one of those missions. What about the other?" Jax asked, eyes on me.

Working to keep a straight face, I held up our catch. "Come on, Jax, you think we'd come home empty-handed?" I said, voice light and playful. "What about you? Any luck?"

Cassie began to bounce on her toes. Her exuberant smile lit up the forest, and I forgot to be annoyed.

Actually, I had to hold in a laugh.

"You'd be so proud of me!" she exclaimed. "I got my first deer! I was hoping for a quail, but then we came across a deer and Jax made me try. It took three shots to actually hit it, but I got it!"

"That's great!" I said, only then noticing the animal next to Jax's pack. It was a decent size, too. Okay, I could admit I was proud of Cassie. She'd come so far in the last weeks and, regardless of the fact that part of me was jealous of her, I couldn't deny how amazing she was.

"Let's get back," Eric said. "We have some cooking to do."

As we stepped into the yard, I noticed three figures walking up the driveway.

"Remy," I said. "Louis is here."

Remy grinned and joined his friend. I tried to escape into the house, but James called out.

"Reena?" James said, leading Lenard toward me. I started to back away, but the steel in James' gaze made me pause. He wasn't going to allow a repeat of last night.

Stopping in front of me, Lenard said, "I'm sorry for the way I acted. I worry about my nephew, and he's demanding to be here. Because of you. It won't happen again." It sounded like the words hurt.

"Yeah," Eric said. "Because you won't like what happens if you do."

With a sigh, James led him away.

Over the next hour, we prepared the food. Some were grilled for dinner, and the rest was set up to be smoked. The aroma of the meat mixed in with the oak chips we'd found made my mouth water.

All but Lenard helped. He stood off to the side, glaring at the group. I tried to ignore him, but every so often a shiver would run up my spine and I'd find him staring directly at me. His nose would flare, and a look I didn't understand would flash across his face. Longing? Hunger? I didn't know, but it was creepy.

Once we were all around the fire eating, I decided it was time. The two curved concrete benches which encircled the fire held most of us, but I sat in a chair between the two, Lily and Sean flanking me. Everyone was distracted with their food and conversation was on hold. So, I spoke up. What better time was there?

Setting my nearly empty plate aside, I whispered, "It's time."

Lily leaned in and rested her head on my shoulder for a second. Sean smiled gently and nodded his encouragement.

"Hey, I need to talk to everyone," I said, projecting my voice. "About a few things."

All eyes lifted to me, and I felt like I had on stage at my fifth-grade talent show. Terrified.

"First, I'm not going to say sorry about last night." I faced Lenard. "I meant to antagonize you. I wanted to see what your true intentions are. You've been trying to get my measure since day one, and now you have it. I'm not afraid of you, but if you're going to stay with us— travel with us—then we need to figure something out, or we will never get there."

A glint of a smile and a slight tilt of his head, Lenard agreed.

I turned and scanned the group. I took a deep breath, then said, "I have made the decision that Lily and I will be leaving here in two days' time. Some others have already agreed to come with, but it's up to the rest of you if you want to join."

"Reena, you can't leave," Kim said. Shock and concern had her sitting straighter.

I cut her off. "The supplies here will not last all winter, especially now that there are so many of us. But it's not just that." I looked down at my hands, cracked and dry, and couldn't help but think they mirrored how I felt inside.

"Reena, honey. I know you think..." Kim tried again.

"Let her talk, Mom," Eric said. He sat across the fire, his elbows on his knees. He sent me a smile of encouragement.

"A lot has happened over the last few weeks. I think we've all been trying to figure it out, but I realized today that it boils down to one thing."

"And that is?" James asked. He looked as happy with me as Kim.

"The Source."

A rainbow of emotions flowed through the group. Jax, shock. James, confusion. Remy, interest. Cassie, excitement. Lenard, need.

"This is what I know. Remy, help me out if you can."

He sat a little straighter.

"The piece of Goliath that entered our atmosphere has two parts. The shell and The Source. The Source is made of a swirling, purple and yellow metallic liquid. I think the ash was part of The Source that burned off. It fell on each of us, absorbed, and for some reason—for a few of us at least—initiated certain abilities. Abilities that seem to be linked to our natural characteristics."

I looked at Lenard, continuing, "Lenard was right. The Source is power, but a power that we don't understand. It's dangerous, and we don't know what it, or these abilities, will do to us."

Jax's eyes were transfixed on me. I could feel the intent behind his gaze. I glanced away, organizing in my head the best way to continue.

"Everyone's felt the pull to The Source, but it seems like those with these abilities are pulled more strongly. But, based on what you've all told me, my pull is even stronger yet. I think that has to do with my specific ability. Remy's is nearly as strong, but I interfere with it."

"Why the two of you?" Jax asked, his voice flat.

"Because he's my polar opposite," I said simply. I summarized the conversation I'd had with Remy earlier, and the epiphany that had come from it. So, I asked Remy to pull out his magnets and demonstrate.

He moved where everyone could see him, away from the concrete seats they occupied. As he focused and worked the magnets higher and higher, something unexpected happened. A metal chair several feet away slid across the ground to stop right behind him. Without thought, he sat down on it, dropped the magnets back to his palm, and relaxed back.

We were speechless. I think every head was tilted to the side, mouths agape.

"What?" he asked at the looks.

"How did you do that?" Cassie asked.

"Do what?"

"You moved the chair to come up behind you. It was nearly ten feet away," Lenard said, his eyes bright.

Remy's confusion was obvious as he examined the chair and the lines in the snow it had made.

"I don't know."

What did this mean? Was this a new power or an extension of... Lily elbowed me in the side. *Right. Back on track.*

"Back to the point. Watch what happens when I do this," I said, bringing the attention back to me. I took the magnets, then showed them how I could do the same thing, but on the reverse poles. "That's why we feel a pull to each other."

Remy winked, and I rolled my eyes. I began to pace in front of the fire, my constant need for movement overtaking me.

"Ever since the workshop, though, I've had this need to head south. It's so strong it's almost painful. Sitting here, staying here, feels wrong. The only reason I've been able to come up with is it feels like something's wrong at The Source. It needs me—us—to fix it."

I met James' eyes. "I know this is hard to hear, and you're going to fight me on this, but I think Dad was trying to tell me something with his last words. '"Stand strong. See what you can see and set it right because truth will always point you home.'"

Jax straightened. "You don't know that. They're just words. For all you know The Source could be nothing. This is dangerous, Reena."

"He's right," James said.

"Dad knew about my powers. I think he was telling me that I needed to set right whatever is wrong with The Source." *That if I did, I could find myself again.* I pressed my fist to my chest. "I feel it, in here. I *have* to go and fix it."

"Or you could just want the power for yourself," Lenard snapped. He glared a hole through me.

I met his fierce stare. "I don't want power. I want to survive. And yes, it could kill me, but I don't think it will. I don't understand the reasons yet, or what, if anything, we're supposed to do. All I know is that it involves me and Remy. Actually, I think we need all of us."

"This is insane, Reena," Kim said.

"I know, but I'm going. I'm heading to Las Vegas and the ocean."

"The ocean?" Louis asked, speaking for the first time.

"The Source and the piece of Goliath that holds it is somewhere in the Pacific Ocean. When Remy and I repelled each other at the workshop, we saw something. I saw a vast ocean with a shimmering island of gold and purple. He saw waves that burned and froze. We both felt its power."

"And who do you think would ever go with you, little girl? Would you risk their lives for yours?" Lenard asked.

"Honestly, Lenard, I'd be surprised if you didn't come. Especially with how much you want it, but to answer your question, I don't expect anyone to risk their lives for me. Eric and Sean have already agreed to go, but they don't have to come to Goliath or find The Source. That's up to them."

James, Kim, Jax, and Cassie all turned to Eric. He just shrugged.

"She's family, and she's right. Reena's always had this weird sense for things we don't understand. Which has just gotten stronger since the ash. We've all learned to listen to it." He met his father's stare. "I know you don't like the idea of her and Lily going off alone, but it's her choice. She's a few months from eighteen and more adult than most. I trust her, and I'm going."

"Listen," I said, trying not to bristle at their protectiveness. I appreciated it, I did, but I had to do this. "If you don't want to go, you don't have to. If you want to come with us, then split off, that's fine, too. I'm going and so is Lily. I've already started gathering supplies, but tomorrow will be a big day. We need to get ready."

I lowered myself back into my chair. Lily nodded, and we waited. They deserved a moment to allow everything to sink in. I stared into the fire; the golden flames flickered high. I was about to head to bed when someone spoke up.

"I asked you on the mountain if I could go with you. Is that offer still on the table? A pyro can always come in handy." Cassie wiggled her fingers.

Smiling, I nodded.

A low gruff voice came from next to her. "You know you don't even have to ask. We can all feel something's wrong, and we won't let you go alone," Jax said. He looked up at me from under his eyelashes, and I caught my breath.

In my periphery, Kim and James were nodding in agreement.

A twitch of an uncertain smile flashed at the corner of Jax's mouth. Reluctantly, I returned it.

That was good enough for me. I stood, said good night, and headed into the house. For once, no one followed.

Chapter Twenty-Six

Every single person agreed to go, including Sydney and Camden. That brought the group to thirteen. Huge! This was going to be an interesting trip. We spent the next day tracking down supplies. With the help of the mayor, we even found a few more heavy-duty backpacks we could use. We also decided to take the litter, allowing for more supplies to be carried and insuring no one person was overburdened.

At dinner, we sat down and made a plan. From what we'd learned while listening to the ham radio, the flooding had destroyed all coastal areas as far inland as Nevada. We couldn't corroborate this, of course, but it was all we had to go on. So, we decided to first head to Madras, Oregon, a small town of what was only maybe six thousand. From there, we would decide if we wanted to take the highway leading through the mountains straight to Ontario or go through Bend and the lower lying areas. I'd listened in and added my opinion but left when Lenard had started to argue. Really, I was going to take the path that felt right, whether or not he agreed.

Needing a moment, I headed outside, choosing a path that would take me on a small loop around the property. A soft breeze brought the smell of clean pine to my nose, light and fresh. The crunch of snow under my boots whispered in combination with the wind rustling the trees. This was my favorite part of being in the northwest.

I swerved through the trees, fretting about my decision. Was I making the wrong choice by going? In putting everyone's lives in jeopardy because of some stupid feeling? Would we even be able to make it? The first leg alone was over a hundred twenty-five miles, and that was the shortest leg of the trip. A total of four days and only if everything went perfectly.

If only we had a car that worked. Then it would take hours. Unfortunately, all the vehicles we'd tried were useless. James and Lenard said that it was probably because the EMP fried all of the cars' electronics. They'd gone over in detail about how cars worked and the different parts that had probably been affected. I didn't listen to all the details. Instead, I only took note of their debate of whether an older vehicle, with fewer electronics, would work with minimal repair.

"Hey," a voice said from behind me, pulling me out of my thoughts. I turned to see Jax. His hands were tucked into his pockets, and his eyes were down. He looked nervous.

"Hey." I approached, stopping to lean on the tree beside him. Not wanting to be the first one to speak, I bit my tongue.

After a long moment, he sighed and said, "You know this is crazy, right?"

"What?" I tried to hide a smile. My tone made the edge of his lip quirk up. "Believe me, I know. It's four hundred and fifty miles to Ontario and then another three hundred and fifty-ish to Las Vegas. What was I thinking?"

I ran my hands through my hair.

"Do you really feel like you need to go? To find The Source?"

"Yes. It's driving me crazy. I have to find it because something is wrong."

"Yeah, I know. I feel it, too."

"Seriously?"

He shrugged. "I didn't think that everyone else was feeling it. Since we've been hiding whatever I can do so that Lenny doesn't find out, I couldn't tell anyone. But I've been thinking a lot and trying to practice like you told me to. You're right; there is a pull."

He paused, then looked down at me. He brushed a hair back from my face. I couldn't move.

"Not just to The Source," Jax whispered. "But to you, too. I know. I know you're not interested." His last sentence was said very quickly.

That's not exactly true, I thought. I hung my head, unable to fight or hide the regret I felt. In that moment, I wished I could understand what was happening between us. That I was strong enough to work through my feelings.

"You're my best friend, and I'll go with you. Protect you. Always. And not just because I know there's something that's important and probably dangerous about The Source, but because it's you. My Reena."

My heart jumped. He thought of me the way I did him. *My Jax.* I bit my lip, and his eyes tracked the movement.

I shifted toward the deeper forest. A few moments of awkward silence passed between us as we watched the trees sway in the breeze.

"Have you been able to control it yet?" I asked.

"No. Maybe. I don't know."

"Don't worry, it doesn't affect your cool status. Especially since you weren't all that cool to begin with." I grinned at him, and my heart swelled when he nudged me back playfully. I sobered. "Maybe you're just too important to understand it all yet. You're the final key that we can't see where it fits." I pushed off the tree and began walking. He followed me.

"I have a question," he said. "Why do you want Lenard to come with us?"

I huffed, "I don't. I want him as far away as I can, but Remy won't come if he doesn't."

"Remy," he spat, irritated.

"I know you don't like him, and that's fine. Honestly, I agree, but for some reason, he needs to be there. Lenard, on the other hand..."

"We need to watch out. He's been acting stranger than normal. And the way he looks at you and Cassie. It's not right."

"I know," I said, changing direction to head back to the house. "I still don't know what to think about this whole Remy thing. It's weird."

We headed up the stairs to bed. Before I entered my room, I watched Jax stroll down the hall to disappear through his door. Right before he passed from view, he looked back, catching my eye one final time.

When we were kids, our families went on road trips. Quick weekends or weeklong adventures, it didn't matter. They were a blast. We spent the time laughing and playing games. At least until we reached the point of no return and our irritation with each other hit our limit. That was when the arguing and games of torture started. I'd loved and hated these trips all at the same time.

This? This was different. Traveling with thirteen people, most of whom were not family, was painful. Hundreds of miles by foot over just a few days without adequate shelter, food, or running water was a completely aggravating ordeal.

We didn't make it to the first real town until the fourth day; over eighty miles from the house. Our goal had been three days, but a dangerous thunderstorm had hit on day two, stopping our progress. As we hunkered down in a small cave, away from the wind and rain, the bickering and bitter side conversations started. Everyone was sore and hungry.

Lenard had nearly started a fight with James when he'd asked for some of the pain medication for his soreness. James refused, saying that there was too little to waste. He'd ranted and raved to anyone who would listen. Unfortunately, Cassie, Remy, and Louis did. Louis seemed to just blow off what Lenard said, but Cassie seemed to agree. I was surprised when the more I watched, the more engrossed she became. It worried me. I'd thought she disliked Lenard, too.

Only twelve hours after hiding in the cave, I pushed to leave our makeshift home, the wind and snow be damned. I was convinced that if we didn't, I'd kill someone.

It was early afternoon on that fourth day when we approached a small town. We decided to take a path around it, away from the main streets in order to keep our presence unnoticed. With the trouble Dad and the others had, we didn't want to chance it. So, we made camp about a half mile east of town in a thicket of trees that topped a small hill. This spot allowed us some protection from the wind as well as blocked us from civilization.

Once set up, I noticed Cassie, Lenard, and Remy talking quietly again. I didn't know what they were talking about, but the looks they shot at some of the others made me uncomfortable. Once, Cassie had looked my way and caught my eye. Not wanting to get involved or frustrated with her, I got up from my seat and walked to a large rock that overlooked the camp. I faced away, wanting only quiet.

"Reena?" Sydney whispered, not wanting to startle me.

Internally, I sighed. "Hi, Sydney."

"Sorry to bother you, but I haven't really been able to speak with you since we left. I wanted to say I'm sorry about your dad and mom." Her voice was sad. Mom and Dad had been Sydney's friends. Their loss hurt her, too.

"Thank you." With all the effort I could muster, I pushed down the tears pressing at the back of my eyes. I didn't want to feel the pain. I just wanted—no, needed —to keep moving forward. I took a deep breath. "You know, Sydney, this is going to sound crazy, but I don't think Mom's dead."

Her surprise was apparent. "Why do you say that? I thought James said there was no sign of her."

"There wasn't."

She waited for an explanation. When I didn't provide one, she spoke. "I remember a time I went hiking with your mother at the Grand Canyon for a girl's weekend. We'd stashed water on our way down like you're supposed to, but at some point, we'd gotten lost. We couldn't find the trail back out. After a cold night under the stars, with all the water gone, your mother suddenly got this strength in her. She was always strong, but this was something else. It pushed us both to continue, to not give up. We stumbled around for hours, then suddenly, she stopped, turned in a circle, and pointed. Without a word, she walked a few hundred yards and bent down. She'd found one of our water bottles, and she'd found the trail out. Four days later, she found out she was pregnant with you."

I straightened. I'd never heard this story before.

"I see that strength and determination in you. Your father saw it, and the others see it too," she said. "You're just like them."

I couldn't speak. Sydney brushed the hair away from my face in such a motherly fashion that I felt new tears sting my eyes. She gave me a quick hug, then retreated.

I leaned back on my arms, the wind picking up. It brushed my skin and whipped my hair. The cold of it burned my cheeks as thoughts of my mother and father ran through my head. Sydney's words made me feel closer to what I'd lost.

I sat there for hours fiddling with my bow and looking out at the high desert which surrounded us. It had trees that were shorter and less dense, allowing for a clearer view. As the sun fell beneath the horizon, small fires lit the night sky. I watched them flicker, reflecting off the thick clouds and adding deep shadows to the darkness.

When someone came to relieve me from watch, I startled. I was a little sad to look away. I walked back to camp and realized almost everyone was asleep.

Kim and Remy, who were also on watch, appeared out of the darkness. Kim headed straight to the tent while Remy approached me at the fire. He wanted to speak to me, I could tell, but, without a word, I sent him a smile and followed after her.

Chapter Twenty-Seven

The next day, we headed south toward Bend. There were no signs of flooding yet, and we hoped that the path to Las Vegas would be clear. We chose our path between towns carefully. For areas with no sign of life, we followed the highway. If a building crossed our path, we gave it space. Cars sat abandoned along the highway, which made the trek eerie. They stood like sentinels, quietly watching the world move forward as they faded from existence.

We passed a crash field for a 747 airliner. The sight had been terrifying, the bodies heartbreaking. I picked up a small doll whose hair had been burned off and face had melted on one side. That had caused my chest to constrict.

Jax took the object from me and buried it with gentle hands in the ground as if it were the child who once loved it. When he stood, I popped up on my tiptoes and kissed his cheek. Then he brushed a tear I didn't know I'd shed from my cheek. We said nothing, just continued on our way, death a common sight now.

Our pace was slow after that. I stayed apart from the others as I had in days past. Remy tried to apologize for upsetting me the night before. I accepted it, but my growing insecurities surrounding Remy and Lenard told me trusting him was no longer possible.

"The town up ahead is too large to walk around. I think we should head straight through," James said.

"I agree," Kim said. "Plus, we could use a night out of the cold. Maybe we can find somewhere safe to stay."

I shook my head. "It's too dangerous. What if there are Deranged here? Like the ones before."

It was a term that had stuck. The people who had attacked Dad weren't the only ones we'd heard about acting strangely. Maybe it was just a fluke, but with more and more stories we'd overheard of people being attacked, I was beginning to believe it was something more.

"You can't be afraid forever," Lenard said. He walked past me. As he did, he leaned in and sniffed me.

I shivered. *What the hell was that? This was the second time he'd done that.* I looked to see if anyone else had seen it, but no one had.

Eric appeared at my side, leaned over, and whispered in my ear, "I am starting to think Lenard is Deranged." When Eric saw my expression, he stiffened. "I'm just kidding, Reena."

I felt sick, the heaviness in my chest like a weight on my diaphragm. Maybe Eric was right. Maybe whatever was wrong with Lenard was getting worse, and soon we'd have bigger problems on our hands.

Irritatingly, I'd lost the argument. So, through town we went. The first set of people we passed were walking from building to building. They waved, and Kim waved back. A few others just watched us suspiciously, but none approached.

We'd planned to break camp outside of the town proper, but when we reached the far end, we found a small airport. It was deserted. I stopped and stared toward the runway off in the distance. There was something about this place. Something important was supposed to happen here. The longer I looked, the more certain I became.

"Hey, guys," I called out. Those walking up ahead stopped and looked back. "I think we should stay there. It's off the main highway and looks easily defendable. Plus, if it hasn't been cleared out, there might be food."

It took me forever to convince the others, but after some very excited discussion, they agreed. Plus, with the sun already beginning to set, our day was almost over. Winter in the north meant much shorter days than I was used to.

Everything was dark inside the building with no indication that anyone had been here in weeks. We traveled along the outer wall of the main building, entering an area that would allow for a good view of the runway.

A few airplanes sat unmoving, awaiting passengers that would never come. Snow and ice from past storms crawled up tires to wrap around their landing gear. Giant icicles dangled from their wings. Cars and trucks sat forgotten both in the parking lot and along the tarmac.

"I say we stay in this room. There's plenty of space for all of us to spread out, but there we'll only need two on watch with so few exits," Eric said.

"I agree. This is the best spot so far," James said. He dropped his bag and motioned to the rest of us. "Make yourselves comfortable."

I eased the bag off my back. As mine was one of the newer bags, I held more supplies, so it was heavy. I stretched, releasing the tension in my lower back.

"I'm gonna go look around. Eric, you wanna join me?" I asked.

He nodded, and we disappeared into the terminal. We wandered in silence. When I squeaked at the sight of a tiny coffee shop near the end, Eric jumped. I giggled and ran for it.

The front shelves and drink fridges had been emptied, but the ones near the back had plenty left. Those here when Goliath hit must've grabbed anything on their way out but hadn't returned since.

"There's coffee!" I said, rummaging through the cupboards.

"Grab all of it," Eric said. "I can't believe we ran out."

"Done. I never realized how much these little coffee shops would come in handy. Or how excited I would be to find one."

Eric laughed. "Right?"

I enthusiastically gathered several pounds of coffee, tea, and snacks up in trash bags I'd found. I also gathered every bottle of water, energy drink, or protein bar I could find.

Eric went to search a nearby restaurant for food. While he was gone, I grabbed some other items that I'd been wishing for.

Deodorant and Chapstick, finally! I thought. I also gathered a hairbrush and all of the medications and batteries that were still up on the wall. A sweatshirt that was a little lighter and could easily be added to my bag was included in my haul. In case Cassie and Lily wanted one, I grabbed two that seemed about the right size. It was more than we needed, but the group could decide what they wanted to keep or just use for the night. The rest we would leave behind.

"How do you think you're going to carry all that?" Eric asked from behind me.

I turned and smiled as he pushed a cart that was full of items. I giggled at the bottles of beer that sat on top of some random food items.

"You get coffee; I get a beer."

I swear he was drooling. We loaded up our stash and headed back to the group.

Everyone cheered as they dug into the food and drinks. We ate more than we should have, but after such a long trip, it was nice to splurge on a good meal. For the first time in days, we were full. Per Eric, there was still more food in the restaurant, guaranteeing we could stock up before we left.

"How are we going to transport all of this?" Sydney asked.

I shrugged. "What we can't take, we'll leave behind for someone else." None of us wanted to abandon necessary supplies, but what option did we have?

James spoke up then. "Would any of you be interested in resting tomorrow? I have an idea that might make our trip a little easier."

"What idea?" Eric asked.

"On our way in, did you notice the hangars? Or the buildings farther out?" he asked. Eric nodded. "Well, I think I saw a few large trucks parked near them."

"Dad, none of the cars we've tried so far work," Jax said from his place along the wall. He held a beer in his hand. Silently, I wondered when Kim and James would notice or if they'd even care.

"Right, but if there's any place that might have supplies to get them working, this would be it. Let's take tomorrow and try. See if we can get one working. Maybe we can make it part or most of the way to Ontario in a car. If we fail, then we get a day of rest. We're all tired, sore, and could use a break."

"It might be worth a try," Louis said. "I can help. I used to help my dad with cars. I don't know how much

I remember, but I'm willing to be an extra set of hands."

"Great. Anyone not want to stay here tomorrow to see if we can get one working?"

A general murmur of agreement spread through the group. Even if it ended up just being a day of rest, it was worth it. We needed it.

There was only one person who didn't seem excited about the proposition. Lenard was glaring at James. I don't think it was the day of rest that bothered him, but that James alone had decided it.

As if sensing my glare, his eyes flashed to me. He spat in my direction and scowled at me until I broke eye contact.

I listened to the group talk about how they would fix the truck. Not really understanding most of what they said, I stopped listening. I would be fine walking. Not having anything to add to this conversation, I got up and walked back toward the small shop to get a book. I loved to read, and it had been a while since I'd had one all to myself. The shop was right around the corner just past the bathrooms. I'd be fine on my own.

The heavy clomp from my boots echoed in the dark hallway, the only light from my flashlight and the far-off windows. I reached the wall of books and magazines, excited about stocking up while here. I picked one up, opening it to smell the pages. I know, weird, but I loved the smell of books. My thoughts drifted to all the adventures I would soon experience.

I scanned the titles but jumped when a hand grabbed me. Startled, I spun. Wide, angry eyes burned into me. I sucked in my breath of surprise. Sweaty fingers wrapped around my wrist.

Lenard.

I stepped back automatically, hitting the display behind me. Books fell to the ground. I went for my bow, hoping to hit him with it, but realized it wasn't there. I'd stupidly left it back on my chair.

With a wicked grin, Lenard wrenched my wrist and slammed it against the wall above me. He pressed his forearm to my chest, holding me in place. His body molded against mine. I could barely move. I went to scream, but his other hand covered my mouth. I flailed and tried to free myself. He twisted my wrist, causing a burst of pain to shoot up my arm. I cried out, the muffled sound quiet in the dark.

I'd been a fool. I might be taller, but he was stronger, especially since he'd taken me by surprise.

His hot breath licked along my neck. The feel of his nose against my skin made a shiver of fear roll through me. I cringed away. The light from my fallen flashlight shone toward us, distorting his face with shadows. It added a deranged quality to his features. When he spoke, his voice was quiet, grave with intent.

"I can see why Remy is fascinated by you. You're beautiful," he said.

"Let go of me," I said, muffled by his hand. I struggled again.

"But what he doesn't seem to get is that you are weak. You aren't willing to make the sacrifices that need to be made to win this game."

I bit his hand. With a curse, he released my mouth, grabbing my face and squeezing it between his fingers. My cheeks ached with the pressure.

"Game?" I asked. "This isn't a game."

"Oh, yes, it is. It's a game of survival, and I intend to win. I will get The Source, and I'll not only survive, but I'll thrive. I will have power. So much power. And I'm going to take yours first." Each word was forced through his teeth. Even in the dim light, I could see the insanity in his eyes.

Deranged, I thought.

"You're crazy. Maybe the reason The Source didn't choose you is because you aren't worthy. It knew you were unstable."

He let out a growl, and I could feel it through my chest where he pressed into me. When he spoke, spittle sprayed into my face.

"And when I have the power, I will kill you."

I turned my face away. My entire body shook. I tried to get control of it but couldn't. I did not want this man to touch me, but I was trapped. I let out a cry for help.

Instantly, he slapped me across my face, cutting it off. Blood leaked from where he'd split my lip. I gasped. A sob caught in my throat. I had to get out of this.

My knife! Only then did I realize that, though the arm at my side was pinned, the hand was still loose. I could move it, if only a little. I shifted it slowly down toward my belt as Lenard was distracted. His touch trailed up my body from my hip, up my side to tangle in my hair.

Tears came to my eyes. My hand crept closer to what I knew was hidden there.

He yanked my head to the side, pressed the pad of his thumb to the blood at my lip, and then licked it clean.

"You taste like power." His voice vibrated with cruelty. His pupils constricted as he let out a sigh of relief. I whimpered and renewed my attempts to struggle.

Just a little farther, I thought. *Almost there.*

A shout from the left startled us. "Hey! Get off her!" Remy's voice reverberated through the hallway.

Right then the switchblade in my belt flew into my hand. In one motion, I opened it and kicked upward, aiming for his groin. The hit landed solidly, and he let out a cry of pain.

He pulled away.

I shoved my shoulder into him and swung my knife at his face. My aim was good. Red gushed from the slice across his cheek. Blood splattered my shirt. He let out a scream of pain and staggered back. I didn't slow or stop. As he released me completely, I moved. Bringing up my elbow, I slammed it into his temple. He fell to the floor.

I heard running steps and voices coming toward us, but I didn't care. I ignored them all. I was already moving toward my attacker.

No. My victim.

I kicked Lenard in the side. Once. Twice. My anger and fear overtook me. Hearing my name again, I stopped kicking and knelt on his chest, pinning him. My knife pressed into his jugular.

A trickle of red escaped from under my blade. He shrieked as I dug my knee deeper into his chest. The knife nicked his neck again, and he froze.

"Do not think me a weak, helpless girl," I spat. "Because I promise, you ever touch me again, you ever talk to me again, and I swear to God, I will slice your throat open and dance in the blood spilling from your body. Do you understand me?" The harshness in my voice scared even me. I didn't recognize it. It was someone I didn't know. Someone strong and cruel. Someone as dark and twisted as the man in front of me. Lenard's eyes went wide.

I stayed there, the knife pressed to his throat, waiting for his response. His breathing was labored as he fought the weight of my knee on his chest.

When no response came, I asked again, louder this time, "Do you understand?"

He choked a strangled "yes."

I pulled the knife back a little. I stared hard into him, looking for any sign of deceit.

Suddenly, a hand touched my shoulder, and I jumped backward away from them. I swung the knife up at the newcomer and retreated farther into the store. The figure skittered back from my blade.

When I looked up, a crowd stood a few feet away, staring at me with concern, the many flashlights they held illuminating their faces. Everyone was there. Everyone, a look of shock and horror in their eyes.

I began to shake. My breaths came hard and quick. Painful. My hands trembled so violently the knife fell from my hand with a loud *clink* on the tile floor.

Remy took a step toward me.

I skittered to grab the knife again, then shuffled backward, the wall hitting my back.

"You stupid whore!" Lenard screamed. He held his face, trying to staunch the blood pouring from the gash. His other hand, already swollen. "How dare you! How dare you!"

Before I had the chance to even register what he'd said, Remy kicked out, silencing him. Eric and James rushed forward, grabbed him, and dragged him away.

As they passed Jax, he rushed forward, fists clenched, but two figures stopped him. In my darkened haze, I couldn't tell who. One leaned in and said something, which caused his gaze to shift to me. I barely registered, my brain still focused on the sound of Lenard's angry cries echoing through the hallway.

Remy squatted down to my level.

"Reena." Remy's voice was gentle. He stepped forward again.

"No!" I screamed, my voice shaking. I lifted the knife protectively. The blade shook in rhythm with my body. I gasped at the sight of my hands covered in Lenard's blood.

"Remy, get back," another voice demanded. It was familiar. Comforting. In my fog, though, I couldn't figure out why until a small form stepped forward. Kim.

"Everyone back. Go back to the terminal and wait," she said, but no one moved. "Now!" She ordered.

They jumped and started away. Lily stayed behind. She walked up to Kim, exchanged glances, then Kim nodded in understanding. Lily wasn't going anywhere.

Only one other disobeyed. Jax stayed where he'd been when Kim, I now realized, had kept him from attacking Lenard. He shook with fury, but it was the concerned shock written over his face that cracked something inside me.

"Reena, honey, I need you to drop the knife." Kim approached me with hands up, as you would a dangerous animal.

I blinked quickly. I took in a deep breath. And another. Long moments passed, and eventually the shaking slowed.

Again, Kim asked me to drop the knife. I wanted to, but my fingers wouldn't listen. When my hand finally responded, a weak cry left my lips. The knife fell from my fingers, clattering to the ground, the metal glimmering. Even in the dimness, the dark crimson of Lenard's blood was plainly visible. Kim took a few steps toward me.

"Reena, it's okay. We've got you." Her hand caressed my face.

A terrified squeak escaped my lips. From one breath to the next, all energy drained from my body. I slid to the floor.

Kim knelt to my right. Her arms encircled me, and I leaned into her embrace. I felt Lily on my other side. She slipped her hand into mine. Realizing Lenard's blood would get on Lily, I tried to pull away and wipe it off. She refused.

"It's okay, Reena," she said, keeping hold of my hand.

"Reena, I need to know. Did he hurt you?" Kim asked. I shook my head. "He didn't hurt you? Are you sure?"

"He was going to. He caught me off guard. I should have been smarter. I..."

"No, Honey, this isn't your fault."

"I... I shouldn't have been over here by myself. I didn't realize that anyone saw me go. If it hadn't been for Remy, I'm not sure I could've gotten that kick in to get him off me. Then the knife..."

Lily squeezed my hand. "You did what you had to. He'll think twice before he comes near you again."

"Not that he'll get the chance." Kim growled.

You did what you had to, I thought. The conversations I'd overheard the last few days with Cassie, Lenard, and Remy came back to me. It mirrored what they'd said. Was I like him? I shook my head as if it would release that fear.

"I need to get out of here," I said, pulling away from Kim and Lily to stand.

When I straightened, I realized that Jax still hadn't moved. He took a step forward, but then stopped. With wobbly legs I approached him, Kim and Lily flanking me. Jax's eyes watched me, his face a mask of anger. It was physically hard for me to look at him. I felt stupid. I felt dirty. Was he mad at me? My arms hung down at my sides, my head down. I couldn't look at him, but I also couldn't walk away.

"I was vicious. Cruel," I whispered.

His hand rose slowly to my face but hesitated as if afraid I would flinch. I held still, unable to meet his eyes. His hand brushed my face, pushing back the hair.

"I'm so sorry I wasn't there to protect you," he said, so quietly I had trouble making it out. My breath hitched. He kept his hand on my face until I repeated in a whisper,

"I was vicious and cruel."

"No. You were amazing and strong. You protected yourself." When I started to shake my head, he added, "You're not like him."

Kim inhaled sharply at the realization of what I truly thought.

I took a reluctant step closer to him. His hand fell to my shoulder, but he didn't push me. I wrapped my arms around him, and without hesitation, he pulled me to him, his face pressing to my hair. He held me, repeating in my ear, "you're not like him" over and over. I didn't cry. I just stood there, listening to him whisper to my soul. His warmth and support brought the trembling to a complete stop. My breathing finally returned to normal.

A shift in the shadows caught my attention. I looked toward the terminal, where everyone had disappeared. I could see the outline of two people looking around the corner. I stepped back and gave Jax a small smile.

"Can you get me something to read? That's why I came over here. I..." I swallowed hard. "You know what? Never mind."

"I'll grab something. You go back, and I'll bring it to you." With one last brush of my cheek, he stepped away.

With Lily by my side, I headed back at a slow crawl. Reaching the shadows where I'd spotted movement, Cassie and Remy stepped into my path.

"Are you okay?" Remy asked. His face was stricken.

"Yeah. Fine. Thanks for coming when you did."

"I didn't do anything. You did."

"You yelling made him step back, giving me the opportunity to get away. Not sure what would've happened otherwise," I admitted, glancing away.

"Is Jax all right?" Cassie asked, not looking at me.

"Yeah. He's just having a hard time resisting the urge to beat the crap out of Lenard. You know how protective he is of Lily and me."

"A little too protective of you, isn't he?" Her voice was so quiet I almost missed it.

"What?" *Had I heard right?*

She turned to me with a sad smile. "I'm just glad you're all right. Lenard's crazy. Thank goodness you know how to protect yourself."

Her comment brought me back to my fight with Lenard. It made me feel awful to think that I could do that to someone. Even someone who was going to hurt me. But she was right. I was lucky my dad and Jax demanded I take self-defense lessons. When I was a freshman in high school, I'd been mugged on the way home from a concert. Jax had been so furious that I'd walked to my car without anyone. He talked my dad into starting them. I'd hated them and been angry with Jax for proposing it, but I'd taken it seriously. The moves they'd taught us were fun to learn and effective. I guess I just proved that.

"Yeah. Well," was all I could say.

Reaching the terminal, I felt every eye on me. Instead of looking down, I met the stares. Some were impressed. Some were scared. I just couldn't tell if the fear was for me or of me. I stopped when I met the eyes of James and Eric who, the last time I'd seen them, had been helping to drag Lenard away.

"Where?" I asked.

"We have him restrained. He's in a room on the other side. Dad got him stitched up and tied to a desk."

"He doesn't deserve medical treatment," Lily snapped. I flashed her a scolding look.

"No, but don't worry. That cut is gonna hurt like hell for a while."

I nodded, still not wanting to acknowledge what I'd done. "Can you go talk to Jax? He needs calming down," I said to Eric.

"Okay." Eric leaned in and kissed my forehead. "Go get some sleep. Someone will be with you at all times. Though I'm not sure if it's necessary with how well you fight."

"You better remember that," I said in a sad attempt at a joke. I still felt numb, and my voice was too flat.

Sean led us to the far side of the group where I'd set up my sleeping area by the window. When I sat down, Sean handed me a washcloth to clean the blood off my hands.

Lily grabbed another one. She leaned in and wiped my face. "You have a split lip. Did he hit you?"

I gulped at the reminder of how Lenard had first hit me, then licked me. Why? And I had to push down the urge to panic all over again.

"Reena. Can you see it?" Sean asked. He was speaking better than usual, but his speech was still too quick. "Cassie and Remy?"

Back home, Sean had told me to watch everyone and how they were changing. He thought it was related to the abilities we all had. He'd been concerned that the more we used them, the more they would affect us.

"Yeah, Cassie's acting weird."

"And Remy's been practicing any time no one's watching. Even he's acting stranger than usual," Lily added.

"I've been hearing Remy and Lenard feeding Cassie lines, trying to turn her against you. No one else, just you," Sean added.

"Why? I'm nothing special."

Lily shot me a look. "Are you kidding me? Yes, you are. The whole group takes what you say and truly listens. You're the closest thing to a leader we have— though you don't seem to know it."

"But I'm all right. Relatively anyway?" At least I hoped I was. I hadn't noticed any major change in my behavior. Had I?

"Yes, but you're different from the rest. You only show physical damage after you really push your powers. Like when you heal someone," Sean said.

Different. I rubbed my face, thinking about what he was saying. *It was true. I seemed able to push myself further than the others.*

"Maybe my body has just figured out what this is. It seems like when I work my abilities, there's some outward effect instead of an internal reaction. Like the ice on the ground in the hospital or the trees in the forest."

"Maybe," Lily said. Her skin began to pale.

"Okay, that's enough, Lily, drop the focus. I want to rest."

Lily smiled. She knew I didn't like her using her power. Especially with knowing the effects it had on people. We fell silent, but they stayed with me. Sean the guard for us both.

Sometime later, Jax, Eric, and Cassie returned. I was calmer now and just wanted to relax. Lily and Sean had gone to help Kim with something after I'd insisted. So, I sat alone, Louis watching over me from afar. Eric looked tired. Jax still looked angry.

He approached with a few magazines and four books. I smiled at the armful and moved over to give him some space beside me.

He set them down, then sat next to me. Cassie sat on his other side. The choices of reading material made me laugh. He'd gotten me some interesting options.

"I know you have varied tastes, so I grabbed some I knew you'd like, and some Cassie thought you might like."

I picked up what could only be called a trashy romance novel. The half-naked man had abs that were obviously Photoshopped. His hair blew in the wind, and he wore chaps that promised more.

"Really?" I asked, trying not to laugh.

"That one was me. It's actually really good. I think you'll like it," Cassie said. "It has cowboys."

"I figured. Okay, I'll read it first. That way we can make inappropriate jokes about it on the next leg of the trip. Try to see how uncomfortable we can make Jax."

She grinned. "I wanted to bring the *Sexiest Men Alive* magazine, but he said no." The disappointment in her voice made me chuckle.

"Why would she need that when she has us around?" Remy asked, taking a seat next to Eric on one of the chairs in front of us. Eric rolled his eyes.

"Cocky much?" Cassie asked.

"Oh, come on. It's not just me. I mean, look at Louis over there. How can you resist him?"

Louis had fallen asleep sitting up. His face was slack, and a line of drool dripped from his mouth and onto his shirt.

"Sexy," Cassie agreed.

"Oh, yeah. And I have to say, the snow pants and parkas are so my thing," I said sarcastically, shifting to lean on Jax.

His arm wrapped around me; his hand moved to rub my lower back. His touch comforted me more than I wanted to admit, and my nerves settled. Then, exhaustion hit me in a wave. I yawned and I moved to lie down. I stretched my legs out away from Jax, then settled my head on his thigh.

Cassie watched me, and a moment later, she imitated my position, her head on Jax's other thigh. He didn't mind. His fingers ran up and down my arm, lulling me into sleep. My eyes became heavy, and my breathing slowed.

I was almost asleep when I heard Remy say, "It's got to be hard having two women fight over you." Remy tried to sound jovial, but his voice had a hint of jealousy.

"They aren't fighting over me," Jax said.

"You have two beautiful women sleeping on your lap, and you say they aren't fighting over you?"

"Cassie is, maybe, but Reena... Even if she were, she's my best friend. It would be weird."

I opened my eyes as little as I could. Eric still sat next to Remy, lounging back. His face was impassive. He knew the truth. Remy shook his head, irritated, and got up.

"You tell that lie so well, Little Brother."

"It's not a lie," Jax whispered. "She's not interested."

"You know her better than that. There's just a lot going on, and she is trying to stay strong. Doing a hell of a job, too."

I felt Jax's hand brush through my hair, the motion so tender.

"That's not what I got from her slapping me in the face."

"That was you being an idiot," Eric said.

"Oh yeah, Eric? And what do you know?"

"I know that you know her better than that. Open your eyes and look at her. Stop being stupid," Eric snapped. He stood and walked away.

I could hear Cassie's soft snores as she slept, but it was Jax's breathing I paid attention to. With Eric's last comment, it had sped up. Still, his hand played at the hairs along my temple. Once he calmed his breathing, he moved Cassie's head off his lap and gently guided mine onto a jacket. He leaned down and whispered in my ear.

"I wish you could see that I'm the one not good enough for you." His lips pressed to my forehead for a long moment. Then he walked away.

Chapter Twenty-Eight

For such a small airport, they had great facilities. We'd been exploring the airstrip and found four large hangars filled with top-of-the-line equipment. Next to them along the landing field were small planes of all shapes and sizes. From the look of it, no one had been in the area in weeks.

"This one might work if we get it to the hangar," Louis said about one of the few potential trucks we'd found.

"I'm not sure that would get us far. Plus, I doubt everyone would fit in it," James said.

"I agree with James," I said, strolling past them. I stared off into the distance, where another set of large buildings stood. Excitement ran through me as I noticed a line of maybe thirty trucks surrounding them. There was something else there too, but I wasn't convinced I was seeing it correctly.

"I think I might have a better idea," I said, interrupting. I squinted, as if that would clarify what I saw. No help. I sighed, then extended my senses, hoping I could learn more about these vehicles or the area around them. The others joined me.

Aha! I knew it. Someone was moving around.

"We have to be careful," I said.

"What is it?" James asked. "Wait, are those military trucks?"

"Looks like it. And a lot of them. Even a few tanks."

"Tanks?" Remy asked, stepping forward.

"Yeah, but that isn't what concerns me."

"Then what does? What can you see?" James asked.

"The only difference between what you see and what I see is the energy, if there is any, and"—I paused —"there are three people moving around. Remy, can you verify?"

"I see two," he said. He paused, then continued. "Nope. You're right. Three."

"Can you tell anything about them?" Cassie asked.

"No, we're too far away. It's not a military base or anything; it looks like just another hangar, but that can't be right. Can you guys tell what's behind the building?"

"No," James said.

"Did you see that?" Remy asked suddenly. "At the far side on the left?"

"A dog," I said, nodding. The low-lying movement ran from an opening door and out to one of the people, only to circle the building. I watched as it ran the perimeter. "A big dog."

I had a bad feeling about this. I rubbed my eyes and turned to James.

"I don't think everyone should go. Eric, why don't..." James said as he started to walk.

I stopped him. "I'm going, too. I can tell you if anything weird is going on."

Just like that, everyone started arguing. Remy wanted to go instead of me, stating that it was too dangerous to send our best hunter. Cassie wanted to go because she was a good weapon with her fire. Everyone, including Sean and Louis, added their opinion on who should go. I watched in amazement as the order we'd held all day disintegrated. We needed someone to step up and take charge. I guess that person was me.

"Everyone, stop arguing," I snapped. I stood tall, my hands on my hips. "Remy and I are going so that we have an extra eye on the situation. Jax is our protection. And James, you're the speaker for the group. Louis, take Lily back to camp and check on Sydney and Camden. Cassie, Sean, and Eric will hang back and watch. If everything goes fine, then we'll need you to get the hangar ready."

Eric nodded. "I agree. We don't need them thinking we're attacking. Too many might cause that."

"Exactly," I said.

After some final grumbles, that's what we did. Jax, Remy, James, and I headed toward the long line of trucks. The others watched as we disappeared.

"Make sure you both stay behind me," Jax said.

"And what are you gonna do, Jax?" I had to bite back a retort at Remy's condescending tone.

Jax clenched his jaw. "If needed, save your ass."

He didn't elaborate. He just stood tall and proud. As we walked, I felt the power he began to pull from around him. The air tingled near him, the hairs on my arms standing up. Remy grumbled under his breath, completely unaware of what was happening next to him.

Remy is so oblivious.

We were two hundred yards out when a man dressed in winter camouflage stepped from behind the closest truck. He had a rifle slung over his shoulder, and a pistol clipped to his belt. His hand hovered near it. A small scar at the corner of his mouth quirked his lip up, making him both handsome and more feral. The dog stepped in front of the man, his growl deep and menacing.

With quick motions, I informed the others of where his companions were. Their energies varied from the blue of the man in front of us to a red of someone behind the far tank.

"Hello," I said sweetly, almost instantly breaking from the plan. "You know, it's not polite to point guns at people."

His eyebrows rose in question. "I'm not pointing a gun at you. Yet."

"No, but your friend over there has a rifle pointed at me and the gentleman over there"—I pointed in the direction opposite the tank—"has a pistol aimed at my friend here. We're not here to fight. And I don't appreciate it. It's rude."

"Don't forget about the woman on the roof," Remy said. I looked up, and yes, there she was, the nose of her rifle just visible.

The man seemed surprised by our easy identification of his companions. "Then why are you here? There aren't any supplies. It's not like shooting ranges keep much food lying around. Anything else you might find has already been claimed."

Shooting range, ah. That explains the odd-looking equipment behind the building. I stepped forward to stand next to Jax. He stopped me from going any farther.

"We're interested in one of your trucks," James said.

"What?" The man laughed. "Why? None of them work."

"We figured that, but we want to try to get one running. We'll be heading out in the next few days and having one or two of these would make things a great deal easier. That's of course if you aren't using them."

While James talked, my focus fell on the dog. The dog growled at James and the others as they spoke, but as I watched him, he focused on me. He was a mutt. Some large breed mix that reminded me of a wolf or a Siberian husky. He was beautiful. The black mask of fur that surrounded its one blue and one golden eye made its face just a little unnerving. Its ears stood up, twitching every so often.

James' voice faded away, the conversation suddenly unimportant. The dog took slow steps toward me. It tilted its head right to left, as if trying to hear something. I could feel the interest in its gaze. I stepped forward, the dog only a foot away now. Not wanting to startle it, I held perfectly still. It leaned in to sniff my hand. I heard Jax's warning, but I didn't listen. I knelt to its level, then made eye contact with the beast.

When its long, wet tongue shot out and licked my face, I laughed. After wiping the drool off my cheek, I reached up and touched the dog's face. His eyes closed, enjoying the sensation of hands on his ears. The dog continued to lick me, and I began to scratch its neck.

"Well, aren't you a sweet boy?" I asked the dog. He knocked me over and half crawled into my lap, demanding more attention. I adjusted the bow I always carried on my back, ensuring I didn't break it or be impaled by it.

Giggling as he snuggled me, I looked up to find everyone gawking. Even those who, seconds before, had been pointing guns at me, had come out from their hiding spots. They approached slowly, weapons pointing to the ground. I stopped laughing and worked to stand up. The dog pushed me down again.

"Okay, okay, boy." I kissed his snout, then said, "I think we've freaked your owners out enough. Go sit next to them. Make them feel better."

To my astonishment, that's exactly what he did. He walked over and sat at the foot of the man in camouflage, a doggy smile on his face. The man looked at me like hell had frozen over, and I was the one who'd caused it. Or, like I was the devil incarnate.

"What did you do to my dog?"

"Nothing," I said, confused. "He's a good boy."

"No, no, he ain't," the man who'd been hiding behind the tank said. "In fact, he doesn't like anyone. Ever. He tolerates Jeff, but only barely."

This man was short with brown eyes that overlooked a prominent nose. He had short-cropped, jet black hair. As if to prove his point, the dog growled at him. Jeff put his hand down on the top of the dog's head and scratched. The noise stopped, but only grudgingly.

"This is Miko, and I'm Jeff. That's Cleat and Sam; Sonja is up top. What's your name, miss?"

"I'm Reena, and these are my companions, James, Jaxson, and Remy." I gestured to each as I spoke.

"I would like to say it's nice to meet you, Miss Reena, but to be honest, I'm a little worried about what you did to my dog. I'm not sure if it means I should trust you or shoot you," he said honestly. "Miko doesn't like anyone."

"It would be a waste of bullets. We aren't here to hurt you or take what's yours. Like James said, we're here for the trucks, and your dog is loyal to you."

Jeff thought about that for a few moments, his fingers still in Miko's fur.

"Now, James said you're in need of two trucks, correct? What are the four of you going to do with two trucks?"

"We have others resting back at our camp. We've been traveling from the north and are headed toward warmer weather. When we saw the trucks, we thought it might be worth a shot." Jeff squinted as I mentioned the others.

"Based on the way you're acting, Jeff, I get the feeling like you've had some trouble around here. Am I right?" Jax asked.

Jeff and Cleat looked at Jax as if seeing him for the first time. They took in his height, then the size of his shoulders. Standing next to the slimmer and shorter Remy, he looked huge.

I had to hold back a smile at the look Cleat shot Jeff. Snickering, I said, "Don't worry, Cleat, you get used to our size eventually."

Cleat grinned. "Y'all are some big people."

Jeff smirked at our teasing, then got back on topic. "Yes, we've had a few people come through town. Most moved quietly though without incident, but a few groups seemed"—he paused—"Deranged. They attacked the main hall and killed a few people."

Deranged. That word again. Who were these people?

Jeff continued, "That's why we're out here. Our leaders decided we needed to gather as much protective gear as possible."

"By protective gear, you mean guns," I said.

"Yes."

"And did your leaders request any of the trucks to be brought back?" James asked.

"Nope, they're not much use in their current condition. Right now, they have more important things to focus on." He took a long breath to gather his thoughts. "Here's the deal. In exchange for letting you take two trucks, and if by some miracle you get them to work, we want to know what you did. Cleat can help you. He has some mechanical experience."

"That sounds fair. We could use all the help we can get."

"But I want Miss Reena to give me her word. No offense, James, but Miko has a good sense of people. I've never seen him act like that with another person."

The group fell silent as they turned to me. Internally, I sighed. *Why in the world did this keep happening? Even strangers were now looking to me for advice, for my word.*

"You want my word that we'll not bother you or your supplies, and show you how to get the truck working if we succeed? Okay, then I want a guarantee of safety while we're here. We do not want your supplies, but that does not mean you aren't interested in ours." I stood at my full height. "While we work to get the trucks working, you will keep your people from bothering us. If you do this, we'll leave your people and your stash of 'supplies' alone. We'll be out of your hair in two days."

Sam and Cleat looked at Jeff as he thought about what I'd said. His brows were pinched in concentration, making them look like two giant caterpillars on his face. His brown eyes were thoughtful. Just as Jeff was about to speak, the door to the building behind him slammed open.

A man in a blood-red coat rushed out. "How dare you come back here! How dare you! You killed my sister, you bastards!" the man screamed, running toward us.

Jeff cursed. Cleat and Sam stepped in his path, but he swerved easily around them. Just as he passed Cleat, the man pulled his arm up to reveal a gun and pointed it straight at me.

Jax immediately placed his hand on my back. In the next second, a wave of energy spread up my spine. It made my whole body tingle.

The gun went off. Three quick pops pointed straight for me. Energy burst from Jax as he stepped between me and the oncoming attack. The wave of energy thrust from him, expanding as it had that day on the mountain.

I heard Remy and James cry out as they were pushed toward the ground and out of the line of fire. Without meaning to, I unfocused my eyes, hoping to see everything. My breath caught.

Jax was holding a shield of energy. It encircled us in a steady sphere of pale green light. With each pulse I felt against my skin, the light and strength of the sphere was reinforced. James and Remy were on the ground behind the protective bubble of power. Safe enough for now.

Three flashes followed by ripples in the colored light. Something small fell to the ground.

Holy crap buckets, Jax was fast. He'd pulled up the shield quick enough to stop bullets!

I looked over Jax's shoulder to see Cleat tackle the man in red. Jax's eyebrows were furrowed in concentration, his face straining with effort. Keeping his hand on my back, Jax led me forward. He walked to stand next to our assailant. Suddenly, another burst of energy flashed from him. It pushed Cleat to the side, then pinned the man in red to the ground. The shield pushed harder until the man stopped and looked up.

"Listen!" Jax shouted. Getting hold of his anger, he spoke softer, calmer. "We're not the people who killed your family, and I will not let you kill mine."

The man in red squeaked sharply, terrified and unable to see what held him down. Miko stepped into the sphere next to me, then began to growl at him, too.

Good boy, Miko. I growled along with him, though not as convincingly.

"You shot at us," I said. The voice from the night before was back again, harsh and cruel. I lifted my bow and aimed for his chest. "I don't know who you are, and I don't especially care. You're the second person to try to kill me today, and I'm getting real tired of it. Listen to me now. I am not the person who killed your sister, and neither is anyone in my group."

I held my stance, the arrow pointed for his heart. His eyes reflected terror back at me. Good.

"I have made a deal with your friend here, and we will abide by it." I took a deep breath, hoping my next choice was the right one. "And the first way to do that is by letting you go. But, Jeff." I didn't take my eyes off my prey. "I would highly recommend that your friend here gets away from us and has his gun taken away. I will not let him try to kill me or anyone else again. He comes at me, and I will put him down."

My eyes lifted to Jeff for just a second. He assessed me, my tone, my stance, my integrity. He nodded. I lowered my weapon, then lifted my hand to Jax's arm.

"That's enough, Jax. Let go."

For two long breaths, Jax held it, then slowly, I felt him pull his energy back in. A small amount of power lingered over my skin, a thin layer of protection. I squeezed his arm and stepped around him to face the others. Jax's fingers stayed pressed to my back.

"And what is a young girl like you gonna do?" the man asked. Cleat yanked his arms behind his back, but then—in an almost comical way—it seemed to dawn on our attacker that neither Jax nor I were hurt. He shrunk back into Cleat.

With a wicked smile, I said, "You've already seen what one of us can do. Do you really want to find out what I can do?"

"How?"

"That's none of your concern. What is your concern is getting away from us."

Jeff nodded to Sam. "Get him out of here."

Sam did as he was told, the two men disappearing back inside the building.

To Jeff, I asked, "Well, do we have a deal?"

Jeff's eyes were narrowed as he looked at me. His gun had been lowered but was ready and waiting. A few minutes passed as he debated. Finally, he holstered his gun and held out his hand to me. I shook it.

Jeff was good to his word. Two trucks were provided as well as some extra parts he'd found inside. He and his men even helped to push the first one the half mile to the hangar. That had taken all of us; the damn truck was massive.

When we got there, Eric had everything organized. The toolboxes had been pushed over for easy access, a table with the extra parts set up near it. He'd even set up a fire to warm the large room and prepared lunch.

Eric asked how everything went, but we stayed silent. It was on everyone's minds, but we all knew that was not the time to discuss. The group spent the rest of the day looking over the truck. I sat with Cassie and Remy as the others worked; we were completely useless. Eventually Jeff and Sonja went back to the range.

As night approached, I told Jax that our band of slackers were heading back to camp. Cassie gave Jax a quick kiss on our way out. As she walked away, Jax met my eyes. In that instant, I wished I'd been the one he'd embraced. That I'd been the one he'd kissed.

We walked back to the terminal in silence. Remy looked ready to burst with questions. So, I wasn't surprised when a few minutes into the walk he broke down and started throwing questions at me. We told Cassie what happened and, after a minor freak out, I assured her Jax was fine. Remy was shocked we'd known all along, but also seriously impressed at Jax's skill.

We entered the terminal and found Sydney working on a fire. Inside. It was set up at the end of the great room, a broken upper window allowing the smoke to escape. It was a smart idea. Having the fire inside and contained made the whole room warmer. Sydney was cooking some sort of stew over it, and my stomach growled at the scent.

Kim sat with Sean near the fire, Lenard tied to a chair next to them. A bright white bandage covered his cheek. He leered at me as I passed, but I ignored him.

After replaying the day to both Kim and Sean, I retreated to my bedroll. I pulled out the book Cassie had picked out and began to read. Unable to sleep, I spent the next few hours with my nose in the book.

Jax came back late, everyone already asleep. Even Lenard, who had been moved to the ground and tied to a railing along one of the walls, snored quietly. Jax sat between Cassie and me, leaning his head back, exhausted.

"Lie down. I'll take watch," I said.

"You're tired, too."

"Yes, but I have this amazing novel to keep me awake," I said, winking. "I'm sure that this will keep me plenty alert."

I started to read aloud until the section became so inappropriate that I had to stop. I started to laugh, and my face reddened. He just grinned, then moved to lie down next to me.

I reached out and, without thinking, played with his hair. It was just as I'd done when we were children. So many nights we'd spent together reading. Our parents would find us sleeping on the couch. Me, sitting up, a book in one hand and the other tangled in his curls. Him, as fast asleep as I was, a book on his chest. I snorted. His beautiful eyes scanned me.

"A good part?"

"No," I said, grinning. "Do you remember when we were maybe twelve or thirteen and you were staying at our house? We were both reading and almost in this exact position. I think I was reading the first Harry Potter?"

"And you braided dozens of tiny braids in my hair as I slept?" The irritation in his voice made me chuckle. "It's not funny. It took me days to get them all out because Mom wouldn't help. She said, 'if you let Reena do that to you, it's your own fault.'"

I laughed out loud, quickly covering my mouth with my hand to muffle the sound and keep from waking the others. An uncontrolled grin spread across his face. I leaned down to him.

"I could do it again." I reached out to grab a lock of his hair.

"No, no, no!" He grabbed both my hands, inadvertently pulling me closer. We froze at the nearness.

My gaze locked on his lips. I couldn't help it; I was drawn to them. Forcing my gaze up to his, I found the same longing mirrored in his eyes.

His thumb ran along the sensitive skin at my wrist. Without breaking eye contact, he brought my hand to his lips, and he kissed my fingers.

Sparks shot up my arm. A sharp breath forced its way out. With that, he released my hands and rolled to face away. I sat back, trying to catch my breath. I shifted so that he could rest his head on my thigh.

He welcomed it. He ran his cheek along my thigh, then sighed deeply, his hand resting on my knee. I reached out again to play with his hair. It was so soft. His body relaxed at my touch, and when his breathing slowed with sleep, I reached down to add one braid right at the base of his neck just behind his ear.

I watched over him until early morning when Sydney took over watch. The world faded away right as the sun began to peak over mountains.

Chapter Twenty-Nine

The sun was high when I awoke. The sound of everyone moving around pulled me from my restless sleep. I scanned the space, slowly settling back into the land of the living. Jax stood with Remy discussing heading back to the hangar. Cassie dug through the bucket of supplies, Lily was reading, and Lenard...

"Jax," I said, and panic filled me. Recognizing my tone, he turned.

"What's wrong?"

"Is it just me, or are we missing someone? Please tell me you moved him to another room." My voice rose in volume; my breath quickened. Everyone searched for the man who'd been tied to the wall.

"Who was watching him?" Jax asked.

"Sydney and Camden," Kim said, her voice worried. "Maybe they went to the bathroom or something."

"Please tell me she's armed," I demanded.

"He wouldn't hurt her," Remy said.

"The bruise from where he struck me would say otherwise," I said harshly. "We need to find them."

Everyone was up and moving. I bent to gather my bow and arrows, then confirmed that the three knives

I'd been carrying the last few days were still in place.

"Reena," Remy said quietly to me. "He wouldn't hurt her. He isn't cruel; he just made a mistake with you. He's just fascinated by you for some reason."

"Remy, you need to get it through your head that he *is* dangerous. Not just to me, but to everyone. There is something wrong with him, and it's getting worse. Right now, he's with Sydney and Camden, and we don't know if they're armed."

Before he could say anything that would piss me off, I stalked away. His loyalty to Lenard was ridiculous, and my patience with it was coming to an end.

We split into two groups. I kept Lily with me but made Jax promise to protect her first. Sean also agreed to watch out for her. Regardless, Jax stayed glued to my side.

A few minutes in, we found Camden unconscious on the far side of the airport. A large gash along his scalp oozed crimson down his face in dark streaks.

I ran, skidding to my knees beside him. He was unconscious but breathing. I pulled a cloth from my bag and pressed it to the wound. Sean appeared on the other side of him.

"Hold this. We're gonna to keep looking. Sydney has to be here somewhere," I whispered.

Sean nodded, then pressed the cloth to the wound. Camden moaned. Stepping away, I headed toward the back doors, which led outside. Jax stayed close, his hunting rifle drawn. Deeper we went. Along the far wall, a door flapped in the wind.

I signaled to Jax and Remy. They nodded and— keeping myself covered—I scanned the tarmac outside. The window here spanned from waist to ceiling and through it, I saw a small body lying on the concrete. A puddle of dark blood pooled below it. No others were in sight. I rushed to her.

Sydney lay face down. I rolled her to her side, and she cried out in pain. I looked to her chest where several knife wounds leaked a bright red.

"Oh, Sydney, what happened?" I grabbed another towel from my bag and pressed it against the largest wound on her chest. She coughed, and pink lined her lips.

"Lenard tricked me. I-I knew better." She choked, then asked, "Camden?"

"Fine. Sean's with him." She nodded. I grabbed her hand, and she squeezed gently.

"Keep him with you. I beg you. You're all he has left." She gasped for breath.

Jax knelt on the other side of her. Lily stood a few feet away, her face stricken.

"Of course," Jax said. He placed his hand on her shoulder. She reached up and grasped it. "We'd never leave him."

My eyes never left Sydney's as she struggled to breathe. The sharp rattle brought tears to my eyes. I didn't know what to do. I wish I could've taken away her pain. She coughed, and blood sprayed from her mouth.

In a harsh whisper, she said, "Your father was so proud of you. He told me on the mountain how strong you are. He said you couldn't see it, but you are. I know Camden will be safe with you."

I shook my head, not understanding.

A second later, fear filled her eyes. She gasped, and blood gurgled from her mouth. One last spasm, and Sydney was gone. The light she'd held faded into the abyss. My throat closed as I felt the energy leave her. I felt her life leave her.

"No!" I screamed, pressing my forehead to hers. "No, that son of a..."

Gently, I placed her on the ground. I stood up and began searching for that worthless piece of garbage. Tinted footsteps led out and away from Sydney's corpse, but the trail disappeared as it reached a frozen stretch of ground.

My feet pounded against the earth as I searched for any movement. *I need to find him. I need to...*

Kill him? No. No, I didn't want that. I couldn't want that. If I did, that would mean that I was like him. In that instant, I swore I would never be like him.

I kept searching the distance, needing to know where he was. Needing to make sure he didn't hurt anyone else.

Nothing? He has to be here. He couldn't have gotten far.

"Reena, I'm sorry." Remy had come up behind me. His voice shook.

"Sorry? Sorry?" I half-screamed at him. "Your uncle, whom you continuously support, just killed a good, honest woman, and you're sorry?"

My fury was like a pulse in my veins fighting for a way out. My jaw was clenched, my hands tightened into fists.

Jax called out to me. I saw him near Sydney, indecision and pain written on his face. He glanced from me to Lily, to the door of the building, and back. Come help me, protect Lily, or get backup?

Lily ran to the door, calling out for help. Seconds later, Cassie, Kim, and Louis rushed out. They stopped in their tracks upon spotting Sydney.

"I know I was wrong, Reena, but maybe he had a reason," Remy said.

"A reason? A reason for this?" I lifted my hands up to show the blood that covered not just them, but my arms as well. "There's no reason for this. You don't kill innocent people. Ever! What frustrates me most, Remy, is that you buy into the crap he spouts. You even believe that it's all right to hurt others as long as you get something out of it!"

"That's not exactly true, and you know it," he yelled back.

"Do I?" My entire body shook with anger. "You said so before we got here. I heard you. You have some freaky attachment to your uncle and why, Remy? Why?"

Remy was only a few feet away then. The power in the air crackled and hissed around us. A warm breeze spun, circling and speeding up with each word we flung at each other. From the corner of my eye, I saw sparks blink in the air.

"He's all I have left. I know that's not an excuse, but why don't you of all people get that? Either way, Reena, I know this is *not* right." Remy gestured to the blood.

He tried to move closer, his body at an odd angle as if he walked against a strong wind. More sparks lit my periphery. He reached for my hand as if to take it.

"You need to calm down. You're not gonna help anyone like this."

Right as he was about to grab my hand, I screamed, "Don't touch me!"

With both hands, I shoved him. The moment I made contact, a loud *boom* erupted from the connection.

The pressure that had filled the air erupted, shooting a blast of energy in all directions. Lights of all colors burst outward, a visual representation of the power that exploded through the touch. Remy and I were thrown into the air. The repellent force flung us more than thirty feet back.

Instantly, an image hit my mind, blocking out the sights in front of me. Jax stood on my left between me and what had to be The Source. His face was strained, his arms extended. The sky was dark with swirling gray clouds, and the ground vibrated with power. I shifted my gaze to find The Source, purple and gold, swirling within a shimmering shield of Jax's green. The shield-covered Source hovered several feet above the ground when Jax screamed for me to finish.

Finish? I looked down at my hands to see a light streaming from them. It pushed into the ground, where it disappeared. I could feel where it reappeared far ahead of me, somewhere behind Jaxson. It arched high into the air, only to turn back to me, once again connecting with my skin.

My back slammed into something hard, and the vision disappeared. My breath was forced out as a parked plane stopped my progression. I slid down, falling nearly ten feet to the cold, hard ground. Sprawled on the frozen concrete, I coughed and choked, struggling for breath.

Across the way, Remy was motionless on the ground. Jax was pushing himself up to a seated position, having been thrown backward as well. Everyone else stood by the open door, arms up as if to shield themselves, their shock absolute.

The world spun; a new kind of headache pounded between my eyes. Black fog impeded my vision as darkness closed in. The last thing I remember was Jax running toward me, Kim and Cassie trailing behind. Then everything went black.

Chapter Thirty

My memory of the next few hours are just bits and pieces. There were flashes of things; Jax picking me up and carrying me, voices mentioning Remy, warnings of Lenard, and the noise of the hangar. Mostly though, I remember blackness and pain.

I came to as a warm cloth was moved gently over my hands. My eyelids were heavy, but I forced them open. I lay on a cushion on the floor of the hangar. Cassie sat next to me, gently washing the dried blood from my skin. Her blond curls were pulled up into a ponytail, her face sad. Lost in her quiet thoughts, I couldn't help but find her beautiful.

I tried to speak, but only a groan came out. My fingers twitched, and Cassie's gaze shot to me.

"Reena?" she asked, realizing my eyes were open. "Jax, Kim! She's awake!"

Pain shot into my temples at her volume. I winced. She placed a gentle hand on my head.

Whispering this time, she said, "Sorry. I should've known that your head would hurt with what you just went through."

"What?" I tried to sit up, but the moment I moved, pain erupted in every muscle of my body. And in a few muscles I didn't know I had. My entire body must have been bruised.

"You need to stay down." Carefully, she pressed my shoulder to the mattress. With no energy to fight her, I collapsed back, exhausted.

"Let me finish this," she said. She grabbed my other hand and wiped it clean.

As she did, I noticed Lily sitting near my feet. She paled as she watched Cassie wash the blood away.

"What happened?" I croaked.

"Honey," Cassie said. "You flew thirty feet, then fell another ten to the ground after you hit the side of a plane. You need to rest."

Jax, Eric, and Kim ran up to us. Even the sound of their steps on the ground felt like hammers to my skull. They knelt by my side.

"How long have I been out?"

"About three hours," Jax said. "How are you feeling?"

"What did Cassie say? Like I flew thirty feet, then fell ten more after hitting the side of a plane." A smile quirked my lip. "How bad am I injured?"

"No broken bones that we can tell," Kim said. "We were hoping you could tell us."

"Just sore, I think. But my head... Any chance you can help me sit up?"

Cassie and Kim said no, but Eric and Jax helped me to a seated position. My head felt like it would burst with the pressure. My body screamed until I was up and no longer moving. I took long breaths, hoping to settle my stomach.

"Here, take these," Kim said, holding out some Ibuprofen. "It's not much, but it will help."

She was about to drop them in my hand when I looked down and realized that the blood was still there.

Subconsciously, I let out a pained noise. Immediately, Cassie started to clean my hands again.

"Don't worry, Reena, I'll get it," she said.

"Oh, Sydney." My voice cracked. "Where's Camden? Remy? Lenard?"

"Remy's sleeping as far from you as possible," Jax snarled. "He seems fine but hasn't woken up yet. Camden's awake, and he's as well as can be expected. But Lenard's gone."

"We've let Jeff and the others know. They sent someone into town to warn everyone. Cleat's been helping around the clock, and we're almost ready to start the truck up. Jeff and Sonja have joined us to help keep an eye out for Lenard. The hangar should be easier to defend than the terminal," Eric explained.

"Why are they helping us?"

"They saw your blast. After finding out it was you and what happened, they decided to join us. Miko hasn't left your side since," Cassie said.

I looked to my right, and sure enough, there was Miko.

"What do you mean 'they saw your blast'?"

"Well, you kinda lit up the sky with that display of power. To be honest, we can't decide if we should be impressed or scared," Cassie said.

I thought over what Cassie said as Miko's eyes stared at me curiously. I lifted my hand, and he got up and came to me. I scratched him gently behind the ear as he settled himself against my thigh. His soft fur comforted me, but it couldn't take away from the sadness inside.

"This can't be happening. I—we—need to find Lenard. He's dangerous. I need to find him." I moved to stand, then thought better of it. One, it hurt. And two, the moment I'd shifted, four hands and a growl held me in place.

"You need to eat and rest," Kim said.

My temper flared. "No! I need to do something," I barked, slicing the air with my arm and extending my fingers.

A quick burst of tension shot up my arm. When it reached my hand, something weird happened. A screwdriver that lay on the floor about ten feet away skidded toward me only to fly into my hand. I blinked at it, then brought it closer. My fingers were still spread, and the screwdriver sat glued to my palm.

I didn't move. All my anger and frustration gone in an instant as shock took over. Everyone around me sat in stunned silence. I reached up and pulled the screwdriver off. Taking a breath, I set it on the ground.

"Cassie? What did you put in that water?" I asked softly.

"I don't know, but I want some."

"It's not funny," Jax said. "Reena, you need to stop using your abilities. You're gonna hurt yourself. Hell, you already did. You had blood seeping from your ears already once today. I need you to rest."

Sighing, I nodded. He only wanted what was best for me. I knew that.

"Cassie, can you go get her some of the stew, please?" Jax asked her.

"Sure." Cassie stood, taking the bowl of red water with her.

Jax sat next to me. He wrapped his arm around my shoulders, and I leaned into him. Eric came to sit on my other side, but Miko growled, not willing to relinquish his spot.

"You're going to eat and then sleep. If anything happens, we'll wake you up, deal?" Jax's hand gently rubbed my arm. "We need you at your best, especially with Lenard still out there. And we don't want that happening again."

"That only happens with Remy, and you know it. I can't really do anything with these abilities. I can't even protect myself."

"That you know of. You probably have more to learn," he said, then kicked the screwdriver. I leaned my head on his shoulder, exhausted. Kim patted my leg and stood.

"I'm so glad you're all right. I don't know what we would do if something happened to you," she said.

"That's why Jeff gave us something to help keep you safe. Well, first he asked us if you knew how to use it," Eric said. He slipped a cloth-wrapped handgun into the space between Jax and my leg. "We assured him that you did, and that you'd only use it to protect yourself."

"But that wasn't the deal. We promised not to take any of his weapons."

Eric stared into my eyes, willing me to listen. "We aren't. You are. We told him what's been going on, and he offered it to us. No one else knows. Jax has a rifle, so does Dad. Mom has her pistol, too. This one's yours, and it's easily concealed."

"I don't like this," I said.

"You don't have to. You're going to do it for me and for Lily. We need you safe," Jax explained.

I held his eyes and thought. I knew he was manipulating me, but what could I do? He was right. We needed as much protection as we could get.

"Okay. Fine, but you know what that means, right?"

"What?" he asked cautiously.

"You owe me the *Sexiest Men of the Year* magazine *and* two candy bars."

He laughed, and then nodded. "All right, all right, but you know that if Cassie sees that magazine, you'll never get it back, right?"

"It's not Cassie you'll have to worry about," Lily said, deadpan. She'd spoken with her eyes lost in a book.

I giggled and couldn't help remembering the times over the last few months that we'd read gossip magazines together. It was weird to have my baby sister noticing boys, but it was fun to watch her grow into a woman.

"Apparently, it's for all of us," I said. "Consider it scientific research to compare the manly men of our group to the model types. I think it should provide hours of discussion." The teasing smile I gave him made his eyes light up. Kim snorted and walked away.

"Kim, you can borrow it too if you want," I hollered after her. She raised her hand in a "no thanks" gesture and continued to walk away, her soft laughter trailing behind her.

The stew Cassie brought me was warm and savory. The candy bar Jax retrieved was sweet. My headache lessened, and my mood improved tremendously.

I slept for an hour more, taking comfort in the furry warmth of Miko as he sat guard next to me. Lily stayed too, reading quietly as she watched over me as I slept. She had grown so much these last weeks.

The sound of the truck trying to start finally pushed me to rise from my spot. It grumbled in protest but came to life just as Lily and I approached it. Everyone cheered. Eric spotted me, then came to give both of us an excited hug. Cassie sauntered up as well.

"I knew I ended up with you for a reason," Cassie said. "You guys are amazing."

I grinned, then walked around the truck to get a good look at it. The truck was huge. The front cab held only a few people, but the back had a large canopy that arched over rails that protected the back. Benches spanned each side with a fair amount of space between them.

This would easily transport all of us.

As I walked around the back to look inside, Remy stepped into my path. The moment he saw me, he took a nervous step back. He was fine except for some stiffness as he walked. Based on his eyes and the way that he cringed as the cheering continued, his head hurt as badly as mine did.

"Are you going to blow me up again?" he asked.

"Are you going to piss me off again?" I realized then that everyone had stopped cheering and were staring at us.

"I didn't mean to make it worse," Remy said. He dropped his head.

I thought about that. I could see that in his way, he had been trying to calm me down. I'd been out of control, and I'd blamed him for everything. This was as much my fault as his.

"You okay?" I asked.

"Other than a few bruises and some road rash from skidding across the ground, I'm fine. You?"

"Sore all over and my head." I rubbed my temple.

"Yeah. Got that too." He shot me a half-smile.

Jax appeared at my side. He placed his hand on my back and steered me away from Remy. He didn't say anything, and I didn't fight. As we walked, I looked back to see Cassie join Remy. He said something, and her eyes narrowed in a glare. She watched us for a moment, then shook her head and turned away.

Chapter Thirty-One

T hough the truck starting had seriously improved morale, the sadness of losing Sydney and the fear of what Lenard would do next was still on everyone's minds. Every time someone laughed, it was hollow; every time someone smiled, it was forced, and every thought was of next steps.

Together we laid out that plan. James and Cleat were convinced fixing the second truck would take half the time. As it was always better to have a backup, and considering the number in our group, this became a priority. Also, knowing that we'd be able to take more supplies with us, it was decided that anything usable would be retrieved from the airport.

The biggest concern was the threat Lenard posed. It was impossible to tell what he was up to and what he might do to get what he wanted. So, it was decided to split into three groups where no one would be left alone.

"Camden?" I asked, sitting next to him.

He leaned against the back wall, his head down. The tear tracks on his cheeks were dry, but visible.

"I wanted to see how you're doing."

"You know how I'm doing," he said.

"I do." I understood perfectly. I leaned my head back, gazing at the ceiling. "Which is why I'm here. I don't handle sitting still well. I work better with a focus, a goal. I have a feeling you're like that, too."

"Okay."

"We have three groups. One going to the terminal, one retrieving the truck, and the last staying here to protect camp. I want to give you the choice."

A few heavy breaths, and he said, "I can't go back to the terminal, but I want to be useful."

"I figured as much," I said, placing a hand on his arm. "Then why don't you head out with Eric and Sean? Get some air."

"Who's staying here?"

"James, Jeff, Sonja, and Remy."

"Then I am definitely not staying."

I could see that. Remy was just another reminder. I patted his leg, stood, then helped him up.

"Thanks." He lowered his gaze again.

"You're family, Camden. You're stuck with us now."

"Great." He lengthened the word teasingly. I chuckled.

"Eric? This troublemaker is with you," I said, gesturing to Camden.

"Awesome." He flung his arm over Camden's shoulders. "Then let's get going. Reena, Jax? Be careful."

Nodding, we met Cassie, Kim, and Lily near the back door. Our group was going to weave through the other hangars and exit out the side door in hopes that anyone watching would miss us. Then, Eric and the others would head out separately.

Once we exited, we took turns running from obstacle to obstacle and across the landing strip. Then we disappeared into the terminal. We tried to stay hidden as best we could, not wanting anyone watching to track our movements or know how unprotected the hangar was.

Working quickly, we gathered everything into the rolling bin Eric had used the first night there. Food, drinks, and anything else useful were stuffed into it. A few bags were filled as well with medicine, tape, Band-Aids, and even a few extra books.

As we left, I couldn't help but glance back to where Sydney's body had lain. Jax told me that he and Sean had gone back for the body. They had found a beautiful resting place for her, then taken Camden to say goodbye. My heart hurt at her loss, but I pushed it down.

We took a little different path back, weaving through the line of parked planes along the edge of the landing strip. We were just about to run for the trees behind the hangars when shots rang out. I ducked, then tried to determine where the shots came from.

"Lily, get down!" I yelled, shielding her with my body and the cart.

"Toward the hangar," Jax said.

Two more bursts filled the air. Kim motioned for us to follow her. Leaving the cart, we rushed back toward the doors. Instead of heading in, she led us around the length of the building to the parking lot. It made sense. We couldn't make it across the open space of the landing field with people opening fire.

Before we left the shelter of the structure, I stopped and turned to Lily. "Lily, I need you to go back to the terminal. You know the conference room right off the main walk? There's an office near the back. I don't think anyone noticed it. Go hide."

"Reena, I—" Lily said.

"No," I snapped. "I need you, Lily. I can't lose you, too. And right now, the only way I can protect you is to hide you."

I pushed her toward the door, but she planted her feet, her expression terrified.

"I can help. I don't want to be left behind," she pleaded.

"We won't leave you behind, ever. But I need you to be safe. If we're thinking about protecting you, we might get distracted."

She stared at me for what seemed like forever until another burst of gunfire made her jump. She hugged me harder than she'd ever done before. She sent Kim a look, and then went to Jax.

"You protect her for me."

"I will," he said.

With one last, fond glance to each of us, she turned and sprinted. We watched her until she disappeared through the doorway, her dark hair blowing out behind her.

Just then, a cold breeze hit my face. In the air, I felt the static of an approaching storm. The smell of ozone filled my nose like a promise of the changing tide. I looked west to see a large black cloud arching high into the heavens. As if on cue, lightning streaked across the sky. The wind picked up and I knew—knew it deep in my chest—that this storm would break us or save us.

Perfect, I thought, *let's just add one more thing to today's list.*

Cassie, Kim, Jax, and I started to run. We took the long way, meandering through the parked cars and down the road that led back to the hangar. We ran hard and fast, taking cover wherever we could. Every so often, another blast of gunfire resonated through the thick air.

"It sounds like they're playing with them," Kim said.

"What do you mean?" I asked

Jax said, "That they're testing Dad and the others. Or maybe they're trying for a distraction?"

"Do you think it's just Lenard?"

"Can't be. He's crazy but not suicidal," Cassie said.

We made it the last thirty feet to hide behind the far wall of the first building. Kim went to the edge as if to look out. I motioned her to move and pointed to my eyes.

"I might be able to see more than you," I said, immediately pressing on my ability. My vision changed; it was second nature now. Kim didn't like it, but she did as I asked.

I scooted past her. Then as carefully and quickly as possible, I leaned around the edge of the building. The first thing I saw was the man in a blood-red jacket. He crouched behind a pickup truck about fifty yards from the door of the hangar. He had a shotgun in his hand, and several other weapons attached at the belt and shoulders.

"You've got to be kidding me," I said, and pulled myself back behind the wall and out of sight. "Remember Jeff's friend Red? I have a feeling that he didn't get our previous warning."

Jax leaned his head back against the wall and sighed. "How many are with him?"

I reached into my pants and pulled the pistol out, released the safety, and waited. Again, I peered around the corner. The moment I exposed myself, a gunshot hit the wall right next to my head. I retreated immediately, cursing.

Four, maybe five, including the man in red.

The others jumped as the metal popped with the impact of another bullet. I backed away, then turned to run, the others right behind. I slipped the key into the door we'd exited before, which led into the first hangar. We followed the line of the wall, reaching the far door easily.

Now would be the hard part. A fifteen-foot gap separated this building from the next.

"Jax, it's your turn," I said.

He stepped to the front, and I felt him draw on his power. "When I open the door, they'll shoot. Be quick. I'm not sure how long I can hold this."

"Everyone, touch him. If we're connected when he creates the field, it will surround us too," I said.

"Really?" Kim asked.

"The few times he's used it, it gave us about six feet of spherical coverage. We only need a few seconds to cross and get into the next door."

They nodded, then pressed their hands to his back. He swung the door open and pushed out with his shield. I watched as it encapsulated us in its light. He huffed as the first shots rang out, bright flashes erupting against his shield.

We moved together, reaching the door in seconds. Again, I found the key and slipped it into the lock. The barrage of bullets came at us with unyielding accuracy. Jax's breathing quickened and sweat lined his brow.

"Reena, hurry. This is a lot harder than it looks."

"Got it!" I pushed Cassie and Kim through the door.

I grabbed Jax's belt loop and yanked him into the room, feeling him drop the shield the moment the door shut. We hurried away from the damaged walls, not wanting to get hit by any lucky bullets that got through.

Jax was pale, his face tired. Shoving the pistol back in my belt and under my shirt, I touched his hand and used what little power I had to provide him with a boost of energy.

"We need to get to the others. Now," I said.

"We need to take out the shooters," Cassie said, a growl in her voice.

"And how do we do that exactly?" Kim asked.

"We—" But Cassie was cut off.

The *click* that echoed was both familiar and menacing. It doesn't matter if you've never held one in real life, you've heard the sound before. It is a sound that sends fear thrumming through your veins. One that haunts your nightmares and promises death. The click of a weapon being cocked.

I froze, instantly knowing that a gun was pointed at my head. The barrel pressed to my skull.

I'm so stupid. How did I not see this coming?

Jax, who had been between the others and me, tried to step forward but I shook my head. He stopped, his attention on the man behind me.

"Miss me, Reena? We didn't get to finish our one-on-one," Lenard's slimy voice said.

Inside, I shivered. I sent Jax a look that said, *get the shield up and protect the others.*

Luckily, he understood, and a half second later, light separated us. His face was calm, but his eyes shone with fury.

"My dear Reena," Lenard said, inches from my ear, his breath hot on my neck. "I told you I would take you, and now I will."

He touched my hair, twirling it around his dirty finger. He grasped my neck hard and forced my face to look back at him over my shoulder.

"But as you've made me angry, I'll make sure everyone sees it." He sniffed my neck, then whispered, "How do you smell so wonderful?"

I closed my eyes, panting. What I'd seen in that dilated gaze was nothing human. Something had happened in the last few hours. Lenard was no longer who he'd once been. He'd changed into something damaged.

Deranged... I tried to figure out what I could do. *Nothing. Yet.*

He grabbed my shoulder, digging his free hand into my skin. He gestured for the others to head toward the exit. Then used me as a shield between us.

Cassie opened the door, then Lenard led us out from between the buildings. The man in red waited, leaning back against the truck he'd previously hidden behind. A wicked grin spread across his face when he spotted me.

"I see you found what you were looking for," the man in red said.

"Almost," Lenard agreed.

Three others held strategic positions in an arch around the large door, two men and a woman. Their guns were pointed at either us or the hangar.

I glanced up to the window of a large metal door to find James watching. James' rifle was pointed at Red. I spotted Remy and Jeff on the far side.

I had to think. I had to figure a way out of this. First, we needed to distract Lenard. Then I needed to disarm him. Finally, we needed to incapacitate the other shooters. Easy, right?

Okay, Reena. Be strong. You can do this.

"What do you want, Lenard?" I asked, demanding his attention.

"You know what I want. I want The Source. I want the power."

"Then what do you need us for?" Cassie asked.

"You? Nothing. Well, I suppose I need the truck. I'll take your stuff, too. I would also like to retrieve my nephew, but that isn't wholly necessary."

"And Reena?" Kim asked.

"Well, Reena is a special case, isn't she? Remy's fond of her, and I think he'll follow more willingly if I keep her as a present. And to be honest, I just want her."

His hand slid down my back to wrap around my waist, pulling me against him. With the gun still pressed to my back, he leaned forward to run his teeth along the arch of my neck.

I cried out as he bit down, blood pooling at the wound. He moaned, licking it up.

"What the hell, Lenard!" Jax screamed. He stepped forward, and the gun shot up. I shook my head violently; the sting of the bite brought tears to my eyes. I pushed them down. I had to stop Jax, or Lenard would shoot him.

"No," I said. I swallowed hard and tried to breathe. Tried to stay calm. I mouthed, "Deranged."

Jax's eyes widened in surprise, then hardened as determination filled his gaze. He knew as well as I did that, if what I suspected were true, then we had to be very careful.

"And if I don't go?" I asked bitterly, trying and failing to keep the fear out of my voice.

"Then I'll kill you."

I need out. I need out. Find a way out! Got it...

"Why are you all doing this?" Kim asked Lenard's lackeys.

I heard her but wasn't paying much attention because Cassie had met my eye. I wiggled my fingers a minuscule amount, then looked at Red and his companions. The corner of her mouth quirked up, letting me know she understood. She shifted to gently touch Jax's side.

He'd seen the exchange, so when I mouthed "mom" and "help," then glanced at the cover of the building, determination lit his eyes. With one quick nod, I knew we had a plan. I just hoped Kim would listen and find the others to help.

"Lenard promised to take us to The Source," Red replied.

God, I hope this works. I focused on pushing all my emotion down, harnessing it for what was to come. I needed to recreate what happened with the screwdriver, but with Lenard's gun instead. That was my only hope. I just had no idea how to do it. I held onto my fear and anger, forcing that energy into my powers, and slowly I felt the air change.

Lenard's hold loosened minutely as he addressed Red. Which is why the movement of my hands, my body, went undetected to the maniac holding me.

I carefully arched away from him, pointing my palm toward the gun at my back. I spooled the energy I'd been collecting and shot it into my hand, reaching for the metallic structure of the gun he held.

Nothing happened. Deeper into myself I went. More energy, more emotion, more desperation.

One more time.

The gun ripped out of Lenard's hand and slammed into my palm. My fingers wrapped tightly. In the same movement, I threw my right elbow at his face. It hit square in the cut on his cheek. He screamed out in pain as red spewed from the reopened wound.

And so it began.

Heat exploded behind me. Orange fire shot from Cassie toward Red. He ducked behind the truck and fumbled with his weapon, but soon took aim.

I spun and grabbed Lenard's wrist, yanking it around behind his back, then placing him between me and Red. Lenard flung profanities at me as he tried to struggle, but I had him. I began to back away toward the hangar.

That's when the gunfire started again. Red's companions began firing at Cassie. As they did, new columns of fire shot their way, forcing them to take cover.

Shots rang out from the hangar, Jeff and James. The woman who'd shot at us earlier fell to the ground. She writhed in pain. Her weapon clattered to the ground next to her. Again, I forced power into my palm, aiming it at the gun she'd dropped. It didn't work.

Jax reappeared, running back into the fray after rushing Kim to safety. He reached the downed woman and disarmed her. She scurried away while Jax took cover behind a small maintenance vehicle. Bullets slammed into the metal protecting him.

Pop, pop, pop. I flinched, the noise deafening with the hangar door so close.

Lenard took advantage of my reaction. He flung his head back as if to hit me, causing my hold to loosen. I pulled back. He twisted, and my hand dropped away. His other fist connected with my ribs, and I grunted.

I swung with my own punch, but he blocked it. His other arm swung fast, slamming into my face. I sprawled on the ground, my cheekbone burning. The gun slid away from me.

The front door to the hangar slammed open; Remy and the others ran out. James and Jeff provided cover for Cassie and Jax while Remy ran toward his uncle. He tackled Lenard.

"Lenard! Stop this," he cried. Lenard pushed Remy off, then stood.

"You don't get it, Remy. The Source should be ours. We deserve the power. Deserve to have people grovel at our feet," Lenard said.

"There's another way."

"Can't you see? They lie. They want power; everyone wants power. Especially her. She tells you lies because she wants to keep it for herself."

"That's not true," I said. I sat up, engrossed in their exchange.

Behind them, Cassie advanced on the three men along the far side. Fire of bright orange spiraled toward them, a tornado of light and death. The air behind her was being sucked into the torrent to feed the funnel of flame. Crystals of ice began to form on the ground behind the vortex. Large shards grew from the concrete stabbing up and out, great spears of glittering ice.

Cassie's hair whipped violently around her head, making her look like an avenging angel. Her face was both beautiful and terrible as she stepped closer and closer to her competitors.

With my power, I saw energy radiate from her small form, reaching up and up into the sky. A burst of light blinded me as lightning hit the ground near her. When it did, the funnel surged hotter, the fire turning a pale yellow.

Cassie's pulling the air and power from everything behind her. Holy monkey balls, how is she doing that?

Lenard kicked out, hitting me in the side. Remy stepped between us. He pushed Lenard away.

"She is lying to you, boy. She wants power for herself!"

"That's not true," he said, but with hesitation.

I gasped when I realized Remy was considering his words.

"Remy, I don't, I swear. I don't want any of this!"

Remy looked down at me as if considering. Lenard leaned in and whispered into his ear. "Look at her; can't you see it? She's a liar. I tasted it in her blood."

He'd tasted... No, get up, Reena. Get up!

"With my help, we can take her power, Remy. We can take it from her."

I jumped to my feet, backing away farther. I pulled the gun from my waistband.

"No," Remy screamed, blocking my view of Lenard.

"I will kill you, girl," Lenard yelled. Lenard pulled out a knife, raised it, and ran for me. The crazed look in his eyes sent shivers running up my spine.

Even then I didn't want to kill him. I just wanted this to stop. I wanted to be safe, my family to be safe. I took a long, deep breath and lifted the gun. I aimed for Lenard's legs and pulled the trigger.

Once. Twice. A third time. The first one missed, but the second and third disappeared into his thigh. He staggered backward.

Remy's scream filled the air as he barged toward me. I braced myself, knowing exactly what would happen next. I could feel the emotion, the pure and diluted energy, between us. *This is going to be bad.*

Remy slammed his palm into my forearm and the gun fell to the floor, but not before light burst us apart. We repelled each other, power pushing us away.

The impact threw me backward, and I hit the hangar door only a few feet away. Shooting lights spread from both of us, an explosion of color. I slid to the ground. Remy was thrown farther. He skidded along at an unexpected angle, coming to a stop near Red.

What I didn't expect was how far the repellent force would travel. It expanded, catching Lenard off guard. With his already injured leg, it pushed him off balance. He slipped and began to fall. I reached for him as if I could stop it. Lenard's body fell directly into the ice crystals behind Cassie's fire vortex.

A cry escaped from my lips, and horror filled me. The pressure settled deep into me as I watched Lenard die.

The moment he'd stumbled into Cassie's wake, he grabbed at his throat, coughing and choking as if there was no air. Ice began to grow over his eyes and mouth. His face turned blue, and his eyes bulged. White crystals spread up his legs to wrap around his waist and only a second later, the light in his eyes disappeared.

"Cassie, stop!" I screamed, praying she would hear me. *Maybe there is still time.*

Jax cried out, and from the corner of my eye, I saw him fall. He moaned as he grasped his arm. The man Jax had been fighting laughed, then reached for his belt and pulled something off it. He brought his hand up to his mouth and pulled a pin out of a grenade.

"No!"

I tried to stand, but pain shot through my lower back and leg. Groaning, I crawled forward, needing to get to Jax. My head felt heavy, and the world spun. I must have hit the door harder than I thought.

Remy was getting up, too. I called to him and pointed at the man who was about to throw the grenade. If he let it go, it would not only kill Jax, but Remy and Cassie as well.

Remy understood.

"Reach for the truck and push," I shrieked.

Stretching out my hand, I focused on the truck the man sat behind. Remy imitated me. I took my fear for Jax and the others, my love for them each, and pooled it deep within me. I felt the metallic structure of the truck and pushed as hard as I could. Remy did the same.

Nothing happened. The man behind the truck raised his arm and began to throw.

I took a long, deep breath, tasting the ozone on my tongue again. I closed my eyes, reaching for the energy of the storm, for the power I needed, but was in short supply. Static electricity was everywhere, and I called it to me.

One breath. Two. My body hummed as I gathered it, and right as the man was about to let go, I screamed, forcing all of myself at the truck. As I expelled everything I had, lightning joined my power. I screamed in pain as it surged through me.

The truck slammed into the man, then flipped through the air to land on the other side of him. The sound of his head hitting the concrete will stay with me forever.

The grenade rolled a few feet away, toward the demolished truck. Time slowed as I counted, waiting for the explosion. The *boom* of the grenade—when it came—was deafening. The blast slammed into the maintenance truck Jax hid behind. His head hit the side, and he slumped forward.

Cassie, however, had been fully exposed. The shock wave threw her backward, pieces of concrete and metal hitting her across the front of her body. Small cuts appeared on her face and arms. I held my breath until she pushed herself up and looked around, dazed. She was pale. Blood ran down her face from her nose and ears; several cuts along her eyebrow wept. She swayed but didn't stand. After a few breaths, she collapsed.

Barely able to lift my head, I scanned for Jeff and James, but couldn't see them. The man they'd been fighting with had fled during the fight. They must've chased after him. Red lay on the ground and cried. The smell of burnt flesh and the sight of his red, blistering skin told me why.

I hurt everywhere but forced myself to face Jax. He was on the ground, blood drenching the shoulder of his shirt. His face was pressed against the asphalt. In the wind, his hair moved gently, and at the base of his neck I could see a single, small braid.

I crawled toward him. Pain radiated up my legs and along my spine. My skin stung as if a thousand wasps had taken their anger out upon me. My ribs ached as my lungs expanded.

I didn't make it even a few feet before Remy stalked up. He staggered, and I knew he wasn't unaffected by the battle. He looked different somehow, darker, angrier. His eyes flared as he took me in.

"Jax," I whispered, reaching out, wanting to touch him. Needing to know he was okay.

"You shot him. You killed him," Remy said.

I collapsed to the ground. My head turned to where Lenard's body stood encapsulated in ice — his body hard, frozen solid, and his eyes dark. The terror in his expression locked forever in death.

Tears filled my eyes.

"No," I said. "I didn't want him to die."

"Yes, you did, and he was right, wasn't he? You want The Source for yourself."

"No," I said again. *How could he think that?*

Remy shoved his boot under me and flipped me over so I faced up.

"Well, you're not going to get it. I'll get there before you do, and I know what I need."

He leaned over to enter my line of vision. He brushed a tendril of hair from my face.

"Jax. He's the key, isn't he? I don't know how, but I don't care. You took my family from me, and now I'll take yours from you. And you can't stop me." Remy stood.

His smile was cruel, disturbed. It scared me. Remy pulled back his leg and kicked me in the temple.

Chapter Thirty-Two

"Reena? Reena!"
I could hear the voice but couldn't find it. The world had been dark for so long; my mind was a mess of confusion.

Something wet hit my face. A series of cool beads which brought me back to consciousness. The smell of rain and smoke burned my nose. My throat ached as I swallowed. My body was in so much pain that there was almost nothing else. I tried to remember what happened.

"Reena!" It was Kim's voice.

"Jaxson!" I screamed. Opening my eyes, I shot to a sitting position. As I did, my body wavered, swaying violently. Small, strong hands grabbed my shoulders, holding me up.

"Reena, where's Jax?" Kim's face tilted in front of me. I tried to shake it off.

Where was Jax? Where was Jax! I glanced toward where Jax had lain. He wasn't there. I scanned the hangar. The large door was open, and the truck was gone.

"Cassie? Remy?" I asked.

"I don't know. And the working truck's gone," she said, terror rising in her voice.

My breathing quickened, and my eyes became wet.

"What happened?"

Eric, James, Jeff, and the others walked hesitantly, examining the damage. Demolished vehicles, red stained concrete, and small fires burned where Cassie's fire had touched.

Jeff limped, and James held his right arm carefully against his body. James led a man in his late twenties, his body burnt in patches across his chest and face. His hair was singed. The bruises on his chin stood out against his pale skin.

"Remy must've taken them," my voice cracked. "He took Jax because of me. He took him! And Cassie. I couldn't protect them."

The tears streamed down my face, mixing with the blood and rain that slid down my skin.

"No." She stood and ran to the others. In quick words, she relayed what I'd said. They all spread out to look for anyone left.

Jax... I need to find him. I need to save him. My Jax.

I sobbed his name, then tried to get my feet under me. I was about halfway up when my legs gave out and I fell. Eric caught me right before my head hit the ground. I looked into his worried eyes.

"I love him, Eric. I love him and couldn't protect him. I tried. I told him I wasn't good enough." My voice was lost in the sobs that racked my body. I was so cold.

Eric's arms slid behind my back and under my knees. He lifted me and took me away. The agony of the realization worse than that of my battered body.

Chapter Thirty-Three

Jax was not the only one who had been taken. The female who'd been shot said that Red and the man in his early twenties had helped Remy carry and tie up Jax. They'd placed him in the back of the truck. Then, Remy had woken Cassie and led her to the truck as well. Cassie had been in a daze, but after the recap, some believed she'd volunteered to go. I didn't know what to believe.

When I was finally able to stay awake for longer than a few minutes, I found that James and the others had worked on the second truck all night. It was around ten in the morning that they finally got it started. That was good, too, because I had been on the brink of losing it.

Eric had removed me from the room a few times for bothering them. Apparently, they didn't appreciate being berated with questions and told to "hurry the hell up." I knew they were doing the best they could, but the pain in my chest was just too great.

I had to find Remy and get Jax back. Watching Jax on the ground in pain, fighting next to me as he always did, and trusting me to be strong enough, had made me realize how stupid I'd been. Finally, I saw the truth. I loved him. There was no resisting it, no denying it. I had always felt this way; I'd just been too stubborn to admit it. So, I would find him, tell him, and be the person he always believed I was.

While I slept, Jeff and Sonja had gone into town and told them what happened. The injured woman was treated and taken back with the body of a man named Chris. He'd been the fifth man in Lenard's group. His body had been covered with blisters and the damage extensive. He'd died huddled behind an old, battered truck. The sight of his mangled corpse had made me sick to my stomach.

In thanks and apologies, the leaders had sent some food and water for us to take. I helped load the truck with the supplies we'd collected. Lily had brought many of them over when Kim had gone to get her. We'd then collected a few large containers we'd found and siphoned gasoline from all the abandoned vehicles. We hoped that this would be to our advantage. We had a full tank and some reserves.

At one point, I'd fallen to my knees as grief and fear hit me hard. Lily, who had been with me, held me while I cried.

We were more than twelve hours behind Remy when we finally loaded up to leave. Jeff and Cleat wore their backpacks as they joined us for a goodbye. We thanked them and apologized for pulling them into all of this.

"Reena? James? If possible, we'd like to go with you. I think we can help," Jeff said.

Everyone was a little shocked by the request, but of course we agreed. They threw a large bag up first, then climbed in after. It clanked on the metal floor. I looked at them questioningly.

"Just some tools that might come in handy when we get Jax back," Jeff said. I felt tears come to my eyes but pushed them down.

When we get Jax back.

A sad smile lifted his lip, and he patted my shoulder. They took a spot next to Sean, then Miko hopped up next.

I stepped out of the hangar; the rest of them loaded up. I walked over to the last place I saw Jax, bent down, and touched the red stain on the ground, his blood from the gunshot wound in his shoulder.

I will find you, Jax. I thought. *Because I need to tell you the truth and apologize for being so stupid.*

Steps approached, and Eric said, "We'll find him."

"If it's the last thing I do," I said seriously.

I turned and started for the truck. We went to the front cab and got in. Eric started the engine, then looked at me. As we pulled out, I pointed in the direction we would go. Where we would find Remy. Where I knew Jax would be. I could feel Remy, and it was only a matter of time before I found him.

It didn't matter what it took. I would get him back, then protect him and all those I love from anything that would harm them.

Then, and only then, I would do what my father told me to. I would see what I could see and set it right.

Thank You for Reading Source Awakening!

I hope you enjoyed the first installment of the Source Rising Series. If you did, I would sincerely appreciate it if you could leave a review. Reviews help authors more than you know and it would mean the world to me! Or, head over to TraceyCanole.com to check out my other projects!

Book two of the Source Rising Series, **SOURCE IGNITED**, will be released April 2022! I can't wait for you to see what happens next!

SOURCE IGNITED

They all want a piece of her—her polar opposite, the love of her life, and the lunatic.

Reena Novak will do anything to get her best friend Jax back, even if it means sacrificing herself. Her chosen path is harder than she expects, and it draws the attention of the ones she fears most—The Deranged. Now that they have her scent, they'll never stop hunting her.

Her mission has not changed. The Source calls to her, and she needs to know why because things are changing in the world. The ever-increasing storms, strange migration patterns, and that feeling of wrongness in her chest is getting worse. As her powers grow, the more she senses something's coming and fears she won't be able to protect those she loves.

Reena needs her polar opposite by her side, but Remy still blames her for his uncle's death. More importantly, The Deranged are closing in. It's time to get to the coast, convince Remy to join their cause, and find a way to The Source. Perhaps, with the help of some new friends and a few miracles, Reena can put the pieces together before the damage is too great to repair.

About Author

Tracey Canole is a YA & Adult, Science Fiction and Urban Fantasy author. She writes stories that take you on an adventure, drawing you into her characters and their experience. Tracey loves stories that are based in reality, but have a fantastical element allowing the reader to go somewhere they never expected.

When not writing, she enjoys reading and dabbling in many different art forms, such as painting, ceramics, and even singing. But her absolute joy is found in exploring the world through hiking and camping with her husband and two children.

For more about her, and her other projects, head over to her website at TraceyCanole.com

S

Made in the USA
Monee, IL
22 January 2022